ANDREA SEPTIÉN

THE
SUNLIT
RUINS

THE ARCHIVES OF THE FORGOTTEN
BOOK 1

Publisher: Bandele Books
Interior Design: Vellum
Editors: Antoine Bandele, Callan Brown
Cover Design & Illustration: Mibl Art

ISBN: 978-1-951905-33-0 (Ebook edition)

ISBN: 978-1-951905-34-7 (Paperback edition)

ISBN: 978-1-951905-35-4 (Hardback edition)

First Edition | July 4, 2024

CONTENTS

A young adult series that chronicles the journey of Ada and Miry, two Mexican-American cousins from opposite sides of the border, who find themselves in a world they never knew existed.

A cross between Coco and The Kane Chronicles, this series delves into the philosophy of the city of Teotihuacán. Follow Ada and Miry in their quest to uncover ancient secrets, reforge family bonds, and learn who they truly are.

If you enjoy this story and are interested in the rest of Ada and Miry's adventures, you can join Bandele Books' e-mail alerts list. We'll send you notifications for new book releases, exclusive updates, and behind-the-page content.

Visit this link:
antoinebandele.com/stay-in-touch

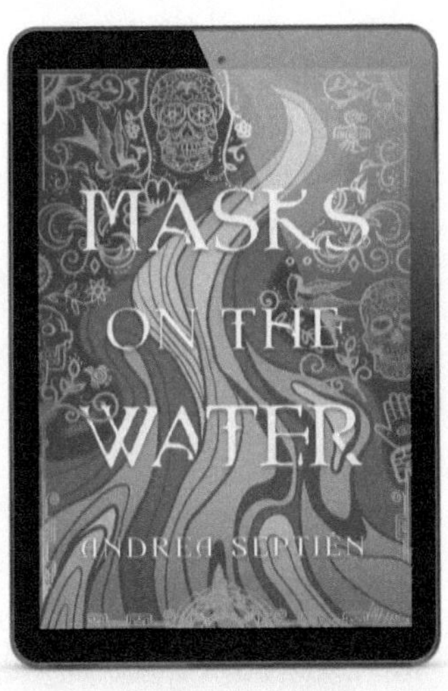

The creature appeared underwater. That's all they knew.

Lorenzo Zavala, a disciple of Chalchitlicue, the deity of the lakes, was sent on a simple mission: Go to Lake Huetzalin in the south of Mexico City, analyze an unknown creature, and report back to the archivists.

By his side was Daniel Merino, his best friend and a disciple of Tláloc, the deity of the rain. But when the two of them reach the lake, Lorenzo discovers the the true danger is much closer than he realized.

Using the power of the deity of the lakes, Lorenzo must use all of his skills to save his best friend. Can Lorenzo triumph against this new threat? Or will he lose the person closest to his heart?

Find out in this prequel short story to The Sunlit Ruins, a young adult fantasy based on the philosophy of the city of Teotihuacán.

Visit this link to read the prequel story:
https://www.antoinebandele.com/book-page-masks-on-the-water

PRONUNCIATION GUIDE

<u>Characters</u>

Chal·chiuh·tli·cue - chaal'chee'tlee'kway

    Da·niel Me·ri·no Gu·tié·rrez - dan'niel / meh'ree'no / goo'tieh'rez

    Gua·da·lu·pe Rey·es-Riv·er·a - gooah'dah'loo'pey / rey'e-hz'riv'err'ah

    Hue·hue·té·o·tl - way'way'tay'oat'el

    Fer·nan·do Riv·er·a Or·te·ga - ferr'naan'doh / riv'err'ah / or'tey'gah

    Lo·ren·zo Za·va·la Már·quez - low'ren'so / sah'vah'lah / maar'cuez

    Mir·an·da Don·ald·son Riv·er·a - mir'aan'dah / don'ald'son / riv'err'ah

    Tlá·loc - tlaa'lock

    Tí·o Luis - tee'oh / looees

    Tí·a Lu·pe - tee'ah / loo-pey

    Tí·o Ri·zo - tee'oh / ree-so

    Tí·a Sa·ra - tee'a / saa'ra

    Quet·zal·có·a·tl - kuet'zal'ko'a'tul

<u>Locations</u>

    Chap·ul·te·pec - chaap'uul'teh'peck

    Co·yo·a·cán - ko'yo'ah'caan

    Teo·ti·hua·cán - tey'o'tee'oo'a'caan

<u>Terms</u>

    Grin·ga - green'ga

    Ha·da - aah'daah

    Nie·ve - kneeeh'veh

    Prof·es·or·a - proff'ess'or'ah

To Usama, my wonderful husband,
who was only slightly annoyed that I dedicated my first publication to
my cats instead of him

FOREWORD
HOW I STUMBLED UPON A SHARED UNIVERSE

In 2021, I wrote a modern young adult fantasy based on the mythology of my ancestors, the Yoruba people of present day Nigeria and Benin. The story was inspired by my favorite childhood stories, from books, television, and theatrical films. That inspiration resulted in a best-selling novel (which has also been optioned for a motion-picture adaptation at the date of this writing). The tale follows the adventures of TJ Young and his interaction with the Orishas—West African deity spirits. But I didn't want the world to feel too small, too narrow. Even when I wrote early drafts of the first novel in the series, *The Gatekeeper's Staff*, I hinted at a larger world beyond TJ and the Orishas. And that hinting is now being uncovered—or in other words, this is how I accidentally stumbled onto a shared universe.

Imagine a world where the Mesoamerican, Yoruba, Norse, Yokai, and Celtic pantheons collide with our contemporary reality. The Old Gods Stories take inspiration from ancient belief systems, folklore, and mythologies, weaving them into a tapestry that is both mesmerizing and evocative. It's a place where the fantastical meets the familiar, and where the extraordinary is just a breath away.

In this shared universe, readers will encounter a cast of diverse heroes and heroines, each with their unique gifts and destinies. Ancient deities walk among mortals, magical artifacts possess unimaginable power, and epic battles unfold against the backdrop of family drama, coming of age stories, and strange mysteries.

I am thrilled to introduce the talented author, Andrea Septién, as she takes the helm of the second full series within The Old Gods Universe.

Andrea's strong voice and mastery of storytelling will transport readers into the heart of Mesoamerica, where the old deities attempt to reign supreme once more. Her richly woven narrative will unravel the intricate layers of family dynamics while exploring the depths of these mystical entities.

Prepare to be enthralled, as Andrea's words breathe life into the pages. If this is your first story in Old Gods Universe, this is a great place to start. And after reading, I hope you continue with Andrea's stories and all the rest in the shared universe. If you've read other stories in this space, then you already know that you're in for a treat!

Join us on this incredible journey, where the legacy of the old gods meets the vibrant spirit of today's youth, forging a tapestry of adventure, magic, and timeless wisdom.

Antoine Bandele
Creator of The Old Gods Stories

HOW I ACCIDENTALLY KICKSTARTED THE CATASTROPHE

ADA

I STOOD TALL IN A CRUMBLING CAVERN I NEVER KNEW existed, back-to-back with the one person I never thought I'd trust my life with.

"I need one more minute!" Miry yelled. "Think you can handle it, *Fresa*?"

"Ha!" I yelled back. I threw my left arm out in front of me and smiled. My nails extended themselves into razor-sharp needles. My fingers faded from brown to green, their skin hardening into masses of thick-skinned cacti.

"You need a minute?" I shouted. "I'll give you two!"

I should probably introduce us. My name's Ada Reyes-Rivera. Your friendly Mexican-American from Phoenix, Arizona. My less friendly cousin is Miranda. Miry, for short. Unlike me, she actually grew up in Mexico City—where most of this mess took place—and where both of our lives changed forever.

So make some popcorn, snuggle into your favorite blanket, and get reading. Because we've got a lot to go through.

July 9th

THIS WHOLE LIFE-ALTERING DISASTER BEGAN WHEN I TOLD my Uncle Luis I'd never been to the pyramids of Teotihuacán. We were sitting in his house in central Mexico City when he brought it up, and he laughed in shock when I told him I didn't know that Mexico even *had* pyramids.

"No way, Hada," he said, nearly spilling *salsa verde* onto my new sundress. He turned to my Aunt Lupe, who was busy setting the table for dinner, and grinned. "*Mi amor*, tell the family that tomorrow we're going to Teotihuacán! Hada's never been!"

I don't know Mexico City that well. Chalk it up to my mom barely getting any time off from the hospital, or to my dad always dealing with calls from other social workers. We visit every Christmas, and we try to go for two or three weeks in the summer, but I can't say that I'm familiar with the place. And I can definitely say that I wasn't familiar with Teotihuacán.

And that's how I ended up squished among four of my cousins in the backseat of a car that only had room for three.

I peeked out of the window—ignoring my little cousin's jabbing elbows—at the vast space that lay between Mexico City and the famed pyramids. It was fairly sparse, populated with only stout trees and long patches of somber, yellowing grass. The nearest buildings were a group of concrete houses off in the distance, built into the sides of low mountains that overlooked the plains. But the biggest change was the color of the sky. It was easy to get used to the gray-tinged skyline of Mexico City. But out here, far away from the cars and trucks and smog, the sky gleamed a bright, beautiful blue.

We pulled into a half-empty parking lot a little away from the entrance, moving off the cobblestone road and onto a large clearing of packed red dirt. My little cousins and I jumped out into the sun and stretched out our aching legs.

Smoothing down my skirt as my uncle ran to corral my younger cousins, I enjoyed the first breath of fresh air I'd had in over a week. A few paces away was a stout building that separated us from a dozen market stalls selling brightly colored fabrics and souvenirs. The pyramids were nowhere in sight — not even when I stood on my tiptoes.

Aunt Lupe walked over to my youngest cousin, Clara, and dragged her by the ear. Clara winced and shuffled over obediently.

I'm convinced that this is the reason my aunt keeps her nails so long.

"Hada," Aunt Lupe called out to me, still holding onto my cousin's ear. "*Hazme un favor* and check that Clara and Eduardo didn't leave anything in the car."

I gave her a smile I hope didn't seem forced and checked the inside of the car, ignoring the stares we got from another family that had parked next to us.

"There's nothing!" I yelled. I stretched up and slammed the car door shut, and my eyes landed on another one of my cousins.

Miranda stood on the other side of the car as she shook out her waist-length hair, using her fingers to comb out the knots that had formed on the drive. She has brown skin that's a shade or two lighter than mine, small eyes, and a mouth that's perpetually stuck in a bored frown.

"You know you can use a brush, right?" I asked Miranda. "I mean, I *assume* you know what a brush is."

My cousin rolled her eyes and continued to detangle her hair with her fingers. "No one asked you, Fresa."

Despite being born on the exact same day 15 years ago, Miranda and I act more like familiar strangers than cousins. Maybe it's because we grew up on different sides of the border. Or maybe it's the fact that we only really see each other twice a year. But considering we're cousins and both Mexican-American, I expected us to have more in common than just passports and a birthday.

I was wearing flats and a bright pink skirt; she was wearing jeans and a black t-shirt. I have short, curly hair that turns into a lion's mane at the mere sight of a brush; she wakes up with long hair that looks like it gets ironed every morning. I almost always wear a full face of make-up; she nearly stabbed her eye out that morning when I dared her to try putting on mascara. I use Apple; she has Android.

I could go on.

"Why are you even calling me a strawberry?" I asked.

Miranda smirked. "Because you're a fresa."

"What does that even *mean*?"

"I thought you guys were the mature ones," a guy with a plain red shirt and a huge fraying backpack said. Miranda and I groaned as he pulled her over to where I was.

"Act nice," Fernando said in English, but you can tell from the way he pronounces "nice" as *"naice"* that he's not a native speaker. He's tall, with pale skin, short hair, and over-sized glasses that make him look like the nerd he is. He's also Clara and Eduardo's older brother, and the eldest of the five Rivera cousins.

"She started it," Miranda said.

"And she's jealous." I buttoned up my pink sweater. "I bet you she wishes she looked like something other than a mannequin at the Vans store."

Miranda crossed her arms and feet, conveniently showing off the Vans logo on her sneakers. "Says the one who's brought a skirt and flats to the *pyramids*. You did hear my dad tell you where we were going, right?"

"*Ay, ya,*" Fernando groaned. "Can't you go *one* day without fighting?"

Miranda rolled her eyes. "Can't *you* get off our backs, Fer?"

"Really," I said. "It's not like we're kids, Nando."

"I know you don't like sharing a room—" Nando

suddenly snapped his fingers, perking up at our shared misery. "Ah, I know! Instead of fighting, you can complain together!"

Miranda and I gave each other a look. Like hell that was gonna fix things, but at least it would get Nando off our backs.

"Okay," I said to him. "I promise we'll try to get along. But only if you promise to take me to the mall later!"

Nando laughed. "I guess I don't mind being your chauffeur again." He shuffled the backpack on his shoulder, and the *ASU* keychain he hadn't taken off bounced along with it. "Come on, Tío Luis and Tía Lupe are going in."

Nando skipped to join the rest of the family at the entrance. Miranda and I trudged on after him.

WE FOLLOWED OUR COUSINS THROUGH THE ENTRANCE AS MY aunt avoided the many guides who stepped up to offer her tours. We walked into a building at the end of the market. It was just two stories high with a several-year-old banner that hung from the roof.

"Ah!" I yelled as my foot stepped on something small and hard. I pulled off my shoe and a little pebble fell out of it.

Miranda glanced at my shoe with an "I told you so" look.

I huffed and slid my shoe back on. "At least I'm looking good. *And* I was ready on time. Really, it's not that hard to get up early."

"It's summer vacation," Miranda droned. Despite the fact she grew up in Mexico City, she speaks English with an American accent similar to mine. "I should be in bed. Or at least in the sleeping bag I call my bed."

"You're just grumpy you lost to me at *Smash*."

The battle for who got to sleep in Miranda's bed was long and treacherous, but after Nando suggested a *Smash Bros* match to stop us from ripping the bedsheets, I finally laid claim to the bed I rightfully deserved.

"Wasn't fair," Miranda said. "Fer stayed with you and Tía Mira in Arizona. I had no one to practice with."

"Jea—" The word froze in my mouth the moment I stepped outside the building.

Before me was the beginning of the ancient city of Teotihuacán. A stone pedestal two stories high greeted us, surrounded by overgrown grass that threatened to take it over. Just behind it was a set of stairs that led up to a high wall, even taller than the pedestal. Miranda and I walked past vendors selling hats and pendants from stalls set up on the pebbled road. Then we climbed the rocky stairs.

Ahead was a vast expanse of land and stone. Tall walls surrounded a huge square courtyard covered in even more dried grass. A stone pedestal sat right in the middle, empty, with staircases on each side. Similar structures stood alongside the courtyard's raised walls, but none of them were as tall as the pyramid directly opposite us.

On the far wall of the courtyard was a tall pyramid with the same stone steps as the rest of the site. Its tip was so damaged that it was more like the top of a hill than a pyramid, but it was still recognizable. It still felt as important as it must've been hundreds of years ago.

"Yeah, it's big." I jumped as Miranda appeared next to me. She walked out into the courtyard and called out behind her thick curtain of hair. "And it's why wearing flats was a bad idea."

I was going to say something back, but Nando came up behind us with the rest of the family in tow, so I, unfortunately, had to shut my mouth.

"Over there, we have the big pyramids." Aunt Lupe gestured to the long road that led through the ruins. "The pyramids of the sun and the pyramid of the moon. To get there, we have to go down this long road called the Avenue of the Dead. But first we go here."

My aunt led us down the long staircase that took us to the sunken courtyard and continued narrating. "All of this is the *ciudadela*. It's the area in front of the *pirámide* of Quetzalcóatl, and it was the center of all of Teotihuacán." She said it fast and quick, like she'd heard it and said it a million times before.

My little cousins had started an impromptu game of tag, but after my aunt grabbed Eduardo by the ear, the cry of pain was enough to get the two of them to settle down.

"All those buildings were temples." Aunt Lupe pointed to the structures atop the walls. "Most were destroyed and—ah, *¿cuál es la palabra?*"

"Ransacked?" my uncle supplied in accentless English.

"Yes, ransacked." Aunt Lupe kept us walking, and we eventually came to a stand at the side of the pyramid.

A pyramid that looked like it'd been cut in half.

"This part," my aunt continued as she pointed at a wall and staircase that wasn't connected to the rest, "was built later. Someone added it to cover the real thing."

My eyes landed on the true face of the pyramid. Dozens of stone snakes with manes of opulent feathers lined every step. They were facing forward, like they were protecting the pyramid from the wall that tried to cover them up. A black railing kept me roughly a foot away from it.

I gripped the safety rail. Maybe if I just hopped over and took a quick peek—

"*Eduardo, ¡ahí está cerrado!*" Aunt Lupe screamed at my little cousin. Eduardo sheepishly covered his ears and backed away from the railing that "blocked" us from the road that split the real and false pyramids.

Okay, so maybe I *shouldn't* jump over the railing.

For reasons that I wouldn't understand until much later, Aunt Lupe immediately led us away from the pyramid, and I was too scared of her nails to protest. We started heading back toward the staircase we had come down when I saw some people climb that stone pedestal in the courtyard's center. More early morning visitors had started arriving, and many of them were posing for photos with the pyramid as the background.

"Ooo! Can you take my picture?" I said to the family member closest to me.

Aaand unfortunately, that family member was Miranda.

"Huh?" she said.

I sighed and held out my phone. "Just take my picture."

"Or else?"

"I'll tell Nando you're the one who doesn't want us to get along."

"You think he'll believe you over me—?" Miranda suddenly cut herself off and took the phone from my hand. "Yeah, he would."

I turned around and victoriously climbed up the steps. Careful to not get anything in my shoes, I waited for a chance to stand in the pedestal's center. On the ground, Miranda held up the phone with a single hand.

"Smile," she droned.

I shook my hair out, put my hands on my hips, and busted out the biggest grin just to spite her. "Cheese!"

You know… I never thought that the keyword for a life-altering catastrophe would be "Cheese!"

The ground shook. It was rough, jostling me sideways. Even Miranda jolted in surprise, having to shuffle around and regain her footing.

I lasted less than a second. And as fast as it had happened, the ground suddenly steadied itself beneath our feet. I looked around me, but no one else seemed to have been affected by it. The other tourists were happily chatting away and taking pictures. The only one who seemed shocked as to what just happened was Miranda, and that's the only reason I was certain I'd felt anything at all.

"Just a little earthquake," Miranda mumbled as she handed me back my phone. "You'll get used to it."

She turned and walked back to the courtyard's staircase, and she kept turning her head toward the people casually milling about. I stuffed my phone in my cardigan's deep pocket and stalked after her.

Uncle Luis and Aunt Lupe were buying trinkets for my little cousins just outside the ciudadela, and the vendor happily swiped the credit card on a tiny terminal as my cousin Clara held a black stone necklace up to the sky. Behind them was the remaining stretch of long road. A large brown-green hill stood tall in the distance, and more stone walls seemed to beckon us forward to an enormous stone pyramid that was right at the end.

"*¡A las demás pirámides!*" Uncle Luis shouted, his American accent as blatant as his bright blond hair.

Miranda cringed.

Aunt Lupe corralled Clara and Eduardo toward the long road—Nando, Miranda, and I not far behind. I crossed the stone wall that enclosed the courtyard we'd just come out of.

That's when I first heard it.

It wasn't much, just a little tingle in my right ear, but then a voice echoed in my head. Low and purring.

This way, a man whispered in accentless English.

I jumped and turned around. The road stretched on far beyond me, leading me away from the pyramid at its other end. It was just grass and trees, with a highway far in the distance, but the voice in my head pulled me toward it.

There's something you must know, it said. *Follow me.*

I did. Part of it was because I rarely heard other people speak English when I was in Mexico, and part of it was because I was honestly curious. But I've already been yelled at enough for this decision, so I'd really appreciate it if I didn't get judged more than I already have been.

Rocks crunched under my feet as I made my way down the road. "Hada!" I heard Aunt Lupe yell behind me. "*¡Es por acá!*"

"Ugh," Miranda groaned. "I'll get her."

I kept walking, following the mysterious voice down a slope that took me farther away from the voices of my family.

"Fresa, didn't you hear my mom?" Miranda asked as she ran up to me. "I know you can't speak Spanish for shit, but in case you didn't notice the *giant pyramid* behind you, you're going the wrong…"

Miranda's voice trailed off the instant I saw the puma. More specifically, a puma with eagle wings as long as its body. It stalked toward us from behind a tall tree and bared its teeth.

Its breath smelled like rotten flesh.

"WHAT THE HELL?" MIRANDA HISSED.

The creature crouched low to the ground. Its eagle wings folded themselves above its scraggly and matted fur, and it let out a deep growl.

"You see it, too?" I asked, not taking my eyes off the… eagle-puma? Pum-eagle?

"Yes, I can—*agh*!" Miranda yelled as the creature slashed at her hand.

"You okay?!" I said. The two of us stumbled backward, away from the creature. "Miranda, are you—"

The pum-eagle cut me off with another growl. Its lips quivered, and it pounced.

It aimed for Miranda again. She turned to run, but the pum-eagle was too close. It would grab her. It would attack again.

And there wasn't anything she could do to defend herself.

"Look out!" I yelled.

My mind went blank as I watched the creature pounce

toward my cousin. Maybe that's what triggered it, or maybe it was a fight-or-flight thing. Or maybe it was pure desperation to keep the beast away from my cousin and me. I don't know, but whatever it was made my chest burn and rumble. A stream of energy flew out from my heart, through my extended arm, and prickled at the tip of my finger.

A needle the length of my hand grew from my nail bed. And like an arrow loaded into a crossbow, it flew out and struck the creature right between its eyes.

The creature jolted and crashed onto the floor. It let out a high-pitched whine and swiped at its forehead, flailing about a few feet in front of us.

I lifted my hand and looked at my index finger. Extending from its nail bed was a long needle, like those on razor-sharp cacti.

"Ugh… this isn't my color," I said numbly.

The creature roared in front of us. It swiped at the ground beneath it, ignoring the needle in favor of pulling itself back onto all fours.

"Hit it again!" Miranda yelled beside me.

"What the hell is going on?" I asked.

"Just *do it*!" she yelled.

The pum-eagle launched itself into another leap.

Miranda gripped my wrist and pointed my finger straight at the creature. A sense of blazing hot energy rumbled in my chest again, and I sent it straight toward my nail. Another needle shot out, and thanks to Miranda, it was aimed straight at the beast's eye.

The creature vanished in a plume of smoke the instant the needle hit it. The projectile flew past the empty space and down onto the road, bouncing harmlessly against the stone.

Miranda let go of my wrist. I looked over at her, but she wasn't looking at me. Or even at the spot where the creature had disappeared.

She was looking up at the sky.

The bright morning blue was gone. Above us were storm clouds as black as obsidian, twisting and turning amongst each other. The sky itself had shifted to a shade of deep purple, and in place of a brilliant yellow sun was the moon, shining down in rays of silver-white light.

"I… am *so* confused," I said.

Oh, poor past me. Right now, a purple sky and a vanishing pum-eagle are the *least* of your issues.

2
____

I HATE IT HERE

MIRY

You know, when I woke up this morning, I didn't expect my question of "why the hell am I here?" to turn into "where the hell *is* here?"

I guess I could have asked the weird puma, but it was dead. We killed it. I think.

"*What the hell is happening?*" I muttered in Spanish.

Ada turned to me like she was about to stab me with her needle nail. "Oh, come on!" my cousin yelled in my face. "You know I can't speak Spanish!"

"I wasn't talking to you, Fresa!"

"Then who were you talking to?"

"Myself!"

Ada shook her head and paced around the faded dirt road that led us away from the pyramids. "Okay, I don't wanna freak out, but I'm kinda freaking out!" she yelled. "What the hell is going on?"

"That's what I—" I stopped myself before I could finish that sentence. "I think you could at least give me a clue as to *what is happening*. Since when can you shoot *needles* from your fingers? What the hell is *that*?" I pointed up at the sky swirling above us in shades of violet.

"I…" Ada trailed off.

"Hm?" I asked, but Ada didn't answer. She was staring off into space behind me. "You what—"

"Miranda," she squeaked. "Look behind you."

"What—"

"Just!" Ada yelped. "Just look!"

I turned around.

My jaw dropped open.

The ruins of Teotihuacán are huge, spanning several kilometers in length. When we arrived at the archeological site less than an hour ago, the long road had been surrounded by overgrown grass, aging stone, and the remnants of a once vibrant civilization.

But now it was back. Really, it was *back*!

The ground beneath us was made of smooth stone instead of chunks of gravel. Most of the grass was gone, replaced by stone floorings that shined under the moonlight. To our right was the sunken courtyard, but it was glimmering. Every surface was made out of polished stone, alternating between light gray and deep red colors. There were even small pyramid-like structures lining the edges of the courtyard, and I *know* that those weren't there before. I've come to Teotihuacán too many times not to.

But the biggest change was the pyramid.

The sunken courtyard, or as my mom always calls it, the ciudadela, has a single small pyramid. It isn't the biggest in Teotihuacán, and it sure as hell isn't the most famous, but it's still there, just beyond the podium that sits in the middle of the ciudadela. And now it was *shining*. The gray rocks glimmered under the violet sky, so bright and brilliant that it was like the pyramid had been carved out of silver.

"That," Ada whispered, "is *beautiful*."

I snorted, not taking my eyes away from the ciudadela. "For once, I think we actually agree on something."

A heavy silence fell between us.

"Miranda," Ada said in a strained voice. "We came here with Aunt Lupe and Uncle Luis, right?"

"Yep."

I turned back to the long road that led to the rest of the ruins, or at least what used to be ruins. Now it was more like the shining, beautiful city it once was, but it was empty. Devoid of any and all life.

"They were right there." I pointed my finger toward the empty road where my parents used to be. "With our cousins, a bunch of vendors, and a crap ton of tourists."

"But… We're still in Teo-tee-hooa-can."

"It's *Teotihuacá—*" I dropped my hand and took a deep breath. If Ada couldn't get her Spanish pronunciation right after 15 years, there's no way I could fix it now. "Yeah… We're in Teotihuacán."

I looked behind us to see if another building had suddenly popped up out of nowhere, but there was nothing. It was just the same dirt road as always. My mom always said that Teotihuacán extended far beyond what was left of the ruins that existed today, but whatever magic that'd cleaned the pyramid and fixed the roads didn't reconstruct what was missing.

My skin crawled. "At least… I think we're in Teotihuacán."

"Dude, your hand!" Ada yelled.

I blinked and looked down. There were three slashes the size of my ring finger on the back of my left hand. Now that the shock of getting scratched by a weird puma and seeing that the sky changed color had worn off, I felt the sting of the wound. Drops of blood fell to the ground.

"Here!" Ada rummaged through her purse and pulled out a tissue. "Stop the blood flow!"

I took the tissue and pressed to the wound. "It's not that bad," I said numbly.

"You're *bleeding.*"

"It just a scratch. Literally." The wound wasn't deep at all, and there was only a tiny amount of blood coming out. It wasn't any worse than getting scratched by our cat.

"Are you sure?" Ada asked.

I nodded.

I've been through something way worse.

It didn't take long for the blood to dry up. I shoved the tissue into my pocket and looked around. If there were more winged pumas around, I needed a weapon.

On the road were pebbles and bits of scuffed-up grass, but just a couple paces away was a thick branch roughly the length of my leg. I picked it up.

Ada raised her eyebrows.

"What?" I said, and I adjusted my grip on my weapon. It was a bit awkward to grab, but not heavy. "You have your weird nails; I have a stick."

Ada ran her thumb over the tip of her needle nail, the tip of which just barely extended past the end of her right pointer finger. "My thing's cooler."

WE WALKED TOWARD THE DISTANT PYRAMID. ADA WAS faster than me, and I almost yelled at her for not taking the time to check the road behind us.

Every nerve in my body buzzed like they'd been electrocuted, and I had to grab the stick extra tight to stop my hands from shaking. I could almost imagine it again. A tall, lanky man, skulking out from behind a corner and reaching his hands out to grab —

No, I thought. *There's a time to panic and a time to act.*

I repeated the phrase in my head, over and over, as Ada and I made our way down the quiet road. Before, there had been chatter: tourists asking to get their picture taken, vendors selling bracelets and necklaces, and our little cousins cheering and asking my mom a million questions. But now, everything was quiet.

At least until a very loud and very familiar voice cut the air. *"AAAH!"*

"Fer?" I said.

"Nando?" Ada said.

Ada and I turned back to the ciudadela, and we saw Fernando running and screaming for his life.

From the top of the staircase that led down to the sunken courtyard, Ada and I watched as our cousin sprinted across the large square. At the side of the courtyard was a pack of five or so pumas, all of them with giant eagle wings sprouting from their backs. The winged pumas walked slowly, pushing Fer deeper into the courtyard and away from the only staircase out of the ciudadela. They weren't chasing him, not yet, but they were stalking him.

"Shit!" Ada and I said at the same time.

We turned to stare at each other in surprise, because she and I are *never* in sync, but then Fernando screamed again.

"¡¡Niñas!?" Fer yelled. Even though he was going deeper into the ciudadela, his voice was loud enough to carry over. "Run!"

"We're coming!" Ada yelled back. She started sprinting down the staircase, and I sprinted after her.

Fer saw us coming and did a double-take. *"Qué*—No! Don't run *toward* me!"

My sneakers and I reached the bottom first. The winged puma closest to the staircase turned to face me. It growled, its muscles tensed beneath its thick fur, and it pounced.

"Aaargh!" I yelled. I swung my stick like a baseball bat. I aimed for the creature's head, but I timed my swing too early. The weapon collided with one of the puma's front legs.

I know I should've been scared—better yet, I probably should've been terrified—but even though my hands were shaking, I was focused. Alert. Maybe it's because I was fighting off a creature instead of a man. Or maybe it's because I had a weapon to defend myself with. Whatever the reason, it let me push back. Fight instead of freeze.

The force of the blow was enough to send the puma tumbling off-course. Its massive claws scraped the flooring, creating deep, long gashes into the solid stone.

"*Agh!*" I ran and swung my weapon again. I aimed for the neck, but I missed and instead hit the puma's feathery wing.

The creature disappeared. The moment my stick touched it, it burst into a plume of smoke. My weapon *thunked* against the ground.

I noticed the other one too late. The second winged puma charged at me from the sky, flapping its massive eagle wings.

I didn't have time to raise my stick for a full swing. Instead, I used the momentum of my body to turn myself toward the winged puma and pull my weapon into an upward slash.

The next second happened in slow-motion. As I stared into the puma's snout, a razor-sharp projectile pierced its nose. The creature roared in pain, and then my weapon grazed the tip of one of its sharp claws.

The puma vanished into a haze of mist. I gasped. The tip of my stick *thunked* against the ground as my arms drooped down.

I spun around and saw Ada. One of her flats was askew on her foot, and she was pointing at the space where the winged puma had been.

"Wow," she breathed. "I am *so* happy I didn't hit your head!"

I was about to give a comeback when our cousin screamed in pure panic.

Right. Fer. Our cousin, who was currently being stalked by the other three winged pumas.

"Cover me!" Ada broke out into a run, her frilly skirt swishing around her as she sprinted across the ciudadela.

I gritted my teeth. "Yeah, I'll just cover you with a *stick*."

I overtook Ada immediately for two reasons. One, I'm more fit than she is, and two, I was the one in tennis shoes. That meant that I was the first to see Fer get cornered.

Fer was standing in the middle of the courtyard's stone pedestal, and the pumas walked around it in slow, menacing circles.

As I ran the fifty or so meters it took to get to the pedestal, my mind processed what had just happened. It made sense how Ada's needle could kill the pumas, but there was no explanation for why my *stick* could kill them. It was like it just *vanished* the instant the second strike had hit.

Wait, I thought.

It just takes two *hits*.

Why the two hits? I had no clue. But I wasn't complaining.

It's a good thing that Fer was pleading with the pumas not to eat him, because that meant they didn't notice me running.

My stick hit the puma on my right. It grazed its tail. By the time the puma's head had turned around, I was already swinging my weapon again. My second strike hit its back leg. And just like before, the puma vanished.

The other two pumas rushed toward me. I raised my stick to bat away the one closest to me. By the time I'd readied my weapon again, a lightning-fast needle struck its hind leg.

A barrage of ten-or-so needles flew toward the remaining creatures. Three made contact, causing the pumas to vanish in a plume of mist. The rest of the needles bounced off the pyramid.

I leaned forward and loosened my grip on the battered stick. My black hair fell around my head.

I just smacked a goddamn puma, I thought. *I did that… with a* stick!

To my right, Fer was checking over his body, like he was making extra sure that his red t-shirt wasn't hiding any bloodstains, and he'd lost his dorky backpack. To my left, Ada was panting like she'd just run a marathon.

The needle on Ada's nail bed glistened beneath the shimmering purple sky. I had no idea how she could even do that, much less how she could shoot out so many that she could turn her hand into a pseudo gatling gun. I was suddenly afraid of her.

But worse, I was jealous of her.

"Why… did that work?" Ada asked.

"They're a two-hit K.O.," Fer said numbly. "You just have to hit them twice and they die."

I almost rolled my eyes. "Of course *you're* the one to make a video game reference."

"Hada, how did you make that thing with you nail?" Fer asked. His glasses were crooked on his face, and they reflected the sky's brilliant purple light. "And what the *frick* just happened?"

And before I ask why the hell he was saying "frick", a thunderous growl echoed throughout the ciudadela.

It came from behind me. I turned to the sky, shining in a series of violet hues, and saw a mass of shadows swooping down.

It was a horde of winged pumas, beating their enormous eagle wings.

And they were heading straight toward us.

3

——————————

I REALLY HATE IT HERE

MIRY

"Run!" Fer yelled.

"This way!" Ada said. She rushed toward the long staircase we used to go into the ciudadela, and Fer and I ran after her.

Another winged puma flew across the courtyard, only to land at the bottom of the ciudadela's staircase. From the center of the courtyard, the creature was just a prick in the distance. But it was large enough for us to see it stalk toward us.

"Not this way!" Ada yelled, doing a 180-degree turn that made her slip in her shoes.

But there was nowhere else to run. When we looked behind us, we saw that more of the winged pumas had started circling the ciudadela, lining up the high wall. They were surrounding us, but they weren't attacking.

They're cats, after all. They like to play with their food.

"To the pedestal!" Fer yelled, his Mexican accent thick with panic. "*¡Ahora!*"

Fer isn't an athletic guy. But he's four years older than us and way taller, so he had no issues pulling us up the shining steps to the ciudadela's pedestal. When one of Ada's shoes slipped off her foot, he hauled her up the rest of the way.

"My shoe!" Ada cried. Fer pulled her back before she could go and get it.

"Shoes!" Fer gasped.

By the time Fer had pulled off his Converse, the winged pumas had begun their charge.

I counted five of them, then ten, then 15, then *20*, running or flying across the courtyard. They crossed the enormous distance fast enough to make 50 meters seem like ten. Ada let out a barrage of needle nails that sailed through the air. Some of them hit, most of them didn't, and at least three of the creatures burst into mist.

The winged pumas kept coming, and it was only the immense distance between the pedestal and the outer wall that kept them from swarming us.

Ada spun around to aim her finger at any ball of fur and feathers she could see. Fer and I were forced to spin with her so we wouldn't get impaled. Needle after needle sprouted from her nail bed, but Ada was panting and her hand was shaking.

One of the creatures running on all fours dodged Ada's needle barrage by flying up into the air. It was getting close, roughly ten meters away, so Fer gripped his shoes, pulled back his arm, and threw his Converse into the air.

The first one went wide. The second one grazed its wing. Ada finished it off with a needle to its chest.

"I'm out of shoes!" Fer cried.

Another puma bounded toward us from the side. One of Ada's nails clipped its wing. But it was still climbing up the pedestal, so I spun around and threw my stick at it.

The creature vanished into mist. My weapon shattered into splinters.

"Shit," I hissed.

"I could use a little help here!" Ada shot another barrage at two creatures that came flying from the eastern side. Her needle nails kept flying, but they were taking a second or two longer to grow.

"What do you want me to do?" I pulled my Vans off my feet and chucked them at a puma roughly five meters away. Both of my tennis shoes hit its back, and the puma vanished.

"I-I don't know! Something!" Ada's movements were getting sluggish, like she was moving through water instead of air. "I got weird powers! Just—try to get some, too!"

The crowd of winged pumas thinned out. But more creatures circled the perimeter, casting long shadows into the sunken courtyard. The creatures I'd originally counted were slowly getting picked off, but now I counted at least 20 backup pumas at the edges of the courtyard, waiting for Ada to run out of steam before charging in.

I gulped. "Try *how*?"

"Just try something!" Ada kicked off her remaining shoe. Fer picked it up and chucked it at a winged puma that was flying down from above.

He missed. By a lot.

I closed my eyes and gritted my teeth. "Give me something to work with!"

"I felt something!" Ada sent out another barrage of nails. "It was just me and it—and it felt like my body had to do…"

"Something?"

"Yeah!"

An eerie quiet came over the ciudadela. I didn't have to open my eyes to know that all the creatures that had charged at us were dead, but I could also feel the stares of two dozen other creatures waiting at the edges of the courtyard. Waiting.

My body shook. The slashes on my hand started stinging again.

I knew that if I couldn't do something, the creatures would attack. They'd get us, and they'd do a lot more than just slash my hand.

And that's when I felt it. A warm, swirling feeling in my chest that tugged at my consciousness. It was a kind of energy I had never felt before, one which was pushing at my ribs and telling me to use it. To do *something*, even if I didn't know what that something was.

So I acted on instinct. And my instinct was the stupidest thing I could've done.

I opened my eyes, stood beside my cousins, and threw my arms wide open.

"Come *ooon*!" I yelled at the growling beasts. "Come at me, *cobardes*!"

The taunt worked. Some of the pumas broke into a sprint. Some took flight with their massive eagle wings. They ran at us from all sides, crossing several meters in the span of a single second. Fer screamed and threw his arms around our shoulders, prepared to use his body to protect us from getting mauled.

I focused on the creature closest to us. One who was flying through the air with its claws extended. It was ten, maybe 15 meters away from us.

That one, I thought. *Twice in a row, at its face.*

The warmth in my chest flew up to my head. The puma suddenly recoiled backward and scrunched up its nose, as if recovering from a sudden hit, before vanishing into mist a moment later.

I had no idea how I did that. But I knew that if I stopped to think about it, I wouldn't be able to fight off the rest before we got overrun. I was calm and focused, just like I was when the winged puma was a second away from pouncing on me.

So I got to work.

The other creatures weren't fazed by their friend turning into mist. They kept charging at us in the same pattern, and that let me hone in on them faster. I stepped out from under Fer's arm and focused my gaze on the puma who was running on all fours.

That one, I thought. *Twice, at its back.*

A prickling sensation twinged on my head. It was like getting poked by a steel pin, twice in a row. The creature I was looking at jumped in surprise before vanishing into the air. The same thing happened when I honed my gaze on the next creature, and the next, and the next.

I heard the flapping of wings and turned my head to the southern sky. Four more of the creatures were getting dangerously close to us, so I concentrated on them.

That one, I thought of the puma roughly ten or so meters away. *Twice, at its left wing.*

The prickling sensation returned; twice in a row. The creature cried out before poofing into mist.

I kept going. First with the creatures in the air, then with the creatures running at us from the west. Every 'attack" was happening almost as fast as I could think it. Unlike Ada's needles, my projectiles were tiny and invisible. The pumas couldn't dodge my attacks, but I still aimed for large parts of their bodies to make sure I kept hitting my mark.

"What are you doing?" Ada asked, sounding exhausted and awed at the same time.

I didn't answer because I didn't know what I was doing. And because I was too focused on the pumas. Everything felt controlled and precise. As I took down the creatures one by one, I vaguely wondered if this was how snipers felt. Picking off their targets from high in their tower.

I kept going until there was only one creature left. It came at us from the east, and it made a massive leap into the air. It spread out its wings and circled us overhead, likely thinking that, by going around us, it could escape my shots.

Twice, in its right wing.

The puma flinched. Its growl was cut short as it faded into the nighttime air.

The danger was gone. So was my adrenaline.

My knees gave out on me as I sunk to the pedestal. The prickling sensation on my head vanished as the ends of my hair brushed the smooth surface of the stone pedestal. I took in ragged breaths that made my throat ache.

The focused calm that quelled my nerves fled my body, leaving me shaking on the floor. I was suddenly acutely aware that a pack of vicious hybrid creatures had stalked us, ran at us, and nearly mauled us.

And somehow I took down 20 of them.

"Miranda," Ada said slowly. "What… did you *do?*"

"Y-You tell me," I said. My words were coarse, rough. Like they'd been pulled from the depths of the earth.

I know. The voice, speaking in perfect, unaccented English, said. It was the voice of a man, and he spoke with a measured cadence of someone who commands power.

It made every hair on my arms stand on edge.

Fer's face was scrunched up like he was puzzling out a math problem, and his arm tightened itself around Ada's shoulders. Ada was spinning her head around like a lost owl, searching for something. So they could hear the voice, too.

It has begun, the voice said. *Your magic has awoken, but you have cracked the seal. And now you must repair it.*

Part of me wanted to yell back and ask who the hell he was, to beg for anything that could tell us what the hell he meant by that. But his voice was so commanding, so sure of itself in its words, that the other part of me felt like an idiot for questioning anything at all.

Seek out the Archivist named Daniel Merino Guitérrez, the voice continued. *He will guide you to the truth about the gods, and he will help you on your journey to seal the spirit whom you've set free.*

Welcome, future Archivists, to the world of Teotihuacán.

Then the voice was gone.

I blinked, and I was suddenly staring up at Ada. She was still standing, and I was still kneeling, but now I was kneeling on dirt that was filtering its way into the ends of my long hair.

Ada and I weren't on the stone pedestal anymore. We weren't even in the ciudadela. We were at the edge of the road that marked the unofficial end of the archeological site, right where we were at the start of this whole mess. The sky above us had switched from purple to bright blue.

All that happened, and do you want to know what my first thought was?

What. The. Hell.

What can I say? Life-threatening situations really bring out the inner poet in me.

4

YEAH, I CAN'T SING IN SPANISH

ADA

BEING THE MIDDLE KID SUCKS.

Yes, I know that I'm an only child. So is Miranda, but on that little trip to Teotihuacán, she and I were the middle kids. So while I was still reeling from the shock of getting transported to a different world, Nando was the cousin Aunt Lupe interrogated after he came running out of the ciudadela with all of our shoes.

"Fernando," Aunt Lupe said sternly. "*¿A dónde se fueron?*"

Miranda shoved her injured hand in her pocket to hide the scratches.

"A-Ah, Hada wanted to see the pyramid in the ciudadela again," Nando said, speaking English for my benefit. He finished tying up his Converse and readjusted his glasses. "She went running back in; Miry followed, so I had to follow, too! Hada's shoe slipped off, and Miry and I threw our shoes in solidarity!"

And that's how we got stuck with the worst cover story ever. And the worst part of it all? Aunt Lupe and Uncle Luis didn't even question him! Why? Because Nando's 19 and Miranda and I are 15, so that's the story we got.

I was too tired to care. I was even too tired to ask why

Nando didn't just tell the adults everything, which is what the goody-two-shoes usually does. I think the only reason why we didn't get lectured is because Clara and Eduardo started laughing at us.

They stopped laughing when Aunt Lupe twisted their ears.

THE CITY AROUND US HAD GONE BACK TO BEING RUINS. Shining stones were replaced by weathered rocks, and tufts of stray grass wove their way through what was left of the long path.

When we reached the two main pyramids at the end of the road—not just the small structure in the ciudadela—I was barely aware enough to realize we'd made it to the fabled pyramids of the sun and moon. They were huge, at least a hundred feet tall, and I was already overwhelmed by the massive amount of stone stairs that led to the top.

Thankfully, we couldn't actually go up them. Apparently, you could a few years ago, but so many people had climbed up the steps that they were starting to wear away at the pyramid, so the site banned people from walking up them. It's the only bit I remember of that part of the trip, and that's because I was so happy that I wouldn't be forced to climb even more stairs.

I wish I could say I was reflecting on everything, on the pum-eagles, the fight, and the fact that I could turn my nail bed into a mini Gatling gun that shoots cacti needles. But I can't. I was too exhausted to think of anything, or to take in the rest of the enormous ruins. I only had enough energy to shuffle my feet forward, letting stray pebbles sneak their way into my flats, and reluctantly trudge away as the blazing sun beat down upon us.

At some point in time, I noticed that Nando had found his stupidly big backpack. He was walking and chatting with our aunt and uncle as if nothing had happened. He might've been fumbling his words a bit, and he was smiling a bit too much for it to be natural for him, but it was enough to convince our family that we weren't hiding something as big as fighting off wild pum-eagles.

But maybe it was good that he was the one keeping our family entertained, because Miranda and I were silent. My body felt like it'd been through a marathon, and it was a struggle to keep myself moving. Miranda wasn't much better. She kept rubbing her throat, and she almost tripped on the stone steps that lined the long trek to the pyramids.

As we kept walking beneath the heat of the blazing sun, I found some of my energy came back to me. The heat was inviting, and I soaked it up like a lizard taking in the sun. I took off my bright pink cardigan so I could take in every drop of the summer warmth as I rubbed at my nails.

After leaving the world of the purple sky, I took what was left of the warm feeling in my chest and pushed through my pointer finger. It made the cactus needle that was growing out of it revert back to its usual nail bed state. The only thing that was strange about it now was the lack of orange nail polish, but I could still feel a connection with it, and even though I instinctively knew it would take all the energy left in me, I was certain I could make the needle grow back again. It wouldn't be easy. It would hurt. But I could do it.

Once I had enough energy back, I walked up to Nando. "Dude, what happened—"

"Not now, Hada," Nando whispered. He looked over at Aunt Lupe and winced. "Later."

I reluctantly shut my mouth. I'm not close with my aunt, but I know her well enough to make sure I don't get into trouble while she's around. And I definitely consider getting sent to a different world as "trouble".

When we finally got back to the car, the five of us cousins crammed ourselves into the back seat. I got squished between the door, Nando, and Clara, who plopped herself onto my lap, and then we were off.

"How did you like the pyramids, Hada?" Uncle Luis asked from the driver's seat.

"And how are your feet?" Aunt Lupe asked. "You didn't bring the best shoes to come to Teotihuacán."

"My feet are okay," I said. But they were stiff, so I stretched out my toes. Well, as much as I could with a seven-year-old on my lap. "But either way, fashion is worth the pain. I was the best-dressed person there and you know it."

Uncle Luis laughed. "I won't argue with that! Later you can give me some styling tips. Us Americans gotta stick together, you know?"

The car sped up as we merged onto the highway. I let out a quick yell and wrapped an arm around Clara's waist, making an impromptu seatbelt.

Not for the first time, I wondered why this whole seating arrangement was allowed here. At least in America, they'd make everyone sit in actual seats. With actual seatbelts!

"*¡Me estás apretando!*" Clara said as her fingers grabbed at my arms.

Nando leaned over. "She says it's too tight," he said, even as I watched him tighten his own arm around Eduardo, keeping his nine-year-old brother firmly in his lap.

"Hada, it hurt!" Clara said, her accent emphasizing the "u".

"I'm sorry," I said slowly. "Would it make it better if I… do *this*?"

I started tickling Clara's side with my free hand, and the kid started laughing and screaming right away.

"*Nooo!*" Clara screamed as laughter filled the small car. "*¡No dije que hicieras esooo!*"

Clara laughed even louder as I kept tickling her, and soon enough, Nando joined in on the fun by tickling Eduardo. The kid was yelling in Spanish, so I couldn't make out exactly what he was saying, but knowing him, it was probably something about being too old to get tickled. Soon enough, everyone in the car had joined in the laughter.

Well, everyone except one.

With how cramped we were in the backseat, I couldn't see Miranda. But I didn't hear anything come from that corner of the car. No laughter, not even a chuckle.

When Aunt Lupe asked if anyone wanted McDonald's, Miranda let out a hard, "No, Mamá," that earned her a sharp stare. And when Uncle Luis asked her if she enjoyed coming back to the pyramids after so long, all she said was, "Yeah, Dad," before falling back into a pensive silence.

"Now that we have Hada trapped with us," Uncle Luis said, "I say we put on some music for her. What do you say, *mi amor?*"

Aunt Lupe sighed fondly. "Juanga or Lola Beltrán?"

"Hmmm," Uncle Luis said. "Lola! Ah, can you put on —"

Before my uncle could even finish his request, the sound of a trumpet backed by violins burst through the car's speakers.

"*¿Cómo supiste que quería esa?*" Uncle Luis asked. From his reflection in the car's mirror, I saw him give my aunt an enormous grin.

Aunt Lupe laughed. "*Porque es la que siempre pides.*"

I was about to ask Nando to translate for me when a woman's rich, deep voice burst into song. I didn't recognize the jaunty melody, and she was singing too fast for me to pick out any words I might know.

"I don't think I know this one," I said.

"Of course you don't," Miranda said in a low voice, one I definitely wasn't supposed to hear.

My aunt and uncle didn't notice. They were already singing along to Lola's voice, to a song Nando said was "La Tequilera", and after a few bars, I hummed along to the melody. It was fun joining in with my aunt and uncle, but I felt the enjoyment slip away as fast as it had come. Because when the next song came on, Nando and his two siblings jumped in, singing Spanish lyrics in off-key harmonies. It was another song I didn't know, and I was easily drowned out by Clara and Eduardo's high-pitched voices.

I was stuck there, awkwardly humming along to unfamiliar tunes in a language that should have been familiar, for the rest of the drive into Mexico City. The only one who sung less than me was Miranda, and that's because she stayed silent the whole way back.

I'VE NEVER FELT LIKE I WAS FULLY PART OF MY FAMILY. Yeah, I see them every now and then, but there was always something different about me. Different language, different accent, different life. They even spell my nickname differently!

You see, most of my family spells my nickname H-A-D-A. Though the 'H' is silent. I didn't mean to name myself the Spanish equivalent of "Fairy" at five years old, but it's the nickname that stuck. Plus, it's better than watching non-Spanish speakers try to spell "Guadalupe".

Unlike my parents, my aunt and uncle had actually given my cousin a sensible name, one that any coffee shop employee can write without you having to spell it out. Mi-ran-da. Nice and simple. Something that even American kindgarteners would like.

You see, my mom and my aunt are close. Close as in I-will-name-my-child-after-you close. That's why I got Aunt Lupe's name while Miranda got my mom's.

I've always wished it were the other way around.

Miranda's name is good. Miranda's name wouldn't get mispronounced by teachers. Miranda's name works in English. She's the one who lives in Mexico, so she should've gotten the super Mexican name. Right?

No. I got it. I'm pretty sure the name was convenient when

Miranda lived with Uncle Luis' parents in Boston for a year, but I've always been too resentful to ask.

Speaking of Uncle Luis.

Uncle Luis has gone full native, or at least as native as a White American in Mexico can get. He's a business analyst who met my aunt when he was traveling Mexico on a gap year, and he's been in love "with both Mexico and Lupe" ever since. And he genuinely loves this place. He learned the language, the culture, and can even sing more *rancheras* than my mom. His real name is Lewis, but my family, being my family, has always called him "Luis". Instead of being offended, he took it in stride. He even introduced himself to my mom as "American Luis".

Needless to say, my family's been a fan of him ever since. Especially my mom. There's even a running joke that if my dad wasn't around, she'd go and steal Uncle Luis from my Aunt Lupe. Then we had the running joke that if my mom steals Uncle Luis, Aunt Lupe gets to steal my dad.

And the weirdest thing of all? My Aunt Lupe, who thinks that puns are stupid and fart jokes are childish, finds this all *funny*. And if I'm being honest, I find it funny, too. It helps that Aunt Lupe and Uncle Luis are the only members of my extended family who seem to remember that I can only speak three or so lines of Spanish. Probably because my uncle had to learn it from scratch. Out of everyone on this side of my family, they're the easiest ones to talk to.

Miranda used to be easy to talk to. But now she didn't want to talk to anyone. Much less me.

We weren't always at each others' throats. We actually used to get along, to the point where nine-year-old me thought of her as a friend. But when we were ten, we had a fight.

It's been five years, and we still haven't recovered from it.

5

——————————

BETRAYED BY NANDO!

ADA

When we finally got to Uncle Luis and Aunt Lupe's house in Mexico City, Miranda made a beeline for the kitchen. Nando followed her, and I'd recovered enough of my energy to stay right on his tail.

"Nando, what the hell happened?" I asked as we walked into the tiled kitchen. My mom and dad weren't in the city at the time—they were on a cheesy couple's trip in a state called Aguascalientes—but the rest of our family was in the living room. So I tried my best to keep my voice to a low whisper. "We were at the site, then we were suddenly in a beautiful and messed up world. And then I got—"

"Nothing happened," Nando said.

My mouth fell open. Even Miranda, who had been gulping down water like she'd been in a desert, set down her water bottle.

"What do you mean 'nothing happened'?" I asked. "I have cacti needles in my fingers. Miranda has weird mind powers—"

"I do *not*," Miranda interrupted, "have weird mind powers."

I ignored her. "And we got *attacked*—"

"No, we didn't." Nando grabbed my shoulders. "We didn't

get attacked. You don't have cactus nails. Miry doesn't have mind powers, and—and nothing!"

"Nando, you're not making sense," I said. "You were there. You saw—"

"Hada, *please*." Nando's hands tightened themselves around my shoulders. "Nothing happened. Not until… Until I can figure something out. So stay quiet, and I'll figure out what's going on. Okay?"

I bit my tongue.

Who are you to order me around like that? I thought. *You're my cousin, not my dad.*

I wanted to say it. I really, really wanted to say it. But the more I stayed silent, the more I wanted to concede and get Nando to stop staring at me like I'd asked him to hide Clara's dolls.

"Who made you king of the castle?" Miranda asked.

I spun to face her, pulling myself out of Nando's grip.

Miranda gave Nando a suspicious glare. "Why're you trying to tell her what to do? You're her cousin, not her dad."

"Huh?" I said. Because here was Miranda, telling off Nando, all to defend *me*.

Nando winced. "*Miry, se que esto te está enojando—*"

"*No estoy enojada.*" Miranda sucked her teeth. "But I will get angry if you keep talking to us like we're kids. We're not Clara and Eduardo. If you want us to pretend like all that didn't happen, you need a better reason than 'because I said so'."

"Because I'm asking you to," Nando said. "As a favor to me."

If it'd just been him and me, I might've said "yes". Because this was Nando asking, and he and I are close enough that I usually go along with his suggestions.

But Miranda was there. She had her arms crossed in front of her chest, and her face was twisted into a deep scowl.

"No," Miranda said.

Nando gave me a pleading look, but I shook my head. If he

couldn't convince Miranda to go along with this, then there's no way I could convince her.

But more than that, I actually agreed with her.

Nando pinched the bridge of his nose. "Nothing happened. Remember that. Unless you want to drag our parents into this mess."

Nando sighed and left the kitchen.

Miranda and I stood there. I let the awkward silence extend for five seconds before I couldn't stand it anymore.

"Hey," I said. "I know we… have our issues, but I kind of saved your butt at the pyramids, and we both have these weird power things, so do you wanna have a—"

"Temporary truce?" Miranda let out a breath through her nose. "If it means we get to ignore what Fer just said and figure out what the hell happened, then yeah. But he's right about one thing. If we tell our parents, they'll take Fer's side and tell us to stay away from this."

"Right." I nodded and clapped my hands once, relieved that I didn't have to waste time pleading my case to her. "Okay, let's do this! I'll look up stuff about Teotihuacán!"

"No, *I'm* looking up stuff about Teotihuacán." Miranda chugged down what was left of her water before stalking her way to the staircase that led up to her room. "Because unless you wanna tell me that your magic nail gave you the power to understand websites in Spanish, you're probably going to struggle even with the archivists stuff."

Miranda paused at the first step, and her hand curled itself around the railing.

"And for the record," she said, "I saved your ass, too."

You'd think that having a dad named Jorge Reyes would mean that I know how to speak my family's language.

Yeah, no. He's a third-generation Mexican-American who barely speaks more Spanish than I do.

He and my mom met at university. He was failing calculus; she was in the mathematics club. He went during open tutoring hours and fell in love at first sight. He asked her where she was from, and after learning she was from Mexico City, he told her, "*Eres muy hembra.*"

My mom then spent ten minutes correcting his pronunciation and explaining that he'd called her "very female." He waited until she was done to ask her out. In English, thankfully. And after he visited Mexico City and got my Aunt Lupe's approval, the rest was history.

My parents are great. Yeah, I know that's a weird thing for a teenager to say, but they are. Their jobs keep them busy, and maybe that's why I actually like hanging out with them. Sure, it means that my mom never had the time to teach me Spanish, but they genuinely like being parents. They used to tell me all the time that one day I'd get a brother or sister.

I didn't get either. But that's okay, because when I was 14, Nando moved to Arizona for university.

Nando's the oldest of us cousins, and boy, does he act like it. Unlike Clara and Eduardo, he's the only one who inherited my Aunt Sara's white skin. Despite him being 100% Mexican, he's pale enough to the point where people in Arizona look at the two of us and think *he's* the American one.

Since neither Miranda or I have siblings, Nando automatically assumed the big brother role for the both of us. He's also the tallest of us, but with his giant square glasses, he's not really that threatening. But he is smart. Smart enough to get a scholarship to Arizona State University that covers 80% of his tuition.

Nando studies a lot—you kind of have to when an academic scholarship is paying most of your international student fees. But somehow he always found time to both hang out with me and play enough *Call of Duty* that he gets the highest kill count in every match. In the span of one year, my cousin became the fun older brother I always wished I'd had.

It's why I was so confused when Nando didn't want to help us out.

Maybe I was naïve, but I was hoping that the cousin I'd grown so close to would be on my side. That he'd look for the answers with me. And instead of him, I had Miranda. The cousin I've fought with more than I've fought with my own parents.

Yeah. I already knew that this was going to be interesting.

BETRAYED BY THE INTERNET!

ADA

I TRIED, OKAY? I REALLY, REALLY TRIED.

I spent hours searching on Google. *Hours*. I searched "archivists". I found Archive of Our Own. I went into an incognito tab. I still found Archive of Our Own. I tried combining the keywords "archive" and "seal", but all I got was my results page filled with AO3 fanfics, and I refused to click on any of them.

That's how the rest of the afternoon went. I typed in keyword after keyword, combining terms like "archive", "archivists", "purple sky", "puma", "eagle", "pum-eagle", "cactus", "nail", "cactus-nail", "invisible nails", and "what to do when you suddenly get magical powers". I didn't find anything. And to make matters worse, my last search led me to a Reddit thread that suggested I either go seek professional mental help or go cleanse myself at the nearest church.

I groaned and collapsed onto Miranda's bed. My cousin was still at her desk, typing away search after search. She'd shoved in her earbuds as soon as she settled down at the desk, ignoring me completely in favor of her Dell laptop.

I even tried looking for Daniel Merino Guitérrez on half a dozen social media sites, but I had no idea which Daniel was the one we were looking for. It didn't help that I spent half an hour searching the name "Daniel Guitérrez" before remembering that Mexicans here have two last names by default.

That's why my cousin's full name, Miranda Donaldson Rivera, doesn't have a hyphen. Donaldson is her *first* last name. The reason my name is Guadalupe Reyes-*hyphen*-Rivera is because America only uses the one last name, and my mom insisted on giving me the Rivera name somehow.

If you think our names our long, Nando's full name is Fernando Rafael Rivera Ortega. The guy has a first name, two last names, *and* a middle name!

I shut off my iPad to give myself a break. The new song in my playlist started, and I let my eyes drift around the bedroom.

Miranda's room was the definition of a tomboy mess. Despite her desk and closet being half-empty, the room was covered in loose papers, disorganized sneakers, and wrinkled hoodies. The sleeping bag she'd been using was rumpled in a corner, right next to a banged-up skateboard with worn wheels. Stray strands of her waist-length hair curled into the light gray carpet, just begging someone —*anyone*—to bring in a vacuum.

There was a cluster of used notebooks hanging precariously over the edge of the desk, next to an old drawing tablet I'd yet to see Miranda use. The only part of the room that was semi-organized was the area around her bed, and that's because it was the territory *I* had claimed for myself.

Still, in spite of the mess, it was nothing compared to the clutter on the walls. Posters of skateboarders I didn't recognize clashed with bright green handkerchiefs, photos of a protest that filled the streets of Mexico City, and cut-out newspaper clippings. The only things that were familiar to me were the occasional *Dark Souls* and *Final Fantasy* prints, but those were gaming franchises I hadn't played yet.

There were some suspiciously empty sections around the room, roughly the size of large posters. There was also a bag in

Miranda's closet sealed shut with a suitcase lock. She didn't mention it, but she didn't need to. That suitcase was clearly a *do not touch* item, and Miranda hadn't left the room long enough for me to seriously consider brute-forcing the lock's combination.

There was also a giant banner that stretched across half of the wall. It was purple, with a huge symbol of Venus in the middle. I'd been tempted to ask Miranda why exactly she had that banner, but I held my tongue. It probably had something to do with a Mexican event or something. If it was important, then I'd practically be begging Miranda to roll her eyes at me.

Well, sorry I don't keep up with news from a country I don't even live in. Sorry I didn't grow up here. Sorry I'm not like you, a proper Mexican teenager who knows Spanish and never gets told she's "too American" by other Mexicans.

Ugh, just thinking about it all was giving me a headache. Making sure I paused my music so Miranda couldn't hear it, I pulled my headphones off.

"This is hopeless!" I said loudly. "I can't find anything about archivists or pum-eagles. I can't even find anything about magical powers other than this weird stunt that happened in New York last summer for a film shoot."

Miranda pulled out a single earbud. "Pum-eagle?"

"Yeah!" I said. "That puma with the eagle wings. Puma, eagle, pum-eagle!"

"I'm not calling it that."

"Oh, so you think you have a better name?"

"Winged puma."

"That… Whatever. Pum-eagle is still cooler." I sighed. "I've got nothing."

"I do."

"It's just impossibl—wait, *what*? Let me see!"

I scrambled off the bed and over to the desk. Miranda quickly pressed something on her phone, likely hitting pause on her own music, before hunching over her laptop again.

"Finally found something that doesn't talk about Aztec gods." She smirked. "Main gods of *Teotihuacán*. Quetzalcóatl, Tláloc, something called the flayed god, and the great goddess. Apparently, she looks like a spider."

"Uh, I know Quetzalcóatl. That's the one that turns into a huge snake with feathers, right?"

"At least you know that one," Miranda said. "Tláloc's the god of rain, and apparently the other two are pretty unknown because a lot of the history of the city's been lost to time. It says that—"

A red text box flashed across the screen, covering almost all of the web page behind it. Words in Spanish floated in the text box, and beside me, Miranda burst into a stream of phrases and curses that I had no way of understanding.

"Hey, you promised a truce!" I said. "That means no speaking Spanish at me!"

"I wasn't talking to you," she grumbled as she furiously tried to click on the text box. "And that wasn't part of the deal."

"It is now. And what the hell is going on with your laptop?"

"Nothing."

"It's something!"

"It's just a weird virus." Miranda refreshed the page. When the text box appeared again right before the page loaded, she closed it and restarted the entire browser. "Most of the websites I've found are either useless or super sketchy, so one of them must've messed with my laptop. It's the only way I could get anything related to Teotihuacán and not Aztec stuff."

"What's the difference?" I asked.

"The Aztecs came after Teotihuacán. They were still around during the *conquista*, and they were way more documented. Teotihuacán was already a ruin by the time the Spanish arrived."

I hummed. "And you didn't wanna tell me you found this website?"

"There wasn't anything to tell!" Miranda scrolled through her search history and brought up the website again. But just like it had before, the bright red text box blocked our view of the web page. "This was the first site I found where I could actually read part of the article before the bug shut me out of it."

The name of the site was in Spanish, so I peered around the edges of the text box to see if I could get a clue as to what it was. I couldn't see any text, but there was an edge of a photo that was awfully similar to ads that promised live chats with beautiful women who are *definitely* looking for singles in my area.

"This… seems kinda sketchy," I said.

"If I could just get this virus off, I could actually try to figure out what the hell that voice was talking about," Miranda said.

"Hmmm. Well, maybe if you told me what that pop out is saying, I could help!"

"You're an Apple user, Fresa. What do you know about tech?"

I hardened my jaw. "You promised a truce."

Miranda's fingers froze above her keyboard. After a moment, she sighed. "Website blocked," she read out. "Enter keyword."

I nodded. "May as well give it a shot!"

"Hey, don't touch my —"

I typed in *"archivist"*, and a small *"x"* appeared next to the word. Miranda pulled the laptop away from me and typed in *"archivista"*, and the *"x"* appeared again. I immediately tried *"archivists"*, and Miranda tried *"archivistas"*, but both gave us the same red *"x"*.

We went at it for a while, typing in a version of pyramid, magic, puma, pum-eagle, and winged puma. What I typed in English, Miranda retyped in Spanish. What she typed in Spanish, I retyped in English after guessing what the word meant. I was wrong half the time, but still.

Miranda typed *pecho*. Another "*x*" appeared.

"What does that mean?"

"Chest," Miranda said. "That's where I felt… my magical thing. I felt it in my head, but that was after. The first time was in my chest."

"Maybe it doesn't come from our chests!" I pulled the laptop to me. "Maybe it comes from…"

I typed in "*heart*". I got an "*x*". I typed in "*corazon*", one of the few Spanish words I actually know. I got another "*x*". Miranda typed in "*corazón*" with the accent over the "o". She got an "*x*", and I stuck my tongue out at her.

"I don't know what else it could be," I said. "We've gone through everything! And it isn't even the cheesy option! Try 'blood' next. Maybe that's—"

"Warm."

I blinked in confusion. "Yeah? I guess blood is warm because it's in our bodies."

"I felt warmth in my chest right before I used my magic." Miranda bit her bottom lip and typed in a new word into the text box:

calor

The laptop chimed.

The red text box blinked out of existence, but it didn't take us back to the sketchy website. Instead, it took us to a new page. The screen flashed green as words in big tacky letters— in the kind of font you'd see in a website from the early 2000s —pixelated into existence.

"Welcome, future Archivist," Miranda translated, and I could hear the smile in her voice, "to the world of Teotihuacán."

I laughed. "Told ya this would lead to something!"

"If you wish to uncover the truth of your powers," Miranda continued, "and the truth of Teotihuacán, prove yourself. Find the clues. Find your answers. Find the deities of this forgotten city."

Below the giant tacky letters was a smaller line of text, but I didn't need to understand Spanish to know what I was seeing.

It was an address. Somewhere in Mexico City.

"We need to go there!" I said, already running back to my iPad to pull up the address on Apple Maps. "This isn't a virus —it's a clue!"

"It's a virus that's also a clue," Miranda said. She tapped her fingers against her desk. "And it's almost dinner. How are we supposed to just 'go'?"

"Just say one of your friends invited us over for dinner," I said, zooming in on the location on the app. The address was a particular store in a mall in the south of the city. At least, I thought it was in the south. "Sometimes I bring Nando to my best friend's place because they both play *Call of Duty*. You can just say we're going over for a *Mario Kart* tournament or something."

Miranda sighed. "That's gonna be a hard sell."

"What? You think people wouldn't want me over for dinner? Or is it because you know that I'd probably win your friends over to my side the moment I—"

"It's not *that*." Miranda ground out the word in a tone I'd never heard her use before. It was harsh. Bitter.

"You said *truce*—" I began, but as I lowered my iPad, the words vanished from my tongue.

Miranda was staring into her laptop, her body still. The muscles in her arms were taut. Like she was ready to throw a punch at the device. As I walked back to the desk, I caught a glimpse of her face behind her long hair. Her pupils were dilated, and she was biting her lower lip so tightly that her brown skin was starting to turn red.

"Okay." Miranda took in a long breath and pulled her hair behind her shoulders.

"I think I can make it work," she said. "An old friend lives in that neighborhood, and I think we can convince my mom to let us go in an Uber so that she doesn't get someone to drop us off. The problem is getting from there to the actual address. We can't take another Uber because that'll send a notification to my mom, and it's too far to get there on my skateboard. We can probably call a taxi to take us the rest of the —"

"Why do we even need a taxi?" I asked. "You guys have public transportation, right?"

Miranda stared at the laptop screen, and the far off look in her eyes returned. "Yeah…" she said quietly.

She started biting her lip again. If we were close, I might've asked what was going on. But we weren't, so I just stood to the side and waited for the tension in her arms to fall away and her eyes narrow back into focus.

It's been a while since that day. I still regret not saying anything.

"Great!" I said so we could move on from the subject. "We can use that. What's the bus schedule like?"

Miranda's fingers froze above the laptop again.

And then she started *laughing*.

"Hah! Schedule!?" Miranda snorted in disbelief. "You're not in Arizona anymore, Fresa. Time you get used to that."

7

TWO TEENAGE GIRLS TRAVELING ALONE. AT NIGHT. ON PUBLIC TRANSPORTATION.

MIRY

Yep. That happened.

The bus decided to show up about 30 minutes after we arrived at a non-descript corner of a large street. The Uber had dropped us off about three blocks back, and Ada and I were waiting beneath a streetlight at the side of the Periférico. Cars, motorcycles, and buses whooshed past us as I half-listened to my music through one earbud.

I didn't take my eyes off the street around us, not even when there was no one walking down the sidewalk. Ada wasn't paying much attention. The most she would do is sigh in exasperation as the minutes ticked by before turning back to her phone. If she noticed how much my leg was bouncing, she didn't comment on it. She probably thought that I was just as impatient as her. And if that's what she was thinking, I wasn't going to bother to correct her.

The green-and-white bus finally rumbled down the street just as the sun was starting to set. I yanked my earbud out and twirled the cord around my finger.

"Is that one ours?" Ada asked. "But it's not gonna stop for us. We're not even at a bus stop—"

I stepped forward and flagged the bus down. It stopped right in front of us.

Ada's mouth dropped open.

"We *are* the bus stop, Fresa." I forced myself to smirk past my growing dread and panic. "Time to get used to it."

I pulled myself into the vehicle and swiped the spare bus card we keep in the kitchen drawer. I paid Ada's fare, too, because the *gringa* still kept forgetting to carry cash and coins. We settled into a couple of seats a little ways away from the door, and I slid a single earbud back on.

My foot tapped with nerves as I took in the rest of the bus. It was fairly empty, with only half a dozen people beside us. Most of them were middle-aged, probably heading back home from work, and they were all at least two rows separated from us.

It was too late to get off now. We were on the bus, and if Ada could handle it, then I could, too. I wasn't 12 anymore. I could do it.

I wanted to. I had to.

We were a few minutes away from our stop when two guys strolled onto the bus. They were about 20 years old, and the bus driver barked at them to pay for transit after they tried to slip in without swiping their cards.

Despite it being summer, I'd pulled on an old gray hoodie before leaving the house. I was getting hot, but the comfort of anonymity was worth the sweat. I'd pulled the hood over my head to hide my face and hair, but Ada was still in the same clothes as earlier. Her bright pink sweater stood out against the dull and worn bus seats, and the two guys spotted her immediately.

Two equally slimy grins spread across their faces.

"*Hey, babe,*" one of them said in Spanish as they walked down the bus aisle. Toward her. Toward *us*. "*Your sweater's cute.*"

My chest shook as my heart rumbled in my chest. These guys were getting close. Too close.

Ada looked up from her phone. She was still listening to whatever music she was playing, and thank god her AirPods were hidden beneath her thick curls.

The other man reached out his hand across the seats. Like he wanted to touch Ada's shoulder. Or something *else*.

"Pink looks good on you —"

"Chinga tu madre, asqueroso," I growled.

The guy pulled his hand back, but he definitely wasn't sorry. Neither was his friend. Instead, the two of them just laughed and walked down the aisle. They jostled a little as the bus restarted its motor and kept going down the road before crashing down into their seats.

They were directly behind us, leaving just a single row of seats in between. It was close enough to keep my senses on alert and my heart thumping in my head.

I turned off my music with shaking fingers.

"Weirdo," Ada mumbled. She tapped her AirPods to pause the music before reaching down to the stupidly bright pink purse she insisted on bringing. She opened the bag and took hold of the iPad inside it. "So I've been thinking, maybe the reason why —"

"Don't pull that out!" I hissed, still very aware of the creeps that were right behind us. "Not here."

"It's not like someone's gonna steal it," Ada said. But after seeing that I was serious about this, she reluctantly dropped the iPad and zipped the purse up again. "Okay, okay. So as I was saying, I've been thinking."

"You think?"

"I do, actually. You should try sometime." Ada gave me a cheeky smile. "So I've been thinking, maybe there's a reason that virus hit your laptop. You were looking up stuff about Teo-ti-hoo-acan, but I wasn't. You can check my search history, which I wanted to *show you*, but now you'll just have to take my word for it."

If I wasn't distracted by the whispering of the creeps

behind us, I might've rolled my eyes. I'd even tried searching the websites on my phone, but the same thing happened when I opened them on my laptop. Same virus. Same keyword. Same everything.

I risked a glance behind us, and sure enough, the two of them were taking us in with nasty smirks. I caught the whispers of their low conversation.

"How old do you think the one in the sweater is?"

"She's younger than the other one." The creep laughed. *"But you can tell she takes care of herself, no?"*

My throat went dry, and I felt the entire back of my neck go wet with sweat.

"—my guess is that one of those tabs triggered the virus," Ada continued. "And after you got it, it showed up on every tab about Teo-ti-hoo-acan you opened."

Ada noticed that I was still glancing at the creeps, but she didn't ask the question that was obviously on her mind.

I wasn't sure if I even wanted her to.

But Ada's explanation made sense. When I clicked on sites that took me to explanations about Aztec or Mayan gods, the virus didn't pop up. It's only when I got to the explanations about gods from Teotihuacán specifically that the virus and its bright red text box appeared.

"Maybe it's a virus that only got activated when you opened a website that had the name of the ruins," Ada continued. "Or it's a virus that was on every page about the ruins and just popped up each time. It's trying to keep us from finding information about the ruins unless we go to this place. Like a scavenger hunt."

"Or a trap."

"Do you always have to be so pessimistic?"

The creeps were talking louder now, and I didn't have to strain my ears to hear their next words.

"Which one would you rather have?" one of them said.

"The pretty one, obviously. You can have the bitch."

The fear and nerves I felt when I was surrounded by the winged pumas crashed into my chest, but it was worse. Way worse than before. Waves of adrenaline and panic coursed through my hands and fingers, and I had to ball them into fists to keep myself from shaking.

There's a time to panic and a time to act. I forced myself to remember. *Panic can wait. Act until you're safe.*

Just outside the bus, the mall came into view.

"Miranda…" Ada said hesitantly, glancing at my shaking fists. "Are you —"

I grabbed her arm and pulled her out of the seat. Ada stumbled as she reached down to grab her purse, and she nearly tripped in her flats as I pulled her to the front of the jostling bus.

The creeps behind us whistled as they caught sight of Ada's short, frilly skirt. I turned to the bus driver to tell him to let us off here, but he was already slowing down to let in a group of people who were standing at the edge of the sidewalk.

I pulled the two of us off the bus and ran down the street. I didn't stop to see if the creeps had also gotten off the bus, or if anyone else was following. I just ran until Ada and I finally got in view of the mall's entrance.

We were both panting by the time we'd climbed the steps into the Perisur mall. Ada was gasping from exhaustion.

I wasn't.

Ada pursed her lips, accidentally scraping off some of the bright pink lip gloss. But instead of demanding to know what was going on, all my cousin said was, "Miranda… What were they saying?"

I pushed down a ball of bile that popped into my throat. "Stuff."

Ada waited for me to say more.

"It's —" My throat closed up. "Let's just go. The place we're going to closes at nine."

ADA AND I WEAVED OUR WAY THROUGH THE SUMMER crowd. The sky was dark by this point, but the mall was still bustling with people. Groups of teenagers who were heading to the movie theater laughed at inside jokes, parents exited the food court with their sleeping toddlers in strollers, and young 20-somethings exited the many stores with armfuls of shopping bags. It was a decent amount of people for the mall, and I savored the feeling of blending in with the crowd as we made our way to the escalators.

I took off my hoodie and tied it around my waist. Mexico City's in the mountains, so we only really get two or so weeks of "hot" weather. I'd felt some of the heat when we went to the pyramids, but it wasn't too bad in the city right now.

I wiped the sheen of sweat off my neck as we got on the escalators. Ada, on the other hand, seemed perfectly comfortable in her fuzzy pink cardigan. Considering Ada would probably get cold in Hell, it checks out.

The *"cafebrería"* was just a little ways away from the escalator. El Péndulo wouldn't be the first location I'd pick as a place for a scavenger hunt, but even I gotta admit it's a nice shop. It's a chain of bookstores with a bunch of locations around the city, all of which also come with a coffee shop to chill out at.

This particular Péndulo opened up to a long bookstore illuminated with bright white lights. Rows upon rows of plastic covered books beckoned us farther into the store, with everything from fiction to biography to kid's fiction filling the shelves. There were two employees behind the counter, another by a shelf, and two more in the café area. It wasn't as busy as other sections in the mall we'd pushed through, but there were a decent amount of people running their fingers over the many book spines.

"Time to find that clue," Ada said.

I looked over the dozens of bookshelves and sighed. "It's gonna take ages to check every—"

"Ah, *dis-cool-pa!*" Ada flagged down an employee near the front of the shop. It was a man who was probably in his mid-20s, but when he turned to us, he didn't give us a nasty smile. He was just tired and ready to close up the store.

Ada gave me a "it's your turn" look.

I sighed again. I unclenched my fists—I hadn't even realized that I'd done that. *"Do you have any books about Teotihuacán?"* I asked the guy.

The man twisted his face and shook his head. *"Teotihuacán? Don't think so, miss. But let me check."*

The employee shuffled over to a computer in the middle of the store. I groaned.

"So… I'm guessing that's not good?" Ada asked.

"Yep." Ada crossed her arms and waited for me to add more. "He says he'll check."

"I can *see* that."

"Then why are you asking?"

"I—Shut up! Wait, what about that guy the voice mentioned? Daniel Merino? Maybe there's a book by him somewhere!"

I had to admit, that was a good idea, so I asked the employee to check. He did, but he quickly confirmed that they didn't have anything written by a Daniel Merino.

"I'm sorry, miss," the employee droned as he stared blankly at the screen. *"It seems that there are no books about Teotihuacán. But I could show you the ones we have about the Aztecs and Mayans."*

"It's okay," I said with a shrug. I went to go find whatever section these "Archivists" might've hidden something—

"Maybe it doesn't have to be about Teotihuacán itself!" Ada said to the guy. "Hm, maybe something that references Teotihuacán? You said something about Aztecs and Mayans, right? Maybe something in those books talks about Teotihuacán?

Sorry, I know it's gotta be late for you, but we'd really appreciate it if you could help."

The man blinked rapidly as he took in Ada's words. He wasn't annoyed, but he definitely had no clue what she was saying.

"Miranda," Ada stage-whispered, "a little help here."

"Dude, the guy's tired. Just leave it. We can find it ourselves."

"Maybe, but it's worth a shot. And we're already talking."

I groaned again. That's right. I forgot that Ada actually *likes* to talk. At least in English.

I translated Ada's words to the employee. He took in Ada's grin, gave her a nod, and typed something else into the computer.

"There might be one thing," I translated the employee's words for Ada, "but it's not a lot. Is that okay?"

Ada nodded. "That's totally fine! I mean, *sí! ¡Por fav-or!*"

The employee cracked his first smile at Ada's genuine enthusiasm. After quickly rechecking something on the monitor, he took us down the store until we got to the archeology section. At the very bottom of the shelf were two thin books that were packaged together in plastic wrapping. They were pressed between two large encyclopedia-like volumes about Mayan history, so much so that I didn't even notice that they were there until he pulled them out and gave them to Ada.

"*¡Moo-chas gra-cias!*" Ada said, as she took the books. "You've just saved us a bunch of time. Thanks, José!"

I wondered when Ada had gotten his name when I realized that José had a big name tag pinned to his shirt. José didn't need me to translate that last bit, so he just nodded and said, "You're welcome," in slow English before heading back to the front of the store.

"See?" Ada said. "It pays to be polite."

I sighed and read the titles of the two books in Ada's hands. *The Origins of the Mayans* and *The Origins of the Aztecs*. It wasn't exactly what I'd call a clue to the Archivists of Teotihuacán. And to make it weirder, neither of them had the author's name on the cover.

I quickly double-checked the rest of the shelf. Ada joined me in our search around the archeology section, but sure enough, there really was nothing about Teotihuacán. Not even a random clue doodled onto a shelf.

Ada was practically peeling the plastic off the books by the time we went to pay. The cashier rang up the price, and I shook my head in disbelief.

"*You sure it's not missing a zero?*" I asked the cashier as I took in the number on the card reader. The woman shook her head, so I pulled out my wallet and gave her a ten peso coin.

"That was cheap," Ada said, already heading over to the coffee shop portion of the *cafebrería*. "But hey, more money for food!"

I strolled behind Ada as we went to get our belated dinner. The cashier smiled at us, but I didn't say anything. I was so done with the day that I didn't have the energy to pretend that I enjoyed doing the mandatory "hi's" and smiles and "how are you's" that make you not seem like an asshole who just wants their coffee.

And then there's Ada. She bounced up to the two cashiers and gleefully took in the long dinner menu, asking them what they thought was good. She asked it in English, of course, but the cashier with red glasses was doing her best to reply in half-formed English sentences. Soon enough, Ada and Lourdes—that's what Ada called the cashier after reading her name tag—were figuring out which was the best thing to order.

I inwardly laughed at the irony of Ada picking the California sandwich until my own stomach rumbled in anticipation as I read the ingredients. I bit my lip and ordered the *enchiladas* instead.

"*And a cappuccino,*" I said to the cashier. Ada blinked like I'd just asked for a nuke, and I held myself back from rolling my eyes. "Coffee. Want any?"

"Now? But it's after eight!"

"Our coffee is good," Lourdes said in heavily-accented English. She was a few years older than us, but she was so short that it might've been her heavy makeup fooling me. "Or you can have a frappé with chocolate."

"Ooo! That sounds even better!" Ada said.

My cousin has a weird ability to be cheery even when she's tired, and it's the kind of vibe that people here like. Her energy bubbled out of her, so much so that when Lourdes pulled out the receipt for our food, she tried to give it to Ada instead of me. Even though *I* was the one who paid for it.

I grabbed the paper with more force than I meant to, partially snatching it out of Lourdes' hand.

"We will… *llevarlo*," Lourdes said when she couldn't find the word in English, "to your table."

"Thanks!" Ada said, as she pulled our newly-acquired books out of her large purse. "Come on, Miranda. We've got some reading to do."

Lourdes' eyes widened when she saw the books. She reached into her pocket, but the other woman working behind the counter hissed that she wasn't allowed to take her phone out during a shift.

The moment was so brief I barely noticed it, but I didn't pay it any mind as Ada and I went over to one of the tables. It's a moment I look back on a lot, because maybe if I'd thought on it, we could've prevented the whole disaster that followed.

But I didn't.

Ada and I scanned the two books, each of which were just over one hundred pages. Ada skim read to see if she could spy the word "Teotihuacán" anywhere, and I got to work reading the actual book to see if there was a clue hidden in the text itself.

We barely took note of the food as we tried to find something—anything—hidden in the text of the two books. But even as we drank our coffees that were six times more expensive than the stupidly cheap books, we didn't find anything in our initial brief reading. The only new information we did find was on the interior title page. It said that the books were written by a guy called Fabián Pérez Santibáñez, but Ada searched his name online and found nothing.

Before we knew it, nine o'clock arrived and José came over to gently kick us out. Ada turned around to wave goodbye to Lourdes, but she was gone. We didn't even notice her leave.

8

THE HUNT BEGINS

MIRY

We were almost home when I first saw our new set of stalkers.

It was past ten o'clock, nearing 11, and Ada and I were on our second bus of the day. The plan was to ride it until we got to the spot the first bus picked us up, text my mom to say we were leaving, then call a taxi to take us back home.

That plan went to crap when we were still a few blocks away from our stop. Ada was scrolling through her phone. She'd angled it away from me so I couldn't see the screen, and all I could tell from the occasional bright flashes was that she was watching something colorful.

I had my hood pulled up and a single earbud in, but I wasn't listening to anything. And I'm damn sure that's the reason I noticed them.

There were two guys at the very back of the bus. One of them was roughly in his late 40s, while the other was 20-something. They didn't give us the nasty smiles that the creeps did, but when Ada stood up to quickly rearrange her skirt after it'd gotten a bit rumpled, I heard the two guys shuffling around. After seeing Ada sit back down again, they settled back into their seats.

My neck started sweating again.

I got out of my seat and moved a row or two down, as if I was heading to the exit to tell the driver to drop us off. Ada quickly scrambled behind me, but before we reached the exit, I shuffled us into a pair of seats closer to the door.

I pretended to look out the window, using the reflection to spy on the back of the bus.

Sure enough, the two guys at the back were quickly shuffling back into their seats.

A memory returned to me.

A memory of a man, tall and wiry, following me to the bus station. Following me on the vehicle. Following me down the streets, only slowing down when a man called out to him and asked him what he was doing following a 12-year-old girl.

"Hey, Miranda." Ada tugged on my sleeve. "You okay? You're literally shaking."

I shoved my trembling hands into my hoodie's pockets. "Tell the bus driver to let us off."

"What?" Ada pulled her AirPods out and slid them back into their case. "I thought you said we weren't there ye—"

"*Now.*"

Ada's face went from concern to confusion to fear in a span of two seconds. She ran down the aisle right away, even leaving her purse on the floor. I grabbed it and threw the strap over my shoulder, and as Ada mimed to the driver to get him to let us off, I took my first good look at the two men.

I caught them rising from their seats. The man in his 40s hid his face beneath a Cruz Azul baseball cap, but I could see his thick mustache flecked with white hairs. Next to him was the 20-something-year-old. Like me, he was wearing a hoodie with a hood up despite it being summer, though it was covered in flecks of multi-colored paints. I caught sight of a thick black beard, and he gasped when he realized I spotted them about to head down the aisle.

To follow us.

To stalk us.

The bus stopped.

I didn't even stop to thank the driver before I was practically pushing Ada down the steps. I didn't stop to look around before picking a random street and walking down it, my pace almost a light run.

"Miranda," Ada said, keeping pace with me even in her terrible shoes. "Tell me what's going on. And not in the vague and annoying way you usually talk about—"

"I think someone's stalking us."

"What?" Ada said. "Are you *sure*?"

I wasn't sure. It could've been just a coincidence, or my mind playing tricks on me. The men might not have even gotten off the bus.

The street was dark, and even with the lamps, it felt like every shadow extended itself farther down the road. I glanced behind me.

And I saw them.

Two men, one in a hoodie and another in a Cruz Azul cap, peering at us from behind a corner.

My breath hitched. They *were* stalking us.

They were *actually* stalking us.

Beside me, Ada gasped. "W-What do we do?"

"Keep walking," I said, turning away from the corner and back down the street. "Find a crowd."

But there were no crowds. We were near a residential area, but this was a shopping street. Everything around us was closed, from the hardware store to the candy shop. Even the road was empty, with only the occasional car passing through.

Nowhere to hide. No one to ask for help.

Ada and I kept walking. To where, I wasn't sure, but I didn't stop to check. All I knew was that I couldn't lead them home. Not again.

Not like I led the other one.

Ada and I turned a corner, and that's when I started running.

My cousin and I ran down a long street that led away from the main road. I ran across the street to the side that had better lighting, in case someone could see us and help.

I kept the pace up, hoping to make a gap between us and the men, but they were matching our speed. I couldn't slow down. Not now. Not when there were more people following me. Not again.

Ada glanced back, and she nearly tripped out of her flats. "A-Are those… *daggers*?"

I followed her gaze. The two men had come down the street, several strides behind us. They were under one of the streetlights, and both of them had shining black daggers hanging from their belts.

The sound of a whistling projectile flew past my ear, and the man in the baseball cap cried out as a cactus needle scraped his left arm.

Ada's arm shook as a new cactus needle slowly extended its way out of her pointer finger's nail bed. Her breaths were ragged and her face was scrunched up, but she kept her eyes trained on the man in the baseball cap.

The man in the hoodie turned back to his friend and said something to him in Spanish I didn't catch.

I felt for a warm feeling in my chest, just like I did back at the pyramids. I found it right away, and I channeled that energy up to my head. At the pyramids, my projectiles made the winged pumas disappear in two hits. I didn't know if it would do the same to the men, but they were stalking us.

And I was terrified.

Twice in a row, I thought, *at the man's chest.*

I felt the sensation of a metal pin pricking my head twice in a row, just like it did at the pyramids with the winged pumas. The man in the hoodie recoiled as something hit his chest.

But unlike with the winged pumas, the man didn't disappear.

I launched out two more projectiles at the man in the hoodie, but all he did was stumble a bit as they hit his chest. Ada yelled as she shot out another needle, and this one pierced the older man's lower left leg. The man cried out in pain, but he didn't disappear.

At the pyramids, all we needed to do to get rid of the pumas was hit them twice with anything. But we had hit these men with our projectiles, but they were still there.

I couldn't make the threat disappear this time.

The man in the hoodie rushed to help the older man slide down on the floor, but Cruz Azul shook his head and pointed his finger.

At us.

"Run!" Ada yelled.

I couldn't.

At the pyramids, an unnatural sense of focus filled me. Even when I was staring down enormous winged pumas with sharp nails. But that focus, that feeling that I could fight back, fled me. Because I didn't have a weapon on me. I didn't have a huge stick to bat the men away. And whatever my projectiles were, they were doing nothing to the man in the hoodie who was now easing the older man onto the ground.

My mouth went dry. Numb.

"Miranda, come on!"

I barely felt Ada grabbing my arm and pulling me away from the men. I vaguely heard the younger man cry something out, but I didn't register the words. All I could feel was the vague sensation of my feet hitting the floor and barreling down the street. We ran down the long streets, every house blurring more and more as we got farther and farther away.

The voice of the younger man echoed behind us. He was yelling something in Spanish, but my head wasn't registering any words. All it could think was *run*. Run, run, run, *run*.

I didn't know where we were going. Or how far. My brain had shut down to the point where I was relying entirely on Ada's guidance, and she pulled me down random streets I didn't recognize.

Ada suddenly yanked on my arm and pulled me to the side. I slipped at the sudden motion, and Ada barely held me upright.

I gasped, and bits of my vision suddenly came into focus. We weren't running anymore, and Ada and I were panting heavily. We were in a small alleyway littered with discarded tissues and empty chip packets, hidden from the street view by a tall stack of boxes.

"I think we… outran him," Ada said, taking a quick peek out to the street between big gasps of air. "I think he got so distracted by the old guy… that it gave us a good head start."

Ada stuffed her hand into her purse and pulled out her phone.

"Nando… hey," Ada said between heavy breaths. "We need… your help. What—no, we're… not getting dropped off! We took a bus."

My heart pounded in my head. Ada kept speaking, but I couldn't focus on any words.

"Yeah, I know—I *know*—just listen!" Ada yelled into her phone. "There's someone following us."

Moments from three years ago played again and again in my mind.

"I don't know!" Ada yelled. She tugged on my arm. "Miranda, what street is this—"

Memories of a tall man with a slimy smile following me along my bus route, again and again, until he could track me all the way to my house. Memories of me running to my home and shutting the door behind me. Memories of me falling to the floor in tears from the relief I felt at being safe.

"I'm sending you our live location," Ada said. "Just hurry! *Please.*"

The moment I saw the man waiting for me on the corner of my street. The moment he reached out to grab me and touch —

Ada yanked on my arm again. "Hey, Nando's coming," she said, firmly and quickly. "We outran the guys from the bus, and Nando's coming. We're gonna be okay."

Ada was exhausted. Her shoulders were drooping, her left foot was almost slipping out of her shoe, and she was still panting. The very tip of a new needle extended from the nail bed of her pointer finger, and though it was growing, it was growing slowly. Like at the end of her massive nail-barrage at the pyramids. Maybe she'd run out of nail to grow, or maybe she just didn't have the energy to make any more.

But even though she looked tired, she wasn't scared. A little freaked out, sure, but she wasn't panicking like I was. She was calm and completely confident that we would actually be all right.

I swallowed what little bile was in my mouth. It wasn't enough to feel completely calm, but it was enough to keep me from losing myself in my head again.

A light chime rang out in the alleyway.

I spun around to the source of the noise, my hand curled into a fist. But then I realized that the noise had come from Ada's phone.

"Nando's… almost here!" my cousin said, sounding equal parts surprised and relieved.

I stared at the edges of the discarded boxes that separated us from the alleyway entrance. I vaguely heard the shuffling of footsteps, a man's voice calling something out, but everything sounded far off. Who knew where Ada had hauled us to, but she somehow did manage to get enough distance between us and them.

"Nando's here," Ada said after another chime echoed in the alleyway. "He says his car is right around the corner."

Ada was still panting; I was still shaking.

"We just gotta run out there and get in the car." Ada

fumbled a bit as she straightened out her skirt and sweater, but she did it either way. "No stress. Yeah?"

Goddamnit. If Ada could put on a brave face during this mess, then I could, too.

So I reached up, pulled Ada's purse off my shoulder, and gripped its straps as if it were a bat. "Y-Yeah."

Ada raised her pointer finger. The new needle was still slowly extending itself outward, but it was grown enough for Ada to launch a single shot.

I tightened my grip on Ada's purse until my fingers turned red.

Then the beautiful noise of Fernando's 1999 Volkswagen Jetta sputtered into the alleyway.

Ada and I sprinted out at the same time. Her foot slipped on an empty packet of chips, and I rushed to grip her arm before she could fall. The blazing lights of a car grew brighter as it rushed down the street, and I could just vaguely note the faded green paint.

"*Wait!*" a man yelled out in Spanish.

I didn't recognize the voice, but when I turned my head, I saw him. The man in the hoodie, running toward us from the opposite side of the road. The man's left hand twitched, inching closer to the dagger that hung from his belt.

Ada's needle scraped his left forearm.

"Go! Go! *Go!*" Ada yelled as the man cried out in pain. She caught her balance and sprinted after the car, and I followed.

Fer's car skidded to a stop just two paces in front of us.

"Hada! Miry!" Fer screamed. "Get in!"

Ada went to move to open the passenger side door, but then someone from the inside opened the door to the backseat. Ada hopped in. I ran to join her, but a sudden scream stopped me before I could.

"*¡Daniel!*" the hooded man yelled.

The adrenaline carried me through the next moments. I ran, hauling myself and Ada's purse into the backseat of Fer's car. The hooded man screamed again, and Fer hit the gas a second before I heard something scrape along the side of the car's door.

Fer drove faster.

"*Are you okay!?*" Fer said in Spanish from the front seat, turning away from the road for a fraction of a second to check that we were in the car. "Are you okay!?" he asked again, this time in English.

"Y-Yeah," Ada stuttered. "I'm good. I'm all good." She straightened her skirt again and turned to me. "You?"

I gulped despite having no water in my mouth. "I guess I'm good."

Ada sagged in relief. "Sweet." Her eyes drifted to her purse I was still holding, and any relief she felt was replaced by shock when she saw that, sometime during all this mess, the zipper had opened all the way. "Crap! My stuff!"

Ada yanked the purse out of my hands, but immediately cheered when she pulled out her fully intact iPad and the two books we'd found.

An unfamiliar laugh echoed in the car. "Good to see your books are okay," an unfamiliar voice said in accented English.

I spun around to find a guy with gelled hair and a clean-shaven face sitting in the passenger seat.

"Who the hell are you!?" Ada yelled, raising her pointer finger at the man. I took hold of her purse's straps and moved to throw it.

"*Hey, it's okay.* It's okay," the man said calmly. "I'm a friend. Promise."

"You didn't answer her question," I said, ready to throw the bag into the man's face. "Who the hell are you?"

"Okay, okay. Just don't hurt me," the man said lightly. "My name is Daniel Merino. And I think you've been looking for me."

9

WE LEARN STUFF! KINDA

ADA

"So that's what you were doing?" I said to Nando as his ancient car jolted down the nighttime street. "You went to find Daniel!"

When a disembodied spirit had told us to find a guy named Daniel Merino, I had no clue what he looked like. But considering we were tracking down a group called the "Archivists", I didn't expect to meet a guy who looked like he was on his way to an old-school rock concert.

Daniel Merino was a 20-something-year-old guy with brown oily skin, gelled hair, a long scar on his left bicep, and an AC/DC shirt that was so faded I could barely make out the name. He didn't exactly seem like the guy who would wander into a dusty archive and pour over stacks of books, but then again, he was the one the voice at the pyramids had told us to find.

"What did you think you were doing?" Nando stared at me from the car's mirror, but the impact of his stern glare was lessened by his giant glasses. "Sneaking out?"

"We got permission," Miranda muttered beside me.

"Lying to your parents?"

"Oh, so did you tell them you were gonna meet with a weird guy who really needs a new shirt?" I shot back.

"*Oye*, this band is a classic!" Daniel said. He had a Mexican accent that came out in every word, but it wasn't nearly as thick as my mom's or Aunt Lupe's.

"And taking the bus on your own?" Nando's eyes shifted toward Miranda. "I thought you said you'd never do that again?"

I blinked. "Huh?"

"Never mind that," Miranda said quickly. She kept her grip tight on my purse. "Who are you and why did the weird voice tell us to find you?"

As much as I wanted to know what the hell Nando was talking about, I, begrudgingly, had to accept that Miranda had her priorities straight.

"My name's Daniel," he said. "But you already knew that. I'm part of a group called the Archivists of Teotihuacán."

"Well, I've never heard of it," I said.

"You heard it at the pyramids," Miranda said.

"I mean I'd never heard of it *before*."

"That's how we like to keep it," Daniel interrupted, cutting off the beginning of my new argument with Miranda. "We're a group of disciples who are blessed with magic from the gods of our country."

"So this is actually magic?" I confirmed. "I'm not suddenly mutating into a plant?"

Daniel laughed and grinned. "I hope not. That would be awkward to explain to your family, I think."

"Gods? There are actually gods?" Miranda asked cautiously. "But the website we found calls them deities. Those books do, too."

"Deities, gods. Same thing. I just prefer one word to another." Daniel sighed and glanced over at Nando, who was carefully navigating the dark streets. "It's a whole debate within the group. I was telling your cousin all about it. Some like to use it, others don't. But whatever you call them, they exist. And they give us magic."

I stared down at my pointer finger. The one that turned my nail bed into cacti needles. I'd half-started to wonder if it was a curse. Maybe I was turning into some sort of freak, or maybe I really did need to go cleanse myself in ultra-purified water. But getting confirmation that it was actually magic felt good.

This was magic. And if magic is actually real, then it makes sense that gods may be, too.

The warm feeling in my chest, the sudden ability to do things I'd never dreamed of, the sense that there was something extraordinary happening to us—if that's not magic, then what is?

"People who are chosen by the gods are granted magical powers by the being that chooses them," Daniel said. "Everyone's powers come out differently, but there are some similarities between disciples of each god."

Next to me, Miranda lowered my pink purse. But she didn't loosen her death grip on the straps.

"But I ran out!" I said. "I ran out of magic! At the pyramids, I was making nail after nail after nail! And now…"

I rubbed my finger again. I'd managed to form and shoot two nails, but it took all the concentration I had to create them. The low thrum of magic hummed in my chest, but it was more subdued than it was before. I'd only be able to create one more needle before I started feeling like the second incarnation of Sleeping Beauty.

"Powers come at a price," Daniel said. "To do the things we can do, we need an energy source."

"What's mine?" I asked.

"Depends on who chose you," Daniel said. "Disciples take in energy from their source and hold it in their bodies. If you have enough energy, you can use magic. If you don't… you don't have a very good time."

Beside me, Miranda brought a hand to her throat.

"So what's your power?" I leaned forward in my seat. "Who's your god? Deity? God-ity?"

Daniel flourished his hand. "Tláloc. God of rain. Or *deity* of rain. Your choice."

"So which gods are there?" I asked. "I know that Quetz guy."

"Quetzalcóatl," Miranda said sharply.

Yeah, Quetzalcóatl. That's pretty much the only guy I know. If I remember right, he was known as the feathered serpent. A being who ran across the sky, jumped into the sea, and promised to return one day. I can't remember if he was born a man or was always a god, and I couldn't even remember what exactly he was the god *of*.

Honestly, the only reason I knew about the guy is because he's the most famous Mexican god there is. But that Tláloc guy he mentioned? Never heard of him.

By this point in my life, I'd accepted that I wasn't a good Mexican. I didn't know the language, barely knew the culture, and definitely didn't know anything about gods and pyramids and the lack of bus schedules. Call me whitewashed all you want, but at least I never pretended to be more Mexican than I am.

But at that moment, when I could feel myself diving into this world of Mexican gods and magic, I wished I knew more. And despite technically being Mexican since birth, I wondered if it was enough for me to justify even being here. Maybe I was too American to belong here at all.

Still, I wasn't about to admit all that in front of Miranda. So I kept those thoughts shut in my head and said, "But I don't know any other gods."

Daniel sighed. "And it is not for me to tell you."

"Huh?" I said.

"*What?*" Miranda clipped.

Daniel let out a long breath. "The Archivists have a tradition. An… initiation, of some kind. Once a disciple is chosen, they must go and uncover the truth themselves. They have to go on a long…" His voice trailed off as he searched for the word.

"Scavenger hunt?" I suggested.

"Goose chase?" Miranda drawled.

"Yes!" Daniel said without specifying which idea he'd said "yes" to. "It is all to show that potential disciples have curiosity. That they have the motivation and the will to join the Archivists." Daniel turned to Nando. "Are you *sure* you didn't feel anything? Nothing in your chest?"

"Nothing," Nando said. His fingers tightened themselves around the steering wheel as the Volkswagen Jetta groaned when it went over a speed bump. "But I heard a voice at the pyramids."

That's when I realized that maybe Nando was just as confused as Miranda and I were. Sure, he'd told us to stay out of this without specifying why, but I figured that there was something he knew about the voice and our new weird nail and mind powers.

But when Nando knows stuff, he doesn't stop talking about it. He drones on about it for hours and hours, even when he's in the middle of an online match. Nando had barely said a word the whole car ride, and he was hanging on to every word Daniel said.

But that still didn't explain how the hell he actually found Daniel Merino.

"How can we trust you?" Miranda asked.

"Here's how you know you can trust me," Daniel said, taking his time to look over at all three of us before continuing. "That voice you heard at the pyramids… it told you to find the Archivists of Teotihuacán, right?"

The three of us nodded.

"And that same voice also told you to find *me*." Daniel smirked. "If I wasn't a Archivist you can trust, then why would it tell you to find me?"

"How do we know we can trust the Archivists?" Miranda asked.

"We can," Nando said. "I did some research. They're a legitimate organization."

Miranda and I looked at each other. If Nando said he researched, he probably did. I mean, this is the guy who happily spent a full day researching pesticides to make sure our blueberries in Arizona didn't come from a farm with dodgy chemicals.

"Nando, it's not that I don't trust you," I said, "but can we get confirmation on that?"

Yes, said a voice.

The voice of the man who spoke to us at the pyramids.

Miranda, Nando, and I jumped in our seats. The car swerved and sputtered, and Nando frantically moved to straighten it out.

Daniel speaks the truth, the voice continued. *He is an Archivist, he was sent to find you.*

The car shook. The metal creaked, the tires swerved, and all four of us were thrown about in our seats. Miranda and Nando gasped, and Daniel hit his head on the roof of the Volkswagen. I frantically grabbed the seats to steady myself.

He is here to help you come into your powers.

The car stopped shaking.

My heart was beating like a hummingbird's, but I found my voice and yelled out, "Are you a god? Is that how you can talk to us? Are *you* the one who picked us?"

I am a god, the voice said. *But I did not pick you. I am only here to guide you because the spirit is growing restless. If he escapes his prison, he will attack this city with all of his power. And he will make the earth rumble until it collapses into dust.*

IT TOOK THE FOUR OF US A SOLID TWO MINUTES TO TAKE IN what just happened. Daniel was the first to recover, and he rubbed his head as he looked us over. "Are you okay?"

We all mumbled shaky "okays". Even Nando's car only sputtered once before rumbling down the road again.

"Is that confirmation enough for you?" he asked.

I nodded. I was shaken and a bit scared, but I should've been *terrified*. In less than 24 hours, I'd gotten attacked by pum-eagles and stalked on a bus. And yet, adrenaline energized my body like a battery.

This feeling, my dad would call it bravery. My mom would call it the kind of fearlessness that led me to breaking my arms three times before I was eight years old.

"I'm guessing you can't tell us who that guy was?" I forced some energy into my voice to drown out the nerves. "Why was he speaking in English?"

"What does that have to do with anything?" Miranda asked.

"Wait, he spoke in English to you, too?" I asked.

"What does that matter?"

"I dunno. Thought he'd speak to you in *espa-ñool* since you like to complain about English."

"Only when *you're* talking."

"*Niñas*," Nando said sharply from the driver's seat. "Not now."

Daniel ran a hand through his gelled hair. "I don't know why he spoke to you in English, but I can say this: he spoke to you because we need you to find the Archivists. Fast. The truth is, the Archivists do not have many members, and we need all the help we can get."

"Then why don't you go recruiting?" I asked. "If you're so desperate for new people, shouldn't you be looking for anyone who might wanna learn magic?"

Daniel groaned. Loud. "If we could do that, this would be a lot easier."

"What do you mean?" Miranda asked.

"Do we want more people? Yes. Would it make *everything* easier? Yes." Daniel groaned again. "But that isn't an option, because there isn't much magic to go around. When a disciple is chosen, their soul becomes connected to the magic of the earth. Deep, *deep*, magic. When you connected with your power, you found it easy to use, yes?"

Miranda and I nodded.

"That is the true strength of our gods," Daniel said. "The magic is easy to access, but difficult to control effectively. The power the gods give is great. Yet it comes at a cost."

"There can't be too many disciples," Nando said. "Every disciple gets access to a magical current in the earth, but there are few of them. If you have a limited resource, you need to make sure that the disciples you choose for life are actually going to apply themselves to the magical world."

"You learn fast," Daniel said.

"Yeah, he kind of does that," I said.

"Doesn't make this whole thing less dumb," Miranda added.

"It *is* dumb," Daniel agreed. "But it's what we've got. If we could wave requirements and let more people in, we would. But with how the magic is divided, there just aren't many spots for new disciples. And when someone does leave, it takes forever to replace them."

I nodded along. "So the gods choosing us is like getting an invitation to a super exclusive club, and this scavenger hunt is the Archivists' way of double checking the gods' choice."

"Exactly," Daniel said.

"The voice said we unleashed a spirit," Miranda said. "You're saying you need... *us*. Really? Without telling us anything useful? Just how desperate are you that you need help from a couple of teenagers?"

"If it makes you feel better, most Archivists get chosen when they're teenagers," Daniel said. "There's a theory that it's the perfect balance between childhood and adulthood. Teenagers are more likely to control their magic compared to children, but they're young enough to still have faith in the world."

"So you come to tell us that gods are a thing, and you won't tell us which ones are interested in us?" I asked. "That is *so* unfair."

"Correct!" Daniel grimaced. "Sorry, but that's just the way things are for us. It's what I went through, and I found it as annoying as you do."

"You're saying we're on a trial run?" Miranda asked. "We only have a fraction of our actual powers. And to unlock the rest, we need to figure out which god picked us and why?"

Daniel nodded. "*Así es, Miranda.*"

"*Miry,*" Miranda replied immediately. "*Me dicen 'Miry'.*"

Daniel chuckled. "*Así es, Miry.*"

"I'm Ada, by the way," I said before he could call me "Guadalupe". "If we're sharing nicknames."

"Ah. Then I am just 'Daniel'."

"So what happens if they don't figure it out?" Nando asked. "What happens to them?"

"Their powers will be lost," Daniel said. "Forever."

I ran my finger over my nail bed. Whatever was happening to me, it was weird. It came out of nowhere, but it's what let me fight back the strange beasts at the pyramids. And if Daniel and the voice were right, something Miranda and I did unlocked a spirit.

If that was the case, then these nail projectiles were my main weapon. And like hell was I losing that.

"What does this spirit do?" I asked. "How did we unseal it? Why can it make pum-eagles?"

"Winged pumas," Miranda said.

"Demons," Nando said with a shudder.

Daniel clicked his tongue. "We don't know."

Wait…

"*What?*" the three of us cousins said at the same time.

"We don't know how the spirit does it," Daniel said quickly. "And we don't know how you unsealed it. But we know it's gaining power. Those creatures you saw, you only saw them in the Spiritual World, yes?"

"*Spiritual World?*" I said. "There's an actual, real Spiritual World?"

"There is," Daniel said. "And if this spirit is left to wander, then it will gain the power to create those creatures in our world."

"What other powers does the spirit have?" Miranda asked in a low voice.

"Well…" Daniel paused for a moment to think. "It can lead others into a lie. Make them turn their back on the people they were supposed to protect. That man who tried to attack the car… He was one of the people the spirit took from me."

Miranda gripped the back of Daniel's seat. "You know him?"

Daniel nodded without turning to my cousin. "He was my best friend. If I am being honest, I'm not just here to ask you to stop the spirit. I'm hoping that, if you help, maybe you… maybe you can also save him."

Daniel turned away from us to gaze out the passenger side window. "*Bájame aquí.* My car is around the corner."

As much as I wanted to press for more information about this weird "friend" who likes stalking people on buses, Nando was pulling over. The engine *popped* loudly as Nando shifted the car into park.

"But we don't know what to do," I said. "We found some weird books, but there's nothing in them about Teotihuacán!"

"Maybe you have to look a little closer." Daniel grinned at us again. "Your cousin has my number. He can call me when you know where you're going next. Or if you need backup. Like I said, I'm here to help."

"Why don't you just come with us now?" I asked.

Daniel and Miranda raised their eyebrows at me at the same time.

"You know what, yeah. I see how you could fit the weird stalker-ish profile," I said. "We'll call you when we know where to meet you."

"Sounds good." Daniel opened the door and stepped out of the car. "Get home safe."

And with that, Daniel shut the door and headed down the street.

"So where are we going now?" I asked Nando. "Aunt Lupe's house?"

Nando heaved a long sigh and turned to Miranda. *"Miry, ¿cómo vas?"*

I turned to Miranda. She was gripping the back of the passenger seat with one hand and my pink purse in the other. "I'm good," she said quietly.

I barely, just barely, noticed the shake in her voice.

"You're not." Nando reached into his pockets and pulled out his phone.

"What are you doing?" I asked him.

"Telling your parents that you're not going to Tía Lupe's tonight," Nando said.

"Where are we going, then?" I asked.

"My house. I think… I think that Miry needs to see a familiar face."

10

ALWAYS CHECK WHAT COMES AT THE BEGINNING

ADA

"Hey, Abuelo," I said to my grandfather. "You look good. Chill."

"He's literally sleeping," Miranda whispered beside me.

"Well, yeah!" I whispered back. "That's the best time to look chill."

Miranda, Nando, and I were in my grandparents' room. Well, ever since my grandmother died two years ago, it's technically only been my grandfather's room, but it didn't seem like it.

If someone were to ask me where my grandparents lived, I would've said a library. The room we were in was lined with tall bookshelves that covered two entire walls. Most of the books were over 30 years old, but some of the tomes on the top shelf were even older. The entire room smelled like old pages and aging leather, and I briefly wondered if this was the archive the voice wanted us to find.

On the queen-sized bed in front of us was my grandfather. He wasn't a tall man, and all three of his kids ended up being taller than him. Nando overtook him in height when he was 15. Abuelo had a clean-shaven face, patchy white hair, and a snore that was so loud I wasn't afraid of waking him up. He was asleep by the time Nando had brought us to the house. But that didn't matter much. Not when I hadn't properly talked to him in over three years.

Abuelo's dementia started hitting him when I was five. He'd forget his pens, where he was in his book, and if Abuela had already taken her medicine or not. By the time I was 12, he'd forgotten who I was. He even kept calling me "Mira"—no matter how many times I told him that I'm not my mom.

He doesn't talk anymore. Mom says that his mind is somewhere else now. I know she doesn't want to say it, but I can tell that she's happy that Aunt Sara and Uncle Rizo are the ones who stepped up to take care of my grandparents.

I still remember my mom's face after she came back from Abuela's funeral. I remember wondering if Abuelo had enough of his mind left to remember to feel sad about her death.

Behind me, Miranda stood next to a portrait.

"*Hola, Abuela,*" Nando said. He placed a hand on Miranda's shoulder. "*Mira quién vino a visitarte.*"

"*Hola, Abuelita,*" Miranda said softly. "*Lo siento que no he venido en un rato.*"

On the wall opposite the bed was a shrine. Well, kind of. It was a large table that once upon a time was a two-person desk. Uncle Rizo had covered it with a long tablecloth, old flowers that were due to be replaced, and pictures of Abuela at various stages of her life.

There were black-and-white pictures of Abuela as a child, her wedding photo with Abuelo, formal pictures with my mom and her two siblings, and a giant group picture of the family we took the summer after Clara was born.

Traditionally, the shrines for the dead only come up when we're getting close to the Day of the Dead in November, but Uncle Rizo said that the shrine might bring Abuelo some comfort. If you ask me, I don't think he was aware enough to recognize it.

I sighed, turning away from Miranda and the shrine. My

cousin had started talking to my grandmother's picture, so I took the time to peruse the bookshelves.

I placed the two books we'd bought from the bookstore on a shelf as I browsed the titles. Most of them were in Spanish, with words like *"historia"* and *"México"* and *"antropología"* getting repeated the most on the old spines. But there were also some words I wasn't expecting. English titles with the words *"aziza"*, *"Scotland"*, and *"djinn"* kept popping up. There was even a thick scroll tucked behind a geology book. I took it out and carefully unrolled it.

"Hada!" Nando hissed. "Don't touch things without permission!"

I winced at the sound of Nando's harsh voice. "Sorry. I didn't realize—"

Nando sighed. "No, no. It's okay. I..." He grimaced and gave me a sorry smile. "Go ahead. Abuelo would've given you permission to read those."

I nodded skeptically and furrowed my eyebrows as I looked over the scroll in my hands. "Since when does Abuelo own a Torah?"

"You recognized it?" Nando asked.

I shrugged. "I took a guess. There aren't a lot of languages that look like Hebrew. It has a real specific alphabet, like Korean does. Could Abuelo even *read* this?"

"A little," Nando said. "He liked researching religious texts, and he'd already read the Quran by the time he got this. Did you know that a lot of Hebrew and Arabic texts don't write down the vowels? They assume that people will be able to recognize the word by just reading the consonants. It's a trait of a lot of Semitic languages, actually."

"Nando, you're a computer science major. How the hell do you know anything about Semitic languages?"

"Because it's interesting!" Nando smiled, but it was brief. "And because Abuelo sometimes talked about it."

As I rolled up the scroll and put it away, Nando walked

over to the bed. A portion of the thin blanket that covered our grandfather had fallen off his shoulder, and Nando moved to cover him up again.

Abuelo stirred. Just when I thought there was a chance he could actually wake up, he suddenly let out a deep, *looong* snore.

Nando laughed, but it was sad.

In the corner, Miranda was still talking to the shrine.

And I was looking at books I had no interest in reading.

Out of the five of us cousins on this side of my family, I was easily the one least attached to our grandparents. Miranda and Nando grew up with them, and Clara and Eduardo literally live in this very house, but I was the kid who grew up in America. It didn't matter that Abuela and Abuelo spoke English—I just wasn't here that much.

When Abuela got cancer and Abuelo's dementia got bad, yeah, I was sad. But I wasn't the one whispering to a shrine or the one adjusting the blankets over my grandfather. I was just... there. I didn't know what to do, say, or feel.

I kind of wish I did. Because even if it meant I felt sad, at least I could feel like I properly cared about my own family.

"*Creo que estarías orgullosa de mí,*" Miranda whispered to Abuela's portrait. "*Bueno, en la mañana. Hoy en la noche... no me fue tan bien. Ada me tuvo que ayudar. Creo que hizo un buen trabajo.*"

I shook my head as I processed that bit at the end. *Creo que hizo un buen trabajo.* I didn't fully understand what she said, but I got the general idea.

I tugged on Nando's sleeve. "Did... did Miranda say something nice about me?" I asked him. "That I did a good job?"

"Hada, shhh!" Nando said. "Let her talk alone—"

"It's okay." With her back still turned to us, Miranda sighed. "Yeah. You did good today. With the stalkers."

I blinked and rewound the moment in my head. Was Miranda... actually saying nice things about me? *Out loud?*

"Why did you even go on a bus?" Nando asked. "After what happened, you said you'd never do it again."

Miranda sighed again, and that confirmed what I suspected.

When Miranda and I were running from the stalkers, she was shaking. At first, I'd assumed it was just nerves from getting, you know, stalked. But this was Miranda. One of the chillest people I know and the girl who took on a horde of pum-eagles head-on. She wasn't just scared of the stalkers—she was terrified.

And the only reason why I can imagine she was terrified is if that kind of thing had happened to her before.

"Miranda," I said. "What happened?"

"Doesn't matter," she snapped. "I just learned to steer clear of public transport."

Nando winced. "Miry—"

"It doesn't *matter*," Miranda said firmly. She turned around to face us. Instead of glaring at Nando like I expected her to, she took a deep breath and lowered her voice. "Fer, thank you. For picking us up. You… You really helped."

"*No hay de qué*," Nando said. "I'm here if you need me. I was just lucky that Daniel told me to meet him close by."

"Now I might have to thank Daniel, too." Miranda gave him a tiny smile, and Nando grinned back.

And I was just… there. Don't get me wrong, I'm glad that Nando understood what was going on. But once again, this was a situation where I couldn't do anything but nod and look solemn.

This is my family. And moments like these make me feel like I'm not really a part of it.

Miranda turned back to the shrine. She was whispering even quieter now, and there was no way I could eavesdrop again unless I was right next to her.

"So…" I whispered to Nando. "I'm guessing that Abuela helped with… something."

"Yeah." Nando took off his glasses and rubbed his eyes. "After Miry… Look, it's not my story to tell, but I *can* say that Miry spent a lot of time with Abuela. She made her feel safe when no one else could. So when Abuela's cancer got bad, I brought Miry to see her. Every day."

"Every day for how long?"

"About a year." Nando slid his glasses back on. "Until… Until Abuela died."

Miranda kept her eyes on the shrine.

I didn't know that Miranda was *that* close with Abuela. But then again, I hadn't known much about her since we were nine. I used to be able to to ask her stuff, even when I could tell that her English was slipping. Then 2018 came along, and suddenly we were yelling at each other in languages the other person couldn't understand. Her year of living with Uncle Luis' family in Boston was supposed to fix all that.

It fixed Miranda's English; it didn't fix anything else.

"So are you gonna tell me how you found Daniel?" I asked because I was curious and because I desperately wanted to change the subject. "And don't you dare tell me you found him on Facebook!"

"No," Nando said. "LinkedIn."

I rubbed at my eyes. No way I heard *that* right. "Haha. Very funny."

"No, seriously. LinkedIn."

I sputtered. "O-Okay. LinkedIn, I guess. But how did you find him on *that*? And why did you tell Miranda and I that we shouldn't be getting into this? Why shouldn't we tell our parents about this?"

"Hada—" Nando started.

"We could always tell *your* parents," Miranda drawled, and I jumped at the sound of her voice. I didn't even realize she was paying attention to us. "Tía Sara and Tío Rizo are right down the hall."

Nando sighed. "You know how Daniel said there are things he can't tell you yet?"

I groaned. "I know where this is going."

"There are things that I can't tell you," Nando said. "Just give me… two days. *Two* days. That's all I ask. Please."

Honestly, as annoying as that whole thing was, I know I would feel god awful saying no to that. Nando had literally just proven that he had our backs when we needed him, and now he was asking us to trust him.

"All right," I said. "But only if you agree to be our driver."

Nando blinked. Miranda glanced over her shoulder, her face barely visible behind her curtain of hair.

"Until this is over, we need someone to drive us," I said to Nando. "Drive us, and we'll let you keep your secrets for a couple days. I mean, unless you want us to take the bus again."

I said that because of two reasons: first, it honestly sounded more efficient to go around the city by car. But second… I'd seen just how much our little bus adventure had shaken Miranda. I still had no idea what was going on, but I knew that I didn't want to see her go through that again.

"Okay." Nando chuckled lightly. "But just so you know, I was going to offer to drive you, anyway."

That earned him a smile from both of us.

Nando yawned and stretched his arms over his head. "I'm going to bed. I put blankets in the living room for you."

"Thanks, Nando," I said. "Good night."

"*Buenas noches,*" Miranda said quietly.

Nando pointed at the books we'd bought earlier that night. "And no more reading before bed. We're getting up early." And with that, he left the room and swung the door closed.

I, of course, immediately went back to the books.

"If you don't want me to do something, don't tell me *not* to do it," I said to myself as I picked up the books. *Los Orígenes de los Mayas* and *Los Orígenes de los Aztecas.*

If we couldn't find anything in the book itself, then maybe

we could find the publisher. If we found out who owned the rights, we might be able to see if there were other books that could help.

I opened *Los Orígenes de los Mayas* and went to the copyright page. I squinted my eyes against the Spanish text.

And something stood out.

"Miranda," I said. "Hey, Miranda!"

"What?" Miranda hissed.

"Get over here!" I held out the open pages. "This is the copyright page of the book, right?"

"Yeah?" Miranda said slowly.

"Then… am I imagining this, or does this bit say 'Teotihuacán'?"

Miranda rushed over and scanned the page.

Her eyes went wide.

"'Future Archivists,'" Miranda translated. "'Congratulations on finding the next clue. But your search has only just begun.'"

I laughed in amazement. We'd found something. We'd actually found something!

"'The Mexico you know is composed of deities,'" Miranda read out, squinting so she could understand the miniscule print. "'Beings of sky and earth that make up the world around us. They have existed for centuries, across many civilizations, as representations of the world we live in. And if you are reading this, then they have offered you power. They have offered you a challenge.

"'Prove your worth to the deities. Prove your resolve. Learn about the world of Teotihuacán, and discover who it is that blessed you with your power.'"

"That tracks with what Daniel said." I traced my thumb over my nail bed. "Looks like he's legit."

Miranda shrugged. "'If you wish to know more about the deities of Teotihuacán,'" she read out, "'the cradle of our philosophies and civilizations alike, find the clue, release your magic, and behold the tethers that bind our world.'"

When Miranda didn't continue, I peered over her shoulder to see the next line in the section. I suppose I was expecting a riddle Miranda was struggling to translate.

I wasn't expecting numbers.

```
LA1 (38)(13)(7), LA2 (50)(20)(2), LA3 (3)(19)
                    (4)
         LO1 / 35, LO2 / 999, LO3 / 500
```

"'38, 13, 7,'" Miranda read the first set of numbers out loud. Her gaze shifted from side to side for a second, and then she gasped. "Page 38, line 13, seventh word."

Miranda took the book from my hand and thumbed through the pages until reaching page 38.

I sputtered in surprise. Miranda had seen the numbers for a total of five seconds, and already she was honing in on specific points of the book like how a sonar hones in on submarines.

Refusing to be outdone by my cousin, I picked up *Los Orígenes de los Aztecas* and flipped to the copyright page. Sure enough, it had the same message. Or at least what I assumed was the same message. The words roughly looked the same, but the numbers at the bottom were different.

```
LO1 (55)(7)(9), LO2 (37)(27)(9), LO3(100)(24)
                    (10)
         LA1 / 182, LA2 / 100, LA3 / 4
```

"LA1," I THOUGHT OUT LOUD. "38, 13, 7. IN BRACKETS."

Miranda stopped flicking pages. I vaguely gestured to the new copyright page, and Miranda took the other book from me.

"LA1." I ran a hand through my hair, and my fingers got caught in a knot hidden among the curls. "Slash 182. That's a big one, but not impossible."

I closed my eyes as my brain did the work.

"*Usa su calor, encuentra la señal,*" Miranda said. The sound of flicking pages stopped again. "Use your warmth, find the signal. But it doesn't say *where*."

I opened my eyes. "19."

"What?" Miranda started thumbing through the book again. "Page 19?"

"No, that's the first number. It's—just give it."

I pulled both books out of Miranda's hands and went to the copyright pages.

"The numbers, they're telling us to multiply." I pointed to the first set of numbers we'd seen. "Take the numbers in the Mayan book, LA1. 38 times 13 is 494. That times seven is 3,458.

"And in the Aztec book." I pointed to the second row of numbers. "It shows us how we need to divide it. LA1 slash 182. So, we divide our big number by 182." I flourished my hand. "You get 19!"

Miranda stood there, staring at me like I'd just recited Shakespeare in Spanish, as I did the mental math for the rest of the numbers. Yeah, I could've used my phone, but doing it all in my head was more fun. And as an added bonus, I got to make Miranda look like an electrocuted fish.

"So LA equals 19, 20, and 57," I summarized for her, "and LO equals 99, 9, and 48." I scratched the back of my neck. "But they're just numbers. Not a location."

Miranda blinked, and the shock on her face disappeared.

"Yes, it is." She pulled out her phone and opened a search tab. "LA and LO. Latitude and longitude."

On a GPS coordinate website, Miranda typed in all six sets of numbers. The website reloaded, and a red dot appeared over a map of Mexico City. She zoomed in until the dot settled over a green square.

"The *Plaza de Coyoacán*," Miranda said.

"Looks like we know where we're going next," I said. "How'd you know it was pointing to words in the books?"

Miranda shrugged. "I like puzzles. How'd you realize it was a math problem? And how the hell did you do all those equations without a calculator?"

I shrugged back. "I like math."

"You like math?" Miranda chuckled. "Huh. Who would've thought."

"Brains and beauty." I flicked my hair and grinned at her. "Why pick one when you can have both?"

11

___

MONDAY MORNINGS SUCK

MIRY

JULY 10TH

A BENEFIT OF HAVING THE ELDEST COUSIN ON YOUR SIDE: IF he says that he's gonna take you on a mini roadtrip around the city, your parents don't even question it.

We had no idea how long we'd be in Coyoacán, and we definitely had no idea how long the Archivists' goose chase would go on for. But Fer's excuse bought us a full day in the city. The plan was to go to Coyoacán, find the clue, and hopefully do all that before I could slam the car door off its hinges.

I was in a bad mood that morning. But honestly, Fer shouldn't have thrown us into the car at 6:30am after I couldn't sleep because of goddamn nightmares.

I wanted to sleep in. But Fer had forgotten to tell us that he was dropping Tío Rizo off at work. And Fer insisted it'd be a "super, super quick" stop.

We hit the morning traffic rush. Cars were diverted halfway through the drive because of an accident. People got annoyed, they didn't give other cars the right of way, and it caused a pile up that blocked not just one, but *two* intersections.

We were stuck in that for over an hour. And on the drive to Coyoacán, we got stuck in *another* car pileup because a bus crashed into a truck.

Mexico City traffic. It's great.

It didn't help that I didn't want to be here. After dreaming of stalkers and earthquakes and voices in my head, I'd barely gotten any sleep. I don't scream when I have bad dreams, so I know no one noticed I had them. And I didn't want anyone to know.

Why? Because I didn't want them to see me as weak.

And if Ada could shrug off getting stalked like it was nothing, I could, too. Even if it was only out of spite.

By the time we had reached the borough of Coyoacán, Fer had gone through all of my patience and at least a dozen Bad Bunny songs. And to make everything worse, we left the house before we even got coffee.

"Next time," Ada said, "*I'm* picking the music—"

"No, you're not." Fer pointed a finger at her and another at me. "You're not allowed to pick, and you're not allowed to pick."

Yeah, right. As if I'd listen to my personal playlist with Ada in the car. The princess already judges me enough. No need for her to judge my music tastes, too.

"Jeez, you don't need to get so defensive." Ada adjusted her mint green purse over her shoulder. She'd switched bags so that it could compliment the matching green flats which had little bows at the front. Alongside her orange and yellow sundress that ended around her knees, the whole outfit made Ada look like a multi-colored popsicle.

"If you want me to keep being your chauffeur, those are the rules," Fer stated. "Unless—"

"We are not paying you," I growled.

"Any reason we didn't stop at that McDonald's to get Miss Grumpy a coffee?" Ada asked.

I growled again, and Fer sighed.

"Hada, if we stopped at McDonald's, we'd just make her even grumpier."

Fer said nothing more, and Ada and I followed him down the streets of Coyoacán.

The inner section of Coyoacán feels like a small Mexican town. It's filled with brightly-colored concrete houses, organ grinders that cranked wind-up instruments, and huge trees that shaded the streets and uprooted the sidewalks. The only structures that were taller than two stories were old-school buildings that were constructed at least a century ago. The streets were a mix of cobblestone and stone tile.

It's so green and vibrant that you'd hardly believe you were in the middle of a megacity. But I guess that's the point. It's supposedly the charm of the neighborhood—an escape from the urban gray. But drive a few minutes out of the neighborhood and you're right back to towering buildings.

The three of us weaved our way through strolling couples, locals munching on *pan dulce* from the local bakeries, and the occasional family on their way out for breakfast. Some of them were wearing shorts and tank tops—a tell-tale way to spot a tourist in the city—but most, like Fer and me, were in jeans and short-sleeved shirts. Though it wasn't busy yet, it was still summer. Soon enough, the entire neighborhood would be overrun with Mexicans and internationals alike.

It's a miracle we found a parking spot, and I'm pretty sure the only reason we beat the rest of the tourists here was because we showed up at nine-something in the goddamn morning.

Did I mention I hadn't had my coffee? Or anything to eat? Because I'm not sure if I've made it obvious enough yet.

"We're here! Great!" Ada cheered as we showed up to *El Jarocho*, somehow managing to be cheerful on an empty stomach. "So, what are we looking for?"

"Coffee," I said, stepping into the store.

"You think the clue's in the coffee?" Ada asked.

"I think my patience is in the coffee."

The scent of roasted beans greeted me warmly as we placed our orders. Ada got herself a mocha, I got myself a cappuccino, and Fer got himself a large americano.

"Since when do you drink coffee?" I asked Fer. "You used to drink tea."

"College corrupted him," Ada said. "Now coffee's the only thing that lets him study for finals *and* still play video games until 2am."

"Hey, I don't play for that long!" Fer said. "And the only reason I drink coffee is because *you* kept telling me to try it."

Ada grinned. "You're welcome!"

Fer sighed fondly.

I bit the inside of my cheek.

As an apology for the traffic jam, Fer bought us some of the freshly made donuts. They were almost the size of my face, some of them coated in sugar and cinnamon, others dipped into dark chocolate. By the time I'd scarfed down my second one, I'd *almost* forgiven him.

Ada and I settled down into one of the green benches that were scattered throughout the sidewalks. I drank my coffee, and Ada fiddled with her phone while leaning backward to take in the morning sun.

"Daniel says he'll meet us as soon as he can," Fer said. There was enough room on the bench for him to squeeze in, but he insisted on standing so Ada and I wouldn't get squished. "He lives in Ciudad Satélite, so he has a while to go."

I scoffed.

"Where's that?" Ada said around a mouthful of donut. Some of the sugar had sprinkled into her shoulder-length hair. "Is it far?"

"Too far," I said.

"Is it even in Mexico City?"

"They like to say it is. We know otherwise." I swirled the

coffee in my hands. "Are we sure we can trust this guy? He seemed a bit too excited to meet us."

"Why's that a bad thing?" Ada asked. "If I was in a magical group that needs more members, I'd be excited for new people! Especially if they're here to help put away an evil spirit that turned my best friend against me. And the god-ity confirmed it for us."

I turned to Fer. "He's Daniel Merino of the Archivists of Teotihuacán," he said. "I'm sure of it."

I bit my lip before I could ask Fer exactly how he knew all of that. We had a deal. If he drove us, we wouldn't ask questions for two days.

I was starting to really hate that deal.

A bright *ding ding ding* sound came from Ada's phone. I glanced over. "What's that?"

Ada twisted away from me. "My phone."

"I meant the app on your phone." Ada turned off the phone, but I caught a glimpse of her screen before she hit the button. "Is that... a language learning app?"

Ada sighed. "Yeah."

My body froze to the bench as I processed that.

"Really?" I asked.

"Yeah, really." Ada put her phone away. "Hey, my brain just isn't good with languages. Sue me if I need a little bit of help."

"Huh. Finally learning Spanish." I smiled and downed the rest of my coffee. "Took you long enough."

Ada went quiet.

Here's the thing about my cousin. If you get her talking about something she likes, she doesn't shut up about it. For hours. She's like Fernando in that sense. But she wasn't talking about this, which could only mean one thing.

"You're *kidding* me," I said. "It's not Spanish?"

Ada straightened her sun dress and grabbed the last donut. "No, it's not. Why do you care? It's not like I'm doing it to spite you or anything. Or what, are you just that annoyed that I'm the American who only speaks English? You're American, too, you know!"

I grunted. "Unfortunately."

"Niñas—" Fer started.

"What do you mean by that?" Ada interrupted.

"I mean that you just love bringing it up."

"Jeez, is this about when we were ten?" Ada said. "Are you still holding onto *that*?"

"I hold on to a lot of things." I stood up and threw my empty coffee cup into a trash can. "And if you think this is only about when we were ten, then you really need to get your memory checked, Fresa."

"How should I know!? You're the one who never talks about stuff!"

"And for someone who really likes prying into other people's lives, you sure don't have any motivation to ask me about mine!"

"Niñas," Fer said forcefully. "*Ya*. That's enough."

Ada and I glared at each other. Whatever truce and "bonding" moment we'd had last night seemed to have evaporated into the air, and we were back to the same bickering routine as always.

Other patrons and passersby were starting to stare. I even heard someone mumbling about the loud tourists.

Ada stood up from the bench and put down her coffee so she could straighten out her sundress. "I suggest we split up so we can cover more ground," she said pointedly.

"Agreed," I said.

"Niñas, come on," Fer said, but Ada and I were already walking away. "Hada! Miry!"

I went down the long street that headed toward the main plaza, and Ada took the road completely opposite.

"Hada! Miry! I—*agh*!" Fer cried. "Hada, wait for me! You don't speak Spanish!"

I glanced back just in time to see Fer sprinting after Ada.

I bit my lip. "Thanks, Fer."

I've always known that Fer had a bias. He's always denied it, as has Ada, but I know. This situation was proof. Even before he moved to Arizona for university, he always focused on Ada first and me second. It only got worse after he'd moved, leaving me without the only person I considered a genuine friend in real life.

And I'd be lying if I said that didn't sting.

I stalked down the road that led to the central plaza, feeling even worse than I did earlier. I suddenly wanted to stop. I wanted to stop worrying about this magic, about Archivists and deities and gods. I wanted to not hang onto the word of a literal stranger we met yesterday. And I wanted to stop fighting with Ada.

Because, believe or not, I actually don't like fighting with my own damn family.

You're quitting, a voice said in my head.

I froze.

You're not leaving your cousin to search for the clue, he said. *You're running away.*

"I'm not," I said, trying and failing to keep my voice from shaking.

You are, he said. *You run away from every problem you can't control, Miranda.*

I scoffed. "Oh, yeah? Prove it."

The man laughed. *I think I will. Just don't complain when you realize I'm right.*

I stalked down the street and pulled out my earbuds —

"*Look,*" said the voice of a teenage girl in Spanish, "*I think it's the gringa!*"

12

THIS IS WHY I DON'T LIKE PEOPLE

MIRY

MY HANDS SHOOK AS THE VOICE OF ANOTHER GIRL SAID IN Spanish, *"It is her, right?"*

"Of course it is," the first girl said. *"Who else would it be?"*

My senses went on high alert. My chest tightened, sweat beaded on the back of my neck, and my throat went numb.

I knew those voices. I thought I had put them behind me.

"Hey, McDonald's!" another voice said in Spanish. *"Don't ignore us!"*

I hopped over cracked pavement and weaved between stalls that had been set up on the sidewalk, hoping to put distance between myself and the familiar voices.

"Hey, you don't have to run!" one of them shouted.

The road opened up to the plaza; I picked up the pace.

I rushed across the smooth stone floor, past the large gazebo, and between the preened hedges that made up this part of the plaza. I crossed the street that led into the second half and sidestepped my way around a pair of dogs.

I made my way toward the big fountain in the center of the plaza, the *Fuente de los Coyotes,* hoping to hide myself amid the small crowd of people taking their pictures with it. The place was big and open. But if I could find a corner that turned into one of the smaller streets, I could hopefully get away from these guys and pretend that this never happened. Pretend that I wasn't hearing—

"Miry! Come on!" the girl said in English now. "Don't pretend you don't know me!"

I don't know why that's the thing that made me stop. But it did.

"What do you want, Caro?" I growled without turning around.

"See, the *gringa* only listens to us when we talk in English!" Caro laughed. "I'm just seeing how my friend is."

"Call me your friend again and I'll throw you into the fountain."

Caro stepped forward until she was right in front of me.

Remember when Ada and I needed an excuse to get out of the house so that we could find our first clue? I said that an old friend lived roughly in the area we'd be going to.

Well, Carolina Mendoza was that "old friend".

She's average height for a Mexican, which means she's pretty small. But despite being several centimeters shorter than me, she always seemed bigger. Maybe it was the broad shoulders, the tall forehead, or her huge smile. When we were still friends, I used to like that about her. She'd always boast about how she was the strongest girl in school, and I'd dare her to prove it by carrying me on her back until recess ended or a teacher scolded us. She used to be cool.

Now she's *this*.

"Wow," Caro sneered. "She thinks she can throw me."

I felt her two friends step closer.

"You really think you have the balls to do that?" Sebastián said from behind.

"Of course," Luisa said. She yanked on a strand of my hair. I winced—hard, and I pushed her.

"*Don't touch me!*" I yelled in Spanish. I pulled my hair back and instinctively ran my fingers through it.

Luisa snickered. "She just doesn't want to talk. Donaldson always thinks she's better than us."

"I never thought I was better than you," I said. "You're the ones who think you're better than me, remember?"

"It's not our fault you're stupid," Sebastián jeered.

"I'm *not* stupid."

"Then prove it," Luisa said.

I wanted to. I wanted to tell them to back off and leave me alone. But they always managed to take whatever I say and turn it into a joke, and the fear of them weaponizing my words against me stilled my tongue.

The sounds of the fountain in front of me filled my ears. It was just water, but at that moment, the falling streams sounded as loud as thunder.

"See?" Caro said. "She leaves Mexico for a year and comes back dumber than a clown."

Sebastián and Luisa laughed, and that made Caro grin.

I growled. It didn't matter that I'd only lived in the US for a year. It didn't matter that I hadn't lived there since I was 11. All that mattered was that I came back more different than I already was, and that was enough to turn my best friend on me.

"*Pinche gringa*," Caro said.

"Don't call me that!" I yelled. Sebastián and Luisa laughed again, and Caro grinned wider. "And I didn't leave you! I didn't want to leave! It was my parents' idea and you know it."

"You still left." Caro shrugged, jostling the purse that hung from one shoulder. "One year in *Estados Unidos* and you forgot everything from here. What did you say to Sebas when you met him? *Me gustas*."

I grimaced. It was a slip up. Instead of saying that I liked him, I'd said that I *like* like him. I said that in front of Caro and her two new friends, and I think that's what started it all. Because ever since then, I went from being Caro's friend to being her biggest target.

"It was dumb," I said, "and it happened four years ago."

"*Oye,*" Luisa goaded, "remember when she told the teacher that the first president was Porfirio Díaz?"

"Ugh, shut up!"

"*No way,*" Sebastián said. "Come on, say something funny!"

"No! I'm done being your clown!"

"But your name is McDonald's," Luisa jeered.

"That's not my name!"

Caro reached out to tug on my hair. When we were kids, it was a game we played. She'd tug on my hair and I'd tug on hers. Now it was just Caro's game. "*Calm down, McDon —*"

I slapped her hand away. "Don't touch me!"

"*Oh, calm down, gringita,*" Caro said. "Stop being a *pendeja —*"

"I'm leaving!" I yelled. My temper had reached its limit, and I yelled at the top of my lungs. "Fine! You're right! I'm quitting! I am *done!*"

I wanted to go home. I wanted to get away from here. I wanted to get away from my asshole ex-classmates, from my infuriating cousin, and from this stupid quest! I didn't care that I was proving the voice right. Nothing about these last two days had been fun for me, and I wanted it to stop.

"I'm done!" I yelled. "Now move —"

"I think," a woman said, "that's enough."

I turned and saw a tall woman stroll over to us. She took her time walking around the large fountain, looking over each of us with a calculating and imposing gaze.

"Aw, the gringita had her *mami* come save her," Luisa said.

"I am not Miry's mother," the woman said in a low voice that clearly enunciated every word. "Unlike her, I have a particularly good sense of smell." She smirked at Caro. "And I believe you have something in that purse you should not have. Something… earthy, let's say."

Caro clutched her purse to her chest.

No way, I thought.

"The rumors were true?" I said. "You actually smoke mari—"

"Miry, *shut up*!" Caro yelled.

"Make me."

"Yes," the woman said. "Because unless you leave here right now, I think that Miry should keep talking."

"Why?" Caro asked.

"Because I see a police officer over there," the woman said. She pointed a finger at a man in uniform who was patrolling the area. "And I do not think you are old enough to hold those substances you have in your bag."

Caro and her three friends gulped.

The woman's smirk grew. "It would be terrible if he overheard us and decided to search your bag. Would it not?"

Luisa and Sebastián walked away immediately. Caro stayed there for a moment—glancing between me, the woman, and the police officer—before Luisa and Sebastián gripped her arms and pulled her away.

I turned to the woman.

She had dark brown skin, a pointed nose, and black hair that fell across one shoulder in a thick braid that nearly reached the ground. Her sleeveless green dress flowed gracefully around her, but the hem was wet. As if she'd just walked through shallow water.

"Who… are you?" I asked.

"Someone you will know about very soon."

The woman blinked, and her deep brown eyes shimmered until they turned gold.

I gasped. On instinct, I felt around for the warm feeling in my chest. The heat—magic, that's what it was—came to me immediately. It hummed inside of me, and right before I pushed it up to my head so I could send out my projectiles, something… shifted.

It was like the warmth inside of me was being pulled. Like a metal sphere being guided toward a magnetic current. It pulled the magic away from my head and toward something that was in front of me.

Toward the woman in the green dress.

That's when I was hit by an irrefutable truth. I didn't know how or why, but my magic was telling me that the woman in front of me was something *different*.

Something more than human.

"You're not a person," I said.

"Not really."

I gulped. "… A spirit?"

"Not quite." The woman made an expanding motion with her hands, and that's when I noticed the dozen or so jade bracelets that hung from her wrists. "Think bigger."

I thought back on the words in the books Ada and I had found. "Are you a deity?"

"I have been called that."

I thought back to what Daniel had said to us in the car. "A god?"

"I have been called that, as well."

I bit my cracked lip, so hard I nearly drew blood. "What are you?"

"Let us go this way." The woman turned and started walking, the sound of thin sandals tapping against the stone floor. "I have been craving a *nieve* for a while."

13

I TALK TO A CRYPTIC LADY

MIRY

When I came to Coyoacán this morning, I expected to find a clue. I did not expect to be sitting next to a potential god/deity/monster in disguise while we waited for an ice cream shop to open.

"It has been a long time since I have been in this part of the city," the jade woman said. "It is not one of my usual haunts."

"So… you're a ghost?" I asked cautiously.

"'Ghost' implies that I am dead. And that I was once alive. Ah!" Jade—hey, she didn't give me a name, so that's what I was calling her—smiled as the store opened. Her golden eyes shimmered again until they faded back to brown. "At last. Come, tell me what you like."

I slowly followed Jade into *La Gloria*, an old ice cream store that's been open since the 50s. The workers inside were surprised to see customers exactly at 10am, but they happily let Jade and me inside. She drifted toward the nieves—ice cream that is made with a water base instead of a milk base—and asked for a triple scoop. I hesitantly ordered a single.

"Have another." Jade winked at me. "It's my treat. You may as well take advantage of it."

I told the workers to make my single into a double because

I didn't want to risk pissing off a magical entity. Jade also asked for two water bottles, and she paid them with a small mountain of coins.

I didn't see her pull out a wallet. She wasn't carrying a purse, and her long dress didn't have any pockets.

The woman took her time walking back to the plaza, taking long, slow strides around the large gazebo. I numbly ate my strawberry nieve.

Jade was unconcerned with my very obvious confusion. She just smiled and turned her cone—a mix of lime, mango, and watermelon nieves—humming happily.

My phone buzzed in my pocket. I ignored it.

My mind was on overdrive. It was burning through every moment of the last day, and if my head were a computer, I would've been overheating. I had no idea who this woman was, what she wanted, or why she was here. All I knew was that she wanted something to do with me, and I needed to know who the hell she was.

There wasn't much for me to go on. Part of the reason my original search for information about Teotihuacán led to a dead end was because there was so little information. It was why I'd only managed to briefly read through one single website before the strange virus shut me out.

It had mentioned Quetzalcóatl, Tláloc, the flayed god, and—

"Are you... the Gran Diosa?" I asked. "The Lady of Spiders?"

Jade shrugged. "Perhaps."

"Are you someone else?"

"Perhaps."

"Are you normally this vague?"

"Not always."

I held myself from groaning. Man, is that what *I* sound like sometimes?

"Why are you speaking in English?" I asked, hoping to get her to talk about *something*.

"Do you think Spanish was my native tongue?" the woman asked, finishing off one of her three scoops of nieve. "I know many languages. And if I can avoid speaking the tongue of colonizers, that's what I choose to do."

I grimaced. "So English isn't a language of colonizers?"

"It is. But it's different from the usual one." The woman tilted her head to the side, and the slight motion made the tip of her long braid scrape across the floor. "Do you not have something to do?"

Oh. Right.

The clue. AKA the whole reason why I was here in the first place.

"Yeah, not today. Don't think I'm in the right mood for it." I wanted to run. I didn't want to be here, with a woman who can make coins come from thin air. With the voice of a man following me around in my head. I was scared, and I wanted out. "Thanks for the ice cream, but I'm gonna go home—"

"That would be unwise," Jade said, and her voice turned as hard and cold as ice.

I gulped. "Why not?"

"Because I need you to unlock your powers," she said firmly. "And even if you want to stop, it's too late. The world is turning. Plans are accelerating. A catastrophe is coming."

I might've been imagining it, but the scratches on my left hand burned. "If it's such a big deal, then why don't you step up?"

"I would if I could."

"So what? You get me out of that mess with Caro just so you can guilt trip me into going along with all this?" I kicked at the floor beneath me. "Why do you think that's gonna work?"

"Because I can offer you something in return," Jade said. "Information. About your quest. About Teotihuacán. And about you."

I frowned. "What makes you think I want that?"

"Because you hate when you don't understand what is happening to you."

I nearly cracked my ice cream cone. "You gonna tell me how you figured that out?"

The corner of Jade's mouth twitched. "Perhaps."

She was right, you know. I hate not knowing what's going on with me. And this entire mess with the pyramids and our stalkers was leaving me more and more in the dark.

I wanted answers. And I wanted them now.

"Use your warmth, find the signal," I whispered.

I searched for the warmth—the magic—in my chest and found it immediately. It swirled in me, just like before. It pulled me to the jade woman, guiding me closer to her. But she couldn't be the signal, right?

I thought about the invisible projectiles I launched at the pyramids. I pushed some of the warmth up to my head.

One, I thought. *At… At…*

But I didn't know what I was aiming at. I didn't know where to shoot them or where to look.

The warmth was getting uncomfortable. The back of my neck started sweating, and the hand that was holding my half-eaten ice cream cone felt slick.

"Breathe," Jade said calmly. "In, out. That's it, Miry. That's it. You're trying to use the power the same way you did before."

"How did you know—"

The woman's eyes shifted to gold again. She gazed at me calmly, with the kind of look that makes you feel like you're staring into the eyes of someone who didn't just know you, but understood you in a way that no one else could.

It was as humbling as it was terrifying.

"Did you choose me?" I asked. "Are you the one who gave me these powers?"

"Why do you say that?"

"It's a guess," I admitted. "You could be just any magical being, but if you know how I'm using my magic… then maybe you're the one who gave it to me."

Jade chuckled and kept eating her ice cream. "I do enjoy it when my disciples prove themselves clever."

My throat felt dry. I scarfed down what was left of my nieve in an attempt to soothe it, but also to pretend like I wasn't freaking out about all this. "Is that why you picked me?"

"No." The woman's jade bracelets clinked against each other, and suddenly she was holding out a napkin. "It was a good guess, but I didn't pick you for your intelligence."

I stared at the napkin.

"If you want help, you may ask for it," the woman said.

"Who says I need help?"

"Miry," the woman smiled calmly, "if you don't ask for my help, I cannot give it to you."

I bit the inside of my cheek.

I didn't want to ask for help. I didn't want to admit I needed it. I was 15. I should've been able to handle things on my own. Right? I shouldn't have to need other people to fix my problems.

There is a time to panic and a time to act.

Those were the words that Abuelita told me then. And she was right. There's a time to panic and a time to do something. But…

"What am I supposed to do?" I asked the woman in green, taking the napkin from her to roughly wipe at my sticky hand. "It says to use the warmth, but I… I'm using it wrong."

She smiled, revealing a row of perfect white teeth. "Then instead of trying the same thing and hoping for a different result, perhaps you should try something new."

Slowly, I reached for the warmth in my chest. It greeted me happily, thrumming in my chest. It pulled me toward the jade woman, encouraging me to go toward her even though she was standing right next to me.

But she's not who I was searching for.

I was searching for something else. Something beyond.

"Keep going," Jade said. "And let me help."

I didn't want her help. I wanted to do this on my own. But I wanted answers more than I wanted my pride. So, when a thrum of power surrounded me, I let it stay there. I let it find the thread of magic that moved from my chest to my head. Jade's magic pushed through me, telling me to let my power fill every bit of me.

So I did.

The feeling in my chest expanded until it ran through every nerve in my body. From the crown of my head to the ends of my fingers to the tips of my toes. I made the magic fill me. I made it expand until it occupied every bit of my body. I unfocused my eyes and honed in on my sense of touch.

And that's when I felt it.

It was like a small pulse in the distance. *Plick, plock. Plick, plock.* It was vague, but it was close.

I closed my eyes and I followed the signal.

I didn't know where I was going. I let my feet guide me along, and when I stumbled on the divot in the ground, Jade caught my arm and pulled me upright. Occasionally, she would pull me to one side or tell me when we'd arrived at a step, but she didn't tell me where to go. The sun peeled away, meaning that we must've gone indoors.

I kept following the signal, *plick, plock,* until it was so loud in my ears that it reverberated in my chest and skull.

I raised my hand until I felt like I was touching a ball of electric energy. My hand shook.

The tip of my finger grazed the spine of a book.

14

<hr>

EVERYTHING IS FINE

MIRY

"VERY GOOD," JADE SAID.

I opened my eyes. A wooden shelf stood before me. I was pointing directly at a thin book, roughly the same size and shape as the books Ada and I had found at El Péndulo, titled *El Mundo Antiguo*. It was wedged in between two large encyclopedias about insects from Southeast Asia.

I pulled it out. The hum of energy faded right away, leaving only a tingling sensation in my fingers.

"Congratulations," Jade said. Golden eyes beamed at me. "I wrongly expected you to take another ten minutes."

"Um," I said, "thanks?"

"Shhh!" someone hissed.

I turned to find a disgruntled man surrounded by open books on a wooden table. Around him were several tall shelves stacked with books, old and new, and he made a frustrated signal at an older woman who was organizing a tall stack of tomes.

Oh, I realized. *We just walked into a library.*

The older woman—the librarian—glared at me. She then scowled at Jade, and I could pinpoint the instant she noticed the still-unfinished nieve in her hands.

"I was right to choose you as my disciple," Jade said as she licked her last scoop.

"Shhh!" I hissed. "We're in a library!"

"People's judgement only affects you as much as you let it."

"Yeah. Tell that to the librarian who wants to kick us out."

I grabbed the woman's arm and pulled her toward the exit. I went to tell the librarian that I was checking the book out, but Jade stopped me before I could.

"This isn't part of their collection," she said.

THE TWO OF US STEPPED BACK OUT INTO THE SUMMER SUN. Apparently the library, identifiable by a small sign I only noticed as we walked out of it, was inside the large yellow building that was directly opposite the large gazebo. Jade started strolling her way across the plaza, and I tucked my new book firmly under my arm. Despite the cold ice cream, my throat felt tight.

The woman pulled out one of the water bottles she'd bought. I didn't see from where, but I figured that that was a mystery I didn't have time to figure out.

"Okay, I did the thing. Now you hold up your end of the bargain," I said between gulps of water. "What information do you have?"

"Ask me questions and you'll find out."

It's a miracle I didn't roll my eyes. "I can't ask you why you picked me. Daniel said I have to figure that out for myself."

"Daniel Merino?" Jade hummed and crossed the street that led to the other side of the plaza. "He always did like to jump straight to the answers. At least, that's what my husband says."

"Your husband?" I thought back to my conversation with the man. "But if your husband has contact with him, then he'd be the person who gave Daniel powers." I bit my lip. "So your husband… is Tláloc?"

The woman nodded.

The two of us walked into the more shaded part of the plaza, and I almost gasped in relief as the tall trees shaded us from the hot sun.

"Daniel said that we're supposed to learn who the gods are," I said, avoiding a group of sprinting children. "You're here now, and I don't think there's a rule that stops you from telling me your name. Is it the Gran Diosa? The Lady of Spiders? What? What's your real name?"

"I do not know."

I lowered the water bottle. "Wait, *what*? You don't know your own name?"

"Not my original one."

"But if you don't know your name, then how do you know anything?" I asked. "How do you even know that Tláloc's your husband?"

"Stories," Jade said. "Because people tell our stories."

This time I did roll my eyes. "Yeah, I'm gonna need more information than that."

"There is something you should know about us." Jade strolled down the stone path that led to the plaza's large fountain. "We existed before everything else. Before cities. Before people. We were always here. And we were given form when you gave us names. But those who first named me are long gone. I have new names, but none are the *first* name. That name will never be known again."

"I don't get it."

"The city of Teotihuacán is the origin," Jade said. "The point where so many other cultures you know of, Aztec, Mayan, Toltec, had their beginning. After the city collapsed, people left. Languages evolved, people created new cities, and names changed." She sighed. "Teotihuacán collapsed many,

many years ago. No one remembers the language I once spoke, so no one remembers my name. Not even I."

I bit the inside of my cheek again. "So that's how you can forget your own name..."

"I have the privilege of seeing humans evolve and grow. That comes with a price. You forgot my name, my original stories, and my history. As such, I forgot it, as well." Jade chuckled to herself. "Even Quetzalcóatl forgot his original name, and he is the most well-known of all of us. But that fame comes with its own price. One that he has been... struggling to handle, as of late."

I forced myself to down the last of my water. "But you have a name you go by now?"

"I have many. I have names given to me by people who came *after* Teotihuacán. The stories and names people give us... they shape who we are. Take Quetzalcóatl for example. That name was given to him by the Aztecs."

The woman produced the other water bottle from thin air and held it out to me. I grabbed it but didn't take a drink. "So the Aztecs know who you are?"

"Yes. But I'm different when I'm with them."

"How?"

"It is a different pantheon. So I am a different version of myself."

We stopped just a couple of paces away from the *Fuente de los Coyotes*, right where Caro and her friends had cornered me. The enormous fountain greeted us with a statue of two large coyotes circling each other, one of them poised and calm and the other a second away from howling. Bits of water splashed out of it, but it no longer sounded as loud as it had before.

"How?" I asked. "How are you a different version?"

Jade finished her last scoop of nieve and moved onto the cone. "With those who follow the Aztec pantheon," she said between bites, "I am more... defined. The stories about me are clearer. But the Archivists follow the pantheon of Teotihuacán."

"What makes it different?"

"There are things that they know of my time. But most knowledge is lost. So with you my image is… looser. More free. Pliable, you might say."

"So… you don't remember what Teotihuacán was like?"

I remembered what Ada, Fer, and I saw yesterday. Polished roads, gleaming rocks, and beautiful, shining pyramids.

"I hardly remember it," Jade said. "And I hardly remember what I was like back then."

I bit my lip. "You forgot it. Like you forgot your name."

"Yes."

"So… How do you know that this is what you looked like?" I gestured to her green dress, long black braid, and multiple jade bangles.

I blinked, and the woman's visage shifted.

Her green dress shifted to a dark red. The jade bangles around her wrist morphed themselves into obsidian. Her nails, which were originally bare, got painted red.

Her long braid slowly unwound itself.

"I have many outfits," Jade said as her now-loose hair separated itself into smaller sections. "Many personalities. When I show myself to those who follow the Aztec pantheon, I act and dress more similarly to their idea of me. But this specific form, this specific version of me, is the version of me closest to what I was like when only Teotihuacán existed."

I gulped. "But… you just said you hardly remember what it was like."

"True."

The woman's hair wove itself into smaller braids. In hindsight, I should've been wondering why no one else was noticing. But at the moment, I was too stunned and terrified to even think about that.

"So how do you know that this is the version of you that was present at Teotihuacán?" I asked.

Jade shrugged. "I guess."

"Basically, you're just going off of what others think of you." I bit my lip again, and I tasted blood. "They get to define who you are. That… sucks."

"It's not as bad as you might think." Jade pulled a napkin from the air and held it out to me. Maybe I was the only one who could see her magic because no one else seemed to care or notice. "We always present different versions of ourselves. To our friends, to our family. We show them different sides of us. Use different words. Different languages. We do it to the point where everyone has a different idea of who we are. There may be different interpretations of me, but I found a method to keep myself sane. Do you want to hear it?"

I hesitated before grabbing the napkin.

"If I do not like what they say, then I do not listen."

I couldn't help it. I laughed.

"That easy, huh?" I pressed the napkin to my bleeding lip.

The woman's golden eyes crinkled at the edges. "Those… antagonizers who came up to you… I know that it was your choice to listen to them or not, but if you want my opinion, I do not think they are ones worth listening to."

Something tightened itself in my throat and my chest, but it wasn't my magic.

"Yeah," I said. "Yeah."

At last, the woman's hair finished weaving itself. It had wound themselves into eight perfect braids that hung about her and just barely grazed the floor at her feet.

Eight black braids. Like spider legs.

"Your journey into the world of the Archivists was meant to be much longer," Jade said. "But I am afraid I will have to shorten it a bit."

Despite the napkin, a drop of blood seeped into my mouth. "Is it because of the spirit?"

The woman finished the last of her cone. "Answer me honestly," she said, low and commanding. "When you and Ada were at the pyramids, did you feel an earthquake?"

"Yes," I said.

Jade nodded. "Then it has started. You and your twin have cracked the seal that holds an old spirit captive."

"Wait, how did we even break this 'seal'?" I asked. "And I'm an only child. I mean, Ada and I were born on the same day, but we're cousins. And I'm an hour older than her."

"So you think." The woman smirked. "I've told you more than I would have under normal circumstances. External forces, cosmic forces—always attempt to limit our direct influences on humans, so we only take large risks when absolutely necessary."

"And this is necessary?"

"What do you think?" Jade asked. "After everything I told you, do you think that this is all a child's game?"

I shook my head.

"Would you like to learn more?"

I hesitated.

"You want to quit," Jade said softly. "But that is not a bad thing, Miry. If things get too much for you, you are allowed to quit. Do you know what you actually struggle with?"

I said nothing.

"You struggle with asking for help when you need," Jade said. "So before you quit, maybe try reaching out to someone."

I gulped. "Like Fer and Ada?"

"Like Fer and Ada."

I tugged a clump of my hair. "I… I can try."

Jade smirked. "I am glad to see that at least some mortals are wise enough to listen to me." She pointed at the book I had tucked under my arm. "This clue was meant to lead you out of the city. After a couple more clues, you'd get the instruction to head to the Museum of Anthropology. Go there now."

Jade straightened her back, and her golden eyes shined brighter. "Also, I recommend you watch your back."

I gulped. "Why?"

"Because some of my disciples are calling upon my magic. And I must give it to them."

"Miry!" Fer's voice came from behind me. He ran up to me and sighed in relief. "I've been calling you for—"

"Woah!" Ada exclaimed. "Who are *you*?"

"Are they the same people who stalked us on the bus?" I asked Jade, ignoring my cousin's sudden appearance. "Your disciples, are they our stalkers?"

"You will find out," she said.

"If they are, then shouldn't you be helping us?" I asked.

"Like I said, rarely do we interfere directly." Jade swayed from side to side. "I think I am satisfied with my choice in disciple. Now it is time for you to prove me correct."

The woman stopped swaying. She tilted her head back, her eyes fluttered shut, and her body phased through the solid stone tiles below us.

"Miry," Fer said slowly, "what was that?"

"*Who* was that?" Ada asked.

"I'm not sure," I said. "But I think I should take her advice."

15

CAR CHASES ARE SURPRISINGLY TERRIFYING

ADA

THE CAR RIDE WAS TENSE. BUT I GUESS TALKING TO A GOD-ity in person is a good reason for a mood shift.

I did my best to stay cheerful as Miranda recounted what Jade had said. When I first saw the god-ity, I was genuinely excited. But I wasn't the one who got to talk to the magical lady. And to add insult to injury, Miranda called shotgun, forcing me into the back seat of the Volkswagen.

There was no explicit reason for us to be so on edge, but the three of us kept glancing out our windows, looking around for any pum-eagles that might suddenly show up. We quickly made our way out of the winding streets of Coyoacán and onto a larger road I didn't know the name of. Huge trees and colorful houses were quickly replaced by tall buildings and gray roads.

We went onto a long road—highway?—that a passing sign told me was called Avenida Cuauhtémoc. Even though it was thankfully devoid of the morning traffic rush, we all kept glancing around as Miranda told us about the weird braid lady.

"I'm not sure how much we'll find at the museum," Nando said.

"How come?" I asked.

"Because it's Monday. And on Mondays—"

Nando didn't get to finish that sentence, because that was the moment the first eagle ripped its claws through the car's roof.

"Holy crap!" I yelled as three long talons pierced the vehicle and scratched their way down.

Nando yelled and swerved the car, narrowly missing another car that honked at us.

The Volkswagen groaned as the tires regained their grip on the road. On instinct, I brought up my pointer finger and aimed at the roof. I pushed a surge of warm energy into my nail bed until it became a cacti needle I shot through the roof. The nail made a small hole, but I didn't hear it hit anything.

Instead, I heard a very loud *caw*.

I lowered my window, looked up, and screamed something I never thought I'd say in my life.

"Eagles incoming!"

In the sky were over a dozen eagles. Not like the pum-eagles from the pyramids. No, these were *eagle*-eagles. They were all huge, with enormous wings that had little trouble keeping up with the car. Unlike American Bald Eagles that have white heads, these eagles were completely brown, with yellow-gray beaks and yellow-white talons. They were gorgeous.

And they were all flying directly toward the car.

Nando yelled as he swerved the car across two lanes. The old car bounced as we swerved, and it was enough to knock the eagle off the roof. Cars behind us honked and Nando yelled out *"¡lo siento!"*, but the eagles bent their wings and twirled toward us again.

Another talon scraped through the roof with a loud *hiss*. I ducked my head to avoid getting my hair shorn off.

The force of the scrape had forced the eagle off the roof and into the air directly behind us. It joined the other eagle that had just attacked us, and they flapped their wings in preparation for another attack.

"I'll get the ones in the sky!" Miranda lowered her window and leaned her forehead out, just enough to get a look without getting her head slammed in by a speeding car. "You get the ones that reach the car!"

"Why can't I get the ones in the sky?"

"Because I have better aim than you!"

I gritted my teeth. I stuck my right hand out of my open window and aimed my pointer finger directly at the eagle flying behind us. It was smaller than the pum-eagles were, but it was coming toward us, and I had a direct shot.

My projectile missed.

I launched out another one, and I missed again.

Okay, I thought, *maybe Miranda has a point.*

The two eagles flapped their wings furiously as they flew over our car's roof again. The metal hissed as the birds' talons scraped through it, tearing into the vehicle as easily as if it was a tin can. The Volkswagen's engine groaned as Nando kept us moving, stuttering every time he had to make a big turn that swung us across the road.

I turned to the three car lanes behind us. There weren't a lot of drivers out mid-morning on a Monday, but the few ones that were weren't yelling or pointing at the killer eagles. They just looked mildly confused at our damaged roof.

"Is no one seeing this?" I yelled. "Nando, you see it, right?"

"I see that eagles are trying to shred my car!" Nando cried, his grip tightening itself against the steering wheel. "And don't attack them! They're a protected species!"

"I don't think protection laws exist for magically-powered eagles!" Miranda yelled back, never taking her eyes off the sky.

A set of three talons pierced the roof again. I launched two projectiles upward, and a bird let out a screeching *caw*.

"They're not disappearing!" Miranda cried.

Two birds flapped around in wide, wonky circles. One of them had a single nail embedded in its left wing, the other had two needles embedded in its right. But they didn't disappear.

In the sky, the other ten-ish eagles recoiled as something crashed into their chests and wings. It jolted them and made them fly off-course, keeping them from reaching the car, but they weren't vanishing into mist.

At the pyramids, it only took two shots to make the pum-eagles disappear. But just like with our stalkers, these guys weren't going down.

The eagles recoiled as Miranda launched a new round of projectiles toward them. But they were gaining ground, to the point where they were about two car lengths behind us. Ready to shred us into confetti string. "Nando, can't you drive faster?!"

"Not in this car!" Nando cried. To prove his point, he amped up the speed a bit, only for the engine to sputter and make the Volkswagen bounce up and down. "And we have speed limits!"

"It's Mexico City!" Miranda yelled. "Who cares about speed limits?"

"I do!"

If we didn't get far away soon, the birds would shred enough of the roof to get in. Worst case scenario, we get mauled to death by eagles. Best case scenario, we crash, survive with no injuries, and run away from the eagles *on foot*.

The car slowed down. We were almost at the edge of an intersection, and the light was yellow.

"Don't stop!" Miranda and I yelled.

Nando's knuckles turned white. *"Aaah!"*

The Jetta's engine groaned and popped, but Nando kept his foot on the gas. And just as it sounded like the engine would die on us, our car lurched its way across the inter-section.

Behind us, another car sped up to do the same.

I scrambled to the back window and peered at the other vehicle. It was a silver car that was at least a decade younger than Nando's, and it had two women in it. In the passenger seat was a woman with a high bun and a deep scowl. She had one hand sticking out the window, and her fingers were pointing at the horde of eagles above us. In the passenger seat was a small woman with large glasses and a full face of makeup.

And that woman was very, *very* familiar.

"Lourdes!" I exclaimed.

"Who?" Miranda said in a strained voice.

"The woman from the coffee counter at the bookstore!" I said. "The one who took our order! There's no way this is a coincidence."

Lourdes lowered her window and yelled something, but the wind that raced down the street drowned out her words. Lourdes turned to the woman in the passenger seat and said something else. The woman with the high bun narrowed her eyes at the car and made a swirling motion with her hand.

The dozen eagles let out a single, furious *caw*, and I got two very distinct feelings. One, it was the woman with the bun controlling the eagles, and two, she didn't like us very much.

I stuck my hand out just enough to not get it crushed by another car. I lifted my finger again and pointed at the silver vehicle's front tire, hoping to pop it.

My needle hit the top part of the tire before getting run over. It didn't even leave a scratch.

I gulped.

I almost aimed my needles at the windshield, but I couldn't bring myself to actually shoot. I had no idea if my needles would pierce the windshield. If they did, and they hit the two women...

The thought of killing someone made me gag.

Nando lowered the Jetta's speed just enough to keep the engine from making really-not-good noises, but the car groaned every time he swerved to help keep the eagles at bay.

Miranda hissed under her breath. She didn't take her eyes off the eagles, which she was still pushing back just enough to keep them from swarming the car. The eagles recoiled as each of her projectiles hit. Though her projectiles were invisible, I guessed that she wasn't missing a single shot.

Miranda was holding back the swarm of eagles when I couldn't. Even if I did have my own weapon, there was no way I'd be as accurate as her. She looked focused; she looked determined.

And worst of all, she looked *cool*.

Miranda kept taking her shots, and I felt a familiar feeling of uselessness come over me. Because *Miranda* was good at this. *Miranda* was the competent one. Miranda didn't need Nando to come chasing after her because she didn't know the language. Miranda didn't need help to hold back a horde of eagles, to know when she's being stalked on a bus, or even to talk to her own family.

Because Miranda is Miranda. And I'm me. Uncoordinated, unaware, monolingual me.

And for the who-knows-how-manyth time in my life, I wished I was more like my cousin.

"Where the hell is Daniel?" Miranda asked.

"I can't read my phone while I'm driving!" Nando said. "Hada, read my messages!"

I—relieved that there was something I could actually do—scrambled forward and pulled Nando's phone out of his pocket. "My password is—"

"Got it!" I said as the phone unlocked.

"Since when do you know my password!?"

I ignored him and opened the Messages app. I almost panicked when I didn't see any conversation with a "Daniel", but then I remembered that Mexico uses WhatsApp for whatever reason and opened that.

"I think he says he's five minutes away!" I thumbed through the buttons, thanking the WhatsApp developers for adding icons that let me use the phone without knowing what *Ubicación* meant. "Sending him our live location!"

"What the hell!?" Miranda yelled suddenly.

"What?" I yelled back. "I'm just sending him our location!"

"Not you! The crocodiles!"

I dropped the phone, peered out the window again, and immediately yelled, "What the hell!?"

In the air, just beside the eagles, was a swarm of five crocodiles. They were large green masses that cast long shadows onto the ground. They were long, longer than the car with Lourdes and the other mysterious woman, and they huffed their huge nostrils as they literally swam their way toward us.

"Since when do crocodiles fly?" I yelled.

"I don't know!" Miranda yelled back.

In the driver's seat, Nando just yelled, *"Aaah!"*

The car lurched and bounced as Nando stepped on the gas again. Cars honked at us, motorcyclists gave us the finger, and I'm pretty sure the panic made Nando rush another yellow light.

The silver car with the two women stayed right behind us.

I jolted as Nando swerved to pass a slow car. I took hold of the door to recover from the sudden dizziness, and I found myself staring up at Mexico City's gray-blue sky.

Except... it wasn't gray-blue.

"Miranda, look at the sky!" I yelled.

"Yeah, I know!" she yelled back. "It's full of crocodiles!"

"Just look!"

"Why?"

"It's purple!"

The sky above us swirled in shades of lilac. It wasn't the deep purple we'd seen back at the ruins, but it was still purple. It was like someone had taken the color from the ruins and mixed it with Mexico City's gray-blue hue, turning the sky above us into a gray-tinged lilac.

But there was something else in the sky. It wasn't just a flat color—it was *moving*.

"It's like it's... waving at us?" I said. "Or like we're looking at it from... from—"

"Underwater," Miranda said numbly. "It's like we're underwater."

I thought about the last time I'd seen a purple sky. When that happened, the ruins turned into the shining city it used to be over sixteen-hundred years ago. It brought an old civilization back to the present. It created something I never would've imagined I'd see.

I gasped. "The sky turned purple when we saw the pyramids."

"Yeah?" Miranda said.

"And that's when the pyramids came back!" I said. "They weren't just the ruins, they were the actual pyramids!"

"What's your *point*?"

"Maybe it's not just the pyramids that can come back! Maybe something else came back and brought the crocodiles with it!"

Something *clicked* in Miranda's eyes. "*Carajo*," she said. "*Fer, es—*"

"Texcoco!" Nando said, having realized the same thing Miranda had. "I know, I know!"

"What the hell is a 'Texcoco'?" I asked. "What does that even mean?"

"It means," Miranda said hoarsely, "that if the pyramids can come back, then maybe the lake can come back, too."

16

NEXT TIME, I'M DRIVING

MIRY

"Lake!?" Ada shrieked. "What do you mean *lake*!?"

"Mexico City was built on a lakebed, Fresa," I ground out. "You know that!"

"I do?"

"Great. Another thing you forgot." If I wasn't focused on the swarm of animals flying toward us, I would've rolled my eyes. "Fer, go faster!"

"What am I? Your chauffeur?" Fer asked.

"Our getaway driver," Ada said. "And right now, we are not getting away!"

Fer muttered something to himself before stomping his foot down onto the gas. The Jetta popped and stuttered, but the engine held on as we lurched down the road, and it was only my death grip on the car door that stopped me from getting whiplashed into my seat.

My scalp ached like it'd been waxed. My throat croaked like it'd crawled through a desert. But I couldn't stop. I honed in on one of the beasts that swam through the sky.

One, I thought, *at the second crocodile.*

I channeled a pulse of warmth through my chest and up to

my head, just like I'd done again and again. My scalp prickled, and the crocodile I aimed at recoiled.

The creature fumbled for a moment before going back to swimming in the air. It didn't stay stunned for long, but because Fer was driving, we were able to keep the eagles and crocodiles one car-length away from us.

For now.

I'd been using my magic non-stop. Projectile after projectile flew from my head as I pushed the animals away from us. But the more I used my magic, the more my scalp burned, and I didn't have a chance to stop and figure out why.

"Nando, Miranda," Ada said. "Was there really a lake here?"

"Yes!" Fernando said. "Part of the city was built on Lake Texcoco! When the Spaniards came during the *conquista*, they drained the lake and built on top of it!"

Yep. With all the buildings and cars, it's hard to believe that this used to be a lake. But then again, it's hard to believe that we were actually being chased by crocodiles that were somehow swimming in the air.

"Okay, so these guys brought the lake back," Ada said. "So, what are we supposed to do? Drain it again?"

"We don't have to!" Fer said. "Because the lake didn't cover the entire city! Only part of it!"

"Oh!" Ada exclaimed. "So if we just get out of the boundary of where the lake used to be —"

"We lose the crocodiles!" Fer said.

The engine *popped* again as Fer skidded us off of Avenida Cuauhtémoc and onto Eje 3. The eagles, the crocodiles, and the silver car swerved to keep up.

"Stall them until I can get to *estación Patriotismo*!" Fer shouted.

"Okay—" A fit of dry coughs cut me off. I launched another projectile at a crocodile, and I coughed even more.

"No way," Ada said. "My needles, they—I didn't actually hurt the eagles!"

"You put needles in their wings!" I shouted, wincing at the pain in my throat.

"Yeah, but that should've grounded them! There's no way they should be flying. That's gotta mean one thing: they've got armor!"

I peered up at the eagles. They were too far away to get a good look, but they weren't swaying. They weren't crying in pain, and they weren't slowing down.

Which could only mean one thing.

"They have armor," I echoed, dread filling my voice.

"Magic armor!" Ada said with considerably less dread.

A set of two crocodiles gained traction. They swerved through the air, their tails swooshing behind them as they bridged the distance to our car.

One at each, I thought. I sent waves of warm magic to my head and prepared myself for the sensation of something pricking my head twice in a row.

But I only felt a single prick. And out of the two crocodiles I'd targeted, only one of them got hit.

The other crocodile was still flying toward us. I felt for the warmth inside my chest again, but I faltered. The energy just wasn't coming to me anymore.

I'd failed.

The crocodile reached our car and opened its enormous jaw. Ada—unprepared for me to actually fail a shot—raised her pointer finger too late.

The crocodile chomped the back of the trunk. Bits of metal went flying, and the car bounced from the momentum. It opened its maw to take another bite—

And a sphere of water hit its snout.

The crocodile recoiled and twirled in the air. Before it could right itself, the sphere of water twisted around and burst against its stomach. The water pushed the animal off course and away from us.

A car next to us honked. I spun around to find a blue Toyota sliding into the lane next to us, with Daniel Merino waving at me from the driver's seat.

"*Heeey*, Daniel!" Ada cheered. "A little help here?"

She pointed at the silver car behind us. Daniel gave her a thumbs up.

I turned to the two women in the silver car, and there were no words to describe how absolutely furious they were.

The woman who was giving us a death glare shifted her eyes of doom to Daniel. She immediately snarled and yelled out what was definitely a slew of swear words. And Lourdes, the woman who might've looked 17 if she wasn't wearing makeup, bared her teeth in a snarl as big as that of a crocodile's.

Above us, the dozen eagles and half dozen crocodiles spun away from the Jetta and turned toward Daniel.

Daniel drove like most Mexico City bus drivers do. In other words, he drove like he was the only car on the road. He wove in between the lanes with no hesitation and no warning, making his tires squeak and skid. He sped up and slowed his car at random, making the animals miss their window of attack. And every time an eagle or a crocodile got too close, he'd bat them away with a sphere of water he shot from inside his car.

For the most part, the distraction worked. Lourdes swerved the silver car to Daniel's erratic pace. That let Fer focus on our car, the engine groaning and creaking as the Jetta sped down Eje 3.

Daniel launched a sphere of water directly at the women's car. The woman in the passenger seat rolled up the window, though she kept her fingers pointed toward the sky. I hoped she'd stay focused on him.

She didn't. Instead, she gave our car another death glare and made a twisting motion with her hand. Four of the eagles turned away from Daniel.

"Miranda?" Ada said warily.

If I had any saliva in my mouth, I would've gulped. "I'm out."

"You have to keep going!" Fer screamed. "I'm almost there!"

The four eagles cawed, and the woman controlling them took in a deep breath.

I shook in the passenger seat. I didn't have enough energy in my chest to shoot out another projectile. There wasn't any way I could bat away the eagles.

But there was someone else who could.

In the backseat, Ada gripped the edge of the lowered window. She had trouble aiming at smaller targets—but I was the one who'd been holding back the eagles. Which meant that Ada still had energy left in the tank.

"Ada!" I yelled as loud as my aching throat would let me. "Can you do the nail barrage you did at the pyramids?"

"Yeah?"

"Then get them!" I called out. "Now!"

The woman with the death glare flicked her hand, and the four eagles swooped toward the Jetta.

Ada stuck her finger out the window. Nail after nail *whished* in the air. A sea of needles flew outward, turning the space between our car and the silver one into a minefield of razor-sharp nails. The birds dove to avoid them, but that just led them into the path of another projectile.

The four eagles *cawed* as the needles pushed them off course. The projectiles weren't hurting them, but it did make them scramble in the air. And every time they charged toward us again, Ada met them with a new barrage of nails that flew over our pursuers' car.

I let out a dry laugh of relief, and I very belatedly realized that I still had the extra bottle of water that Jade had given me. I scrambled around until I found it and twisted it open. The first gulp tasted like the best water I'd ever had in my life, and a new sense of warmth filled my chest.

Wait, I thought.

Warmth.

Daniel had said that magic had a power source, and that it needed to get replenished for the magic to get used. After the pyramids, I was so thirsty I couldn't talk for the whole ride home. After shooting what was at least a hundred projectiles, my throat felt like a desert.

Jade had given me water. And to top it all off, she said that her husband was Tláloc. The god of goddamn *rain*.

Oh, I thought. *You're kidding me.*

"Aim at the girl in the passenger seat!" I said to Ada before I put the bottle to my lips and started chugging.

"What? But what if I hurt her!?"

"You won't!" I said. "If the eagles and crocodiles have armor, then I bet you their car does, too!"

Behind us, the silver car was still swerving in time to Daniel's erratic driving. Daniel suddenly sped up in a move that drew most of the animals toward him. The silver car rushed to keep up, and that gave Ada a direct view of the woman in the passenger seat.

A *whooshing* barrage of Ada's needles embedded themselves into the windshield without cracking the glass. As if they had hit an invisible sheet of armor. The needles were spread out enough that the woman flinched. The eagles above us twisted themselves into a calm glide, completely forgetting their mission to shred Fer's car.

The woman with the death glare moved her head to peer around the needles, but Ada sent more projectiles until they completely covered her side of the windshield.

"The crocs are coming!" Ada yelled. I turned around to see

that two out of the five crocodiles had twisted away from Daniel's car.

"That means Lourdes is the one controlling them!" My throat was still dry, but the warmth in my chest came back to me. I took hold of it, ready to push it up to my aching scalp.

Two, I thought as I focused on the crocodiles, *one at —*

"On it!" Ada yelled.

Ada shot a new barrage of nails directly at the other half of the windshield. Lourdes flinched away from the needles, and her car swerved.

I gasped as Ada covered the entire windshield in needle-nails. She was slowing down a bit, but she kept it up with a relentless confidence that let her block the women's line of sight. She was panting, but she still kept at it.

A pang of jealousy rippled through my chest.

I didn't fire my projectiles. With Ada on the job, I didn't need to.

"We're almost there!" Fer yelled.

Fer took us to a new speed I didn't think was possible in this car. If the engine was groaning before, now it was roaring. It creaked and popped and sputtered, making every bit of the Jetta rumble from the force of the acceleration.

Behind us, Lourdes rolled down her window to poke her head around the needles blocking her view—and that's when I saw something in the air between us.

I hadn't noticed it before because I was busy batting away the eagles and crocodiles. But at that moment, when Ada was doing the fighting and I had water in me, I saw it. Rippling currents of water covered the entire car. They rolled around the vehicle as it sped down the road, and they diverted around the needles Ada had embedded into the windshield.

"They're using the lake water as armor!" I said.

"How do you know that?" Ada asked.

"I just do!"

I wasn't sure how they were doing it, but then again, I

wasn't sure how they could make crocodiles swim in the sky. All I knew was that the water from Lake Texcoco was protecting them, and we were almost at its border.

"When I tell you," I said to Ada, "aim at their tires!"

I honed my gaze at the silver car's tires. The rolling, rippling currents were still there, creating a barrier that would push Ada's needles away until the vehicle could run them over.

Wait for it, I thought. *Wait for it.*

The water fell away, exposing the tire.

"Now!" I yelled.

A barrage of three or so needles *whooshed* out of Ada's finger. One of them went wide, but the other two pierced through the rubber.

The tire deflated right away. Lourdes and her companion cried out as the car lost speed. Fer accelerated, and our pursuers' car faded into the distance.

The crocodiles, and the eagles, didn't follow. The lilac sky was blue again.

"*Jajaja!*" Fer cheered as he sped down Eje 3. "You're lucky that I'm a nerd who loves maps, niñas! Woohoo!"

Beside us, Daniel honked; Fer honked back. Ada cheered.

I didn't.

Instead, I collapsed into my seat as a familiar feeling washed over me.

It was jealousy. Pure and simple jealousy.

By the time Ada joined the fight, I wasn't needed. Sure, I'd held off the original onslaught of eagles, but that's something Ada could've done back with her nail barrage. She would've ended up exhausted, but if I'd told her to use the nail barrage at the beginning, she could've handled it herself.

I couldn't.

Because I ran out of energy too fast. And even if I had a million water bottles to refill my magic, my strange invisible projectiles weren't thick enough to block windshields. They weren't strong enough to puncture tires. If it was just me, we wouldn't have gotten away.

Why is it, I thought, *that whenever Ada actually works at something, she always turns out better than me?*

I crushed the empty water bottle in my hand.

Neither Fer or Ada noticed.

17

MONDAY AT THE MUSEUM

ADA

"No," I said as I stared at the sign behind the glass doors. "We did not just get chased halfway across the city for this place to be *closed!*"

I despaired at the sign that barred our entry to the Museum of Anthropology. Behind me, Miranda scoffed in disbelief.

The entrance to the famed museum was impressive. Multiple glass doors lined the entryway, and though the building was only two or three stories high, the gray brick walls made it seem taller. A huge Mexican flag swayed from a nearby pole, and the face of the building had a huge emblem of an eagle standing on top of a cactus. Something about it rung a bell, but I was too embarrassed to ask about it.

The Museum of Anthropology is next to an enormous park. After our little car chase, Daniel recommended that we leave the Jetta at a far-off parking lot to throw off our pursuers in case they somehow caught up to us. It meant that we had to walk for about ten minutes to get to the museum proper, and I was starting to wonder if Daniel was the one leading us on a wild eagle chase.

"I tried to tell you after we got away from those girls,"

Nando said as I took in the museum. "This place is always closed on Mondays."

"I thought you were kidding," Miranda said.

"Why would I be *kidding*?"

Miranda shrugged. "I don't know. Maybe so that we'd give up and tell you to take us home?"

Nando turned to me. "And what did *you* think?"

"Gonna be honest," I said. "I kind of tuned you out once you started lecturing me. I mean, come on, what's the big deal with me figuring out your phone's password?"

Nando groaned and rubbed the spot between his eyes. "Hada, you can't just look at other people's things without permission! You might…"

"Hm? I might what?"

Nando sighed. "Never mind."

"Getting back on topic," Miranda said sharply. "What do we do now?"

The three of us looked at the huge museum. After a solid minute of silence, I asked, "Think we can we break in?"

"No!" Nando yelled.

Someone behind me laughed. "We don't need to break in."

I turned around and saw Daniel strolling up to us. The guy was in bright blue jeans, which contrasted with the ancient AC/DC shirt he still had on from the day before. Now that I was actually standing next to the guy, I could also see he was tall. At least a couple of inches taller than Nando.

"This is where I come in." Daniel pulled out his phone and dialed a number. *"Hola, Chema, ¿cómo estás? Oye, ¿estás trabajando hoy?"*

"Okay then," I said. "While we wait, tell us what we're looking for!"

Miranda shrugged. "Don't know."

"Huh? I thought you said—"

"I said I don't know!" Miranda snapped. I widened my

eyes in surprise. Miranda bit her lip—I could almost say she looked sorry. "Jade just said that this was the place."

That got Daniel's attention. He lowered his phone and asked, "Jade?"

Miranda huffed and ran a hand through her long hair. She repeated the story to Daniel, whose expression got more and more serious as she told it.

"Turns out she's Tláloc's wife," Miranda said. "And she's got something to do with water."

"How'd you figure that out?" I asked, because even though I had my own powers, I still had no clue which god-ity had picked me.

"She gave me a bottle of water. Wouldn't have been for nothing. And when your husband is the god of rain... it checks out."

I rubbed my bare arms and searched for the warm feeling inside my chest. The car chase fight had drained a good chunk of my magic, and where before it felt like there was a warmth that filled me from head to toe, now it felt like half of it had been replaced by an empty void. I'd drunk some water when we stopped to get some duct tape to patch the car's roof, but I didn't feel any kind of boost in magical energy.

But of course Miranda figured her stuff out first. Of course, she's the one who put together the puzzle. Like she always does. She got to talk to a cool god-ity lady while I was wandering Coyoacán like a lost tourist.

Daniel hung up his phone and put it away. "You saw a god in the Physical World?" he asked in a tight voice. "That hasn't happened in a long time."

"You don't get to talk to them?" I asked. "You don't have a weird magic link you can use to call them or something?"

"If there was, I would've called my guy a long time ago." Daniel shrugged. "But it is what it is."

"You didn't need to call anyone to save us, though," Nando said.

Miranda nodded. "Yeah. Thanks. But… what the hell was that?"

Daniel let out a huff of air. "This technically isn't about Teotihuacán, so… yeah. I think I can tell you about this without affecting your powers. How much do you know about the Spiritual World?"

"Let me guess, there are… spirits?" Miranda drawled.

"Teenagers," Daniel sighed. "You said that you saw a purple sky?"

The three of us nodded.

"That's the Spiritual World." Daniel made a circle with his right hand. "Aside from the purple sky and the fact that there's never any sun there, it's a representation of the earth from centuries ago. And it's a place where our knowledge of the past comes to life. For example, think of Lake Texcoco. Texcoco no longer exists in real life because the Spaniards drained it, but because we know that Texcoco existed, it exists in the Spiritual World."

"So, when we were at the pyramids," Miranda said, "and we saw the purple sky, we were actually…"

Daniel nodded. "In the Spiritual World."

"But that doesn't explain the flying crocodiles," Nando said. "We thought that they were bringing the lake back to our real world, but if that were true, they would have flooded the whole city."

Daniel grimaced. "Yeah, that's where it gets complicated. So, you have the Spiritual World." Daniel made a circle with his right hand. "And you have the Physical world." He made a circle with his left hand. "These two worlds are usually kept separate, and the only way you can go between them is with a portal."

"Portals?" I exclaimed. "Wait, can we do that? Can we—"

Miranda glared at me.

"Okay, question for another time." I gestured back to Daniel. "You were saying?"

"I was saying… only portals can take people between worlds. But," Daniel brought his two hands together, making a venn diagram with his fingers, "if you make the portal big enough, sometimes you can bring aspects of the Spiritual World into our world."

"Like the crocodiles," I said.

"And the eagles," Daniel added. "And the craziest part is that, if you have enough control over that portal, you can control exactly what comes through it, and you can move it. And only the people who are in the radius of that portal can see what you've brought over from the Spiritual World."

"So—theoretically, you know," I said, "if you had enough control over this portal thing, you could bring out a bunch of animals and lake water from the Spiritual World to attack people?"

Daniel nodded. "Correct."

"And that makes the sky turn lilac purple instead of diabetes soda purple?" Miranda asked.

Daniel nodded a second time. "Correct again."

"And if you're the only people in the radius of the portal, only you see what's happening?" Nando asked. "Which means, if I get a speeding ticket, I can't say that it was because I was getting chased by a group of killer eagles and flying crocodiles."

We all turned to stare at him.

"You have interesting priorities, Nando," I said.

"That's one way to put it." Miranda scoffed before turning back to Daniel. "You seemed to hold them back well enough."

"Hell yeah! You were amazing!" I said, ignoring how Nando muttered to himself about a potential fine. "It was just water blast after water blast! How'd you even do that?"

Daniel ducked his head, but smirked nonetheless. "My power lets me pull water particles from the air and turn it into liquid. I take that and turn it into water blasts."

"You get that much water from the air?" Miranda asked.

"Summer is the rainy season here." Daniel pointed up at the cloudless sky. "Well, today isn't a good example. But there's still enough moisture in the air."

Nando laughed. "Abuelo really hated that. Always said it was ridiculous that he could never enjoy summer without wondering if it would start raining."

"You talk about him a lot," Daniel said. "Well, you did yesterday. Before we had to pick up your cousins."

Nando smiled, but it was sad. "Abuelo and Abuela helped take care of me when I was little."

Miranda scoffed. "That's an understatement. They pretty much raised you until Eduardo came along." She turned to Daniel. "Our aunt and uncle had him young. I'm pretty sure he was an accident."

"I *wasn't* an accident!" Nando cried.

"Nando," I said, "Uncle Rizo and Aunt Sara had you when they were 20 and still in college. And you're ten years older than your brother. That kind of age difference wouldn't have happened unless you were an accident."

Nando pressed his mouth into a thin line, and I'm pretty sure his left eye was twitching.

I laughed. Miranda held back a snort. It doesn't matter that Nando knows he was an accident. He still gets annoyed every time we bring it up, and his reaction is never not funny.

"I'm glad you guys get along," Daniel said. He smiled, but his eyes were sad.

"Everything okay?" I asked him.

"Yeah, yeah. It was just… strange, to fight against people I know."

I straightened my back. "So you knew the girls that were chasing us?"

Daniel nodded. "Lourdes and Teresa. They were my friends. Should've known that they'd also try to attack me."

"This spirit that we unsealed… the one that took your best

friend from you," I said carefully. "Did it take Lourdes and Teresa away from you, too?"

Daniel swallowed something in his throat. "It did."

I grimaced. "I'm… I'm sorry about that."

Miranda grimaced and looked away.

It might've been the high-speed car chase, or it might've been the fact that I was getting tired of only now discovering things about my own family's lives. But whatever it was, it made me want to talk. To ask my cousin what was going on inside her head.

"Miranda, what—"

"*¡Ey, Daniel!*" a security guard said as he came through one of the museum's glass doors. "*¿Cómo andas?*"

Miranda looked over at me, waiting for me to say something. But the moment was gone when Daniel walked over to the security guard and gave him a one-armed hug. The two of them said something quickly to each other, and Daniel waved me and my cousins over to the doors.

"C'mon," Daniel said. "It's not everyday you get a private tour of a national museum."

18

———————

FAMILIAR FACES

ADA

Picture this.

You walk into an enormous open-air museum with stylized science symbols sculpted onto a giant cylinder, hidden behind streams of falling water that surrounded it like a waterfall. Above you is a square ceiling that covers half of the stone courtyard in the shade, and the other half of it basks in the sun. Rays of sunlight shine down on a rectangular pond that has a sculpture of a seashell in the middle, and the entire courtyard is surrounded by tall walls that lead into the museum's many exhibits. You feel awe; you feel respectful, and you feel curiosity inviting you into the many doorways.

Picture that, and then picture the very eloquent response I had to seeing this for the first time.

"*Woah.*"

Yeah. You heard me. *Woah.*

Nando and Daniel laughed. That wasn't surprising. What *was* surprising was that Miranda didn't. She's the one who usually finds my moments of dumb shock funny, and she didn't even roll her eyes.

"I'm impressed you're here so soon," Daniel said. "This is usually the last stop before…"

"Before what?"

Daniel stuffed his hands in his deep pockets. "Before you can get proper answers."

Daniel strode toward the right hand side of the pond. The three of us followed, and I noticed inscriptions that had been chiseled into the white-gray stone walls. Daniel took us to what was maybe the third or fourth exhibit, which had the word "Teotihuacán" stamped onto it with big white letters, and next to it was the following inscription:

CUANDO AÚN ERA DE NOCHE.
CUANDO AÚN NO HABÍA DÍA.
CUANDO AÚN NO HABÍA LUZ.
SE REUNIERON.
SE CONVOCARON LOS DIOSES.
ALLÁ EN TEOTIHUACÁN.
CÓDICE MATRITENSE

"IT'S FROM THE MATRITENSE CODEX," NANDO SAID. "IT'S the notes the Spaniards made when they came to the new world. 'When it was still night. When there still wasn't day. When there still wasn't light. They reunited. The gods convened. There at Teotihuacán'."

I immediately thought back to the sight we'd seen at the pyramids—in the Spiritual World, apparently. The shining roads, the polished stones, and the glittering pyramids. It was nothing short of majestic, and I could already imagine a gathering there. With beings of power—gilded in colorful robes as they preside over the world around them.

"Gods," Miranda said, her eyes scanning over the words etched into the stone. "Not 'deities'."

Daniel shrugged. "Like I said, it's a debate in the group."

Without another word, he strolled into the exhibit, and we followed him inside.

The first artifact to greet us was a massive block statue of a man with short arms and a square head standing a few feet away from a mural of a hilly landscape. To my right was a section of artifacts protected by glass panes and illuminated by warm golden lights. Most of them were stone carvings of some kind, others were pieces of crumbling pottery. Nando walked over to those immediately, his brain seemingly going into nerd mode at the sight of anything that was over a century old. To my left was another statue, though this one was cylindrical with a flattened sphere at the top. Miranda headed in that direction, but she had no interest in the statue.

Just a few paces into the exhibit was a red wall with the figure of a strange man painted onto it. He had large circular eyes and a beak for a mouth, with yellow arms that peeked down from underneath detailed layers of red and green waves of clothing. Large drops of water surrounded the man, and two smaller figures stood on each side of him, pouring jugs of colorful water into the ground beneath him. But the largest aspect of the whole mural was the twisting, winding vines that sprouted from his head and curved downward like the long branches of a willow tree.

Miranda stared up at the mural.

"I figured you'd want to see this one," Daniel said. "This is the mural of my deity… Tláloc."

Daniel gave us a forced smiled.

"The woman mentioned you," Miranda said.

Daniel blinked in surprise. "She did?"

Miranda nodded. "Apparently, Tláloc thinks you're quick to jump to conclusions. If that means anything."

"I… suppose it does," he said.

I glared at my cousin. "I don't think that was helpful."

Miranda shrugged. "What else was I supposed to do? Lie?"

"Maybe not mention things that you don't think will help other people."

"It's the truth, though. What's wrong with that?"

I groaned and turned away in exasperation. But as I put my back to the mural, my eyes landed on the section of the exhibit right in front of me.

Remember the ciudadela back at the pyramids? The one that had the small pyramid of Quetzalcóatl that had its face bricked up around it? Someone had built a new front of the pyramid, meant to cover the multiple stone carvings that depicted large snakeheads surrounded by opulent feathers. When Miranda, Nando, and I entered the Spiritual World, the pyramid in the ciudadela had shown us the bricked-up side. I didn't get to see the carved serpents in their original glory.

It's almost like the Museum of Anthropology decided they wanted to fix that.

In front of me was a replica of the original face of Quetzalcóatl's pyramid. It wasn't as tall as the real thing, but it still had layers of carved serpents that had been painted green, yellow, and red. They stood proud against the exhibit's wall, shining with the full confidence that they'd originally been created with.

"Okay, this is really cool," I said as my feet pulled me closer toward it.

"You know that pyramid at the ciudadela?" Daniel asked. "It's a recreation of what that pyramid looked like. With all the colors, too."

"Why'd they even want to hide all this?" I asked. "I mean, the pyramid of the sun and the pyramid of the moon were *huge*, but this one's just… *gorgeous*. I don't know why they'd ever want to cover it up."

"Political upheaval," Daniel said immediately. "Politics exists in all times. Back then, it was likely that some important figure had aligned themselves with Quetzalcóatl. Said that he represented their values and customs. They might've even been a disciple of his. But when they got outed from politics, their rivals couldn't destroy the pyramid, so they just covered up all the details."

"Huh," I said. "Petty revenge for the winning party. Gotta say... we humans haven't really changed much."

"No, we haven't," Daniel bemoaned. "I'll see where Fer is. Tell me if you find anything."

Daniel moseyed his way deeper into the exhibit, off to find whatever weird vase that had snatched Nando's attention.

I absentmindedly spun on my heel and wandered around the front area of the exhibit, and my eyes glazed over the statues and ceramics.

It was a bit strange that the woman Miranda ran into didn't give us a hint as to what we were meant to do, and my cousin hadn't given any strategies as to what it could've been. It wasn't like we had a direct order like before.

Use the warmth, find the signal.

I gripped the fabric of my dress in a tight fist. Miranda figured it out, and I hadn't. I'd tried to find the signal by using my magic to create another nail, hoping that it'd activate like a sort of compass and point me to our next clue. I bet that Miranda didn't waste her time on that. She said that she'd used her magic another way, and that led her to the signal.

Well, I thought. *There may be things she can do that I can't, but she's not the only one with magic.*

And I won't let her beat me at that.

I felt around for the warmth in my chest. My figurative magic tank was still roughly half-full, but it felt a bit stronger than it did before we arrived at the museum. I swirled it around in my chest, waiting for my instinct to kick in and tell me what to do.

Come on, I thought. *Miranda said she felt like she'd turned into a sonar, but that made her wander around Coyoacán with her eyes closed. Wouldn't it make more sense if you could actually see the clue?*

I wondered if I should just throw out magic and see if

anything stuck. But then I remembered that Miranda was still in the exhibit, and I held myself back. No way was I gonna let her see that if I didn't know if it would work.

I stood there, thinking, for at least a minute.

You should listen to your heart, Guadalupe, a deep voice said in my head. *You do not fare well when you second guess yourself.*

I JUMPED. *WHAT THE HELL!?*

Do not tell me you've already forgotten me, the man said. *It's only been a day since I first spoke to you.*

When someone jumps into your head telling you he's a god, he's kind of hard to forget, I thought without realizing I was thought-speaking back to the god-ity. *Wait, you can read my mind!?*

Only when I am speaking to you.

Still kinda creepy.

The man laughed. *I must agree, but I am currently limited in the way I can speak to humans, so this is how it must be done. But as I was saying, you should trust yourself, Guadalupe. Trust in your instincts.*

I cringed a little when he called me "Guadalupe". Only my parents call me that, and when they do, I'm usually in trouble. But hey, at least he was pronouncing it right... *What are you even talking about?*

The clue you are searching for. You had an intuition.

Huh? I was just wondering if it'd be easier if we could actually see the clue.

Exactly, the voice said. *Do not wonder if you are doing something foolish, Guadalupe. Or if you will look foolish. Simply do it.*

...What do you mean by that?

I mean that you tend to hold yourself back. When you fear you will fail at something, you do not even act. You freeze.

A shiver ran up my spine. *How the hell did you know that!?*

I know because you're doing it right now, he said. *The magic you have been graced with is easy to pull, but your power means nothing if you cannot control it. And do you know what is the first step to controlling it?*

Nope, I thought. *But I have a feeling you're gonna tell me, anyway.*

I like you. The man laughed again. *The key to controlling the magic of Teotihuacán is to listen to it. Listen to your heart, Guadalupe. Listen to your instincts.*

And just like that, the voice was gone.

So… he's saying I should try to see *the clue.* I let out a puff of air. *No clue if this'll work, but if he says it's worth it, then I guess it's worth a shot.*

I pulled a wave of warm energy out of my chest. But instead of making it flow into my hand so I could make a new needle-nail, I pushed the warmth up to my eyes. I scanned the surrounding area, looking for something that could lead me to the clue.

And I found it right away.

At first they were little pinpricks of light that gleamed and glittered against the stone floor beneath my flats, like bits of golden glitter that had fallen to the floor. There weren't many—maybe just a dozen or so—but they were pointing toward something. I followed the brilliant trail and found myself right back where I started.

The golden lights led me right back to the replica of Quetzalcóatl's pyramid. It was still the same as it always had been, but now there were lines of shimmering yellow-white text written between the layers of stone serpents.

I gasped.

"What was *that* for?" Miranda asked.

"You can't see this?"

"See what?" She walked over and squinted at the replica.

"This!" I pointed at the lettering that just *had* to be magic of some kind. "There's writing here!"

"What!?" Miranda yelled. "How the hell did you find that so fast? How the hell did you even know what to *do*?"

"Just trusted my instincts, I guess. I sent the magic up to my eyes and *boom*! Magic writing!"

Miranda balled her hands into fists. "So you figured that all on your own, huh?"

"Yep." I peered at the letters. "*Buuut* this clue's in Spanish. Okay, write this down! *Eel loo-gaar dell cono-cee-me-en-toe. Eel—*"

"*El lugar del conocimiento, el lugar de la juventud.*"

My mouth fell open as Miranda spoke the words. Though there was no outward show of magic, I knew that she'd done the same thing I did. She pushed her magic to her eyes, and she was reading the clue.

"*El lugar de los gatos, el lugar del deporte,*" Miranda continued.

And she was reading it *perfectly*.

Why you? I thought. *Why are you the one who knows everything? Why are you the one who gets to be best at languages, at being Mexican, at... at everything!?*

"*El lugar del desorden, el lugar de su futuro.* Okay. I've got it. Let's get Fer—"

"Freaking showoff."

Miranda blinked at me. "What?"

"Freaking. Showoff," I repeated. "You just had to butt in and flex."

"I wasn't showing off. I decided to read it because I actually know Spanish and can read faster than you."

"And why didn't you give me the chance to try reading it now?" I asked.

"Because you've had your chance. Four years of chances," Miranda hissed. "Four years to learn my language, *our* language, and you didn't. So sue me for stepping in."

"Oh, as if Spanish is *our* language. It's not like you don't speak English!"

Miranda rolled her eyes and turned away from me. "As if

English would ever be my lang—" Miranda gulped suddenly. "Ada. Get your nail out."

If you hadn't noticed, Miranda has better spatial awareness than I do. That's why she noticed our stalkers on the bus.

And it's why she was the one who noticed that someone else had walked in.

The man had come into the exhibit with his hands raised above his chest, his open palms splayed outward. He was tall, taller than Daniel. His long hair was tied back in a bun, and he had a full beard that was just a bit less impressive than my dad's. He was wearing old sneakers, faded jeans, and a light gray shirt that contrasted his brown skin. A shiny black dagger hung at his waist.

I took a closer look at his sneakers, which had flecks of paint on them. Like the ones on our bus stalker's shoes.

In fact, they were *exactly* like our stalker's shoes.

"*¿Español?*" he asked, coming to a stop several paces away from us. "English?"

"Who's asking?" I raised my right hand and channeled a new wave of warmth to my pointer finger. Out of the corner of my eye, Miranda tensed her arms.

"I'm not here to hurt you," the man said calmly. "I promise. My name is—"

"Lolo!"

Miranda and I jumped as Daniel came bounding out from the inner section of the exhibit. The man narrowed his eyes when he saw Daniel approaching, and Daniel slowed himself down to a cautious pace.

"Don't get any closer to them." Daniel slowly put himself between us and the mystery man.

"I wasn't going to," he said defensively, baring his teeth in an angry snarl.

"Daniel," Miranda said in a tight voice. "Is this guy…"

"Lorenzo Zavala." Daniel's voice came out pained. "A disciple of water… and my best friend."

19

WE SCARE THE NERDS

ADA

"Run!" Daniel screamed.

Lorenzo's eyes widened in panic. "No!" he shouted. "Don't run—"

A giant sphere of water suddenly appeared in front of Daniel. It twirled around our stalker in swirling waves, trapping him inside. Something long and black slashed at it from the inside.

"Get out!" Daniel yelled. He twisted his feet into a fighting stance. "Now!"

I moved to run, but Miranda was still.

"Miranda, move!" I yelled. But my cousin's gaze stayed fixed on the water bubble.

The obsidian dagger slashed its way through Daniel's sphere. The whole thing burst, leaving only light droplets in its wake, and it revealed Lorenzo's panicked face.

"Miranda, come on!" I grabbed my cousin's arm and started running.

The men screamed at each other in Spanish as we ran out of the exhibit. Miranda stumbled. By the time she was running on her own, I was hauling our butts through the courtyard.

"We just need to get to the car!" I yelled. "Then Nando can get us—"

Miranda ground her feet to a halt. With the momentum of me dragging her arm, she nearly fell face first onto the floor.

"Miranda, what—"

"Fer." Miranda looked at me, at the exhibit, and then back at me.

Oh, *crap*.

We forgot Nando.

We ran back into the Teotihuacán exhibit. Inside, Daniel pulled small balls of water from the air and launched them at our stalker. Lorenzo slashed them with his obsidian dagger, making each projectile evaporate after two hits. Lorenzo raised his arm in a large arc. A long stream of water jettisoned from the pond and into the exhibit, forcing Daniel to roll out of the way.

Miranda and I used Daniel's dive as a distraction to rush inside. We tried to run, but there was a thin layer of water that covered the whole floor. If we tried sprinting, we'd slip and maybe crack our heads open.

Lorenzo gasped when he saw us. Daniel conjured a sphere of water to surround him before he could speak. But the giant sphere didn't do much other than delay Lorenzo, because the man made the sphere burst after two quick strokes of his dagger.

Another stream of water burst from the outdoor pond and into the room. It blasted its way toward Daniel, and he was forced to roll out of the way again. Lorenzo shot stream after stream of water that forced Daniel to roll and go on the defense.

Miranda and I slid our way into the exhibit.

Lorenzo's water burst into droplets right before it could crash into the exhibit's glass cases. He saw us running, looked at the water beneath our feet, and closed his unarmed hand into a fist.

The water underneath us froze. And I mean actually *froze*. It was like a chain reaction that started at Lorenzo's feet, crystallizing the liquid into a gray-blue ice cube. But then the ice extended itself, and the thin layer of water that covered most of the exhibit's floor suddenly turned the Museum of Anthropology into a makeshift ice rink.

Miranda grabbed onto the face of one of the glass cases to keep herself from falling. I—who may or may not have been panicking a bit—tried to do the same. But I wasn't as close to the exhibits, and I slipped just before I could grab hold of it.

"*¡Aguas!*" Miranda gripped me by the armpits, stopping my fall a half-second before I could crash into the exhibit.

"I told you to get out!" Daniel screamed.

"Nando!" I yelled. "We gotta run!"

Nando shouted something from deep in the exhibit, followed by a cry of him screaming and a loud *thump*.

"I think he's having the same issues we've got," Miranda said.

The two of us tried to get up, but we fell over after every step. We could hear Nando cry out something from the inside, but we moved at a slippery snail's pace. And to make it worse, every time we made some progress, a geyser of water like the ones Lorenzo was wielding would crash into us. The force pushed us back and sent us spinning on the ice.

"Daniel, can you start winning?" I called out. "Or at least distract Lorenzo a bit more!"

From behind a stone statue, Daniel moved his arms in a new pattern. A black mist formed in front of him. He glanced at Miranda and me. The black mist turned itself into a sphere of water that he shot toward Lorenzo.

"I've had enough of your old tricks, Lolo!" Daniel cried.

"At least they're working!" Lorenzo yelled back.

Lorenzo was on the offense. Lorenzo parried Daniel's attacks with his dagger or small currents of water. With every stream of water launched at Daniel, he was closing the distance between them. The only thing that kept him from winning the fight outright was the fact that he kept circling his water attacks around the exhibit's artifacts.

I wish I could say that I was the one who noticed that. But I wasn't.

It was Miranda.

"This way!" she bellowed.

My cousin used her hands to crawl-sprint across the icy floor. It didn't get her far, but it was enough to get to a pedestal holding an artifact in a small glass box.

"Hey, nerd!" Miranda used the pedestal to pull herself up into a standing position. "You hit me; I fall onto this thing!"

"Don't!" Lorenzo yelled.

A blast of water socked Lorenzo in the face. The man bent backward at the force of the blow, and Daniel's water sphere came back for another hit. It crashed into Lorenzo's back and sent him off balance across the ice.

"I'm not gonna let you hog all the glory," I said. Copying Miranda, I slid across the floor until I was up against another glass case.

"Oh, no!" I said dramatically. "I wonder what would happen if I slipped and fell into—"

"No!" Lorenzo cried.

The distraction was just enough for Daniel to launch another sphere of water at Lorenzo. Before the man could recover, Daniel covered his face in a sphere again. He used the time Lorenzo was momentarily dazed to slide his way over to the glass cabinets closest to him.

A new sphere of water encased Lorenzo. Daniel was sweating now. He'd been launching the smaller water spheres well enough, but these larger ones seemed to take a bigger toll on his energy.

"Go now!" Miranda yelled.

That's when a geyser of water burst in front of us.

This geyser wasn't like the other ones Lorenzo had shot

out. The geysers he made were pulled from the entrance, and this one was coming from *inside* the inner exhibit. It blocked our way to Nando, and it swirled around the exhibits until it crashed into Miranda and me with the force of a tidal wave.

Miranda and I cried out as our legs hit the ice. Just as we tried to pull ourselves into a sitting position, a new geyser of water pushed us to the ground.

I blubbered as water filled my mouth. I had no way to stop the geysers. My needle-nails were fast and sharp, but they were small. There's no way I could use them to fight against water geysers.

But maybe I didn't need to use them to fight back.

I raised my right pointer finger. The nail bed extended itself into a needle, and I slammed it into the ice beneath me.

My needle screeched as it scratched its way into the ice. I yelled as the pressure intensified on my finger, but my grip held firm.

Miranda wasn't as lucky. She crashed into a wall with a *thump* and let out a low hiss.

"Miranda!" I used my needle's grip on the ice to inch my way to her. "Grab on!"

Miranda begrudgingly grabbed hold of my wrist. Rushing water filled my ears, and Miranda's expression went from pained to fear. "Behind you!"

Out of the corner of my eye, another geyser of water headed toward us. I didn't have the grip to pull us away with my feet.

But I did have the grip with my needle-nail.

I pushed a burst of power into my finger. "Grow!"

The magic pushed itself into my needle. It grew longer than it ever had before, yet it kept its grip on the ice. The effect was like a coiled spring. One moment, Miranda and I were lying on the ice, and the next, the force of the needle-nail's growth had us flying away from the rushing water.

Miranda and I crashed into the ice with a groan.

"Are you okay?" Lorenzo yelled, stopping his attacks on Daniel.

"That's my line!" Daniel cried.

Lorenzo sneered. "That wasn't my—"

Daniel thrust out his arm, and a new sphere of water suddenly formed around Lorenzo, cutting off his question to us.

"Agh!" Daniel yelled. "All right! Get Fernando and go!"

Lorenzo slashed his way out of the water sphere. Daniel threw his spheres, Lorenzo launched out his jets, and the two gritted their teeth as they threw themselves into a full-on water fight.

"You have a sword on your finger." Miranda pushed herself into a sitting position and stared my nail. It had expanded to the point where it was nearly as long as my forearm, turning my needle-nail into a quasi needle-sword.

"Looks like it," I said. "Pretty cool, right?"

Miranda shrugged. "Eh."

"What the hell does that mean? Do you—Ugh, not now!" I planted the tip of my needle-sword into the ice and used it to push myself up. "Grab on!"

Miranda hauled herself up and grabbed onto my arm. I pulled us across the exhibit by stabbing my scarily sharp nail into the ice beneath us. It was a stretch to say that we bolted away from Lorenzo and Daniel's fight, but it's the best we could do.

For all the trouble it took to actually get into the exhibit, it wasn't long before we found Nando. He was sliding from glass case to glass case, panting as he tried to angle his slides away from the priceless artifacts and toward the exit.

"Hada! Miry!" Nando called out, his voice hoarse as if he'd been screaming for a while. "What's happening over *thereee*—?"

Nando slipped right before getting to us. Miranda and I lurched forward to catch him.

"Stalker. Here. Daniel. Fighting," I said in a very detailed, very articulate manner. "Run!"

"And if he tries to attack you," Miranda added, "try falling onto one of the exhibits."

"What!?" Nando yelled. "But those are priceless! You can't just fall on them!"

"Right," I said, "you're a nerd, too."

I RUSHED US BACK TO THE EXHIBIT'S ENTRANCE AS FAST I could. Considering I was basically awkwardly gliding us with a giant cactus needle, I was doing a pretty good job. I hoped to glide around Daniel and Lorenzo when we got to the exhibit's entrance, but they weren't there.

They were now in the museum's courtyard, going at it in what I'd call a full water slugfest. Lorenzo was in the middle of the courtyard's long rectangular pond while Daniel was at the edge. Daniel dodged Lorenzo's water strikes when he could, and he alternated between surrounding Lorenzo in a sphere of water and attacking him with smaller attacks. Daniel's old AC/DC shirt was soaked, and Lorenzo's hair was falling out of his man-bun.

The icy floor ended just at the entrance to the exhibit. From the middle of the pond, Lorenzo broke through a new water sphere with his dagger. And from the entrance to the Teotihuacán exhibit, I pointed my needle-sword at his leg.

"This is for stalking us, asshole!" I launched my needle.

The giant nail flew through the air. It flew across the floor between the exhibit and the pond before falling, crashing into the water several feet away from Daniel.

Yeah, considering the fact that the needle-sword was longer and heavier than my normal needle-nails, I probably should've expected that it wouldn't fly far.

I gasped as the energy left my chest. That little maneuver had cost more energy than I realized, and now I was starting to pant like Daniel.

"Listen to me!" Lorenzo yelled from the middle of the lake. "Daniel is lying to you!"

"You're the one following a lie!" Daniel yelled as he formed a new water sphere around Lorenzo. "Get as far away as you can! I'll distract him!"

"What about you?" Nando said.

"I'll be fine! Just go! Now!"

"But—"

"I know the Archivists," Daniel panted. "And I know that Lorenzo's smart enough to bring backup! So go! Now!"

We did. The three of us turned around and booked it to the exit. When we got to the entrance, we saw the security guard who let us in. He was chilling on a chair, headphones in, and mindlessly scrolling on his phone.

"Dude!" I yelled. "Water fight! Do something!"

By the time the guard looked up, we were already sprinting out the door.

20

IF I GO BALD, I'M BLAMING YOU

MIRY

YOU KNOW, EVEN THOUGH IT ISN'T MY THING, I KIND OF GET it when people take forever to pick out an outfit. You wanna look good, and you wanna make sure you're looking like you. I can understand that. I can respect that. But I can't understand why people like wearing shoes that don't cooperate with their feet.

Most of the time, I feel this way about high heels. That day, however, my annoyance spread to the flats that kept slipping off Ada's feet as we ran away from the Museum of Anthropology.

"Ada," I said, as my cousin almost slipped *again*. "I. Hate. Your. Shoes!"

"You're. Just. *Jealous*," she panted.

"Hada, I'm sorry," Fer cried, "but I hate your shoes, too!"

The three of us crossed the road that led us to the park where we'd left the car. We ignored the main entrance to run down the sidewalk that gave us a more direct route, even if it meant almost crashing into a bunch of people. Ada and I were still soaking wet, and my water-logged jeans made it a pain to keep running.

Ada made a new needle-sword grow from her pointer

finger. Fer and I kept telling her to drop it before she accidentally stabbed someone, but she stubbornly insisted on keeping it.

I hate to admit this, but we were lucky that she did. Because as if this day wasn't already a shit show, someone decided that it'd be a great idea to throw spiders into the mix.

What had to be at least a hundred spiders crawled their way down the sidewalk. They were roughly the size of a person's hand, and they rushed toward us at a speed that shouldn't have been possible for their thin brown legs. People shrieked, jumped, and sprinted away. Locals and tourists filled the street with terrified screams, but the spiders ignored them.

I had a bad feeling that they weren't interested in ignoring us, too.

"People are seeing this!" Ada yelled as we did a 180-degree turn away from the creepy bloodsuckers. "I repeat, people are seeing this!"

She was right. Unlike with the eagles and the crocodiles, *everyone* around us could see the hoard of spiders.

"We'll lose them in the park!" Fer yelled. "Go, go!"

The three of us booked it into the entrance of the Bosque de Chapultepec. The wet soles of our shoes clapped against the stone road off-limits to cars that led us into the park.

I immediately saw why Fer was pulling us through here, instead of the main street that'd give us a faster route toward the parking lot. Spanning multiple kilometers in length, the Bosque de Chapultepec is the largest urban park in Latin America—even bigger than New York City's Central Park. If we went down a straight path while getting followed by supersonic spiders, we'd get caught. But if we first ran through a park so big it sometimes felt like a forest, we might lose the horde of blood-sucking spiders.

The spiders were definitely after us. They ignored the panicking park-goers as they followed us. Their legs clicked against the stone as they kept up with our pace.

"This isn't real," I muttered.

Ada pointed upward. "The sky's still blue!"

She was right. The sky wasn't purple—or lilac. According to the info Daniel had given us, that meant that whatever was coming toward us was 100% from this world.

I ground my teeth. "This better not get worse."

The tree line to our right opened up to reveal a big lake that spanned at least a kilometer. I'd honestly forgotten about the Lago de Chapultepec, and now it was here to mock me. It wasn't nearly as big as something like the lake in Xochimilco, but it was water. And our stalker at the museum had used a giant pond to attack us with, yep, water.

Ada groaned. "Miran—"

"Yeah, I know! I jinxed it! Just go!"

The three of us bolted away from the stone path and into the tree line on our left. Roots were sticking out of the ground, but going this way meant we were getting away from the potentially dangerous lake. Still, the rougher terrain made Ada slip more in her shoes. Fer and I had to keep helping her back up.

We kept running, occasionally hearing the panicked yells of other park goers as they noticed the swarm of long-legged spiders. Most screamed in Spanish, some in English, and the couple who was making out between two of the larger trees almost destroyed my hearing after the spiders got too close.

Ada had tripped over another root when one of the spiders took the lead and rushed up to us. It jumped, aiming for the back of Ada's left leg.

One projectile, I thought. *At its body.*

I winced as the prickling sensation pierced my scalp. The spider was a tiny target, but my projectile hit it all the same. The spider fell backward.

Another one! I thought.

I winced as another prickling sensation burst in my scalp. The spider jolted before poofing into a clear mist.

"They disappeared!" I yelled. "They're a two-hit K.O.!"

"Really?" Ada glanced back at the spiders, and her water-logged hair flopped against the side of her head. "Like the pum-eagles at the pyramids?"

"*Exactly* like the pumas at the pyramids," I said.

The spiders stayed on our tail. I knew that I didn't have enough energy to make over a hundred of them vanish. My scalp still ached, and the pain was made even more intense by the fact that it was dragging my thick, wet hair.

With a harsh scream, Ada extended her nail bed needle until it was the size of a sword again. She swung her nail behind us as we ran through the trees. The spiders that did get hit by it were batted away, and the threat of her nail was enough to keep the horde from getting too close.

I gritted my teeth and put some distance between me and Ada's swinging arm, trusting Fer to keep Ada from slipping onto the grass. Of course, Ada was the one who managed to get us out of the museum. Of course, she kept the spiders away. She didn't freeze when she saw our stalker at the museum. I did.

And even though now that the man was gone, I still wasn't the one who could do anything about the horde of spiders.

Fer led us onto another one of the park's roads. But instead of leading us down it, he pulled us straight into the trees again.

"We haven't lost them yet!" he said.

The spiders were still getting pushed back, keeping a gap between them and us that was just less than a meter. It wasn't a lot, and the fear of getting bitten to death was enough to keep my feet moving.

My fear spiked when I saw the woman behind them.

Coming from the park's road we'd just crossed, a woman sprinted through the trees. She was taller than average, with hair cut close to her head, and was in a full workout set—from the tight tank top to the worn running shoes. A face mask covered the lower half of her face, but the wrinkles around her eyes told me that she was at least 40.

And she was running *toward* the spiders.

The woman pointed her hands toward the towering trees above us and twisted her arms in a series of half-turns. Branches *cracked*. A flurry of green leaves fell from the trees above her. The leaves surrounded her lower legs, spinning around her like a small tornado.

The woman reached the hoard of spiders within seconds. The brown spiders tried to attack her, but after brushing up against her spinning leaves, the spiders vanished into clear mist.

"There's—more—magic—people!" Ada panted.

"*Stop!*" the woman called out in Spanish. She sounded nasally, like someone who was holding her nose closed. "*Who are you? Where's Loren—*"

The woman was cut off by a set of coughs that wracked her body. The trees above her rustled, more leaves fell from the trees, and the woman slowed down.

But the spiders were still on our tail.

"One woman down!" I yelled. "One hundred spiders to go!"

Fer kept us moving, hopping over tree roots and ducking under low branches. I wasn't sure where we were going, but we had to be getting *somewhere*.

"*Aaa*—" the nasally woman cried, "*chooo!*"

The moment the sneeze traveled through the park, each and every tree in our general direction shook. The ground rumbled, and tree roots broke free from the ground. Fer and I stumbled as we regained our footing, but Ada wasn't as lucky.

Ada tumbled as her foot got caught on a root. She threw her hands in front of her to cushion the fall, and her enormous nail was the first to make contact with the dirt. The long nail broke in two with a loud *crack*.

"Aaah!" Ada yelled as she crashed to the floor. She brought

her broken nail to her chest, which was now just barely longer than her hand.

Without the needle to keep the spiders at bay, the wave of arachnids climbed their way over the tree's roots. They shambled their way toward Ada, and Ada shrieked as the creatures ran toward her.

"Shit!" I hissed.

The only weapon I had on me was my projectiles, but I was too slow with them. And I wasn't sure if my head could stand the pain of getting rid of a hundred creatures.

So instead of sending the magic within me to my head, I pushed it to my arms. Because if Ada could send her power to her hands and create a strange-ass nail, then maybe I could do something, too.

Twice in a row, I thought. *At—at all of them!*

The magic flowed through my right arm, and a wave of projectiles pulled themselves away from my skin.

The spiders that were a few centimeters away from Ada jolted as my projectiles crashed into them. It wasn't like my precise shots from earlier. This was a group of tiny little things, so I sent out every bit of ammo I could feel on my skin.

Most of the spiders jolted before disappearing into mist. Any lucky survivors that ignored my barrage were crushed beneath Fer's Converse.

I let out an inaudible scream. My throat was dry and hoarse. My entire right forearm throbbed like it had been waxed. I held my arm to my chest and groaned when I saw another spider crawl its way to Ada, ready to jump and sink its venom into her hand.

Twice in a row, I thought through the pain. *At its body.*

The prickling sensation came again, twice in a row, on my right arm. It hit the spider, and the creature vanished.

Fer helped Ada off the ground. They looked at each other, at the spider-free ground, and then at my arm.

I followed their gazes and gasped.

My entire forearm was smooth. Before, I had arm hair across the entire thing. But now it was just… gone. The stinging sensation I felt before—like my arm was being waxed—was actually a damn perfect analogy for what happened.

"You've gotta be kidding me," I said. My arm was slowly turning a deep shade of red.

"Did you just launch…?" Ada said.

"My hair," I said.

"So you're saying that this whole time, those weird things you've been throwing out…"

"Was my hair."

The prickling sensation in my head… that was me pulling out strands of my hair.

My hair.

My. *Hair.*

I wanted to vomit.

I curled both of my hands around my still-soaking tresses. Ada and Fer had matching expressions of pure horror.

Ada winced. "Ouch."

I nodded numbly.

"Okay, you're getting along!" Fer said with a smile that was way too big for the situation. "Great! But run!"

Fer grabbed our arms and hauled us forward. But with Ada exhausted, and me still in shock mode from the realization that I was slowly making myself go bald, we weren't getting very far.

"*Children!*" the nasally woman yelled. "*Where are you—*"

The woman devolved into a fit of rough coughs. Every plant around us shook, and more green leaves rained down from above.

"We need to get away from her," Fer panted.

"Fer, we're in a park," I croaked. "There aren't a lot of places for us to hide."

"So we hide in plain sight," Ada said. "Somewhere they won't think to look for us. Somewhere like…"

"Like that!" Fer pointed at something to our left.

I followed his finger, and ground out, "No."

Just to our left was a large and loud tour group with at least 40 people in it. Some were taking selfies, some were asking the guide questions about the park, and over half of them were wearing the American flag somewhere on their body.

"*No,*" I said again, loudly and firmly.

"That could work!" Ada said. "There's no way workout lady would think to look for us there."

I shook my head. "We are not joining *that.*"

21

———————————————

WE JOINED THE TOUR GROUP

MIRY

FOR AT LEAST TWO MISERABLE HOURS, WE FOLLOWED THE tour group as they meandered through the park. We strolled around the long roads, stopped at every single stall along the way, and listened to the tour guide happily chirp about all the different migratory species that passed through the area. Fer even volunteered himself to translate for a pair of tourists who wanted to buy some *chapulines*, and I got to watch their faces of complete confusion as they ate the seasoned grasshoppers.

Some of the group were confused as to why we were there, but after faking the explanation that we were from another group that we'd lost track of, the tired tour guide let us join them.

Did they ask why Ada and I were wet? Yep. Did Fer come up with the excuse that we accidentally fell into the park's lake? Yep. Did they buy it?

Surprisingly enough, yeah. They did.

The worst bit was when they saw how soaked my shirt was. Because what did one of them have on hand? A loose shirt with a giant American flag on it.

And Fer, very kindly, said that it'd be really rude not to

take it. Especially when they couldn't offer it to Ada, since the t-shirt couldn't fully replace her soaked sundress.

So that's how I ended up wearing a thing that proclaimed to everyone with eyeballs that I was definitely part of the tour group, and I was definitely a goddamn *gringa*.

Fer gave me a sympathetic shrug. Ada laughed behind her hand.

I quelled my gag reflex by downing four water bottles.

The whole time, we were keeping an eye on the surrounding trees. We waited for movement, any rustling or tremors from the ground. For the first half hour or so, the trees would sway occasionally, as the nasally woman called out in the distance. But the deeper we got into the park, the less the trees moved.

Fer had us stay with the group until we were almost at the Castillo de Chapultepec, the huge fortress in the middle of the park. Ada, for some reason, actually wanted to go in.

"No time today," he said as he pulled her away from the giant hill we'd have to climb up to reach the castle. "Maybe next time."

I huffed and trudged along. *At least I don't have to go up* that *thing,* I thought.

But you would, said a deep male voice. *If Guadalupe decided to go, you would follow her just so that she won't show you up.*

My spine went ramrod straight as the voice from the pyramids echoed in my head. *Oh, so now you can read my mind?*

As I told to your cousin, the voice said, *I can only listen to your thoughts when I'm communicating directly with you.*

I glanced over at Ada and forced myself to keep walking like normal. *Should've figured you'd talk to her. I bet you already like her better.*

I don't think it's wise for a god to play favorites.

Are all of you this cryptic and weird?

That is for you to decide. Who am I to tell you what you think of me?

I bit the inside of my cheek. *Did you lead Caro and her friends to Coyoacán?*

They were already there when I was talking to you. I just… gently guided them in your direction.

I snarled. *Pendejo.*

You were about to abandon the quest, the voice said.

So you sicked my bullies on me?

I was reminding you of what truly motivates you, the voice said, and I heard a smirk in his voice. *You like proving that you're better than what others see you as. More than that, you like proving others wrong.*

You're saying I'm spiteful?

I didn't say that. You did.

I gritted my teeth. *How did you even know about Caro? I haven't talked to her since the school year ended.*

I know a lot of things about you, Miranda Donaldson. I'm just using my knowledge to help you get to where you need to be.

If you were really using your knowledge wisely, I thought angrily, *then you'd know not to call me 'Donaldson.'*

If you're so angry, then come tell me that in person, the voice said. *Once you've fully unlocked your powers, you and I can meet. I look forward to that… Miranda.*

And before I could tell him not to call me "Miranda" either, his voice was gone

Jackass.

AFTER THAT, WE WERE FINALLY, *FINALLY* ON OUR WAY TO THE car. During our long trek back to the vehicle, I took in Ada. She had tilted her head up to the sun, taking in the last rays of sunlight before ominous gray clouds glided across the sky.

The moment we were out from under the trees, Ada immediately got a second wind. Her smile got wider, her mood got cheerier, and she even started skipping down the stone roads. She talked with pretty much everyone in the tour group, and whenever she was on a patch of road that got direct sunlight, it was like she got a sudden boost of energy.

Like the kind of boost I'd been getting whenever I replenished my magic by drinking water.

So her energy source is the sun, I thought to myself. *And mine is water. Wonder how that works.*

You might be wondering why I didn't tell Ada that I'd figured out her power's energy source. And do you wanna know the answer? The real, honest, and flat out petty answer?

I didn't want to tell her.

Because during this entire detour, I'd been thinking about the clue Ada found at the museum. I'd been turning the words over and over in my head, and I was drawing a blank. I hated it. Because out of the two of us, I was the one who was good at puzzles. That's what I told Ada last night.

And now I couldn't figure the clue out. Ada was the one who found the clue, and even though I was the one who spoke Spanish, I couldn't find the answer.

So even though I realized that Ada was getting magically charged via photosynthesis, I felt like I was failing. Like I wasn't pulling my own weight in this citywide goose chase.

Fer's car came into view. With the amount of duct tape we'd put on the roof and trunk, the ancient green Volkswagen looked like a car version of Frankenstein. Ada called shotgun, and we drove out of there.

"Daniel just texted you," Ada said, as she read the newest message on Fer's phone. "He says he went to… *Cee-oo-dad Nee-zaa-huuua…*"

"Ciudad Nezahualcóyotl?" Fer asked.

Ada shrugged. "I guess. But I sent him our location again, and he says he should catch up to us soon. We just need to figure out where the last clue is leading us and he'll meet us there."

Ada turned around in her seat and stared at me.

I slumped against the backseat. "What?"

"What's the clue?" Ada asked. "You know, the one you butted in to read? I hope you memorized it, because if we have to go back and read it all over again, it's your fault."

"Of course I memorized it," I said. "What do you think I am? Stupid?"

"No, just annoying."

"*Niñas*," Fer said in a hard tone. "If you keep this up, you don't get to pick any music."

I rolled my eyes. "As if you were gonna let us pick. You hate my music."

"And *mine*," Ada added.

"I don't hate it, I just —" Fer let out a long breath through his nose. "Miry, what was the clue?"

"The place of knowledge," I repeated, translating for Ada's sake, "the place of youth. The place of the cats, the place of sport. The place of disorder, the place of your future." I sighed. "That's all of it."

"Well, knowledge and youth makes me think high school," Ada said. "Sport would work too, since there are sports teams. But things get tripped up by the mention of cats."

"Maybe a vet school?" Fer asked as he turned onto a large street. "There could be disorder there because, um, maybe things get crazy at vet school?"

"Sure, Nando," Ada said. "Any famous high schools with a cat mascot?"

I shook my head and pulled my hair over my shoulder, using it to cover most of the American flag on my wonderful new shirt that I wanted to burn in a fire.

"Mascots aren't as big of a thing here, Fresa," I said, not adding the part where I'd thought of that myself. There are some mascots, but it's not like we go crazy over them like they do in the States.

"Come on, there's gotta be something!" Ada said. "What about sports teams? Any wildcat teams?"

I rolled my eyes again. "Not a thing here."

"What about the lions team?"

"No."

"Leopards?"

"No."

"Pumas!"

"N—"

My brain did the mental equivalent of a car crash. Because with that one single word, everything had fallen into place.

"I'm an idiot," I muttered.

"That's it!" Fer cheered. "That's it!"

"Huh?" Ada asked. "What's it?"

"Pumas! You're talking about UNAAA—" Fer yelled as he suddenly slammed on the brakes, having noticed the yellow light too late.

"UN-what?" Ada asked.

"UNAM," I ground out. *Universidad Nacional Autónoma de México.* Pretty much the best university in the country."

"Oh, cool!" Ada cheered. "Wait, how'd I figure that out?"

"Pumas," I said. "Goddamn pumas."

"Yeah? I thought of those guys because we literally got attacked by pum-eagles yesterday."

"And they're a sports team," I said.

"The Pum-eagles are a sports team?"

"Wha—No! The Pumas are!" I reached up and rubbed at my face. "They're a football club based at UNAM."

"Okay? But that doesn't explain the 'disorder' bit."

"It really does," Fer said.

"Why?"

Fer laughed. "Because they're always on strike."

The light turned green again, and Fer drove the car forward.

I huffed out a dull laugh. "It's a higher education institution with a famous football team that has a big cat as its logo… Now that I say it, it sounds pretty damn obvious."

Yeah. It was.

And I wasn't smart enough to figure it out.

I waited for Ada to laugh, to give me a big shit-eating grin that she does when she beats me at something. But she didn't do that. Instead, she fiddled with the hem of her still-damp dress.

I slumped into the back seat. "Just get it over with, Ada."

"Huh?" Ada asked.

"Say what you've got on your mind."

"I thought you said football wasn't popular here?" Ada said.

"What?"

"I mean, you said that football isn't really a thing here!" Ada crossed her arms. "How can they be a famous team if it isn't a famous sport?"

"Dude, I mean *fútbol*-football. Not *American* football."

Ada's eyes went wide and she turned her head away from me, her damp curls bouncing off her face. "You could've just said soccer, you know."

"I didn't think I had to."

"Why?"

"Because you know we don't call it that here." I huffed out a laugh. "Never mind, I'm dumb. I keep forgetting you forget everything you learn here."

"What's *that* supposed to mean?"

"It *means* that I told you this last summer. And you forgot. *Again*. Like you always forget everything you learn here."

"*Niñas*," Fer sighed. "Do you have to fight now?"

"Not my fault!" Ada said. "Miranda's the one who started it!"

"I'm just reminding you of things you supposedly already know," I scoffed. "But of course, you need a refresher. You don't remember anything I tell you about this place. Or literally any other fact about your country."

"My country?" Ada said, snarling just a little. "*My* country? You're the one who always reminds me that I don't belong here!"

"What?"

"All those times you get on my case about not speaking Spanish! Who cares if I don't? Almost everyone in our family speaks English!"

Fer grimaced. "*Niñas —*"

"What about when *I* couldn't?" I said. "Because when I was ten, I'd pretty much forgotten how to speak English. And the only reason I ever even tried to speak it was so I could talk to you!"

Ada blinked in surprise. Or confusion. "What about your dad?"

"Dad speaks Spanish. You don't. And whatever bits you learned when we were little, you forgot them a long time ago."

"But you know English now, so what's the damn problem?"

I rolled my eyes and looked out the window. Cars piled up as the afternoon traffic rush started. The gray clouds were getting closer.

"No," Ada said. "You don't get to shut up now."

Fer sighed. "Hada, just leave it —"

"Tell me, Miranda," Ada said. "What's. The damn. Problem?"

If it'd been a normal day, I might've had the patience to ignore it. But it wasn't a normal day, and I was in a stupid American t-shirt, so I had a short fuse.

"What if I hadn't learned English?" I snapped. "What if my mom and dad *didn't* send me to the US for a year? What if I *didn't* have grandparents in Boston? If that didn't happen, would you have tried to learn Spanish? Would you have cared enough to try to talk to me?"

"But they did send you," Ada shot back. "You got to learn."

"Yeah, I learned," I said. "*I* switched countries for a year. *I* learned English again."

"And then when you came back to Mexico," Ada said, "you got to practice with Uncle Luis!"

"Tía Mira speaks Spanish. Why don't you practice with her?"

"Yeah, I don't see her much," Ada said. "She's working at the hospital most days, and when I do see her, she's usually dead tired. So sorry for not forcing her to practice with me when I just wanna have a chill time with my mom!"

"And what if *my* parents couldn't speak English?" I asked. "Or what if Tío Rizo and Tía Sara couldn't? Would you try to learn it so you could speak to them? Or what about with Clara and Eduardo? Because their English is slow, and at this rate, they're gonna grow up with no way to talk to you."

"Miry," Fer said, "now's not the time —"

"Oh, so I should do it for the family," Ada said. "Why? It's not like I'm close to them. I barely even got to know Abuelo and Abuela!"

"Oh, so now you care about them?" I said. "You didn't even come for Abuelita's funeral!"

"Because I wasn't in Mexico!"

"Right. Because you were in the good ol' US of A." I rolled my eyes. "When you're not here, the only time you talk to us is when *your* mom is on a call with *my* mom. When was the last time you called anyone yourself? You don't even use WhatsApp!"

"Why do you even use that app? Just use normal call and text like everyone else!"

"You mean everyone else in the *States*. You all think you're so much better off over there. That your way of doing things is better." I huffed. "Guess what? That doesn't fly here."

"You lived in America for a *year*."

"Yeah. As a kid." In a much lower voice, I added, "And I wish I could forget everything about it."

A weird silence came over the car. Fer had pressed his mouth into a thin line, probably hoping that this was the end of our conversation.

"You really hate it, don't you?" Ada said in a tone that made the hairs on my left forearm stand on edge. "You get all up in my case about not learning Mexican stuff, but you… you flat out hate that you're American."

I bit the inside of my cheek. "Oh, yeah?"

"It makes sense. Why you get on my case about only speaking English. Why you cringe when your dad's accent comes out. Even why you hate McDonald's." Ada laughed. "And when we were in *Coh-yoh-a-caan* this morning, you got pissy when I brought up that you're American."

I turned away from the window to glare at her. "I'm *not* American."

Ada grinned. "You are, Miranda *Donaldson*. And you *hate* it."

"Shut up," I growled.

"Make me." Ada laughed again. "Come on, Miranda. Tell me, why don't you come over to America again? Get in touch with your culture."

"Why the hell should I?"

"Because you're half American."

"Doesn't matter."

"By that logic, why the hell should I care about Mexico? Sure, my mom's from here, but I've never lived here. Why should I care?"

"You *always* use that excuse!" I yelled. "I wasn't raised here. My mom never forced me to speak Spanish; I have no reason to learn. Well, news flash, *Fresa*, the reason you get a pass on that is because we've done the hard work to accommo-date *you*. You think that Fer got this good at English just through school? No. He did it so he could talk to his favorite cousin."

Fer winced. "Miry, she's not—"

"You could do it, you know," I said. "And don't give me that BS about not being good at languages. When you actually try at something, you're good at it. And you're not good at Spanish, which means you're not even trying."

Ada opened her mouth but said nothing.

"So don't come complaining that you don't know enough," I continued, "that it's too hard. Because out of everyone in this family, you're the one who's happy to stay as she is and not try to connect with the rest of us. And you know the worst bit? If you did, you wouldn't just be Fer's favorite." I turned back to the window. "You'd be everyone's."

Ada went quiet again, and I pushed down the bile in my throat. I could feel the tension in the quiet car. But then… But then, Ada said something that made me pissed.

"Fucking *green-ga*."

I snarled at Ada. "Don't. Call me. That."

"What? Gringa?" Ada laughed. "But you are one, Miranda. You're a gringa. Just like me."

"I never wanted to be!"

The car swung to the right and screeched to a stop. The three of us jolted against the seat belts, and Fer pushed the gearshift into park.

"Out!" he yelled.

Ada and I blinked. "What?" we asked.

"Out of my car!" Fer bellowed. "I've tried to be patient, but this is enough! I'm tired of hearing you fight. So until you can talk to each other and agree, you'll stop, get out of my car."

"Are you serious right now?" Ada asked. "Nando, what—"

"Guadalupe Reyes-Rivera," Fer said, and Ada stiffened at the sound of her full name. "If you don't get out of this car right now, I will call your parents and tell them about the time you accidentally got high at your friend's party."

Ada stuttered.

I furrowed my brows. "How do you accidentally get hi—"

"Miranda Donaldson Rivera," Fer said, and now *I* was the one who was stunned into silence. "If you don't get out, I'm telling your parents about the time you accidentally ruined Tío Rizo's suit and made it look like Clara did it."

I shut my mouth.

"*Out,*" Fer said.

He didn't need to tell us again.

22

———————

ANGELS IN THE RAIN

MIRY

OUT OF ALL THE PLACES FOR FER TO THROW US OUT, JUST moments after Ada and I almost started the second Mexican-American war, he just *had* to choose the most ironic location.

The American goddamn embassy.

I groaned as I looked up at the tall white-and-gray building. One of the security guards raised an eyebrow at my shirt, and I hugged myself to hide the flag.

I crossed the street, weaving between the cars that were at a complete standstill, and onto the stretch of walkway that separated Paseo de la Reforma into smaller sections. The walkway was made out of concrete, but several parts of it had been reserved for the trees lining the massive street.

"*Woah*," Ada said.

I furrowed my eyebrows. I hadn't even realized that Ada had followed me. I tracked her gaze, and then I saw why she said it.

Paseo de la Reforma is a large street that leads to an even larger roundabout. In the center of that roundabout is the Angel of Independence.

Eagles and cacti are symbols that represent Mexico as a whole, but *el Ángel* is one of those icons that's specific to

Mexico City. It's a glimmering statue that stands on a stone pedestal, with a golden angel holding broken chains in one hand and a laurel in the other. The hand with the laurel is held aloft, almost like the angel was presenting it to us, and her brilliant wings were spread out behind her, as if she was about to take flight. To escape the gray clouds that were getting closer and closer to us.

To be fair, the angel was some distance away. But her beauty was enough to impress Ada. Before I knew it, she'd started walking toward it.

Maybe it's because I knew that Fer wouldn't let us into the car until she and I made up, or maybe it's because I was curious why Ada wanted to see el Ángel of all things, but I followed her.

"You ruined Uncle Rizo's suit?" Ada asked. Her voice was just a bit louder than the cars caught in the late afternoon rush hour.

"You accidentally got high?"

"I didn't—I mean, I did, but—" Ada sighed and ran a hand through her curly hair, which was getting frizzier and frizzier the more it dried. "Look, my best friend had a party, and someone decided to bring brownies."

"You... accidentally got high on pot brownies?"

"Um, kinda?" Ada said sheepishly. "His mom came home early. We heard her car pull up to the house. If she saw the brownies and tried one, my best friend would've been grounded for *life*. There were only three left, so I figured that if she couldn't try one, we'd be fine."

"And you thought she wouldn't notice you getting high?"

"Why do you think we called Nando? I said I had a stomachache, but he knew that was BS the moment he saw me. But he still drove me home and let me ride it out. My friend's mom never found out, my parents never found out, and Nando still thinks I got high on accident."

I scoffed. "He actually let you get away with that?"

"Yeah." Ada grimaced. "He was a bit angry with me, but not… not like he is now."

We said nothing for a while. We kept going down the walkway, occasionally passing by another pedestrian. But with the storm coming, most people were running to hide indoors. Everyone except Ada and me.

"So…" Ada began. "Which one of us is gonna start talking?"

I huffed. "You honestly think it's gonna be me?"

"Fair point."

We kept walking. Though our view was blocked by the many trees on the walkway, el Ángel was slowly getting closer to us.

"I'll make you a deal," Ada said. "I'll start the conversation, and you don't roll your eyes."

I shoved my hands into my pockets, which were still a bit damp on the inside. "Only if you don't call me a pinche gringa."

"I didn't call you that. I called you a freaking gringa—"

"Same thing," I barked. "Different language."

"Okay… But why does that bug you so much? I know you don't like being American, but your reaction to that is… harsh. Even for you."

"…Because it's what my bullies call me."

"*What?*" Ada said. "You have bullies?"

"You're saying that like it's a crime."

"No! I mean, *you* have bullies?"

I let out a breath through my nose. No point in hiding it now. "Yeah. One of them used to be my best friend."

"Wait, that Caroline girl you used to talk about when we were kids?"

"*Carolina*, technically. And yeah, her. I'm surprised you remember her."

Ada shrugged. "You're right when you say I don't

remember a lot from when we were kids, but… some things stick."

"So why don't you remember? Every summer, you and Tía Mira and Tío Jorge come here. We've even brought you here before."

"Really?" Ada asked. "Here?"

"Yeah."

It was when we were seven. Tía Mira and Tío Jorge decided that el Ángel would be a good place for a family photo, and my parents decided to turn it into a mini family trip.

We have a picture of that day. Well, we have a lot of them, but there are two that I remember. One is of the whole family, minus Clara, since she hadn't been born yet, but the other was of just Ada and me. I remember that Ada was so excited to see a golden angel that she put on her glitteriest dress and paired it with a set of fake fairy wings. She was sad that I didn't have any glittery clothing of my own, and when I said I didn't wanna wear one of her dresses, she'd somehow convinced me to put on the shiniest t-shirt I had. A silver one that Tía Sara had given me.

In that photo, we're smiling and posing in front of the angel. I had an arm around her shoulders; she had one around mine, and we were giving the camera toothy grins.

That was one of the most fun summers I'd ever had. And the reminder that Ada had pretty much blocked it out still hurt.

And yet, I wished that I could move on from things like she can. I wished that I could go through life and only care about who I am now, not who I was or could be.

Ada went silent again. We reached the end of the walkway pretty quickly, and we stared up at el Ángel from the edge of the roundabout. There were barriers in front of it that day, who knows what the reason was, preventing people from going up to it like we'd done eight years ago. Still, the golden angel shone at the top. Looking down on us in victory.

The gray clouds loomed above us. A single droplet of rain fell on my head.

"I guess I didn't really see the point in remembering," Ada said at last.

"Not even if it's stuff with your own family?" I asked.

"I didn't mean—" Ada curled her arms around her chest. "I didn't want *that*. It's just... I never feel like I'm enough, you know? And if I'm not enough, why should I focus on that? Why can't I focus on other stuff where I don't need to constantly question if I'm worthy enough of my own freaking identity?"

"You question it that much?" I asked.

Ada sighed. "Back home, people who aren't Mexican talk to me like I'm supposed to be this encyclopedia about Mexico with a fridge full of tamales. When they realize I'm not that, they get *disappointed* in me. And then I talk to other Mexican-Americans, but the moment they realize I don't speak Spanish, they say I'm a white-washed Mexican. I figured, if I'm not enough for either of them now, why should I try to become what I'm not? I don't owe them anything. I don't owe becoming 'more Mexican' for them."

I huffed and kicked at the ground. "They don't know what they're talking about. Outside the language issues, you're Mexican enough as it is."

"I am?"

"More than me. You actually *like* making small talk."

Ada chuckled. "Wow. Didn't know that was a Mexican thing."

More droplets started falling from the sky, but Ada kept walking toward el Ángel. I followed. It's not like we hadn't already gotten soaked that day.

Ada pointed up to the golden angel. "You think she's real?"

"Huh?"

"*Her*. Angels. I mean, we've got our own god-ities. Maybe angels are real, too?"

I shrugged. It was hard enough wrapping my head around the things that happened to us already—I didn't have time to think if other religions or pantheons were real as well.

I crossed my arms over my chest, and Ada noticed how the movement conveniently covered up the American flag on my shirt. "Why don't you like being American?" she asked.

"Because it made me different," I said. It was like the incoming rain was exposing me, melting away the layers of silence and frustration that I'd used to keep others at a distance. "Because some people like making fun of others who aren't like them. The more different you are, the bigger the target."

"But you're Mexican. And you speak Spanish!"

"Yeah, and after a year in Boston with my grandparents, I came back with an accent. Caro found some new friends by the time I came back, and they found me *funny*. By the time I kicked the accent, I was already target number one. I'm finally switching to a different school for *prepa*, but for years… I was the pinche gringa with a short fuse. Heh. Guess I made myself a target."

"Don't give them an excuse to bully you," Ada said.

"Doesn't matter. They did."

"I'm sorry."

"Don't be. It's not your fault."

"Still. I'm sorry."

"… Thanks."

"Also, what's a *preh-paa*?"

"*Preparatoria*. High school. Here it's three years, not four."

"Aaah."

The rain picked up the pace. Loose droplets became a shower, and Ada and I rushed to duck under one of the trees. It didn't give us complete protection, but it was enough to keep us from getting soaked again.

My phone buzzed in my small shoulder bag. It was Fer, worrying about us being out in the rain. I nearly messaged to ask whose fault *that* was, but I figured that we'd put the guy through enough already.

"Is that Nando?" Ada asked.

"Yeah." I sent Fer a text saying we were okay and put the phone away. "He always gets nervous when I leave the house by myself."

"… Because of what happened when you were 12?"

I nodded. "I'm surprised it took you this long to bring it up."

Ada gripped her elbows. "I'm not gonna say that I don't wanna know. I know something bad happened but… I don't want to push because I *know* it's bad. Whatever happened to make you feel like that, you deserve to tell it on your own terms. Not because I push it right now."

"… Thanks," I said. Ada bit her lip, which was the sign that there was something else on her mind. "So what *do* you want to ask now?"

"Why ten?"

"Huh?"

"Why are you so hung up on the summer when we were ten?" Ada said, raising her voice so she could be heard over the rain. "I know we had the fight, but that was five years ago!"

"I hold grudges."

"Yeah, I noticed. So what's this one about?"

I sighed. "It's not about when we were ten. It's about when we were 11."

"Yes, that clears *everything* up. Thanks for the explanation."

"I wasn't done, Fresa," I said. "At that point, I'd lived with my grandma and grandpa for a year. I relearned English so I could talk to you again, but when you came to the city that summer… you didn't learn any Spanish. And I couldn't stop thinking that if I hadn't learned English, we'd be back to where we were a year ago. Yelling at each other with no way to communicate."

Ada huffed. "I see we haven't changed much."

"Yeah," I said. "And then I started the new school year. Caro went from my best friend to my bully, and I… was alone. I didn't have many friends to begin with, and all that just completely changed everything."

"You never told me that," Ada said.

"I didn't want to. C'mon, what's more embarrassing than saying your only friends are online because all your in-person friends turned into jackasses?" I sighed. "And you… we used to be friends when we were kids. And then we weren't. That hurt… and I took it out on you."

"I…" Ada grimaced. "I might've deserved that."

"Maybe a bit," I said. "But not that much. I pretty much iced you out."

"Yeah. And I answered ice with fire. I tore into you every time I could."

"Doesn't make it okay. I hurt you, too. I shouldn't have done that." In a quieter voice, I added, "I'm sorry."

I wasn't sure if Ada heard me, but then she said, "I'm sorry, too."

The rain came down harder. Pools of water surrounded our feet, but neither of us made a move to go back to the car. Not yet.

"Look at us," I said. "Apologizing to each other. Fer would be proud."

"More like shocked." Ada dropped her arms. "Why didn't you tell me all that stuff before?"

"Thought you'd judge me. Didn't want you to see me as the loser outcast."

"Miranda, I've been worried about you judging *me*."

I shook my head. "I wish it were that simple. This whole time I've wished—"

At the same time Ada scoffed. "I mean, I wish—"

"—I was more like you," we said.

At the exact same time.

23

NOTE TO SELF: MIRY GETS SAPPY WHEN IT RAINS

ADA

"WHAT!?" THE TWO OF US SHOUTED.

"There's no way I heard that right," I said. "It's the rain, isn't it? The rain's magic somehow, and it's playing tricks on us."

"We said what we said." Miranda pulled her hair away from her face, letting me see her stupidly shocked face. "Don't go blaming it on an illusion."

I knocked my head to the sides, seeing if I had something stuck in my ears. "For hell's sake, why would you want to be more like *me*?"

"Because you don't care!"

I blinked. "Oh, *wow*. That's a nice thing to say."

"That's not what I—" Miranda let go of her hair. "I mean that you have the ability to not give a crap."

"Still doesn't sound nice."

"I mean it nice." Miranda shook her head. "Ada, it means that you're confident enough in yourself to not give a damn about what anyone else thinks of you."

I kicked at the wet pavement. "If I didn't give a damn, then why would I want to be like you?"

"Okay, maybe you do give a damn, but you still wouldn't

change yourself. Come on, you just said that you didn't care about learning Mexican stuff because you didn't want to change yourself to suit other people."

Yeah, she was right about that. "And that makes you… wanna be like me?"

"Why wouldn't it?" Miranda crossed her arms over herself, conveniently covering up the American flag on her borrowed t-shirt. "It doesn't matter how 'Mexican' I think I am. Or what I do, or how much I know. If I'm not fully Mexican, then I'm just the dumb gringa."

"I thought you were…"

"A proper Mexican teenager? Doesn't exist. Or maybe it does, but I don't know what she's like. I thought I had friends who understood me, but the moment I came back too different from them, I was the outcast. But now I've spent so much time trying to not be the gringa that I don't know how to be anything. All this, this is just me trying to figure it out.

"But you've always known exactly who you are. It doesn't matter what people say or how much they stare, you've always been happy being you. And you wonder why I'm jealous of you."

"No," I said. "I'm the one who's supposed to be jealous of *you*!"

"Why?"

"Think about it! You know all these things about, I mean, everything! You understand everything before I even realize what's going on, and you just know things! You say that you don't know who you are, but you never show it. You've always been, I dunno…" I waved a hand in the air. "Cool!"

Miranda scoffed. "Interesting take."

"But you are! I know you don't think it, but come on. You can skateboard, you never lie about anything—"

"Neither do you."

"Yeah, but you're upfront about it. I've spent my whole life wondering why I'm not Mexican enough for everyone, but you've never even *tried* to be more American."

Miranda scowled and looked away, up toward the golden angel. "That didn't help me fit in."

"Yeah? Well, join the club."

The rain was coming down even harder, and not even the tree above could protect us from most of it.

I straightened out my soaked dress, which was sticking to my skin, and pulled at my water-logged hair that flopped against my cheeks and neck. Miranda was no better. Her hair hung around her in a curtain of black, and the water had fully soaked itself into her jeans. At this rate, the two of us were literally going to start swimming in our clothes.

"You think you're the outsider of the family," Miranda said.

"Yeah." I ran my hand through my shoulder-length hair, wincing as it got caught in a new knot. "I know my parents and I come here every year, but it's not like I'm really close to anyone. I didn't really get to know our grandparents, and I only got close to Nando when he came to study in the States. I barely even know Clara and Eduardo."

"And still, Clara and Eduardo adore you. Everyone in the family does."

"They do?" I asked.

"Hell yeah. I don't know how, but you somehow just get along with everyone here. You even get along better with Fer's parents than I do, and they barely speak English. If you really think about it, I'm the outsider. Everyone here is loud, friendly, cheerful. And I'm… not." Miranda clicked her tongue. "Really, out of the two of us, I think you're the one who should've grown up here."

"Is that why you never wanted to be American?" I asked. "Because it made you feel different?"

"Pretty much. And come on, do you know how many 'McDonald's' jokes I've gotten?"

"McDonald's?" I furrowed my eyebrows. "McDonald's, Mc… Donaldson."

"Yep."

I didn't mean to, but I laughed.

"That's why you hate that place?" I said, unable to stop the flurry of laughter. "That's so… *stupid.*"

I waited for Miranda to roll her eyes and storm off. But she didn't. Instead, she snorted and said, "It is stupid, isn't it?"

"So stupid," I agreed.

"We're idiots."

"No, we're not. People just suck."

"Society sucks."

"True," I conceded. I kicked at a puddle of water that was forming around us, not caring that it made water splash into my shoe. "But you know what… you don't need Mexican society."

"I kind of live in it," Miranda said.

"Yeah, but that doesn't mean you have to play by their rules. Do what you wanna do. Be who you are, even if it isn't 'Mexican' enough."

"Says the girl who unlocked the power of a Mexican god."

"What can I say?" I kicked at the puddle again, but instead of aiming away from us, I aimed the water at my cousin's jeans. "Guess I'm just that good at being Mexican."

"Oh, shut up." Miranda kicked the puddle, splashing water onto my legs in retaliation.

I kicked more water at her, and she did the same. We were both soaking wet, *again,* at this point, but that's what made it fun. It almost felt like we were kids again, nine years old instead of 15.

I couldn't believe it. I was having fun. With *Miranda.*

"You are good at it," Miranda said when we stopped. "Being Mexican. You don't give a damn if someone doesn't like who you are. That's a good thing."

I grinned. "And—even if you hate it—you're good at being

American. Perfectly willing to tell people exactly what's on your mind, even if it's not something they wanna hear."

"Then can I ask something?" she said. "Why'd you start calling me 'Miranda'?"

I blinked. Water fell from my eyelashes.

"You only started using my full name when we were ten," Miranda continued. "Before that, you called me 'Miry'."

"… You never corrected me. You correct everyone else, so I assumed that you *wanted* me to call you 'Miranda'."

Miranda sighed. "Can I say something else?"

"Sure."

"We look like idiots out here."

I laughed. "Back to the car?"

"Yep."

We turned around and walked back the way we came. We didn't rush—we were soaked either way, and we'd done enough running for the day.

"We should probably apologize to Fer," Miranda said.

"Yeah. Never thought we'd piss him off so much he'd actually blackmail us." Remembering that moment, I wondered, "So… how *did* you ruin Uncle Rizo's suit? And why'd you make Clara take the fall for it?"

"I didn't."

"Huh? But Nando said—"

"I told Fer that I ruined the suit." Miranda turned to me, and the lights from the cars on the street gave her face an eerie red glow. "But I didn't. Eduardo did."

"Wait… you're telling me you took the fall for Eduardo in front of Nando, and then made Clara take the fall in front of our uncle?"

"Yep." Miranda shrugged. "Eduardo was six and tripped while carrying a juice box. He'd already gotten in trouble that day, and I knew that Fer would scold him again. It was just an accident, so I put the juice box in Clara's hand and told Tío Rizo that she did it."

"Why not take the heat yourself?" I asked.

"Because Clara is Tío Rizo's special little princess." Miranda rolled her eyes. "Really, that kid could kill us in our sleep and he'd still think she's the sweetest, most innocent girl on earth."

I laughed again. "I hope Eduardo thanked you for that one."

"… I never thanked *you*."

I raised an eyebrow. "For what? Everything I've ever done our whole lives?"

"For saving my ass from those stalkers. I panicked, and you picked up the slack."

"I was only returning the favor," I said. "You're the one who spotted them."

"Guess we make a good team," Miranda said with a smile. "Sometimes."

"Sometimes." I smiled back. "Thanks, Miry."

Miranda stopped, just for a second, before walking again. "Yeah… You too, Ada."

WHEN WE TURNED ONTO THE STREET WHERE NANDO HAD parked the car, Miranda and I saw him peering out from the driver's side window. Next to it was a familiar-looking vehicle, and when we got close to it, two people hopped out of Nando's car.

"Are you two okay?" Nando asked, holding one hand above his head to protect his glasses.

"Even though you're wet," Daniel added. He was using his denim jacket to protect himself from the rain.

Miranda blinked when she saw Daniel. "You got here fast."

"But you're okay?" Nando asked again.

"I think so," I said.

"*Perfecto*." Daniel gave Nando a slap on the back before running to his own car. "I'll meet you at UNAM."

"C'mon, get in the car." Nando pushed Miranda and I toward the ancient green vehicle. "Daniel brought towels, so get yourselves dry before you get sick."

"That's... nice of him," Miranda said suspiciously.

"Dude, he brought *towels*," I said. "If you wanna complain, complain when we're dry."

I called shotgun and cheered at the sight of a fluffy towel on my seat. The duct tape we'd wrapped around the roof was enough to cover up the tears caused by the killer eagles, meaning that the car was miraculously nice and dry. I rubbed the rainwater out of my ear, and Miranda towel-dried her stupidly long hair.

"We're sorry about the fights," I said. "We didn't know it was affecting you that much."

"Yeah," Miranda said from the backseat. "We're really sorry, Fer."

"So... did you make up?" Nando looked between the two of us slowly, almost as if he was considering whether it would be ethical to kick us out again if we said 'no'.

"Yep." I rubbed the towel over my head. "Who knew that Miry could be reasonable?"

"Keep talking and I'll be *un*reasonable for the rest of your life," Miranda added.

Nando's eyes grew to the size of his glasses. "Did you call her—"

When neither of us said anything else, Fer sank into the driver's seat with a shocked laugh.

"Okay. Okay." Nando pulled something from the console. "You've earned this."

And Nando, for the first time since I've ever been in a car with him, handed me the AUX cable.

"Are you serious?" I asked.

"Yes." Nando held up a finger. "But after one song, you

pass your phone to Miry. And it's only until we get to UNAM. Okay?"

I snatched the cord. "I'll take it!"

Nando chuckled as he pulled out of the parking spot. Next to us, Daniel's car did the same, and both cars turned onto the long stretch of road. We were immediately greeted by the red taillights on the road, and Nando's chuckling soon faded into grumbling about "stupid traffic".

I pulled my phone out of my purse and scrolled to my playlist. I was a second away from hitting the first song—

When I remembered that Miranda was in the backseat.

I hesitated. For ages, there were parts of myself I didn't show her because I thought she'd judge me. My musical tastes aren't traditionally Mexican, or Mexican-American, and I had no clue how Miranda would react to it.

But… For the first time in years, I felt like I actually understood my cousin. We'd had a proper conversation that didn't end with the two of us fighting. And I thought that maybe, just maybe, she wouldn't judge me for this.

You don't give a damn if someone doesn't like who you are, Miranda had said. *That's a good thing.*

Well, I thought as I selected the song, *time to see what you think of this side of me.*

I pressed play.

A light melody boomed through the speaker, and after a few seconds, Jimin's voice chimed in with opening lines to "Answer: Love Myself." AKA, the song that got me through eight grade.

Nando groaned. I looked back at Miranda, expecting a similar reaction, but she just stared at the stereo with wide eyes.

"… BTS?" she asked cautiously, lowering her towel away from her damp hair.

"Yeah. I like BTS." I threw my hands in the air. "K-pop's

great, okay? I know it's Korean and not Mexican, but I don't care. They've got great music, great dances, and—"

"Who's your bias?"

Wait…

What?

I slowly, very slowly, turned to Miranda.

"What did you say?" I asked.

"From BTS," Miranda pressed, sounding absolutely, completely serious. "Who's your bias?"

"… Suga," I said.

Realization dawned on Miranda's face, and she pointed a finger at her chest. "Jimin."

And that is the moment when Miry and I let out high-pitched, ear-splitting, car-shaking shrieks of pure joy.

"*Ay,*" Nando hissed as I jumped into the backseat.

"Why didn't you tell me you like BTS?" Miry demanded.

"Why didn't *you* tell *me*?" I asked. "And I don't just like them. I *love* them!"

"Are you ARMY?"

"Duh!"

"No shit, me too!"

We screamed again, loud and high. It was the kind of joy you only get when you find someone as passionate and excited about the same thing you're passionate and excited about. When you're so happy, all you can do is yell and scream. I'd had those moments with friends back home, but not with Miry. Not in years. I didn't even know that sarcastic, brooding Miry *could* scream like that.

And there we were. Loudly singing along with Jin and Jung Kook as they entered the chorus. We were having fun.

We were having *fun*!

Well, Miry and I were; Nando was just suffering.

"It's okay, Fernando," my cousin muttered to himself from the driver's seat. "You only have to listen to this for a nice, *short* drive."

24

KNOWLEDGE IN THE RAIN

MIRY

"That was not a short drive," Fer muttered as we finally reached UNAM.

Ada and I laughed from the backseat. My cousin turned up the volume for the final song, and Fer wound the car down the many roads that composed Mexico's largest university.

UNAM is huge, and its nickname, *Ciudad Universitaria*, was accurate. The campus spans several kilometers. With so many buildings, departments, and even a full stadium, it really did feel like a city in and of itself. Seriously, this place is so big it has its own inner bus service.

At this point, Daniel had pulled ahead of us, leading us deeper through the winding roads of UNAM to the part where we'd—hopefully—get answers. But even though we'd been sitting in the car for another hour and a half at that point, Ada and I didn't really care.

Next to me, Ada was rapping to "Seesaw". In actual *Korean*. She was terrible, but she got the lyrics dead right.

"Ah," she said, rolling her shoulders to the beat, "the songs are *so* much better when you understand the lyrics!"

I scoffed. "So that's why you're not learning Spanish! You're learning Korean!"

"Well, yeah!" Ada said. "Learning Korean is hard as it is. Mixing that up with Spanish is just gonna make me forget which language is which."

"Sure," I drawled, before—badly—singing a line from Natalia Lafourcade's song "Hasta la Raíz."

Ada blinked. "What're you singing in Spanish?"

I grinned. "So… what did you say about getting the languages mixed up?"

"Oh, shut up!"

Had she said that to me this morning, I would've rolled my eyes. But now… I laughed.

In the driver's seat, Fer sighed. But when I caught his reflection in the mirror, he was smiling.

Through the haze of the rainstorm, I made out the serpentine roads that made up UNAM's campus. Structures that ranged from new multi-story buildings to decades-old single-story ones. But even with the blinding rain, I still managed to spot a few posters taped to trees and light posts talking about one of the departments going on strike.

Fer followed Daniel to a small car park. It was a little ways away from a stout building that seemed like it was made out of bricks with a wooden cube on top. Despite the towels and the car's lackluster heating, Ada and I were still kind of wet. Daniel and Fer sprinted out of their cars and rushed to the closest shelter. Ada and I walked.

"Isn't your guy the god of rain?" I called out over the torrential rainfall that was soaking me *again*. I was so done with it all I didn't even try to shield myself.

"Yeah!" Ada, unlike me, was actually trying to protect herself by holding one of the soaked towels above her head. "Can't you make, like, a rain shield or something? I kind of like this dress!"

Just within the entrance to the brick-like building, Daniel sighed. He held open the glass door for Fer, who immediately wiped the water droplets from his glasses.

"I'm all out of power," Daniel said as we got closer. His AC/DC shirt was plastered to his chest, and some of his perfectly gelled hair had come loose. "I used up all of my energy getting away from Lorenzo. I have enough for a spell or two, but not enough to stop this."

With a single finger, Ada pointed up to the sky. "Why don't you just drink the rain?"

Daniel laughed. "You think I want to drink any of this polluted *mierda*?"

Fer appraised his glasses. They were dry, but bits of the glass were slightly dirty due to the aftereffects of the polluted rainwater. He sighed and rubbed them against the hem of his shirt.

I glanced up at the large letters that adorned the building, using my hand to keep the water from entering my eyes. It read:

FACULTAD DE ARQUITECTURA.

"Miry!" Ada shouted. "Come on! You gotta check this place out!"

Fer reached out to pull me inside. "And come in before you get sick!"

"Relax, I'm coming," I said, before stepping into UNAM's Faculty of Architecture.

The outside of the building didn't do this place justice. Once inside, a long hallway stretched out before us, with stone flooring that morphed into large tiles of black obsidian-like rock. The section to our left was open, allowing for the water to come in, but the rain just bounced on an array of gray pebbles, leaving us dry. Farther down the hallway was a statue of a naked man who was punching an invisible opponent in the face, and just ahead of that was a woman walking toward us.

"*Profesora*," Daniel said with a grin. "It's been too long."

"Two years," the woman said. She was around my mom's age,

probably a bit older, with light brown skin, her hair pulled into a low ponytail, and a thick puffer jacket that ended around her knees. When she saw us, she gave us a tired smile. *"And who are they?"* she asked in Spanish. Her accent was vaguely northern.

"Ada, Miry, and Fer," Daniel said. "They're the new Archivists I told you about. Well, Ada and Miry are."

Fer bit his lip and shoved his hands in his pockets.

Another pang of guilt shot through me. This whole time, Ada and I were so preoccupied with what was going on with our powers, we hadn't wondered what Fer was thinking about all this. To be fair, his two-day no-question window was still ongoing, but I couldn't help but wonder.

How did Fer know where to find Daniel Merino? Why was he so insistent on us staying out of this? Why didn't he want to tell our parents?

And why did he agree to help us in the first place?

"And why are we speaking in English?" the professor asked.

"That's because of me," Ada said with a sheepish smile. "Hi, I'm Ada! This is Nando, the nerdy cousin, and this is Miry, the moody cousin."

"Nice to meet you," the professor said before Fer and I could react. "And why are you coming to me?" she asked Daniel. "The Archivists know that I've stopped working with them. And you're supposed to go to the university's library, not here—"

"I know, I know, *Profesora*." Daniel scratched the back of his head. "But this is a... unique situation, and we need an acceptance ceremony as soon as possible. You may not work for us anymore, but you're still an Archivist."

"Which means I can officially accept them to the group." The professor crossed her arms in front of her like she was annoyed, but I think she did it because she was cold. In *summer*. "But why come to me?"

Daniel laughed. "Do you honestly want me to admit you were my favorite teacher?"

The professor chuckled. "I've known that for a long time." She turned to us. "I'm *Profesora* Gabriela Jiménez Bernal. It's been a long time since I've worked for the Archivists, but if it's really necessary, I can perform your acceptance ceremony. Under one condition."

"What's that?" I asked.

Something shone in the professor's eyes, and I suddenly understood the meaning behind the phrase "thirst for knowledge." "It's simple. I want to know everything about your journey."

THE PROFESSOR TOOK US TO A CLASSROOM ON THE TOP floor of the building. There weren't any people to get in our way since it was still summer vacation, but the room we'd been shuffled into was a disaster. Tables had been haphazardly shoved against the walls, all the drawers from the teacher's desk were open, and there was even a set of sequin scarves hanging from the whiteboard.

"Sorry about the mess." Profesora Gabriela said as she rearranged the chairs. "Some of our... *guests* forget to put everything back to how it was."

Daniel helped her move a table. "You should yell at them. Remember the time you yelled at me for losing your book? I'm pretty sure I was scared of you for a month."

"Just a month?" the professor asked with a smile.

"I can't believe you took classes here," Ada said in awe. "I mean, this campus is *huge*. How do you remember where everything is?"

"I only know where this building is." Daniel sat down at

the table. "I didn't go to school here. I actually went to art school."

"You're an artist?" Ada said. "Cool! What do you do?"

"Mostly paintings. But I've done some sculpting and woodwork."

"Is the pay good?" I asked. Daniel gave me a flat look, and I winced. "So do you supplement your pay with money you get from the Archivists?"

Daniel took in a very deep breath, held it in for a solid five seconds, and then let it out slowly.

"If you want to join the Archivists for the money, don't," Profesora Gabriela said firmly.

I narrowed my eyes at her. "You don't look like an art teacher."

"Miry!" Fer hissed. "Don't be rude!"

"How is *that* rude?"

"It would be rude if I were an art teacher," the professor said. "But I'm not. I was actually one of Daniel's magic teachers."

"So you're a disciple of Tláloc?" I asked.

Profesora Gabriela shook her head. "Not quite. I'm a more… general practitioner."

"What does that mean?" Fer asked.

"I'll explain." She signaled for the rest of us to sit at the table she and Daniel had organized in the middle of the room. A tiny rectangle of order inside the chaotic classroom. We sat, and she pulled out a laptop from her bag.

"I'm sure you already know the basics," she said as she booted up the laptop that was *at least* a decade old. "That the deities give us power, that Quetzalcóatl is the deity of light, that Tláloc is the deity of rain, Chalchiuhtlicue is the deity of—"

"Wait, what?" Ada exclaimed. "We haven't heard anything about Quetz! And who's *Chaal-chee-tley-cuay*?"

The professor glanced between the two of us. "You didn't read the books?"

"The first two were pretty useless," Ada said. "We only got one more before going to the museum. The one from Coyoacán. I think it's in the car somewhere?"

"They had to skip a few steps," Daniel supplied.

The professor sighed. "Then I guess I should explain." Once the laptop finally booted up, she typed a few things before turning the screen toward us. On it was a Powerpoint made with one of the generic templates, and the opening slide greeted us with a bold title.

LAS DEIDADES DE TEOTIHUACÁN

"A POWERPOINT?" I SAID. "REALLY? *THAT'S* HOW WE'RE gonna do this?"

The professor glared at me. "If you don't like it, you can leave."

I sighed and slouched in my chair.

The professor clicked over to the next slide, which was a photo of the ruins. "There are many misconceptions around the city of Teotihuacán. The civilization started around 0 CE, and it collapsed around 650 CE. This was so long ago that not even the city's original name and language are known, and it's part of the reason why the deities who emerged from it are so misunderstood."

She clicked to the next slide, which showed an image of the earth. "Many think that Quetzalcóatl, Tláloc, and everyone else are gods. But they aren't. They're the physical and magical representations of the world around us. These deities who have given you power, they are beings of the earth and sky. They are not gods. They are the manifestations of the world itself."

"I… I'm not sure I get it," I said.

Fer sat completely still. I expected him to be the one to jump in with questions, but he kept his mouth shut.

"Um…" Ada said. "Mind giving us an example?"

"This is why I prefer teaching architecture," the professor said under her breath. "Okay, let me give you a basic summary. The concept of a god is that they have power to control something. Poseidon is the god of the sea, so he can control the sea."

Ada and I nodded.

"For us, the pantheon of Teotihuacán, that doesn't exist," the professor said. "Because if Poseidon was part of *this* pantheon, he wouldn't be the *god* of the sea. He would be *the sea*."

"*Oh*," I said. "It's like in *The Last Airbender*."

"Yeah?" Ada asked.

"Yeah. When Princess Yue took over for the moon spirit, she didn't turn into the goddess of the moon. She turned into *the moon*."

"Oooh." Ada nodded, and her damp curls flopped against her face. Fer muttered something about how she and I were definitely getting sick after this, but we ignored him. "So I'm guessing that's why you prefer the word 'deities'."

A moment from our time at the Museum of Anthropology flashed in my mind. "But the inscription in front of the Teotihuacán exhibit said 'god'."

"It's…" Profesora Gabriela sighed. "That's a conversation for another time."

The three of us cousins turned to Daniel, since he's the one who'd been calling the deities 'gods'. He glanced between us and the professor, waved his hand, and said, "Like she said, a conversation for another time."

Ada nodded slowly. "So who are the go—deities?" she corrected when the professor gave her a pointed stare. "Who chose us?"

"Well, we can start with the biggest one." The professor clicked to the next slide, showing a drawing of a long snake with feathers on its back. "Quetzalcóatl, the feathered serpent. Deity of light. He *literally* represents the sun's light, and he's one of the most powerful in the pantheon. You also have Xipe Totec." The professor moved onto a picture of a man with a red helmet adorned with long leaves. He held a tall staff, and his skin was red, as if it'd been flayed. "He is the deity of fertility. He represents fertile land and crops, but also nature in general."

Ada's eyes widened. "My energy came back to me when I was walking at the park. I thought it was my body just relaxing, but when I stood in the sun… that was my magic coming back to me."

"Yep," I said. "You're a walking, talking plant now. Congrats."

Ada snorted. "So either *Sheep-ey Tote-ec* or Quetz picked me… Kinda wish I knew which one."

Ada rubbed her thumb over her nail bed; I stayed silent.

"Huehuetéotl, the deity of the fire," the professor continued, showing us a photo of a statue of a wrinkled man with a large circular plate on his head. "I think you can guess what he represents." She clicked the slide again, showing a new drawing of a man dressed in green, yellow, and red. "There's also Tezcatlipoca, the deity of smoke and mirrors. His disciples are granted the power of illusions, but he doesn't give them to magic users from the pantheon of Teotihuacán."

"Why not?" I asked.

"Personal preference," she said. "He said that someone else was 'stealing his spotlight', so my guess is that he's jealous that deities like Quetzalcóatl are more popular than him. Overall, he prefers picking disciples as a deity from the Aztec pantheon."

Ada huffed. "Didn't know a deity could be picky."

The professor sighed again. "You have *no* idea."

"So, there are disciples for other pantheons?" I asked. "People with magic besides the Archivists?"

"There are," the professor said. "There's even an organization of magical users in Latin America. *La Liga de Latinoamericanos: Autoridad Mágica y Autónoma.* LLAMA, for short."

"Um, they got a name in English?" Ada asked.

"The League for the Latin American Magical Authority," the professor said. "Also LLAMA, for short in English."

"*Cool,*" Ada said. "And do all of them have this weird recruitment system?"

The professor held back a groan. "No, they don't. That is something unique to our pantheon. Our circle of magic users is also smaller. A disciple of the Aztecs can live their whole life not knowing half of the other magic users in their pantheon. A disciple of Teotihuacán knows every Archivist, every affiliate, and everyone's mother."

"Seriously?" I said. "Why the hell is the group so small?"

"Because Teotihuacán isn't well-known," the professor explained. "The more we and others know about Teotihuacán, the more our deities can connect to the magic in the earth. And the more they connect to it, the more disciples they get to pick. In an ideal world, the deities would be able to pick dozens, maybe *hundreds*, of people. But they can't. So this small little group is all we've got."

"Even for a big, catastrophic event?" Ada said. "Can't the go—*deities*, call a state of emergency and just give a whole bunch of people magic?"

"They would if they could." Profesora Gabriela sighed. "The deities want more Archivists. The *Archivists* want more Archivists. It would be so much easier if we had more people. We'd have less paperwork, less cases. We'd actually have time for research instead of spending our time cleaning up magical messes. It's a lot for a small group to handle, and... sometimes it drives people away."

"People like you," Ada said quietly.

"People like me," the professor said. "But back to the deities." She turned to the laptop. "Here we have the two most important deities of Teotihuacán. Tláloc, the deity of rain. And his wife, Chalchiuhtlicue. Deity of lakes."

A photo flashed onto the Powerpoint. It was a mural of two people standing side by side, with water flowing from their outstretched hands. They had green-tinted skin, opulent robes that covered their bodies, and rectangular mouthpieces that covered the lower halves of their faces. They also had enormous headpieces with an eagle head and bright green feathers that filled almost half of the mural.

"Why are they so important?" I asked.

"You've been to the pyramids," the professor said. "You know the pyramid of the sun and the pyramid of the moon?"

Ada and I nodded.

"They're not the pyramids of the sun and moon," she said. "When the original archeologists came to the pyramids, they thought that the pyramids must've been built to worship them, but they were wrong."

She jumped ahead several slides, ending at an image of a map of the archeological ruins. "The pyramid of the sun," she pointed at the large pyramid that was to the side of the walkway, "was built on the line where the sun rises from the horizon. But it was also made to honor Tláloc. Deity of the rain."

Then she pointed her finger at the other pyramid, the one that was at the very end of the walkway. "The pyramid of the moon was built on the line where the moon rises from the horizon. But it was also made to honor Tláloc's wife, Chalchiuhtlicue. Deity of the lakes."

"I had no idea," I said. I'd gone to the pyramids so many times, and yet I'd never once learned about this.

"Few do," the professor said. "Teotihuacán has been gone for so many years that few people really know what life was like there, much less what their spiritual lives were like. The important thing is to keep an open mind and learn about what this place actually was. Who our deities were, as well as who they are now."

I thought about the woman on the mural. Water flowing from her hands and her skin tinted green. I thought of the woman I met in Coyoacán. With a green dress, jade bracelets, and a taste for nieves.

"Jade…" I whispered, "is Chalchiuhtlicue."

Profesora Gabriela furrowed her eyebrows. "Jade?"

"I met her in Coyoacán." I gasped softly. "I think…"

"You think she's your deity," Ada said.

"Yeah. My magic comes from water, and she's the deity of the lakes. It… it checks out."

"Glad you figured it out," Ada said. She pulled at the hem of her damp dress and suddenly stood up. "I gotta go to the bathroom. Be back in a bit."

"Hada—" Fer started, but our cousin was already heading to the exit.

I didn't bother telling Fer he shouldn't waste his breath. Even though Ada and I had our cheesy heart-to-heart, there are some feelings that take a long time to get over.

And I know just how hard it is to let go of jealousy.

The professor sighed. "And just when I was getting to the interesting bit." She turned to me. "And *you* are telling me everything about your meeting with Chalchiuhtlicue."

Great, I groaned. *Now I have to talk.*

25

HOW TO BE FASHIONABLE DURING A MIDLIFE CRISIS

ADA

OKAY, LET ME EXPLAIN.

Yes, I was kind of annoyed that Miry figured out her deity first. Yes, I was glad for her, but still jealous. But even with all that, I honestly—swear to god-ity—*did* need to go to the bathroom.

I walked out of the classroom and found myself with a problem. I had no idea where the bathroom was, and going back inside to ask Professor Jiménez would've undermined my entire dramatic exit.

I looked around for a sign or some summer school student who could tell me where to go. The professor had to have been here for a reason, right? Maybe an extra class or a make-up exam for a poor student who needed to retake their final.

There was a light shining from underneath a doorway to my left. A sign said that it was the *Sala de Profesores*. It was the room that the professor had gone into to get her laptop, though she hadn't invited us inside. Still, *Profesores* definitely meant "professors", so I figured that there must've just been a different teacher in there. Maybe they were working on papers or models or whatever it is that architecture students have as homework.

I peered into the room. "Um... hey? Do you speak English? I just wanna know where the bathroom *iiis*—"

I trailed off, because instead of seeing a teacher sitting at a desk, I'd walked into a full-on closet.

In front of me was a room full of desks, coffee tables, and bookshelves that had been repurposed into clothing racks. Everything and anything, ranging from tank tops to capes to wigs to high-heeled boots to oversized jeans, was stacked in piles of discarded clothing. There was no rhyme or reason to the mess—just a maelstrom of clutter equivalent to the aftermath of a tornado running through an apparel shop.

In the middle of the room was a man. He was kind of tall—around Nando's height—with a stubble beard, dark brown skin, messy shoulder-length hair, and dark brown eyes that hung above deep eye bags. Considering we were in a university, my first thought was that he was a tired grad student who was stressing out over his thesis.

But then I took in what he was wearing.

The guy had brown Texas-style cowboy boots over forest green skinny jeans. His shirt was lemon yellow, which somehow contrasted with the many gold chains around his neck, but matched the gaudy sunglasses on his head. And to top it all off, he had an over-sized, leather-like jacket with a multi-colored snake skin pattern.

It was, in every sense of the phrase, a fashion nightmare.

"Uh, hi!" I said. "I think I'm in the wrong room. I'll just be heading out—"

"It's the snake print, isn't it?" the man said in the tone that made you believe he truly thought the end of the world was upon us. "It's too much, and it's everywhere."

Confused, I took a step closer. Sure enough, the forest green skinny jeans had a faint snake pattern running along them, and even the bright yellow shirt had some thin lines that vaguely resembled snake scales.

"It's... a fashion statement?" I said.

"But it doesn't even work!" The man pulled at his hair. "It's too obvious!"

In a fit of rage, the man yanked the snake-print jacket off. He threw it into one of the many clothing piles, making a stack of trench coats, fluffy scarves, and swim shorts fall to the floor. He switched his yellow shirt for a tie-dye tank top with a low neckline, and just as he pulled it on, a pair of giant wings sprouted from his back.

"Woah!" I yelped. But I hadn't cried out because I was scared.

I cried out because the wings were absolutely *gorgeous*.

They were huge—at least six feet long—and they had to curl into themselves to avoid toppling tall piles of clothing. They had deep brown feathers that ruffled against each other, and every small movement made the wings rustle softly.

I almost touched them when I remembered how much I hated when strangers tried to touch my own hair without permission. It felt creepy, and I realized that maybe it wasn't the best idea to touch someone's spontaneously-appearing wings.

"I am *so* sorry," the snake man said. He held his hands out like he'd made a mistake he wasn't sure how to fix. "I didn't mean to scare you."

"Ah, it's okay! You didn't freak me out that much." I nervously jostled my damp curls. "I mean, maybe a little, but… *woah*. You… You can shape-shift?"

Snake Man sighed and lowered his hands. The thick golden chains around his neck *clonked* against each other. "Yes…"

"That's so cool!" I stepped to the side so I could take in the enormous eagle-like wings. "Are they real?"

"They are," he said.

"Can you actually fly?"

"I can."

"Woah. This is so awesome! Just—How do you have *wings*?"

Snake Man sighed again. "Because I'm a deity."

The next question stayed on my tongue.

I took in the man. His enormous eagle wings, the green scaly jeans he still wore, and the thick gold around his neck. He didn't look like the woman—who was Chalchiuhtlicue, apparently—that Miry had met in Coyoacán. But then again, these guys were representations of the earth itself. Who knows what a common look for them is.

I remembered what Miry did at the park. She said that her magic hummed with Jade, so I figured I could try it for myself.

I channeled the magical warmth in my chest and pushed it to my finger, like I'd done so many times in the last 48 hours. But instead of going directly to my hand, my magic was pulled outward—toward something else.

Toward *someone* else.

My magic was pulled to the man in front of me. It was almost like a tug on my chest, guiding me toward a destination I never knew I was destined to go to. The magic guided me to him, and that's when everything fell into place.

The eagle feather. The snake pattern. Even the warmth in my chest. Whenever I'd felt like my magic had been drained out of me, my energy had always come back after being in the sun.

And according to the professor, there was a deity who was the physical and magical representation of light.

"You're Quetzalcóatl."

The man in front of me smiled, and his dark brown eyes shimmered until they turned gold.

"I am," Quetz said. "It's nice to finally meet you, Ada. Kind of."

I blinked. "Kind of?"

The man sighed and yanked off the tank top, retracting the enormous eagle wings as he did so. "It's not you." He rummaged around a pile of blue and purple clothes. "I just don't know if I'm really me."

"So… you're not a deity?"

"I am!" Quetz tugged on a bomber jacket that was weighed down by an absurd amount of enamel cacti pins. "But I don't know if you're meeting the real me, or a version who's like me but not really me, or a version that's only like this for today because tomorrow I'll be completely different!" He yanked the yellow glasses off his head and stared despondently at the ceiling. "I don't even know if I'm Quetzalcóatl anymore!"

"But… you do *kind of* know who you are?"

"No! I don't know *who* I am!"

I scratched my head. "But the woman my cousin met said that deities are shaped by how people remember them and interpret them. And pretty much everyone knows about you!"

"Yeah," Quetz said. "And that's part of the problem."

His body was suddenly engulfed in light, as if someone had turned on a lamp inside of his body. It was so bright I was forced to shut my eyes.

When I opened them again, in place of a dark-skinned man, I saw a woman. She had light skin, wavy yellow-green hair that cascaded down her back, heterochromatic eyes, tiny jean shorts, and a tight tank top with a neckline that showed off her enormous—and I mean *enormous*, breasts.

"Oh… *wow*," I said, forcing my gaze away from her massive chest. "That's… something."

The woman in front of me closed her eyes and gave me a sleepy smile. "This version of me comes from a Japanese manga"

"I see…" I said. "You okay, man? Um, woman—um, person?"

"I don't know." The bright light shimmered again, and suddenly I was staring at a brown-skinned man with gold chains and a tie-dye tank top again. "Right now, I could be anything and anyone!"

I remembered what Miry said about Chalchiuhtlicue. That because Teotihuacán collapsed so many years ago, they couldn't remember what they were like back then. And that humans' interpretations about these deities are what shaped them.

So, if the deities get shaped by what people imagine of them, and one of them happens to be pretty famous…

"You're saying," I said, "that people have so many ideas and versions of you, you don't know who you're meant to be?"

"*Yes*," Quetz groaned.

Oh, I thought. *So* that's *what's happening*.

The most powerful, well-known, and transcendent god-ity of the mesoamerican pantheons was having a full-blown identity crisis.

"That's rough, dude." I gestured at the office space-turned-closet. "How long have you been here?"

"In this office? Half a year. Maybe more."

"And Professor Jiménez lets you stay here?"

"We have a deal." He kicked at a pile of clothes that cascaded to the floor in a sea of denim and pleather. "In exchange for my knowledge, she lets me use this room as a closet."

I briefly glanced back at the very *unlocked* door I'd just come through. "Does anyone else come in here?"

Quetz chuckled. "All the time. But I just say I'm her cousin."

Quetz shimmered in a sea of light, and suddenly I was staring at a middle-aged man with long hair, a tan bandana, a flower print shirt, and khaki cargo pants.

"But not always," he said, sounding like a stoned hippie. "Sometimes I'm her chill uncle from LA."

He shimmered again, shifting into a woman with knee-length wavy hair, a dress that faded from green to blue to red, and a golden crown on her head. "Sometimes I'm her friend from grad school."

Quetz shimmered yet again, and he was back to being the same man/fashion disaster he'd been when I walked into the room. "And sometimes I'm this."

"I don't even know what that *is*."

"Exactly!" Quetz groaned and collapsed onto the piles of clothing he'd kicked to the floor. "I've been like this for a long time, but recently it's gotten so bad that I've barely been able to get out."

"That can't be good for you," I said. "You're, like, the deity of light, right? You gotta get some vitamin D in you!"

"I should," Quetz bemoaned. "When I'm the version of myself from the Aztec or Mayan pantheons, I work just fine! But when I shift to the version from Teotihuacán…" He waved his hands at himself. "I turn into this."

"Don't know who you are or what you're meant to be?" I guessed, to which Quetz nodded. "Textbook identity crisis. Well, Quetz, guess what, I've got a strategy that I think can help."

"Didn't you have to go to the bathroom?"

"I can hold it." I stepped forward and sat down on a pile of sweaters and faux leather pants. "Okay, first step to getting a hold of your identity is getting a few facts settled. So let's start with some basic questions. What's your name?"

Quetz sighed. "Quetzalcóatl. I think."

"Age?"

"More than two millennia," he said despondently. "Can't even remember the birth date."

"*Okaaay*, so we're staying away from *that* topic. Favorite food?"

"Depends."

"Favorite thing to do?"

"I don't know."

"Uh, favorite movie?"

"*Princess Diaries 2: Royal Engagement.*"

"Out of left field, but I'm not gonna judge. Any activities you're good at?"

"Creating terrible outfits." Quetz dramatically flopped an arm on top of his eyes. "I don't know how you mortals do it. How you just… figure out who you are on your own."

"It isn't easy," I sighed. "I mean, I went through this whole identity crisis thing when I was, what, 12? 13?"

Quetz peeked one golden eye out from under his arm. "Why did that happen?"

I shrugged. "I felt like I was never enough. Never Mexican enough, never Mexican-*American* enough. I mean, that's a pretty big part of me, but not all of me. And everywhere I went, *that's* what people focused on.

"But then I thought, you know what? They don't know a thing about me. The only person who knows me is me. I felt good to realize that. But… I can't say it fixed everything."

"In what way?" Quetz asked.

"Well, the obvious one is that I can't speak Spanish to save my life." I leaned against a tower of tank tops. "I don't know the songs, barely know the food. I come here twice a year, but the only extended family I'm close to is Nando, and a big part of that is because he moved to Phoenix last year. All of it makes me wonder if I'm worthy of my own identity." I scoffed. "Sometimes I wonder if I'm enough to be part of my own *family.*"

Quetz nodded slowly. "If you understand the issues, why don't you try to fix them?"

"I've *wanted* to," I said. "Every now and then, I try something. Learn a bit of Spanish, listen to a couple songs, join in on my mom's calls with Aunt Lupe and Uncle Rizo. But none of it sticks. And…"

"And what?"

"And it's embarrassing!" I said. "I should already be good at Spanish. I should already know something about the culture. I should already be close with my family! But I'm not, and every time I try to fix that, I feel like I'm being judged and get super self-conscious. It's easier to try something no one expects you to be good at than try something you're already expected to do well in. I know it's an excuse, but..."

"You feel like you never live up to who you're meant to be," Quetz said.

"Yeah. And the worst part is that it stops me from even *trying*." I chuckled. "I blame myself, you know. That I haven't done enough. I mean, my grandmother's dead and my grandfather forgot who I was years ago. Even if I did try now, it doesn't make up for the fact that I'm never gonna get to know them.

"It sucks, and I don't like to think about it *because* it sucks. The only consolation I have is that I know who I'm meant to be."

Quetz appraised me, and his lips quirked upward into a small smile. "And you've never wanted to be someone else?"

I chuckled. "Sometimes. But at the end of the day, I'm just Ada Reyes-Rivera. Your friendly Mexican-American from Phoenix, Arizona. And even if I'm not perfect... I like being me."

"You do," Quetz said, and for the first time since I'd met him, he gave me a genuine, full smile.

I let the words sink in for a moment. Because this guy, this deity, was talking to me. Just like Chalchiuhtlicue had talked to Miry.

"Why'd you pick me?" I asked.

"I can't tell you, remember?" Quetz pushed himself into a sitting position, and the many cacti pins on his bomber jacket clinked together. "But I think you can take a guess."

I could. I could take a guess, but there was something that was still bothering me.

"Am I really good enough for this?" I pushed myself off of the pile of clothes. "Dude, I just told you exactly what my issues are! You heard all of that, and you still want to make me your disciple?"

"I do," Quetz said.

"You *sure* about that? Like, really, really, *really* sure?"

"I am."

I let out a shocked laugh. "You picked me to be your disciple because I'm certain of my identity. Even if I don't always feel like I'm worthy of it."

Quetz grinned. "And who are you, Guadalupe?"

I gestured to all of me—my damp clothes, my frizzy hair, and the shoes that kept slipping off my feet.

"I'm a Mexcian-American teenager who hates the cold and loves BTS. I'm bad at languages but good at math. I like dresses, makeup, skirts. And even if someone says I'm too much of what society says that women should like, I don't care. Because even if I'm not perfect, and I've still got a lot of things to learn, I do know one thing… I know exactly who I am. And by the way." I let a smirk grow on my face. "The name's Ada."

Quetz's golden eyes shimmered. "That's right," he said.

And magic burst in my chest.

It was like the sun itself had exploded in my heart, filling every bit of my body with rays of warmth that flowed to the very core of my bones. It rippled within me, from the soles of my feet to the tips of my fingers. When I pushed the magic to my pointer finger, a long cacti needle the size of my forearm jutted from my nail bed.

But I knew I could do *more*.

I pushed my magic into my hands, telling it to expand. Telling it to *grow*. I let the magic envelop my palms, my thumbs, my pinky fingers, and I pushed it out.

My hands turned green as they morphed into thick-skinned cacti. It encompassed my palms, making them grow until they were the size of a small potted plant. It made my fingers longer and thinner, and each one had a sharp needle sticking out of its nail bed.

Still, I knew they could grow even more.

I raised my right hand to the ceiling and stretched.

The cactus on my right arm burst forward. My hand-turned-plant grew upward, with new needles covering the surface of my "skin" as it expanded itself. It grew at rapid speed until it banged against the ceiling. Bits of paint fell off as the impact rocked the room. The impact rocked my body and nearly made me fall to the ground, but even though there was a slight sting, it didn't hurt.

This was it; this was my magic.

I'd gotten my magic!

Behind me, the door slammed open.

"*¿Qué pasó—*" Professor Jiménez said before trailing off.

I turned around to see the professor, Daniel, Nando, and Miry staring at me. Well, it was more like they were staring at my giant cactus hands, but that was technically still me.

"Hey, guys." I waved with the cactus hand that wasn't hitting the ceiling. I gestured to the deity who was still sitting among his pile of clothes. "Meet Quetz. Quetz, these are my cousins, Miry and Nando."

"Hey," Miry said numbly.

"*H-Hola,*" Nando said, taking off his glasses to clean the lenses.

"Nice to see you again." Quetz chuckled and pushed himself off the floor. "I guess I have a new nickname."

I grimaced. "Sorry. Do you mind?"

Quetz shook his head. "Not at all."

"Great!" I cheered. "Oh, and that's Daniel. He's kind of been helping us along the way."

Quetz nodded. "Good to meet you, as well."

Daniel didn't say anything back. He stared at Quetz with wide eyes and shuddering breaths. A shadow crossed his face, and he suddenly tightened his jaw. Like he was stopping himself from saying something.

A pang of sympathy rolled through me. Daniel had told us

that he hadn't heard from Tláloc, his deity, and here I was, right next to mine. Daniel's eyes shifted, and it seemed like he was torn between sadness, anger, and jealousy.

If I were in his position, I might've felt the same.

"Your deity is Quetzalcóatl," Miry said, shifting her gaze from my cactus hands to my face.

"Yeah. And guess what." I raised my left hand toward the ceiling. "I figured out *why*."

I pushed my magic outward, and just like with my right hand, my left hand grew into a long cactus that bumped against the ceiling and made more flecks of paint fall to the floor.

"Can we please not destroy my university?" the professor said into her hand.

Quetz and I winced. "Sorry," we said at the same time.

As Quetz told me to relax my muscles and slowly pull back my hands, I saw Miry smile a little bit.

"I'm glad you've got it," she said. She sounded genuine, but there was still a tone of frustration in her voice.

"Congratulations," Professor Jiménez said as I slowly coaxed my cacti-hands into becoming my normal, non-green hands. "Now that you've officially claimed your power, I can start the ceremony that formally acknowledges you as a member of the Archivists."

"But we still need to activate Miry's power," Daniel said.

"How?" Miry asked, raking a hand through her hair. "I'm pretty sure my powers are from Chalchiuhtlicue, but I don't know why! It's not like I can call her and ask."

The professor hummed.

"Maybe not here," she said. "This is a long shot, and I'm not sure if it'll work… But I think I know a place where she might hear you."

26

SUMMER SCHOOL. YAY.

MIRY

"Why didn't you tell me about this?" Daniel asked.

Profesora Gabriela gave Daniel a sad smile. "Because I knew you'd try it. Again and again, even if you never got an answer."

Daniel nodded, but said nothing.

Ada, Fer, and I shared a look. We were in the teacher's lounge, and Quetzalcóatl had loaned us some of his vast amounts of clothing to replace the damp rags we were wearing.

I was *finally* free of my American flag t-shirt and soaked jeans. But now I had an enormous tie-dye shirt that hung loosely over my body, as well as a set of bright orange bell bottoms.

Did I pick this outfit? No. Was it the only thing roughly my size? Yes.

Ada, on the other hand, had somehow found a yellow maxi dress that she'd trimmed to her size with a pair of office scissors. The dress' hem looked like it'd been yanked out of a paper shredder, but it worked for her.

Since Fer hadn't gotten completely soaked, he was still in the short-sleeved shirt and jeans he'd picked out in the morning. He glanced over at Daniel and rubbed his forehead in thought.

To the side, the guy who was somehow the physical representation of *light itself*, stopped rifling through his collection of snake-patterned tights. Quetz gave Daniel a smile I think was meant to be sympathetic.

I didn't know what was going on in Daniel's head, and only Profesora Gabriela and Quetz seemed to know what was happening.

"All right." Profesora Gabriela stepped around the stacks of clothing, nearly colliding into a set of over-sized hoodies. "The plan is to get you to the Spiritual World. Once you're there, call for Chalchiuhtlicue. There's only a chance that she'll hear you, but it's more likely she'll respond than if you call her from here."

"Okay…" Ada said slowly. "How do we do that?"

"Simple," the professor said. "We make a portal."

The memory of the two women chasing us with eagles and crocodiles flashed in my mind, and I shuddered. They'd used a portal that time, and what came out of that wasn't good.

"Are you serious?" Ada asked. "Cool!"

As you can see, Ada dreaded this whole "portal" thing much less than I did.

"So, how do we make a portal?" Ada asked. "Can *you* do it?"

"I can't. I may have been a magic teacher, but I'm not a disciple."

"What?" Fer asked. He took a step toward the professor, wobbling in place when he almost made a stack of trench coats fall to the floor. "I thought you had to be a disciple to use magic."

"Not necessarily," the professor said. "You have to be a disciple to use a deity's magic, but there are Archivists who use magic without being a disciple. We just have a more… general style. Which I can explain to you later, if you want."

After a moment, Fer nodded. "That... Yeah. That'd be great."

"So, getting back to portals," Ada said. "If you can't make one, who can?"

"A lot of people," the professor said.

I rolled my eyes. "Really? Go figure."

The professor chuckled and *finally* pulled off that puffer jacket of hers. I still have no idea how she didn't feel warm with it on. "Only disciples from three deities can make portals into the Spiritual World," she said.

"Which ones?" I asked.

"I'll give you a hint. They all have pyramids."

"Tláloc," Fer said, glancing over at Daniel.

"Quetz," Ada said, peering over at the deity who was now zipping up a set of gladiator sandals to match his dark gray cowboy hat.

"... and Chalchi," I said.

Ada raised an eyebrow. *"Chaal-chee?"*

"You call Quetzalcóatl 'Quetz'."

"Fair point."

"They have the biggest presence at the ruins, so they have the biggest connection to the Spiritual World," the professor explained. "Disciples of Tláloc and Chalchiuhtlicue can do it the easiest. For disciples of Quetzalcóatl, it's incredibly draining, and it takes much longer, but they can still manage it."

"Can I try?" Ada asked. "I mean, if it's okay. It's just... portals sound *so* cool!"

"I doubt a brand new magic user like you will have the stamina to finish it," Profesora Gabriela said. "But if you want to, go for it."

"Is that a good idea?" I asked. "What if she needs to use her magic again?" The rain was blocking the sun, and sunset wasn't far off. If Ada used her magic now, she wouldn't be able to fuel up again until tomorrow.

"We should be safe for now," Daniel said quickly. "What's

important is getting your powers unlocked as quickly as possible. That's what—what Chalchiuhtlicue needs you to do. Right?"

I nodded slowly. "Right."

He wasn't wrong. We did need to unlock our powers, but I'd felt weird about Daniel from the moment I saw him in Fer's car. Sure, he'd helped us out, but there was something in the way his leg kept bouncing that made me keep an eye on him.

"Why don't you open a portal?" I asked Quetz.

The deity sighed. "I can do it for myself. But..."

"It's been a while since he's taken other people to the Spiritual World," the professor said. "Even deities can have trouble with magic."

"You get so overwhelmed you stop being able to do even basic stuff?" Ada said. "Yeah, I get it."

"Are you sure this is a good idea?" I asked.

"We're in a controlled space," Profesora Gabriela said. "And I have experience teaching beginners magic. If anything gets out of control, I can handle it. If she wants to try it, I see no reason why she shouldn't."

"Sweet!" Ada elbowed me in the arm. "What's the big worry? Best-case scenario, you talk to your deity. Worst-case scenario, you get to be smug about it."

I groaned. "Okay, *fine*. Let's do this portal shit."

Following the professor's instructions, Fer, Daniel, and I stood a few steps away from Ada. That was surprisingly difficult, since most of the room was either cramped with desks or occupied by stacks of mutli-colored clothing.

"Feel the magic in your chest," the professor said. "Feel how it moves within you, calling on you to use it. Channel it through your shoulders, down your arms, and out of your body. But don't create your cacti. Instead, let the energy flow out of you *exactly* as it is. As a pure magical force that wants to return to the world it came from."

"Okay," Ada said, as she closed her eyes and held out her hands. "I can do this."

I smirked. "Unless you need me to step in."

Ada, who still had her eyes closed, smirked back. "Not yet, Miry."

My cousin took in a deep breath. When she let it out, a river of amber magic flowed from her hands.

A trickle of heat seeped into the room. It was slow at first, but as Ada let out more and more of her magic, the heatwave grew. It rushed out of her fingertips, circling the four of us in a bubble of warmth that made the back of my neck sweat.

And around my cousin was an amber colored aura. It surrounded her chest, her arms, and the very tips of her fingers.

When Ada had used her magic earlier, with the needle nails and the needle sword, I couldn't see her magic. But when I walked into the office and saw her turn her hands into giant cacti, I could literally *see* waves of magic surrounding her. And as she was trying to create a portal, I saw the amber glow surround her again, in steady waves of heat and energy.

It reminded me of the time I used my magic to locate the book in Coyoacán. Or to read the hidden message at the museum. It was like a sixth sense that let me pierce through an invisible curtain, laying the world's magic bare before me.

At the time, I thought I could see the aura because that was what happened when a disciple fully activated their powers. Or that maybe it was a side effect of the powers of Quetzal-cóatl. But I wouldn't realize until later that I was dead wrong.

I looked at Ada, swimming in a magical amber glow, and felt the familiar feeling of jealousy climb up to my throat.

We had to go to the Spiritual World because of me. Because *I* couldn't figure it out. And despite the fact that I might've been able to make portals easier than Ada, at that moment, I was useless.

"Think of that first moment you realized you were in the

Spiritual World," the professor said to Ada. "The first moment you saw the purple sky. The obsidian moon."

"The shining pyramids," Ada added.

Beside us, Ada closed her eyes and stretched out her hands. More heat wafted out of her, and the professor hummed happily as the warmth hit her. Amid piles of clothing, Quetz smiled in approval, but he wasn't fully focused on Ada. He shifted his gaze from side to side, like Fer sometimes does when he's in deep thought about something.

"So how are we gonna contact Chalchi in the Spiritual World?" I asked. "Just call out her name?"

"It's an option," the professor said. "It worked for Samuel when he needed to talk to Huehuetéotl. I think they spent an hour playing chess."

I immediately turned to Daniel. "I thought you said that it had been a while since anyone had seen a deity in person?" That's what he said at the museum. After I told him I met Chalchiuhtlicue at Coyoacán.

Daniel winced like he'd been struck.

"What?" Profesora Gabriela exclaimed. "That's ridiculous! Out of all the pantheons on Earth, the deities from Mesoamerican pantheons interact with humans the most."

"It's one of the perks," Quetz added. He absentmindedly kicked at a pile of orange socks. "I don't have to worry about the world going to pieces if I'm not supervising it, and I have less rules about interacting with mortals."

"Case in point." The professor turned to Daniel. "Is this because of Tláloc?"

"What about Tláloc?" I asked.

Daniel *tsked*. "Tláloc... hasn't been seen in a long time. He still picks disciples, but doesn't say anything. None of us have talked to him in years."

The way Daniel said it, he wasn't just sad.

He was *angry*.

A surge of warmth surrounded us as Ada pushed a new

wave of magic around her. The heat grew around us, so much so that my underarms were sweating.

"Hey, Professor," Ada said in a strained voice. "Can I ask you a question?"

"Go for it."

"What were the pum-eagles we saw at the pyramids?"

"Pum-eagles?"

"Yeah! When we got sent to the Spiritual World place, we saw these giant pumas with eagle wings! Is there a legend for that or something?"

"No." The professor paused for a moment. "... No. There isn't. There's no reason a creature like that should exist at the pyramids unless... Maybe..."

"Unless what?" Fer asked.

"Unless they were illusions," the professor said.

Behind her, Quetz furrowed his eyes.

"Did the creatures disappear after you touched them?" Profesora Gabriela asked.

"Yeah," I said. "After we hit 'em twice. But how are they illusions? The spiders that chased us at the park disappeared after we hit them, but they seemed pretty real to me."

"Illusions are temporary manifestations of energy," the professor explained. "They can take the shape of almost anything, and they can affect the real world. But their power doesn't last long. When something touches them, their energy bonds are severed. That's why they disappear so quickly."

"So they aren't actually a threat?" I asked.

She shook her head. "Not necessarily. Because they're illusions, they can take many forms. Let's say there's an illusion of a parrot. You can make the parrot disappear if you touch it, but the parrot can still scratch you and bite you until you make it go away."

"So... you can make illusions of anything," I said.

"Not quite," the professor said. "From what I've heard from disciples in other pantheons, it takes a lot of energy and a lot of time to design a new illusion from scratch. The more complicated the illusion, the harder it is to create. That's why almost every illusion is based on an object, animal, or person that the illusionist is familiar with. But with enough practice, an illusionist could theoretically create creatures that don't exist."

"So the pum-eagles were illusions!" Ada said with a laugh. "Daniel, why didn't you mention that illusions are a thing—*aaah*!"

Around us, the constant wave of magic fluttered. The temperature dipped for a moment, and some of the heat was lost. The amber waves of magic that had surrounded my cousin faltered.

"Calm down!" the professor said sternly. "Stay. Still. Don't think about anything else other than the portal."

"But—"

"Daniel didn't mention it because Archivists rarely deal with them," the professor said. "Don't focus on it. Focus on your magic."

Ada nodded and splayed her fingers outward. She grunted in effort as she refocused herself, and more waves of magic fell out from her hands.

I kept my eyes on Daniel.

The bubble of warmth grew in temperature again, and I could feel the heat expanding around us.

"That's it," the professor said in approval. "You're about a quarter of the way there."

"A quarter!?" Ada exclaimed.

Profesora Gabriela laughed. "I told you it takes a while. Just hold steady and let the magic do its work. But don't expect to show up at the pyramids."

"Why not?" I asked.

"Portals can only take you to the same spot in the Spiritual World," the professor explained. "If you're really good, you can travel within a ten kilometer radius. But we're far away from Teotihuacán. If you want to go to the Spiritual Pyramids, you need to open a portal at the ruins."

"That's inconvenient," Ada grunted out. "If distance didn't matter, this would be the best spell ever! You could get from here to Arizona!"

"Or from Ciudad Satélite to Coyoacán," I said.

Daniel raised his head.

"Very good," said a woman.

A woman who was *not* Profesora Gabriela.

To the side of the room, next to a small puddle that had formed beneath a leaking window, was a woman. She was tall, with a sharp nose, a sapphire blue dress that ended at her feet, and two long braids that nearly grazed the floor.

I scoffed. "Chalchi?"

27

THE CAKE—AND EVERYTHING ELSE—IS A LIE

MIRY

I stared in absolute shock as Chalchi, the deity we were trying to contact, seamlessly wove her way through the waist-high stacks of tank tops and bomber jackets.

"Chalchiuhtlicue!?" Daniel yelled.

Chalchi ignored all of us in favor of walking toward Quetz. Even as I kept blinking and stuttering at the fact that she just *showed up.*

"Hello, Quetzalcóatl," Chalchi said. "What are you thinking right now?"

Quetz blinked and shook his head roughly. "I-I don't know what I'm thinking. Things—memories—everything feels jumbled."

"But you understand that something is wrong here," Chalchi said softly. She placed her hands on his shoulders and squeezed. "You've been keeping an eye on Ada. Just like I've been keeping an eye on Miry."

"When I could." Quetz pressed his eyes into his hands. "Something—I know *something.*"

I stuttered. "C-Chalchi, what—"

"Shhh!" Ada hissed. The warmth around us shifted as Ada

turned to face the two deities. "They're having a moment. Don't ruin it."

Fer was staring at the two deities like he'd just seen a cartoon come to life. Daniel opened and closed his fists, and the professor watched the scene fondly.

"You've gotta be kidding me," I muttered under my breath. We had been going through this whole portal thing so I could get a chance to talk to Chalchi, and now she's just *here?*

Ada grabbed my arm, and it was the only thing stopping me from walking over and asking Chalchi what the hell was going on.

"I don't—I don't know—I don't know anything," Quetz cried out. "I—I—"

"What's my name?" Chalchi asked in a calm voice.

Quetz paused for a moment before whispering, "Chalchi-uhtlicue."

"And what's yours?"

"Quetzalcóatl." Quetz grimaced. "My mind is telling me to remember. But I don't know *what* to remember."

"Don't overthink it," Chalchi said. "Don't go far into the past. Just think about today. What was strange about today?"

Quetz grimaced like he was in pain. "Daniel."

The four of us humans turned to Daniel.

His leg stopped bouncing.

"I *knew* it," I hissed.

"Miry," Chalchiuhtlicue said, "what did you realize about Daniel?"

"He traveled across Mexico City faster than he should've been able to," I answered. "He went from Satélite to Coyoacán in less than five minutes. He got from Neza to el Ángel in less than 30. With *traffic.* He even found the time to get us towels before meeting us at the embassy!"

Chalchi gently placed her hands on Quetz's shoulders. "Quetzalcóatl, is there a spell that would let Daniel do all that?"

"I—" Quetz gasped. "The instant teleportation portal. The only one that can transport you across the country."

"But that's *impossible*," Profesora Gabriela said. "Only the deities have that power, and they can't pass it on to their disciples! At least... that *shouldn't* be possible..."

Daniel laughed. "The power of gods is greater than you think, Profesora."

"Chalchiuhtlicue," Quetz whispered, "is it really..."

"Yes," Chalchi said. "I'm afraid it is."

Daniel was still staring at the floor. He hadn't made a move to run, or fight, or anything. And yet my mind whispered to me.

Run, it said. *Run, run*, run.

But I couldn't run from this. Not when Daniel was right there.

"Why do you keep saying 'god'?" I asked. "I know that was on the inscription at the museum, but the professor, the books, everything else is calling them deities. So why do you keep calling Tláloc a god?"

Profesora Gabriela sucked in a breath.

"You're right," Daniel said. "He isn't one."

"None of us are," Chalchi said firmly. "None of us are gods."

"You keep saying that." Daniel laughed, but there was no humor in his voice. "And yet you play with us. You like to sit back and see us suffer."

"We don't," Quetz said. He still had Chalchi's hands on his shoulders, but he squared his back and stared Daniel dead in the eye. "We care about humans more than is good for us."

"Then why are you here?" Daniel asked. "To mock me? To tell me that Tláloc *hates* me?"

"I am here because my husband cannot be," Chalchi said. "I am here to offer you a chance to turn away from this path you've foolishly chosen to follow."

"Hah! If that's what you want from me, then Tláloc

should've told me this *himself*." Daniel turned to me, to Ada, and grimaced. "I didn't want to do this."

"Don't—" Chalchi cried out.

But Chalchi didn't get a chance to finish her sentence. Because just as she spoke, Daniel raised his hand and snapped his fingers.

There was a blur of blue as I saw Fer run to Daniel and grab his arm, but it was too late.

The world around me spun in a kaleidoscope of brown, yellow, and black. And I suddenly crashed onto a patch of hard, dusty earth.

28

HEADBANGING IN THE DESERT

MIRY

ADA AND I FELL ONTO A DUSTY PLAIN DOTTED WITH DARK green bushes. The ground was hard and cracked, more like the environment you'd find in Mexico's northern deserts than the central mountain region, and even the air felt different. I took in a deep breath and more air rushed into my lungs than was possible in the high, smoggy altitude of Mexico City.

"I didn't do that!" Ada cried immediately.

"I kind of figured," I said, coughing as bits of dust flew into my mouth.

A quick glance upward and I was greeted with a deep purple sky. To my right, the silver moon cast a bright light over the land. We were in the Spiritual World, all right, but it wasn't by our choice.

Ada and I shakily pushed ourselves into a standing position and we rubbed our legs from where we'd crashed to the ground. I dusted the dirt off of my tye-dye shirt.

"You okay?" I asked.

"Oh, yeah," Ada grunted—the entire left side of the yellow maxi coated in a thin layer of dirt. "I just *love* getting thrown through a portal that isn't mine after wasting all of my energy. It's a fun time."

I wish I could say she was exaggerating, but she wasn't. Ada was taking in heavy breaths, like she'd just run a marathon. Considering she used up almost all her magic to finish a difficult portal spell that she never got to finish, that's not a bad comparison.

Ada spun her head around, which made her curly hair bounce around her. "Where's Nando?"

I gulped. "And where's Daniel?"

Ada placed her hands around her mouth. "Nando!" she yelled into the void. "You here?"

"Not so loud!" I hissed. "What if Daniel—"

There was no sound, no hint that anyone was arriving. All I saw was an empty space in front of us, and a moment later, Daniel was standing in it.

He was about ten or so meters away from us, panting and holding his right arm to his chest.

"Your cousin's quick." Daniel rubbed at his wrist, where two long scratch marks were dripping blood down onto the dirt. "But not quick enough."

"What did you do to him?" Ada demanded. She took a step forward, and a wave of amber magic flew out of her pointer finger. It extended her nail bed into the needle sword I'd seen her use before, but even that spell had Ada panting harder than before.

"Nothing," Daniel said. "But he did make me miss my drop."

I barked out a laugh. "Go, Fer."

Twice, I thought in my mind. *At his forehead.*

I pushed my magic to my left arm, and I winced as I felt two hairs from my forearm yank themselves away. They crashed in the very center of Daniel's forehead, making him stumble backward.

"*Argh*," he cried out. "Nice try, Miry. But that trick won't work on me."

He moved his arms in a quick set of twists and turns. He

raised up his chest, puffed up his cheeks, and splayed his hands outward.

We heard the spiders before we saw them. The arachnids shuffled and chittered between the bushes and across the dusty ground.

This was more than the spiders we'd seen at the park. This was a wave so dense that they came at us from the front, our right side, our left side, in droves that scuttled across the desert.

Toward *us*.

"*Shit*," I hissed.

Ada and I bolted into a run, sprinting between the desert's bushes as Ada frantically waved her needle sword behind her. She hit a wave of spiders that got just a bit too close, sending them scuttling about.

"Illusions!" Ada cried. She tripped on the hem of her long dress, and I caught her arm before she could face plant into the floor. "He's the illusionist!"

I gasped as my mind flashed back to Daniel's fight with Lorenzo at the museum. To his fight against Lourdes and Teresa during the car chase. Every time that Daniel used his water blasts, they would dissipate after two hits from Lorenzo's water cannons. When I was watching it, I assumed that his water had evaporated into the air.

But it hadn't.

"Even his water magic was an illusion!" I cried as we ran across the Spiritual World's desert.

"You're right, Miry," Daniel said.

Behind us, Daniel trudged behind the hoard of chittering spiders. At a pace that was trying and failing to match our running speed.

"I hoped we'd be able to use you before the Archivists found you," he said between harsh and angry breaths. "But it seems it's better if you're out of the way."

"Out of the way?" I said. "What do you mean by—"

"Trap!" Ada yelled. "Giant trap ahead!"

I followed Ada's gaze to a large hole that had been dug in the ground. It wasn't "giant", as Ada had hyperbolized, but it was definitely big. It was about 30 or so meters away, and it had been hidden by a set of green bushes that surrounded its perimeter. But now that we were closer to it, she and I could see it.

We turned to veer away from the hole, but the spiders surrounded the dusty earth we were about to cross.

"Do you think the gods will help you?" Daniel shouted. "I worked for the Archivists for *years*, and all they gave me was a dagger! Everything I did, I did for free, because they're too broke to offer anything in return!"

"Chalchiuhtlicue!" I called out to the air. "Can you hear me?"

"She won't come!" Daniel roared. "She doesn't care about you! The gods don't care about *any* of us! I spent so much of my life learning Tláloc's magic, and one day he just disappeared! He doesn't even *try* to talk to his disciples! Not even when we *beg* him to!

"But this god—*my* god—he listens. He answers! And for that, I will do what he asks."

Ada slashed her needle sword at the horde of spiders. We turned on our heel to sprint around the trap from the other side, but the spiders started crowding around that side, too.

With a heavy grunt, Ada morphed the pointer finger on her left hand into another needle sword.

"I could use some help here!" she yelled.

"You think I don't know that!?" I yelled back.

Ada slashed at the spiders with her double needle swords. "I said that my name's Ada, that I like BTS, and that I'm a Mexican-American. After that, I unlocked my powers! Try that?"

I didn't want to. But as the spiders cut off our only escape route, I didn't have much of a choice.

"My name's Miry!" I shouted to the sky. "I'm, *ugh*, I'm Mexican-American and Jimin is my bias! Chalchiuhtlicue picked me! You hear me?"

I waited for a feeling of warmth in my chest. A pressure that would tell me I'd done *something* right.

I felt nothing.

"Maybe switch your bias to Suga?" Ada suggested.

"I am not abandoning Jimin like that!"

We couldn't run. The spiders had covered the only way around the hole in the ground, and the hoard was still coming. Slowly pushing us, step by step, toward the desert trap.

"Why did Chalchiuhtlicue pick you?" Ada cried. She swung her swords, getting rid of the frontline spiders, but the creatures kept coming. We were now less than 20 meters away from the trap.

"I don't know, Ada! That's the reason we came here to begin with!"

"Then—think!"

"What's the point? She's the deity of *lakes*. There's no water around here!"

"So?" Ada swung wildly at the sea of spiders. "It's not like you've been using water so far!"

"I—"

I hadn't.

This whole time, I hadn't been controlling water at all. Even though water was replenishing my energy, it wasn't what I was using to fight back.

If I had to think about what a water disciple's attacks would be, I'd say they'd be something like Lorenzo's water cannons at the museum. I wouldn't say it'd be *hair*.

We shuffled backward as the spiders got closer. Ten meters away from the trap.

I thought back to my conversation with Chalchi at Coyoacán. My bullies were laughing at me, calling me names, and telling me to put on a circus show for them. They wanted to see me as their plaything they could make fun of, and they used the fact that I wasn't fully Mexican to do that.

And Chalchi had stopped them. And she told me that I didn't have to listen to them.

"That's why she picked me…" I said softly. "She wanted to show me that it's okay."

"That what's okay!?" Ada yelled as she swatted her swords at the league of spiders.

"To be different," I said. "To be more than what people see you as."

The spiders pushed us closer. We were two meters away from the trap.

Ada shrieked and sliced her needles too close to the ground. Some spiders *poofed* into mist, and her swords split in two with a loud *crack*.

"*Aaah!*" Ada cried.

"You okay!?" I said.

"That feels *so* much worse than breaking a nail!" she hissed in pain.

The horde of spiders stopped when we were less than a meter away from the hole. Behind them, Daniel trudged his way toward us. "There's an easy way to do this. You two jump in, or I make you jump in." The spiders chittered. "What's it gonna be?"

"Miry…" Ada said tentatively. "I'm out of juice, so please, *please* tell me you've figured it out."

Daniel sighed and rubbed at his eyes. "Miranda Rivera, do you really want to do this?"

I scoffed.

"My name's Miranda *Donaldson* Rivera," I said. "And I might not be fully Mexican, but I've still got the powers of a Mexican deity in me. And guess what else?" I felt for the magic in my chest, and smirked. "I'm real damn tired of people who don't care about me trying to push me around."

And just like that, the warmth in my chest exploded.

It rippled outward, from my lungs to my legs and to the tips of my eyelashes. It was like an ocean had burst forth within me, flooding me with warmth. The magic channeled itself upward. Up my bones, my muscles, through my skull, and to the crown of my head.

Two, I thought. *Part my hair in two.*

I let the magic rush up to my head and to the roots of every hair on my head. Power swirled within the beads of sweat on my head, mixing into the natural oils in my hair. My magic synergized with it, and it expanded to cover every single strand of hair I had.

I pushed everything outward. I could even feel my hair growing, enough to make the longest strands just barely reach my knees. I parted my hair into two separate sections of hair that I fanned out around me. I raised the strands of hair high above my head, letting them extend outward in a sea of black tresses that made me feel like the reincarnation of Medusa.

I wasn't controlling the water from a lake, from a fountain, or even from a water bottle. Instead, I was controlling the sweat on my body. Before, I had used drops of sweat to pull strands of hair out of my head and launch them as projectiles. Now I used that sweat to move and control the hair flowing from my head.

"Woah," Ada breathed.

Daniel clenched his fists. "I see we're doing this the hard way."

And with that, the spiders charged.

I pulled Ada behind me and hunched close to the desert floor. My hair wasn't long enough to attack something on the ground while I was standing, so I bent my neck downward to give my hair the longest range possible.

Through the small gaps in my thick hair, I saw the spiders come close. And when they were just centimeters away from reaching me, I had my hair bash against the ground.

The first wave of spiders burst into mist immediately. They

disappeared under my thick mass of hair, and when the next wave came, I made my hair crash onto the floor with another *bang.*

I smirked. These spiders, these *illusions,* were a two-hit K.O.—as long as it gets hit twice, they vanish. It didn't matter what you hit them with, or how hard. You could even hit them with a strand of hair.

And when I hit these spiders, I was hitting them with thousands.

Death by a thousand cuts, as the old saying goes.

"To your right!" Ada yelled.

I angled my head right and made my hair slam against the ground. A wave of spiders that had charged toward us from that side burst into smoke, and I grinned.

"Spider wave to the left!" Ada called out.

With my head bowed, I followed my cousin's lead as she told me where the nearest wave of spiders was coming from. My hair was long enough that it could take out the spiders before they ever got close, and it was thick enough that I could use it to cover a wide surface around us.

It was working. This half-baked spur of the moment plan was *working.*

Daniel hadn't moved. He didn't even walk toward us. He just stood there with a snarl on his face.

"Last wave!" Ada yelled. "Dead ahead! Think you can take it?"

I grinned.

I brought my hair up, fanned it out as much as I could, and slammed it down onto the dusty earth. And with that, the final wave vanished into the air.

I breathed heavily as tension fell out of me. I was feeling a bit thirsty, but I still had magic in me. In fact, I had a lot more in me. More than I did yesterday.

But my body felt warm. Even warmer than when I'd first unlocked my magic.

"What the hell did you want to use us for?" Ada screamed at Daniel. "Why the hell did you lie to us? Why are we even here?"

I raised my head and winced at the pain in the back of my neck. Daniel was there, standing a few meters away from us and looking… tired. His shoulders hunched over, and he slowly ran a hand over his face.

He didn't summon more illusionary spiders, but the anger in his eyes still burned like the sun.

I stood up and growled, "What. Do. You. Want?"

Daniel slammed one of his fists against his thigh. "I don't have the energy to deal with you." He raised his head to the sky and called out, loud and clear, "*Señor de la Tierra, come to me!*"

A swirling mist appeared between us and Daniel, swarming in a sea of purple.

"That's not good," Ada muttered.

"Ya think?" Sweat pooled at my nape.

From the swirling sphere in front of us, we heard the deep, low growl of a puma.

Ada and I shuffled backward. And just when we saw the outline of a claw pierce its way through the portal, she and I were wrapped up in a swirling sphere of thick orange heat.

A hot wind blew our ridiculous clothing in every direction. It tangled my loose hair into a flurry of knots, blowing it in front of my face to the point where I could barely see. The rush of wind lasted for at least half a minute before finally settling down.

When I could push the hair out of my face, I found myself staring at an old, green Volkswagen Jetta.

Fer's Jetta.

"I gotta be dreaming," I muttered.

I turned to the sky. When we'd left, there was a storm going on. But even though it wasn't raining right now, I knew we were back in our world.

Because between the lingering gray clouds, I could see the colors of a sunset mixed in with the light blue sky.

Ada pushed the frizzy curls out of her face. "No way. We're… We're back!"

"Hada! Miry!" Ada and I turned to the sound of the voice. It was Fer, sprinting his way to the damp parking lot.

We met in the middle. Fer threw his arms around us and pulled us in for a hug so tight it pushed the air out of my lungs.

"You're okay!" Fer exclaimed. "You're okay!"

"Y-Yeah, Nando," Ada croaked, her voice going squeaky due to how tight the hug was. "We're okay! Right, Miry?"

"Yeah," I said, my voice no better than Ada's. "We're good, Fer. Promise."

Fer let out a shaky breath and loosened his grip on us. "You're okay," he repeated. "You're okay."

Our cousin gave us another tight squeeze before letting us go. When he did, I saw bits of dried blood beneath his fingernails.

"Fer, are you okay?" I asked.

"Dude, your hand!" Ada said.

"Don't worry about me," he said. "It's Daniel's blood. I'm okay. And *you're* okay."

Ada and I nodded wearily.

"How are we back?" Ada asked. When Fer didn't answer right away, she glanced my way.

I shook my head. "Don't look at me."

"Look at *me*."

I turned toward the ramp leading into the parking lot. There was Quetzalcóatl, panting in exhaustion as he dragged his gladiator sandals across the wet pavement. Behind him was Chalchiuhtlicue, holding her hands out when Quetz swayed from side to side.

"Quetz!?" Ada yelled.

"Yeah." Quetz stopped and put his hands on his knees. "I… am *never*… doing that again. Portals into the Spiritual World are fine. Portals into the Spiritual World halfway across Mexico are *not* fine!"

I glanced around in confusion. *Is it just me*, I thought, *or are there more cars now than there were before?*

"Quetz, what happened?" Ada asked.

"Quetzalcóatl brought you back," Chalchi said calmly. "He performed a spell he has not attempted in a very long time. I am proud."

"If you're proud," Quetz said, though he sounded like he couldn't quite believe it himself, "then you can fund my next shopping spree." The deity pushed himself into a standing position and turned toward the building. *"Come out of there!"*

A slew of familiar faces exited the Faculty of Architecture.

First was Profesora Gabriela, who had put on her puffer jacket again. Then it was Lourdes, whose makeup was now smudged, and Teresa, the death-glare lady who'd been with her in the car. Behind them was the older woman with the face mask and workout clothes, and she was holding the hand of a limping middle-aged man with a thick mustache and a Cruz Azul cap.

The same cap I'd seen on the other stalker on the bus.

And trailing at the back was a man with long hair tied into a bun, a short-sleeved t-shirt, and old sneakers that were stained with multi-colored flecks of paint.

It was Lorenzo. The man from the bus and the Museum of Anthropology.

Daniel's best friend.

Ada and I were stunned silent as the group came forward. They stopped a few paces away from us, but after Profesora Gabriela nudged Lorenzo's arm, the man stepped forward.

"Are you all right?" Lorenzo asked.

"Yeah…" Ada said.

The memory of him following us flashed in my mind. He was there, on the bus, and I was certain he was there to do something to me.

Ada and I nervously glanced around. "Professor *Heem-en-ehz*," Ada said cautiously. "What's going on?"

Profesora Gabriela sighed. "A misunderstanding. A terrible misunderstanding." She gestured to the men and women around her. "These men and women are Archivists of Teotihuacán, and they were trying to help you."

29

CAN I GET A NAP, PLEASE?

ADA

I huffed in disbelief as I stared at the semi-familiar group of faces. After all the rushing around the city—going from plaza to museum to university—I was suddenly in front of the people who we'd been running away from.

The people who were, apparently, the actual Archivists we were meant to find in the first place!

"I'm sorry for all the confusion I've caused," Lorenzo said. "I truly am."

Behind him, Professor Jiménez and the rest of the Archivists gave us a sea of apologetic looks. They hung back, near the cars, but close enough to hear anything we said. Nando and Chalchi were on the sidewalk and keeping an eye on Quetz, who was sprawled out on the damp floor.

"Ah, it's okay," I said to Lorenzo. "It just sent us on a huge wild goose chase across the city, got us chased by flying crocodiles, and had us almost imprisoned in a giant hole in the Spiritual World. No biggie."

Yes, I was rambling a bit, but I was also dead tired. Okay, not *dead*-dead tired, since I was still breathing. But jeez did I want a *nap*.

Beside me, Miry growled.

An aura the color of deep sea blue extended itself around Miry's chest, enveloping her, her head, and each strand of her hair in a calming glow. I hadn't seen the glow until she fully unlocked the power of Chalchiuhtlicue in the Spiritual World's desert, but now I could see it clearly as her magic made her hair float around her like she was underwater.

When I saw all that, I was immediately convinced that it was a side effect of using the power of a deity of lakes. You know, because it was blue. It wasn't until the next day that I'd realized I was completely wrong.

"Why did you stalk us on the bus?" Miry asked Lorenzo.

"Miry—" I started.

"I'm not dropping these until he answers."

Lorenzo stared at the floor in… shame? "We were there to protect you."

I blinked. "You were *what*?"

"After Daniel left the Archivists, we were worried he was targeting new disciples," Lorenzo explained. "After Lourdes saw you buy the books, she called us and let us know where you were. We were meant to protect you in case Daniel or anyone else tried to hurt you, not… not scare you."

Miry scoffed. "Yeah. The daggers helped with that."

Lorenzo raised his head. "Daggers? We didn't have our daggers that night."

"But they were on your belts!" I cried. "They—" I cut myself off. "Were another illusion. If you didn't know they were there, they must've been an illusion!"

Miry grimaced. "How?"

"I don't know!" I said. "But it makes sense."

"But how did you track us to the museum?" Miry demanded.

Lorenzo sighed and pulled out his phone. "Do you remember the virus when you tried to access websites about Teotihuacán?"

Miry snarled. "You tracked our *phones*?"

Lorenzo nodded. "One of our members created a magical network that connects to any cell phone that gets transported into the Spiritual World. It sends a signal to any technology that gets close to it for two days and downloads a virus."

I scoffed. "Okay, impressive. But that sounds like a lot of work."

"It is," Lorenzo agreed. "It's meant to help identify potential new Archivists so we can watch over them while they complete the tasks. And to stop them from getting misinformation. But the magic is delicate. If you get exposed to too much magic, the signal disappears. And Daniel and I used a *lot* of magic at the museum."

"And you couldn't use that spell to get our numbers?" I asked. "Or send us text messages? You know, so you could call us and tell us what was happening?"

Lorenzo sighed. "Not with your phones."

"Why not?"

"Because your phones were made after 2017, and that was the last time we updated the spell."

I blinked. "Are you saying you couldn't contact us because the spell needs to get recast every time a new phone comes out? And you just, what, forgot about the update for six years?"

"We've been busy," Lorenzo said tiredly. "It's a difficult spell. And it hasn't been a priority until now."

"But if you were at the museum to 'watch over us'," Miry snarled, "why did you attack us?"

"He didn't," I said. "I mean, I'm *guessing* you didn't. You did turn the floor into a real-life ice rink, but it doesn't make sense that you'd attack us if you were there to help. But if it wasn't you, it must've been —"

"Daniel," Lorenzo groaned. "He made his illusions look like water."

Miry turned her gaze to Lourdes and Teresa, who were hanging out near the back of the small crowd. The tips of her hair flicked in warning. "What about you two? Why did you attack our car?"

Lourdes turned to Teresa and whispered something in her ear. Once she was done, Teresa shouted something in rapid-fire Spanish.

"Um, what did she say?" I asked.

"She says they thought our car was Daniel's," Miry translated. "There was an illusion making it look like his. When the real Daniel showed up, they didn't know which car had the real him, so they kept attacking both."

"But why were you so obsessed with attacking Daniel?" I asked them.

Lourdes replied in much calmer Spanish, and Miry translated. "'Because Daniel betrayed the Archivists.'"

"In a way," Lorenzo said sadly. "He abandoned Tláloc. In the name of something he considers to be his true 'god'."

"That explains the mumbling," I said. "What 'god' did he find?"

"We weren't sure," said the older man in a blue cap that had a logo for something called the Cruz Azul. "But I think we know now."

The man was roughly in his mid to late 50s, and he looked like a stereotypical Mexican dad you'd find in Arizona. He was short, with brown skin, a thick black mustache interspersed with white hairs, old loose jeans, and a belly you could see through his polo t-shirt.

The only thing that set him apart was the accent. It was still Mexican, but I'd spent enough time around Mexico City accents to hear the difference between it and a *norteño* one. The northern accent has more of a twang to it.

The older man gingerly stepped forward, but stayed far back enough that he wouldn't get slapped in the face by Miry's hair.

"After what Quetzalcóatl and Fernando have told us," he said, "and what you've seen... We think the so-called 'god' that

Daniel found is a spirit the Archivists have dealt with before. A very dangerous spirit."

I tugged at my dress. "When we were at the pyramids, a voice told us that we cracked a seal and set a spirit free," I said. "That's our fault. Is it actually?"

"He's not free *yet*," the man said. "But he's getting close."

Miry flicked her hair. "And who the hell are you?"

"He's *Jefe*," Lourdes chimed in.

The man—Jefe, apparently—placed a hand on his chest. "Fabián Pérez Santibáñez, disciple of Quetzalcóatl and leader of the Archivists." He gestured to the woman in workout clothes and grinned. "And this is Jessica. Disciple of Xipe Totec and my wonderful wife."

Jessica, who was still wearing a mask over her nose and mouth, waved at us. "Pleasure to meet y—*achooo*!"

The trees to the side of the parking lot shook, and bits of green leaves fell to the ground.

"She's a bit sick at the moment," Jefe explained. "When that happens, she isn't fully in control of her powers."

Jessica blew her nose in a tissue. "I'm getting better!"

"You should be at *home*," Jefe said. "Resting."

Back in the crowd of people, Teresa burst into another string of rapid-fire Spanish. Professor Jiménez and Lourdes said something to her in calming tones, but Teresa shrugged them off and said something else.

"What did she say?" I asked Miry.

"She's talking to Jefe," Miry translated. "She said he should also be resting because he got a needle to the leg."

"Oh!" I winced. "Oh, *yeah*, I did do that. Sorry."

"No need, no need," Jefe explained with a hasty wave of his hands. "I'll heal soon. And it was our fault for causing confusion. We thought that you spoke Spanish."

"We do!" I said. "Well, I don't. But Miry does."

"Then why did you run yesterday?" Lorenzo asked,

sounding genuinely confused. "I was trying to tell you that I wasn't a threat. That we were there to protect you."

Miry let go of her magic and let her hair drop down.

"I..." Miry ducked her head, using her hair to cover her face.

I cringed as I remembered the previous night. At the sight of Lorenzo and Jefe following us, Miry pretty much shut down. It was a flat out miracle I got her running. I remember Lorenzo yelling at us, but he was yelling in Spanish, and Miry was too far in her head to tell me what he was saying.

"It was a stressful night for her," I said. "Getting chased by two random guys kind of set off her nerves. She could barely hear me, and I was right next to her! Right, Miry?"

Miry nodded.

"So no worries," I said. "Right?"

"Right," Lorenzo said immediately. "Still... I really am sorry."

"... Thanks." Miry peeked a single eye out from behind her curtain of hair. "So you're a disciple of Chalchi?"

"Yes," Lorenzo said.

Miry nodded thoughtfully. "... You're good."

Lorenzo smiled a little. "I had a good teacher."

Miry and I immediately turned to Professor Jiménez.

"No, no. Not Gabi," Jefe said. "She's more of a general teacher. Lolo was trained by another disciple of Chalchi-uhtlicue. It's a—*¿cuál es la palabra?*"

"Apprenticeship?" Jessica supplied.

"Yes!" Jefe snapped his fingers. "Apprenticeship!"

"And I'm guessing Teresa was your apprentice?" I said, shuddering a bit when Teresa stared at me like I was about to shoot a needle nail at her.

"Yes," Jefe said. "She was."

"And she's giving me a death glare because I stabbed her old professor?"

"Very likely."

I rubbed my hands over my eyes. "Okay. Brain overload."

"The apprenticeship is explained in the clues," Jefe said. "You didn't read the books?"

"*Ugh.*" I groaned and stalked over to Nando's car. "Books, books, books. Why is everyone going on about these books?"

I yanked on the passenger seat, groaning even more when I realized it was locked. After Nando unlocked the door, I yanked the car door open and fished around the glove box for the book Miry found at the Coyoacán library.

El Mundo Antiguo was like the first two books we found at the bookstore. It was super thin, with a brightly-colored cover, and didn't have the author's name on the front cover. I flipped the pages in a fit of exhaustion and annoyance—

And immediately did a double-take.

I flipped back to the page that caught my eye—the interior title page—and did another double-take. And a triple-take. And a quadruple-take.

I ran over to my cousin. "Miry, look at this!"

"Look at what?" she asked.

"This!" I shoved the book in her face. "Look at the names of the authors!"

Miry gasped. "Roberto Rivera González y María Isabel Cortés Huerta."

"Abuelo and Abuela!" I flipped through the rest of the book, seeing names like Xochiquetzal, Mictlantecutli, and Mictecacihuatl flash on the pages. "They wrote this?"

"Yeah. And you know what that means?" Miry said. "They were Archivists."

"They were," Jefe said. He sniffed and rubbed his nose. "And they were some of the best until…"

"Until *what*?" Miry demanded.

"Their last mission," he said. "When they sealed the spirit."

My heart pounded in my chest.

"What happened?" I asked.

"We can't tell you," Jefe said.

"Why not?" I asked. "They're *our* grandparents. And they were Archivists! Like we are! Shouldn't that mean you *have* to tell us?"

"It's complicated," Jefe said, and I could hear the frustration in his voice. "We aren't allowed to contact your family. At all. Not unless one of you was chosen as a disciple."

"What?" Miry asked. "Why?"

"We can't tell you."

"So if you're not allowed to contact us," I asked, "and you make it *really* difficult to find you, how did Nando find Daniel?"

Lorenzo spun to face my cousin. "Fernando, *you* found Daniel?"

Nando winced again.

Everyone turned to stare at him.

"You said you found him on Facebook? No, LinkedIn!" I said. "Is that actually how you found him?"

Nando pressed his lips together. "Yes," he said, very quietly.

"We have a LinkedIn profile, but under a false company name," Lorenzo said. "We haven't used that in *years*. How did you know to look there?"

"Fer, what are you hiding?" Miry asked. "What are you keeping from us?"

"I..." The chorus of a random Bad Bunny song started playing, and Nando jumped. He fished around in his pocket until he pulled out his phone, sighing in relief as he read the name on the screen. "It's my mom! I have to answer this!"

Nando accepted the call and turned away from us. "*Hola, Mamá. ¿Todo bien?*"

"Wait, Nando!" I cried. "*Ugh*, why is this so *difficult*?"

"Don't ask me," Miry said.

Behind us, the group of Archivists whispered amongst each other, too low for me to pick out any words I might recognize.

"I didn't push him because we made that deal," I said, "but now…"

"Now's the time we get answers," Miry said. "After he finishes talking with Tía Sara."

"Why don't we just talk to him now?"

"And interrupt his talk with our aunt? Do you *want* Tío Rizo to kill you?"

"No, but—"

"*¡No!*" Nando cried out. "*Mamá, por favor dime que no—*"

The Archivists' whispers stopped.

"*Okei, okei.*" Nando sniffed. "*Sí. Ahorita vamos pa'llá.*" Nando nodded into the phone, and a rough shiver passed through his body. "*Yo también. Te quiero.*"

He hung up. "We need to go home."

Nando turned to us, and I swear I'll never forget his face for as long as I'll live.

Because that was the first day I ever saw him cry.

In less than a minute, Nando's face had turned red and blotchy. Tears fell from behind his giant glasses.

"What happened?" Miry asked.

Nando closed his eyes. "Abuelo had a stroke."

The Archivists gasped.

"*Está muerto,*" Nando whispered, and more tears fell from his eyes. "Abuelo… he died."

30

SOMETHING I NEVER NEEDED TO KNOW

ADA

JULY 11TH

SOMETHING I DIDN'T THINK I'D LEARN ON THIS TRIP: funerals in Mexico happen quick.

Not in the sense that they get finished fast. In that sense, it's more the opposite. The funeral lasts all day, with the family staying from mid-morning to late afternoon, sitting or standing around in a room while a large casket sits in the middle. Friends and people who can't be there from sunup to sundown come throughout the day, to pay respect and talk to family. So you talk, see people walk in with tired eyes and black clothing, and try to process the fact that the person in the casket was alive just yesterday.

Because yeah, funerals happen quick.

It happened so quick that my parents just barely made it from their trip to Aguascalientes. They arrived in clothes that were a bit too bright to work for a funeral, but they were the only formal outfits they had packed for their trip.

Aunt Lupe immediately scooped my mom in a hug, and the two of them cried into each other's shoulders.

It was a stroke, according to the paramedics. I don't know how they figured it out so fast. I don't know how I was still focused after getting hugs from people I barely knew just because they knew my grandfather. Miry translated and told me that they were saying sorry, and how hard it must be. Neither of us knew what to say to that.

I didn't pack any black clothes, so I spent the day in a black dress Miry had stuffed in the back of her closet. It was a bit tight around the chest area, but Aunt Lupe gave me a dark shawl to cover it.

Miry wore a dark blue dress that just barely passed the color threshold to be considered appropriate for a funeral. She had her hair in a messy bun so that our parents wouldn't notice that it'd grown in length, but I think that everyone was too focused on grieving to realize.

I felt terrible. Yeah, part of it was because my grandfather died, but another part was because people spent so much time worrying about me. It's not like I was like Miry, who kept staring at the casket. Or like my Uncle Rizo, who kept getting consoled by my mom and Aunt Lupe. Abuelo died, but I didn't get to know him well enough before the dementia kicked in. So I was stuck in an awkward limbo where I was grieving for a man I barely even knew.

After a while, my dad took me for a walk outside the funeral house.

"You look a little overwhelmed," he said.

"Just a bit." We strolled between people marching to attend one of the many funerals going on in the large house. There were clouds in the sky, but they were spread out enough that I could feel the sun's rays slowly replenish the magic reserves I'd drained the day before. "How are you doing?"

My dad sighed. "Better than your mom," he said. "I'm just happy that we were in Mexico this time."

I remembered when my grandmother died two years ago. It was midway through my exam season, and when I'd gotten home from school, Dad told me that Mom had rushed to the airport. He'd stayed behind so that I wouldn't be left alone in the house, and he was the one who broke the news to me.

Back then, I thought it was because my mom wanted to go be with her younger brother and sister. I thought that she didn't take me because I didn't know Abuela well and had finals. Now I realize it's because she was scrambling to actually make it to the funeral.

"Is Mom gonna be okay?" I asked Dad. "After Abuela died, she was… sad, but also something else?"

"She was relieved," Dad said.

"Relieved? Why?"

"Because it meant that the cancer was over."

I thought about it for a moment. About Abuelo, lying still in his bed, his mind so far gone that he couldn't even recognize his own granddaughter.

"I think I get it," I said. "You're sad that they're gone, but glad that they're not suffering anymore."

Dad nodded. "You ready to go back?"

"You can go ahead." I turned my head toward the thin rays of light piercing through the clouds. "I think I need a bit more time out here."

Regardless of what you might think, I wasn't standing out there to hide from the funeral. Or to take in the sun.

I was out there so I didn't have to look at Nando.

Out of everyone at the funeral, Nando was the worst off. My cousin spent most of the day staring at the casket and crying. He could barely even talk to Clara and Eduardo, meaning that my little cousins had to watch their big brother break down in front of them. It got so bad that Uncle Rizo and Aunt Sara had to take turns watching over him.

When I finally went back into the room, Nando was still there with red eyes, messed up hair, and an untucked black button-up. Miry was in a corner of the room, and I joined her. She was there because it was too overwhelming to talk to so many people at once, and I was there because I felt awkward standing around with nothing to do but grieve in public for hours.

Miry's eyes were a bit red, and all I could do was give her a smile I hoped was comforting.

By the time the funeral workers came to wheel out my grandfather's casket, it hadn't even been 24 hours since Nando had gotten the call from our aunt. My mom and her two siblings were saying their last goodbyes before their dad was carted away to get cremated, leaving Miry and me standing in the corner of the room.

"It's finally done," Miry said, sounding emotionally exhausted.

I took another glance around. "Is this really everyone?"

Miry nodded. "You noticed it, too?"

"Yeah," I said in a half-whisper. "None of the Archivists showed up."

"Even though Abuelo was supposedly an important member."

"Yep. I know they said they weren't allowed to contact us, but we've already met them! Shouldn't they have showed up today?"

"That's what I'm wondering." Miry pulled her phone from her shoulder bag. "And we can ask."

"You got their number?"

"Lorenzo gave me his WhatsApp. He said it's so we don't go through this miscommunication thing again, but I think it's because he feels bad for making me think he was a stalker."

"Nice!" I said, my voice a bit too loud for a funeral home.

Our parents, who were still next to my grandfather's casket, turned to us. Even Nando burst out of his funk to look over.

"Sorry!" I said. "I mean that Abuelo was a nice guy. Didn't mean to say it so loud."

"Subtle," Miry whispered.

"Oh, shut up," I whispered back. "Okay, so once we're out of here, you message Lorenzo and get him to spill."

"They won't tell you." Miry and I jumped at the sound of Nando's voice. At some point in time, Nando had walked over to us. He'd stopped crying, but his eyes were still red. That was the first thing he'd said to us all day. "They didn't tell you yesterday, and they won't tell you today."

"I don't care if they don't want to talk," Miry said, and I got a look at her phone's password. "Whatever they didn't want to say, it had something to do with Abuelo and Abuelita. And now they're both *dead*. I want answers."

"And I do, too," I said. "It's one thing if they didn't talk to us when Abuelo was alive, but I think they're the only people in Mexico City who didn't come to his funeral. We at least deserve answers for that."

Nando glanced back at our parents, who were watching Abuelo's casket get wheeled away. "Niñas, don't ask me now. Not when our parents are nearby."

"We're not asking you," I said.

Nando stuttered. "Y-You're not?"

Miry and I shook our heads. We'd made a deal with Nando. He could keep his secrets for two days as long as he drove us around the city. But now that our 48-hour window was almost done, there was no need for us to hold back. Still, after seeing Nando cry, Miry and I made an agreement while we were getting ready for the funeral.

"Nando, we're not asking you," I said. "This is hitting you hard enough as it is, and it's not fair to push you right now. You're the one who's getting hurt by this the most, and... you've already done enough."

"What are you saying?" Nando asked.

"She's saying that we're not gonna be jackasses and force you to talk," Miry said. "But we need answers. So we're getting them."

Nando's eyes went wide behind his over-sized glasses. I can

imagine why. After what happened yesterday, he probably expected us to keep hounding him about whatever secrets he had.

But even I, who only sort of knew Abuelo, was grieving for my grandfather. Nando was practically raised by our grandparents when he was little. I couldn't begin to think how much this was hurting him.

Miry opened up her WhatsApp and scrolled to her chat with Lorenzo.

"I know them," Nando murmured.

Miry and I looked up.

Nando pinched his eyes shut. "I know them," he repeated.

"Know what?" I asked.

"The answers to your questions," he said. "I know why the Archivists didn't come. I know why you're important. I know that… that you can't just reforge the seal. You two are the only ones who even have a *chance*."

"What?" I asked. "*We're* the only ones?"

"Yes."

"Why?" Miry lowered her phone. "And how do you know that?"

Nando glanced back at our parents, who were all hugging each other as Abuelo's casket was wheeled out of the room. "Because I've read through Abuelo and Abuela's notes."

"What?" I said. "Nando, what are you saying?"

"I'm saying… I know. About the Archivists. About the spirit. And I know it because—" Nando gulped. "Because Abuelo and Abuela told me. They told me everything. And you two were never supposed to know about it."

31

THE NERD'S ARCHIVE

MIRY

THE BIG REVEAL HAPPENED AFTER THE FUNERAL. WE WERE back at Tía Sara and Tío Rizo's house, and this time we were in Fer and Eduardo's room. The rest of the family was down-stairs, comforting Clara and Eduardo as they mourned their grandfather. The only reason why us three were allowed upstairs was because Fer had said that he needed time in his room to calm down. I think they were happy that Ada and I had semi-volunteered to keep an eye on him.

Ada and I awkwardly waited for Fer to find whatever it is he was searching for. Getting restless, I glanced around the room. It was a decent size, considering that half of it was occu-pied by Eduardo's football jerseys and discarded sports gear, and Fer's side was definitely the cleanest. His desk and drawers were neatly organized, and even his laptop charger was rolled up on the desk. The only clothes that were out of place were the jeans and shirt he'd worn the day before, crum-pled up by the bed.

There were empty spots on the walls from where Fer had put posters from *Call of Duty*, *Halo*, and another FPS game he probably had at least a thousand hours in. He'd taken all those posters with him when he moved into Ada and Tía Mira's house for university, but he still brought both his Nintendo Switch and his PlayStation for the summer. On a normal day, he might've challenged us to a match.

"All this time," I said, "you knew… everything?"

Fer stopped flicking through his absurd collection of accordion folders and sighed. "I did. Well… Almost everything. I didn't know they were that strict with the difference between 'god' and 'deity'. If I did, I might've known that Daniel…"

He didn't finish that sentence.

"Is this your old school stuff?" Ada asked as Fer flipped through a bunch of yellowing worksheets made for kids in sixth grade.

"Did you keep *everything*?" I asked. There were files ranging from fourth to 12th grade.

Fer paused to wipe a new set of tears. "Yeah. I decided that this would be the best place to hide something in case Eduardo went through my stuff."

"So why did you hide something in the sixth grade folder?" Ada asked.

The flipping stopped. Fer's fingers landed on a set of six or so handwritten pages held together with a clip.

"Because I was in the sixth grade when they told me," Fer said. He held out the pages. "I translated it. Here. Both of you can read it."

Ada immediately took them. Her eyes widened. "Miry… I think you should read this."

"Huh? Why?"

Ada offered me the pages. "Because… It looks like Abuelo and Abuela wrote this."

My throat went dry.

My eyes were crusty from having cried earlier in the day, but I suddenly felt tears push at the back of my eyes.

I accepted the pages. The first three or so were written in Spanish, in perfectly flowing cursive that pretty much no one my age can pull off. Beneath those pages was another set, this time written out in English, and I immediately recognized Fer's blocky handwriting.

I took the English pages, breathed in, and read them out loud.

To whomever reads this,

We are Roberto Rivera González and María Isabel Cortés Huerta, two Archivist disciples from the pantheon of Teotihuacán. If you are reading this, we have died, and we have failed.

On the 11th of June, 2008, we were sent on a mission to investigate an anomaly at the pyramids of Teotihuacán. While we were there, we encountered a spirit from centuries past. A spirit who was trapped behind a seal in the pyramid of Chalchiuhtlicue.

He called himself the Lord of the Earth. He said he was the last true ruler of Teotihuacán, and that he would take revenge on the deities that forsook him. He said that they let Teotihuacán crumble and rot, all while letting new civilizations blossom around him. He is angry, he feels cheated, and he has spent over one thousand years amassing power so that he can do one thing.

He wants to create an earthquake. An earthquake that is bigger than '85. One that will destroy thousands of buildings, kill thousands more people, and cause chaos in all of Mexico City. From what we have seen, and what we felt when we sealed him away... we fear that he truly has the power to do so.

At the pyramids, we had to make a decision. To reforge the seal at the expense of our lives, or to risk the deaths of hundreds of thousands of people. To risk the deaths of our family.

It was an easy choice.

We fear the burden of this fate. When we reforged the seal holding the spirit captive, we felt our souls connect with the magical energy of the world. The invisible lines of magic that call out to every Archivist. When we were in this state, we felt our souls stretch out across the land. They sought out sources of magic to help us seal away the spirit.

And—by accident—we connected with two people. More specifically, two babies. One in Arizona, and another in Mexico City.

Somehow, through the forces of the earth or the magical ties that bind blood to blood, we connected our souls to the souls of our unborn granddaughters: Guadalupe and Miranda.

When we entered the Spiritual World, our daughters had yet to give birth. When we left, we came home to the news that Hada and Miry had been born.

Those girls are twin souls, brought to earth at

the same time, and forever bound together by magic. When the two girls were first brought together, we could literally see the magical energy weaving around them, calling out to its other half.

And we could feel the power they held in their infant bodies.

We have placed a terrible curse upon our grand-daughters. When we tapped into the earth's magic to reforge this spirit, we accidentally tied the seal's magic to our family. We have revisited the ruins of Teotihuacán, and the pyramids in the Spiritual World. We have confirmed that the only people who can touch the seal are us.

And if everything we know about magic is true, then the only other people who could even attempt to reforge the seal are Hada and Miry.

We wish we could say that is all, but there is something else you must know.

When we sealed the Lord of the Earth, he gath-ered enough energy to curse our bloodline. If anyone in our family learns what happened that day in 2008, they will accelerate the seal's magical absorption. It will make us die faster. Because of this, we and anyone who knows what happened that day are unable to tell our family what happened.

Our children know we are cursed, but they do not know why. We cannot tell them.

For years, we hid this secret from our family.

We watched our children curse the Archivists, and when their children grew, we were forbidden from telling them anything about magic. Our grandchildren could go to the pyramids if they wanted, but they were never to know about the Archivists.

The plan worked. It worked until our oldest grandson, Fernando, was nine years old.

He found a copy of our report.

It was careless on our end. Fer was always curious, always poking through our books when we took care of him while our son and his wife were at work. We thought he wouldn't look through old journals children have no business being interested in.

But he did.

By the time we caught him, it was too late. Even though he didn't understand everything, he knew something horrible had happened to us, and we felt the curse grow stronger. We tried to keep him away, to tell him it was all a story. But Fer is clever. He knew we were lying, and only knowing part of the truth was worse than being kept in the dark. So when he was twelve years old, we sat him down and promised that if he could keep this secret, we would tell him about our curse.

We didn't tell him he was the one who accelerated our mental and physical decline. He figured that out himself. It hurt him so much that we begged him to never seek out information about the Archivists or Teotihuacán unless he absolutely had to. It is our fault that he lives with guilt he does not deserve. We could not bear it if he was forced to be reminded of it every day.

We've enclosed instructions at the back of this letter for you to find our official additional report. But before we end this letter, there are some final things for us to say.

To our children: Mira, Lupe, and Rizo. We do not blame you for staying away from the Archivists. This mission has broken your hearts, and by keeping you apart from this, we hope to prevent your hearts from shattering completely. If all goes well, you shall never know that this happened. You shall not feel more pain than what we have already given you.

To our grandson: Fernando. This isn't your fault. None of it is. You were a child; you were curious, and all you wanted was to explore our little archive. This curse is ours to bear. If there is anything we want you to remember, it is that we never blamed you. We will remind you of this every day we can, and we hope you remember that long after we are gone.

To our granddaughters: Hada and Miry. If you are reading this, then we and the magical community have failed you in the worst way. There is now a task only you two can accomplish. It is a burden you should never have to carry. But we have had the privilege of seeing you grow up, and we know that you two will become women more than capable of seeing this through.

To the Archivists of Teotihuacán. We have given our lives to protect this city, and to protect our granddaughters. Now it is your turn to protect our family.

This spirit is prepared to destroy the lives of millions. If our granddaughters succeed at sealing him again, there is a chance that they, too, will suffer just as we have. We have done our best to imprison him, and now it is your turn to do what we cannot.

Use every piece of knowledge you can find. Every ally who knows of this spirit. Go to Peru and tear down LLAMA's headquarters if need be. Do this to accomplish one thing.

Discover a way to destroy this monster. Because if he is destroyed, the seal will no longer be needed, and our family will finally be free from this curse.

Signed,

Roberto Rivera González and María Isabel Cortés Huerta.

MY BREATH SHOOK AS I READ OUT THE LAST LINES.

The spirit that we met at the pyramids has the power to destroy the city. And my cousin and I were the only people who had a chance at stopping him.

But more than that…

"He made Abuelo and Abuelita sick," I said. "This seal holding him back, it drained away their lives."

Fer sighed and lowered himself to the floor, leaning against his bed frame. "It did. It drained Abuela's physical body, and Abuelo's… Abuelo's mind."

Ada sat down next to him. "Nando," she said softly. "You've been carrying this secret… all this time?"

Fer nodded and wiped away a tear. "I thought that if I could contact the Archivists, I could see if they had gotten closer to destroying the spirit. I thought I could help you activate your powers, maybe find a way to stop this spirit before Abuelo died. I—I thought I could *help*… But I couldn't."

"Nando…"

"I'm sorry," Fer said. "If I didn't know, maybe Abuelo and Abuela would've lived longer. And you… You wouldn't be in this mess."

I hesitantly sat down in front of him. "Fer—"

"I'm calling Lorenzo." Fer reached into his suit pants' pocket and pulled out his phone. "Now that you know… they might talk to you."

I could tell from the shocked look on Ada's face that she was as floored as I was. Sure, we knew about this weird seal thing, but the bombshell that it's what made Abuelo slowly lose his mind, and made Abuelita so sick she couldn't even get out of bed…

Anger crawled up my throat, and I didn't push it away.

Lorenzo picked up. Fer put the phone on speaker.

"*Hello?*"

"We know," I said immediately, speaking English so Ada could understand. "About our grandparents, the seal. We know."

Lorenzo hissed. *"Carajo."*

We told him about the letter. "They're right," Lorenzo said. "We tried everything. The only people who could even get close to the seal were your grandparents. And from what we've seen, it's likely you two are the only ones who can fix it."

"But if that's the case," Ada said, "then why would Daniel be trying to activate our powers? Isn't that the kind of thing he *wouldn't* want us to do?"

"Not necessarily," I said. "Daniel said that our powers can be used to reforge or break the seal. Maybe he wasn't trying to get us to reforge the seal."

Ada huffed in disbelief. "He wanted us to *break* it."

"The death of your grandmother weakened the seal," Lorenzo said. "That's when we assume the spirit gained even more influence outside his prison. But until the day your grandfather died, the seal would hold."

"And then you and I come along," Ada said, "tap into the seal's power, and kickstart our own powers. It's like dangling a carrot in front of a really hungry bunny."

I bit my bottom lip. "And we went to the pyramids. Stood on the pedestal at Teotihuacán —"

"And I said 'Cheese!' for a picture." Ada let out a shell-shocked laugh. "If the seal is at the pyramids, then maybe the spirit somehow heard me."

"You and your cousin are tapped into the magical fabric of Teotihuacán," Lorenzo said. "When you spoke on that pedestal, it's very likely you caused a magical ripple that further weakened the seal."

Ada fiddled with the black shawl that hung over her shoulders. "How do we fix this?"

"You don't have to," Fer said.

"We do." Ada pulled the phone out of Fer's hand and spoke directly into the microphone. "What are you doing right now?"

"Preparing to fight," Lorenzo said. "If we're reading the magical energies right, then we have just over 24 hours before the spirit breaks free. If we can't reforge the seal, our only hope is to destroy him before he triggers the earthquake."

"Can you do it?" I asked, leaning over so I could make sure that Lorenzo heard me. "And don't lie to us because we're not adults. Like you said, we're the only people who can reforge the seal, so we need to know. Can you defeat this guy before he creates a massive earthquake?"

Lorenzo went quiet. My temper flared, so I repeated, "Can you—"

"We don't know," he said.

I gritted my teeth. "Shit."

"That pretty much sums it up." Ada took in a deep breath and pushed herself off the floor. "I guess we're going."

"W-Where?" Fer stuttered.

"To fix the seal," Ada said. "I'm guessing we have to go to the pyramids to do that, so we'll head out now."

"Hada…"

"Great. Another road trip," I groaned as I pushed myself onto my feet. "Just when I've had enough of cars. We'll make our way to the pyramids. See you there soon."

"No, wai—" Lorenzo began.

I grabbed the phone from Ada's hand and spoke directly into the mic. "No, I'm not waiting. This *pendejo* made my grandmother go through seven years of cancer. I don't care what you say, I'm getting some payback."

"Save some of that payback for me," Ada said. "If this guy is the reason my grandparents got sick before I properly got to know them, then I'm gonna shove a needle in his goddamn face."

Lorenzo sighed. "Okay. I'll send you the meet up point."

"Great! See ya there." And with that, Ada hung up the phone.

"You're not going," Fer said from his spot on the floor.

"We kinda have to, Nando." Ada dumped Fer's phone onto his bed. "I accidentally weakened this seal, and now there's a weird spirit coming to literally destroy the whole city. The city with *our* parents and *your* siblings."

Fer shook his head tiredly. "How are you getting to the pyramids?"

"Taxi," Ada said immediately. "I've got some money saved up."

"I do, too," I added.

"I'll tell your parents," Fer said, the weight of the threat buckling beneath the desperation in his voice.

"And admit that you're the guy who took us all around the city looking for the Archivists?" I countered.

Fer grimaced. "You can't do this. What are you going to tell them? Why would they let you out of the house?"

"I'm not sure yet. But we'll figure it out." Ada smiled and leaned down to grip his shoulder. "Nando, we've got this. Stay and rest. You've already done enough for us. And... now it's our turn to sort this out."

Ada turned to leave, and I followed. "We'd better change," I said. "And if you dare put on those damn flats again, I'm throwing them out of the car."

Ada groaned. "Yeah, continue the crusade against my shoe choices. You don't see me complaining about—"

"*Carajo.*"

Ada and I spun around. Because she didn't say that, and I didn't say that.

Fer did.

"Fer..." I said. "Did you just *curse*?"

"Yeah." Fer readjusted his glasses and pushed himself off the floor. "Okay. I'm doing this."

"What are you doing?" Ada asked.

"Getting a change of clothes," Fer said as he rifled through a drawer. "It's a long drive, and I don't think I can take another minute in the suit I wore to our grandfather's funeral."

32

GO FERNANDO GO

MIRY

BENEFITS OF HAVING THE GOODY-TWO-SHOES ON YOUR SIDE: they can pull out any excuse to get you out of the house.

After the three of us had changed into outfits that didn't make us look like mourners, all Fer had to do to get us out was say that he needed some time away from the house. That he needed to get away from Abuelo and Abuelita's empty room. He had a friend nearby whose parents were out of town, so he'd go over and spend some time there. Ada and I would go as well to keep an eye on him.

Our parents said okay and gave us hugs before we left. My mom held me extra tight.

"Thank you," Mamá whispered in my ear, "for taking care of your cousin."

I couldn't tell her that it was *Fer* helping *us*.

So we stocked up on water bottles, shuffled ourselves into Fer's car, and headed north.

The road in front of us was clear, and a deep sense of schadenfreude ran through me when I saw the massive traffic jam on the other side of the road. It was drizzling, and dark storm clouds were nearby, but I could still see the sun set behind the mountains. There was just enough light to make the towering buildings that surrounded us shine.

"Did my feet grow overnight or something?" Ada grumbled in the backseat as she tried putting on her sparkly, hot pink sneakers with shiny silver laces.

"No," I said, feeling much more comfortable in my purple tank top, ankle-length workout pants, and well-worn Vans. "It's just that you haven't bought new sneakers since you were nine."

"Haha, very funny," Ada drawled. She'd changed out of the black dress and into a pair of bright blue jean shorts, coupled with a bright green shirt that was long and flowy enough to count as a short dress. She still had her mint green purse with her, and the color combination was so saturated it just barely made the outfit work.

"There's something I still don't get," Ada said once she'd gotten her shoes on. "That letter said we were born at the same time because Abuelo and Abuela tapped into the earth's magical forces or whatever, right?"

"Pretty much," I said. "Dad and Mamá were surprised because I came out a month before I was due. Mamá says I was pretty much already born by the time the ambulance showed up."

"My mom was already in labor at the hospital," Ada said. "But she says that her labor kicked into high gear at one point. A few minutes later and *boom*, I was out! But we still weren't born at the same time."

"I'm an hour older," I said.

Ada scoffed. "You say that as if it's a lot."

"You *were* born at the same time," Fer said. From my spot in the passenger seat, I could see his red-rimmed eyes. He'd changed into his usual jean and t-shirt combo, and it made him look less sad than he'd been an hour ago. "Miry was born at 8:34 PM. You were born at 7:34 PM."

"But that's still an hour difference!" Ada said. "Unless there's a world where 7 and 8 PM happen at the same time."

I groaned as the realization hit me. "There is. *Time zones*."

"Oh, *duh*." Ada groaned into her hand. "Because I was born in Phoenix, and you were born here. And the time difference between Phoenix and Mexico City—"

"Is one hour." I rolled my eyes at our own obliviousness and chugged down half a water bottle. "How did we not realize that before?"

"It's basic math. At least *I* should've noticed that!" Ada said. "It's like one of those answers that's right in front of you and makes you feel dumb for not seeing it sooner. Like with Daniel."

"Hey, *I* thought there was something off about him from the beginning," I said. "And I told you so. A *lot*."

"You did," Ada sighed. "I probably should've taken you more seriously."

I smirked. "*Mmmhm.*"

Ada rolled her eyes. "Yeah, yeah. Rub it in."

"Oh, I *will*. I mean, seriously, the guy was sketchy as hell."

"I'm still annoyed he tricked us like that," Ada said. "More than that, I'm annoyed that you noticed it instead of me. I mean, come on! Between the two of us, *I'm* the people person."

"You're also the one who tries to see the good in everything," I said. "Even people."

"And you only spent one day with him," Fer added. "Daniel was the first Archivist you'd met. You had nothing to compare him to."

Ada loosened her seatbelt and leaned forward. "Nando, you only knew him for one day, too."

"But I talked to him for longer." Fer's fingers tightened their grip on the steering wheel. "About the Archivists, Abuelo, Abuela. He spent over two hours just telling me what the Archivists do now, and I... I believed him. Every word."

"Nando, it wasn't your fault," Ada said. "None of this is."

Silence.

"Nando, you listening?" Ada prodded. "It isn't. Your. Fault."

"Doesn't change the fact that our grandparents died sooner because of me. Doesn't change the fact that you have to…"

I didn't know what else to say to that. I'm not good at comforting people—I never have been. But luckily, I wasn't the only other person in the car.

"Reforge the seal. Yeah, we know," Ada said. "And we can do it. I don't know how, but we've figured things out so far. So… We can do it. And we'll be okay. No matter what."

Fer sighed. "Why aren't you angry with me?"

"Well, I'm not angry with you because it makes no logical sense," Ada said. "You were a kid who accidentally read something you shouldn't have—our grandparents back us up on that. And Daniel's got every Archivist scrambling after him. If he managed to escape a whole magical group, the only way I can be mad at you is if I'm mad at me, too."

Fer tightened his jaw.

"I am angry," I said. Fer sucked in a breath, and I quickly added, "But not at you. Like I said to Lorenzo, if there's anyone I should be angry at, it's the guy who made Abuelo and Abuelita slowly die in front of us. *That's* who I'm gonna be angry at, and there's nothing you can do to change that. You know why?"

My cousin sighed. "Why?"

"Because this isn't your damn fault," I said.

"Gotta agree with Miry on this one." Ada leaned forward and wrapped her arms around Fer's shoulders. "So stop thinking that you've gotta carry this guilt with you, okay?"

A new wave of tears leaked out of Fer's eyes. There wasn't much else I could say, so I followed Ada's lead and leaned my head on his shoulder.

"Okay," Fer whispered. "Okay."

We spent a few minutes like that, the three of us, just

staring at the long road that would take us out of the city. It was a strange calm. The three of us, all with different levels of grief, just sitting there and staring at the setting sun.

Fer was the one to break the silence. "You know, I think I understand why Abuelo used to call you 'twin souls'. You might look different on the surface, but… you're more alike than I gave you credit for. Maybe there's a deeper reason you were forced to be born on the same day."

Fer's words made me think. "I just realized something."

And without giving any warning, I reached back and elbowed Ada in the ribs.

Ada grunted and stared me down. "Hey, what was that for?"

"You're the reason I was born a month premature!"

"Oh, so *I'm* the reason?" Ada poked my armpit hard, making me yelp. "It wasn't a weird magical spirit who screwed over our grandparents?"

"You were already being born. I'm pretty sure that had something to do with everything." I elbowed her again. "Besides, blaming you is more fun."

"Oh, it's on now, *green-ga*!"

She poked me in the ribs, I elbowed her in the arm. She tickled me in the armpits, I faux-punched her shoulders. Fer called out to stop us, but by that time, Ada and I had started laughing like we were kids again.

To be fair, we were pushing and shoving each other like we did when we were nine. I elbowed her, she kicked my seat, and in a few minutes, we even had Fer laughing.

"Niñas," he tried to scold. But Fer's tone was immediately undermined by a belly laugh when Ada missed a kick and got her foot caught between the two front seats.

"We literally just came from a funeral." Ada laughed as she pulled her foot back. "Why are we laughing?"

"Because this is how we cope with death, Fresa," I said,

pausing the play fight so I could catch my breath. "Grieve 'til you cry, cry 'til you laugh."

Ada cackled. "This is so dumb."

"Says the one who's still laughing!" I shot back.

"No fighting while I'm driving," Fer said, slowly pulling himself into the rule-abiding older brother figure. "If you fight, you get out of the car until you can drive yourselves."

"What's the fun in that?" Ada pointed at Fer. "We've already got a chauffeur right here."

I scoffed. "Suit yourself. I'm getting my permit as soon as I can. Someone's gotta teach this slowpoke how to drive faster than 60 an hour."

"You think I can't go fast?" Fer raised his eyebrow. "I'll show you fast." He grinned and put his hand on the gearshift—

"Wait, wait, wait!" Ada interrupted. She reached forward and took hold of the AUX cable. "If you're going fast, you need the right playlist to go with it."

Fer groaned as Ada cycled through her Spotify. "I already let you pick the music. No more BT—"

Fer cut himself off as Ada pressed play on the song. Because instead of K-Pop, the ancient stereos were playing the opening notes to the Eurobeat hit, "Gas Gas Gas".

Fer's eyes widened, and he grinned again. "That works."

And right as the singer started his lyrics, Fer hit the gas and sped us down the road.

WE SHOWED UP AT THE MEETING SPOT JUST AS THE "STAR Theme" from *Super Mario Bros* ended. It was in the parking lot of a hotel just a little while away from the pyramids. We got there about an hour after the sun set, and we somehow outran the rainstorm that was now showering most of Mexico City with buckets of polluted rain.

The Archivists made their way toward us the moment we stepped out of the car. I recognized everyone we saw yesterday, plus an extra dozen or so people that were holding long obsidian daggers in their hands. Most of them were in their 30s or 40s, but there were a few in their 20s. And I think I saw a couple who were *at least* in their 60s.

Lorenzo was the first to reach us. He had an empty one liter water bottle in one hand and a dagger in the other, and he'd pulled his hair into the tightest man bun I'd ever seen. He was also wearing a pair of pants that were so covered in paint splatters... I had no idea what their original color was.

"You got here fast," he said.

Fer sheepishly rubbed the back of his head. "I had a good playlist."

Lorenzo kept a distance away from me and Ada, and I could tell that he still felt guilty about the stalking incident. The logical part of my brain said it was a misunderstanding he'd already apologized for.

The non-logical part of my brain said I shouldn't go near him.

"We're truly sorry about your grandfather," Lorenzo said. "I only knew him for a short time, but he was a good man."

Fer nodded. "He was. Thank you."

Ada gave him an appreciative smile.

"What do we need to know?" I said, not looking Lorenzo in the eye.

Jefe, who was now in full workout gear but still wearing the same blue cap, limped forward. "We have over a dozen people ready to go in, and more are on the way. The spirit is gaining power, so he might be putting up safety measures to keep you from reaching the seal. We're going to do our best to keep you guarded until you can reach the seal, and then... It's your turn."

"Where's Quetz?" Ada asked, her curls swishing around her head as she searched for her deity.

"He's... picking out an outfit." Jefe sighed. "He says he can't go to battle without looking like a proper warrior."

"He's gonna take forever with that," Ada said firmly.

"And what about Chalchi?" I asked.

"She's setting up a border around the ruins," Jefe said. "It will help keep everything contained. She can only make one entrance near the ciudadela, so we'll enter the ruins from there."

"What's even the point of a border?" Ada asked.

"Even if people can't use it, they can still see magic," Jefe said. "But we find that the less they know about the magical world, the better. And we're less likely to get attention from the UCMP."

"The UCMP?" I asked.

"United Council of Magical Peoples. The magical equivalent of the United Nations."

"LLAMA is lax in comparison," Lorenzo added with a scratching of his beard. "UCMP are *very* strict with documentation. They make you fill even more paperwork than what we'll have to report to LLAMA, so we like to keep our magical business as quiet as possible."

Jefe nodded in agreement. "And in case the spirit's power grows..."

"The border will stop any pumas from attacking the areas around us," I finished for him. "Are any other deities here?"

Jefe rubbed the back of his head. "We tried calling them, but only Quetzalcóatl and Chalchiuhtlicue answered."

Ada stuttered. "A spirit is getting ready to destroy a whole city, and they're the only ones who showed up to help?"

"It's more than I expected," Jefe said. "Our deities can't have too much direct influence over human affairs. If they could do everything they wanted, they wouldn't be choosing disciples. The fact that we have *two* of them here means that this is serious."

Serious? Yeah, understatement of the millennia.

I narrowed my eyes at the group of 15 to 20 Archivists. "And this is really everyone?"

"Almost everyone," Jefe said. "There are a few disciples who chose to leave the Archivists without abandoning their magic, but the rest are coming. We're a small group, but we're good. I promise."

"Hey, aren't you forgetting something?"

Profesora Gabriela stepped out from the crowd of Archivists, speaking Spanish. She was in the same puffer jacket as before, and she had a wide smirk on her face.

"What is it, Gabi?" Jefe asked.

"The initiation," the professor said, switching to English. "We usually do this with a bit more ceremony, but we can save that for when you fill out the paperwork."

"Paperwork?" Ada groaned.

"For LLAMA," Lorenzo answered, then groaned just as Ada did. "I told you. There's *lots* of it in our line of work." He turned to Jefe. "Did you get through to them? Can they send any magic users?"

"My phone call has been on hold for nearly 24 hours, Lolo," Jefe said. "I doubt that LLAMA has even read your original report on Daniel."

"I sent that two months ago..." Lorenzo muttered under his breath.

"Let's not think about that right now," Profesora Gabriela said quickly. She held out a hand, palm up, toward Ada and me. "Repeat after me. I knowingly accept."

Ada and I held out our hands. "I knowingly accept."

"And strive to uncover."

"And strive to uncover."

"The knowledge of Teotihuacán."

"The knowledge of Teotihuacán."

"To seek answers of history and magic."

"To seek answers of history and magic."

"And remember those who have been forgotten."

"And remember those who have been forgotten."

As we said those final words, a rush of magic bloomed in my chest. It nearly made me stumble. Beside me, Ada swayed on her feet. It's like something grew in my heart, grounding me into my own skin.

Profesora Gabriela reached into her pockets and pulled out two obsidian daggers. She placed one in my palm, another in Ada's, and closed our fingers around the hilts.

"Welcome," she said, "to the Archivists of Teotihuacán."

There was an awkward silence as various faces within the group gave us serious nods or light smiles.

"That's it?" Ada asked.

"Well, we kind of have a situation going on." I turned to Jefe. "When do we go in?"

"At midnight."

"Shouldn't we be going now?" I asked. "There's someone ready to destroy a whole city!"

"We have time," Jefe said. "We have one day before his magic is powerful enough to break free. So we go when we're strongest. And all disciples of Chalchiuhtlicue and Tláloc are at their strongest when it's midnight. This is our best plan." Jefe winced. "As long as…"

"As long as *what*?" I asked.

"As long as everyone shows up on time."

33

I NO LONGER HATE IT HERE

MIRY

July 12th

Everyone did *not* show up on time.

To be fair, you're talking about a group of Mexicans. The moment you get a large group of us to show up on time is the day we turn into a functional country.

Half a dozen more people showed up before midnight. Another dozen showed up *after* midnight. Even Quetz didn't finalize his outfit until one in the morning.

So, because literally a third of our makeshift army was late, our golden hour to storm the ruins was gone. Going at midnight was our best option, and we instead went with our *second* best option. That option included all of us booking hotel rooms and marching to the ruins at sunrise.

Yes. You heard me. *Sunrise.*

I wish I was joking.

Don't get me wrong, Ada, Fer, and I put up a fight. We were going against the guy who made our grandparents' lives hell, and we wanted to end this as soon as possible.

But then I found out that Chalchi hadn't finished her

magical border because she *knew* that people would show up late. When a deity herself guesses that you're not gonna show up on time, there's not much you can do but accept it.

By the time Ada, Fer, and I shuffled out of our hotel room, the Archivists were *finally* ready. Some of them had jeans and t-shirts. Some came in suits like they were gonna rush straight to work after this. One of them even came on a motorcycle designed to deliver pizzas.

Right before sunrise hit, all of us *finally* made the walk to the pyramids. Ada, as always, was wide awake. She was happily asking Lourdes about how she could summon croco-diles, though she kept her distance from Teresa and her perpetual death-glare. On one hand, Teresa still might've been annoyed at Ada. On the other hand, she might just have a really bad resting bitch face.

Fer ran on nerves and adrenaline. He talked with Jefe, hauling his backpack full of giant water bottles in case I needed to refuel my magic.

Even Quetz joined us on our march to the ruins. The outfit he finally settled on was a set of army camo pants, steel boots with spikes, a bedazzled jean jacket, and a banana yellow motorcycle helmet I *think* was meant to represent the sun.

Was the outfit hideous to look at? Of course.

As for me? Had this been any other day, I would've been half-asleep at this hour. That is, if I'd gotten any sleep to begin with. I stayed awake the whole night, wondering how the hell we were actually going to do this.

I was near the front of the pack, forcing my body to stride forward as we passed the merchants, who were busy setting up their stalls for the day. When we got to the actual entrance, a security guard waved us through, casually reminding us that we only had an hour to get this sorted before they had to open up the archeological site.

Yeah, because magic is apparently so secret that even when

you're preventing a city-wide catastrophe, you've still gotta get your business done before the tourists show up.

As we walked through the entrance, my fingers brushed the handle of the obsidian dagger that hung from my waist. Jefe's wife, Jessica, had given Ada and I leather-like holsters to hang them. Now that I could see its texture over my workout pants, I kept thinking back to that time I'd supposedly seen daggers at our stalkers' hips. The daggers that turned out to be illusions.

I kept trying to remember if the illusion had the daggers hanging from a holster or if they were just hanging in the air. Was the appearance of the dagger meant to scare us enough that we wouldn't look beyond it? Or were there more details I hadn't seen?

I forced the thought from my head. *There's a time to panic and a time to act.*

A shimmering wave of green light welcomed us to the ruins. It surrounded almost the entire ruins in a large dome, encasing everything in a wall of magic.

"Good luck," Chalchiuhtlicue said. Her voice came from the magical dome, which reverberated with each word, and slowly, a small entryway appeared at the edge of the barrier.

We walked through.

Fer got stopped right next to the staircase to the ciudadela, where the pyramid of Quetzalcóatl lay at the bottom. Profesora Gabriela pulled him aside and told him that they'd be staying there. She was staying because her powers weren't combat focused, and Fer was staying because he didn't have any. Fer's eyes grew to the size of his glasses, and it was only the professor's grip on his arm that stopped him from protesting. I grabbed a bottle of water and told him to keep an eye on the rest.

The ruins were almost the same as I remembered them. Long slabs of stones, half-covered in dirt and overgrown grass, stretched across the Avenue of the Dead. The very first few rays of sunlight cut across the land, making sporadic patches of grass glimmer under the morning glow.

It was old. Most of the structures were long gone, and whatever hadn't been ransacked by thieves or time lay buried beneath the hard dirt. It lay entombed. Waiting for someone to dig it up.

But having seen a glimpse of the city when it was alive made the ruins feel different. When you hear about old civilizations that are long gone, they feel distant. But standing there, I suddenly felt the presence of a once great city brimming with life. Something so large and powerful that they managed to create all *this*.

The people who lived here built enough that parts of the city endured the test of time. Enough that, almost a thousand and a half years later, I could see the shadows of a once great civilization. I didn't know what they called themselves. I never would. But I knew that these people were here. I knew that they existed.

"You okay?" a man asked in Spanish.

I faced Lorenzo. He was still in the same paint-splattered outfit he wore yesterday, with his hair tied up and a large obsidian dagger hanging from his holster. I also noticed that he kept a respectable distance between the two of us.

"Yeah," I said, continuing the conversation in Spanish. *"You know, I got dragged here as a kid a lot. Didn't really understand why. But… Now I think I get it."*

"It's beautiful." Underneath Lorenzo's thick beard, I think I saw him smile a little. *"In its own way."*

"Yeah."

"Miran—" Lorenzo started.

"If you're gonna apologize again, I get it, but you don't have to. Except if you call me 'Miranda' or 'Mira'. That's my aunt's name. I go by Miry."

Lorenzo nodded seriously. *"Okay, Miry."*

Some of the other Archivists had started walking ahead of

us. Quetz took the lead, but he got so far ahead that I lost sight of his banana yellow helmet. After double-checking that I could still feel my magic in my chest, I walked after them. Lorenzo followed.

We headed down the road, walking up and down the staircases that made up the Avenue of the Dead.

I WISH I COULD SAY THAT I WAS PUSHING THROUGH THE nerves. But as we went up and down another staircase and saw the pyramid of the moon get closer and closer, I got so nervous I did the most non-Miry thing ever.

I made small talk.

"So, what's the deal between you and Daniel?" I asked in Spanish.

Lorenzo paused when he realized I was talking to *him*. *"He's my best friend,"* he replied in Spanish. *"But he already told you that. If you're asking what happened with him… he abandoned Tláloc."*

"Why?"

"Because Tláloc hasn't been heard of for many years," Lorenzo said. *"He still has his disciples, but he doesn't talk to them. Not the way he used to. Daniel… he's always liked having assurances. Knowing that someone's there to have his back. So when Tláloc stopped talking to him, I guess he thought that… that the Archivists weren't enough."*

Lorenzo grunted as we trudged up another set of stone stairs. *"That's when the spirit reached out to him. He convinced Daniel that he was a god and gave him the power of illusions. By then, Daniel had abandoned Tláloc, and I had no idea. I didn't know anything until a couple of months ago. He faked a magical incident so he could get me alone, and then he tried to convince me to join him."*

I blinked. *"Really?"*

"Unfortunately," Lorenzo said. *"He tried to get me to renounce Chalchiuhtlicue. I refused, and I fought him."*

"You fought him? Like at the museum?" I asked. *"Why'd you do that?"*

Lorenzo huffed, and the corners of his mouth twitched. *"Daniel is… stubborn. When he believes in something, he believes in it all the way. When that happens, the only way he listens to you is if you fight him and make him listen."*

"Seriously?"

"Seriously. The only way I stopped him from getting into a pyramid scheme one time was by punching him in the jaw."

I scoffed. *"Boys are weird."*

Lorenzo chuckled. *"I suppose we are. Or at least… at least Daniel and I are."*

Lorenzo got a faraway look in his eyes, and I scrambled for a question that didn't involve Daniel. *"So… are you a disciple of Tláloc or Chalchi?"*

Lorenzo paused at the mention of the nickname before huffing out a laugh. *"Chalchiuhtlicue."*

"How do you do the water jets?"

"Have you tried doing them?" he asked. *"Let me guess. It didn't go well."*

I refused to answer that question despite the fact that yeah… I did try. When we were waiting for the Archivists and I had nothing better to do.

"It happens," Lorenzo said gently, and I appreciated the fact that he wasn't mocking me. *"Magic manifests differently in everyone, even with disciples of the same deity. Give it time. You'll learn."*

"I don't have a lot of time," I said as we trudged up *another* staircase. *"Are we going this way or through a portal?"*

"No portals yet." Lorenzo's eyes flickered to the dilapidated structures on the sides of the avenue. *"The seal is in the Spiritual World, so it's likely that the spirit had more power there than here. We're going to get you as close as we can to the seal in this world and then portal you to the Spiritual World. Hopefully, you'll run into fewer illusions that way."*

"Can you do them?" I asked. *"Portals, I mean."*

"*I can.*"

"*How?*"

Lorenzo huffed. "*Did you also try to open a portal?*"

I tugged at a clump of loose hair.

I did try to make a portal. I tried for *two hours.*

I couldn't fall asleep, so I tried practicing the magic. At first it was so I could have some extra magic to lean back on, but then I did it because I was so nervous I couldn't think of doing anything else. So I tried, and I failed, again and again. Just as Lorenzo said. I used up so much magic I had to drink four bottles of water to compensate for it.

For some reason, moving the water like Lorenzo did at the museum just wasn't working for me. All it did was leave me confused and needing to go to the bathroom. I didn't say that out loud, of course. Based on the way Lorenzo chuckled to himself, I didn't have to.

"*You were trying to do them the way disciples of Quetzalcóatl do,*" Lorenzo said.

I raised my eyebrows. How did he know *that*?

"*Profesora Gabi told us that she tried to guide your cousin at UNAM. The problem is that you're not a disciple of light. You're a disciple of water.*"

"*What does that mean?*"

"*Have some patience. I'm getting there.*" Lorenzo made his point by staying silent for a moment, and I resisted the urge to roll my eyes. "*We need to have anchor points. Can you guess what they are?*"

"*I don't know. Water?*" I drawled.

Lorenzo sighed and rubbed his beard. "*Teenagers,*" he whispered under his breath. "*You're right. Doesn't matter how much water, but for your first attempts, the bigger the water source, the easier it is. Lakes, puddles, even toilets.*"

"*Gross.*"

"*Oh, yeah. But then you won't need much water. If you get good enough, you can make a portal pretty much anywhere. Even in the driest desert. All you need is to search for the smallest water molecule in the air on the other side, and you're there.*"

I closed my eyes as much as I could while still keeping some view of the ground beneath my feet. I felt around for the magic in my chest and let just a small bit of it flow out into the world. I let it search the world around me for water.

I sensed a drop or two of sweat rimming my brow line, the swish of small water flasks Lorenzo had in his back pockets. And when I extended the magic farther, I could even sense the heavy sloshing of the other one-liter bottles in Fer's backpack. Even though he was all the way back by the ciudadela.

Already, I could feel my magic honing in on something. It wasn't spread out and directionless, like when I tried to replicate the portal spell Ada tried. There was a point I could hone in on — something I could use to push or pull myself to where I needed to go.

I kept searching with my magic. If I could search a little more, then maybe I could find that drop of water on the other side. Maybe I could —

"*Miry. Miry.*" Lorenzo's stern voice made my eyes snap open. "*Not now.*" His voice was soft but firm. "*You can try when we're done with this.*"

"*You knew what I was doing?*" I said, pulling my magic back into my chest.

"*I figured you might try some magic, so… I kept an eye on you.*" Lorenzo motioned for us to walk a bit faster. "*Didn't expect you to try a portal spell right now. If you really want to know, I can teach you properly later.*"

I huffed. "*Have you taught anyone else before?*"

Lorenzo smiled. "*My students.*"

"*You have apprentices? From the Archivists?*"

"*No, I'm not a mentor. But I do teach primary.*"

I laughed.

"*What?*" he said, taken aback.

"*Just… The pants make sense now.*"

Lorenzo sighed. *"This is why I don't teach teenagers."* He went quiet for a moment. *"I know you said to stop, but I'll say it again. I'm sorry for scaring you. I... That never should have happened."*

My throat tightened up. I still remembered him as one of the men on the bus—the guy who chased us through dark streets at night. But he was there to protect us. Even though it wasn't the best way, the intentions were there. And unlike the creeps we did run into, I didn't feel anything off about him. Anything that made me want to run away.

So maybe... Maybe it was really all a misunderstanding. One that he had the strength to apologize for.

"Thanks," I said.

"Miry!" Ada called out. She ran up to me, her bright pink sneakers standing out against the grass-covered stone floor. "What magic was that?"

"Nothing much," I said, switching to English.

"Well, it looked like *something.*"

"You *saw* her magic?" Lorenzo asked. "Were you searching for it?"

"What? No." Ada furrowed her eyebrows. "I just saw her glowing blue again and figured she was doing magic."

"Blue?" I pointed to Ada. "I've only seen you glow orange."

"I glow, too?"

"You saw *what?*" Lorenzo's eyebrows shot up. "When you were doing magic?"

"After Ada fully unlocked her powers, I saw her glow orange when she tried the teleport spell." I furrowed my eyebrows. "That isn't normal?"

Lorenzo shook his head. "No, it—"

It isn't, said a man, his voice echoing in my head.

I recognized the voice immediately. It was the voice I heard at the pyramids—in Coyoacán, and the Parque de Chapultepec.

"It's the spirit," Ada said. "All this time, it was *him.*"

I groaned. "Are. You. Serious?"

Archivists, the man said. Every person around me shook their head wildly, trying to find the source of the voice. *I understand why you would attempt to seal me again. I understand, but it does not make you any less foolish.*

But I must thank you, because you brought Guadalupe and Miranda to me.

Lorenzo gasped.

Lorenzo turned to Ada and me, but it was already too late. By the time he reached out to grab hold of our arms, Ada and I were already in a portal. The world stretched around us, in a sphere of myriad colors, and for the second time in 48 hours, we fell.

Goddamn *portals*.

34

SO NOW YOU KNOW HOW WE GOT HERE

ADA

"I DIDN'T DO THAT!" I YELLED AS I CRASHED ONTO THE hard earth.

"Again, I didn't think you did," Miry groaned next to me. "Where are we?"

I blinked to get my bearings, but saw nothing. It was completely dark. Dark as in I-couldn't-see-my-hand-in-front-of-my-face dark. The scent of something damp and earthy surrounded me, but before I could panic over *where* we were, a voice rumbled in my head.

It seems that you were not needed, the spirit said. *Now I must dispose of you.*

I yanked my phone out of my purse and scrambled to turn on the flashlight. The light illuminated a long tunnel that was about twice my height. It was so long that all I could see in the distance was a dark abyss. The air was stuffy, filled with the scent of damp dirt, and it made me cough on instinct. Miry and I used the walls of the tunnel to push ourselves up —

And that's when the earth started rumbling.

The floor beneath me shook violently, so hard that I almost tumbled back down. Bits of dirt rained down from above as the entire tunnel shook, threatening to cave in on us.

"We've gotta get out of here!" I whipped my head toward both ends of the tunnels. "We've got two options to pick from! I vote left!"

"It doesn't matter—we won't have enough time!" Miry shouted. Bits of the collapsing ceiling got tangled in our hair. "I think I know where we are! There's a tunnel under the pyramid of Quetzalcóatl!"

A loud *creak* sounded above, and a massive crack appeared in the dirt that made up the roof of the tunnel. On instinct, I flung my right hand upward, sending my magic from my chest to my fingertips. My nail beds morphed into needles, and my skin hardened itself into thick green cacti. I made my arm grow until it connected with the ceiling. The crack stopped expanding, but the tunnel didn't stop shaking.

"What do you mean *tunnel*?" I ground out. "Why didn't we see it before?"

"I don't know—maybe because it's *underground*!" Miry shouted. I was actually impressed that she could still be sarcastic while sounding absolutely terrified.

"Yeah, I got that! But where's the entrance? How do you even know we're in that tunnel—"

I cried out as another tremor pressed the dirt harder down on my hand. My sneakers skidded as they worked to find grip on the shaking earth beneath me, and Miry grabbed my arms to keep me from landing flat on my butt. My phone wasn't as lucky. It tumbled out of my hand, and I couldn't grab it without giving the crumbling ceiling more leeway to crush us.

"I don't know!" Miry picked up my phone and shone it up at the ceiling, where another large crack stretched across the dirt. "But my mom told me that they sealed this whole place off way before archeologists discovered it. And I bet it's a damn good place to trap someone with an earthquake!"

I gulped. "So even if we find the exit..."

"It's probably blocked."

After what felt like hours but was logically only a few

seconds, the rumbling stopped. But the damage had been done. More and more cracks spread throughout the ceiling. They went past the area where my cactus hands were holding it together, and deep into the dark tunnel.

We needed to get out. Fast. Even if this was a different tunnel with a conveniently non-blocked exit, there's no way the ceiling would hold long enough for us to make it out of here. That left only one option.

We needed a portal.

I searched for the magic in my chest, but then the weight of the collapsing ceiling got heavier. The sound of crumbling rock echoed in the distance, and I commanded my cactus hand to grow larger. Thicker. It held up more of the ceiling, but it wouldn't hold forever.

"I can't hold this and make the portal spell!"

Miry tore her eyes away from the ceiling. "You don't have to! Just keep me alive for a bit!"

Miry placed my phone on the floor facedown, letting the flashlight illuminate the surrounding space. She closed her eyes and raised her hands, just like I'd done at UNAM. When Professor Jiménez tried to show me the portal spell.

"If I were this guy, I'd make sure we were in the Spiritual World," Miry said shakily. "It's the best chance to make sure we're out of the picture, so I just have to make a portal back to our world."

I thought back to the professor's words about portals. *Disciples of Tláloc and Chalchiuhtlicue can do it the easiest*, she said.

And Miry just so happened to be a disciple of Chalchi.

I grinned. "You wanna take the spotlight for this? Show me what you've got!"

Miry glanced at me, saw my face, and grinned back.

My cousin closed her eyes and whispered something to herself. Right away, I saw blue magic come off her in waves, extending outward from her chest to her head. From her head to the tips of her hair.

Her black hair magically wove itself into dark braids. It twisted and turned, pebbles and dust raining down from the cracked ceiling and into her long tresses. Miry closed her eyes, focusing solely on the portal spell that was our only hope of escaping.

Remember the beginning of this story? Yeah, that's how we got here.

I stood tall in a crumbling cavern I never knew existed, back-to-back with the one person I never thought I'd trust my life with.

"I need one more minute!" Miry yelled. "Think you can handle it, Fresa?"

"Ha!" I yelled back. I threw my left arm out in front of me and smiled as my nails extended themselves into razor-sharp needles. My fingers faded from brown to green, their skin hardening into masses of thick-skinned cacti.

"You need a minute?" I shouted. "I'll give you two!"

With another push, I thrusted my left arm toward the ceiling.

I grunted as the pressure of the dirt fell onto my cacti hands. It was getting closer and closer to crushing us. But I held on.

Because if Miry had the confidence to dive headfirst into summoning a portal spell, then damn it if I couldn't hold back a few rocks.

I hissed as the sounds of crumbling dirt echoed through both ends of the long tunnel. More cracks appeared in the ceiling, getting ready to crush us bit by bit. The pressure mounted, and I straightened my feet and kept my cacti steady.

Miry's almost done, I said to myself. *She's almost done, she's almost done, she's almost —*

"Got it!"

I witnessed the moment the portal burst into being. Miry's hair, which had twisted itself into four long braids, snapped as they spun around her. They moved until a bright circle appeared before us, shining as bright as a full moon in the sky.

"Move it, Fresa!" Miry shouted hoarsely.

Oh, I realized. *I have to* jump *into this one*.

The moment I released the cacti was the moment I felt the pressure of the tunnel come down on us. I didn't have time to think about the split-second I had to get in the portal. Or the fact that I had one shot at this. Or the fact that I wasn't sure if Miry's portal actually *worked*.

I just… jumped.

35

ALL HAIL THE BRIGHT PINK SNEAKERS

ADA

I LANDED FACE-FIRST ONTO A PATCH OF DUSTY GRASS, HALF an inch away from a familiar pair of Converse.

"Nando?" I mumbled.

"Fer?" Miry mumbled beside me.

Nando dropped down and immediately started checking us over. Probably to see if we were bleeding—which we might've been. I think there were rocks in that dirt.

"Hada, Miry!" he cried. "What happened? How are you *here*?"

"Miry! Lupe!" I turned my head to see Lorenzo sprint toward us. His man bun had gotten loose, and it made him look just a bit crazy.

"It's *Ada*," I grumbled as Nando helped me into a sitting position. "Not Lu—Crap! My phone!"

Yeah, I almost died, and I was asking about my phone. It was a near-death experience. Don't judge me.

"I've got it." Miry shoved my phone in my face. "Your hands were busy being literal cacti."

I sighed in relief and took it. That's when I got my first look at where we were.

We were at the ciudadela. Well, almost. We were at the

entrance to the sunken courtyard, almost right where we were the first time we got transported to the pyramids. The only people here aside from us were Lorenzo and Professor Jimenéz, who were frozen in shock. And Nando, of course. He was going into worry-mode and was frantically pulling out the giant water bottles from his backpack.

"You're okay?" Lorenzo asked. He kneeled in front of us and tucked his dagger away. "Where did you go?"

"I have no idea!" I said louder than I should've, feeling the panic of the we-almost-got-crushed scenario seep into my bones. "We were in a tunnel. Miry thinks it's under a pyramid. She opened a portal, and now we're here?" I elbowed her arm. "I thought portals could only take you to the exact spot in the other world? Shouldn't we be in another tunnel?"

Miry gestured to Lorenzo. "I just did what he told me to do," she panted. "Find an anchor."

Right at that moment, Nando shoved a huge water bottle into my hand.

Lorenzo's eyes widened. "The bottles?"

"Yeah." Miry held out a hand to Nando. "*Dame una.*" The moment Nando gave her the bottle, she downed it like it was the first water she'd had in her life.

Above us, Chalchi's dome had turned translucent, encasing the entire ruins like a bubble. It made the sky look brighter by refracting the light of the sun, making it shimmer above the land in hues of orange, pink, silver, and gold.

Wow, Chalchi, I thought. *You've got some really pretty magic.*

I turned to the ruins. In the distance, dozens of Archivists pushed back hordes of pum-eagles that descended on them from both sides of the Avenue of the Dead. I was too far away to see every attack, but I heard the Archivists grunt and shout as they sent out attack after magical attack.

And all of that was blocking our way to the pyramid.

"You did a long-range portal," Lorenzo said, seeming a bit shocked. "For a brand new Archivist, that's amazing."

Miry finished the water and wiped her mouth. "Yeah, well, I got some good advice."

"Yeah, nice job, cuz." I pushed myself onto my feet and started running. "This is cool and all, but now we've gotta get through all *that*. So come *on*. Let's go, go, go!"

"Oh, hell," Miry grumbled. "Great. Now I have to fight pumas *again*."

MIRY, LORENZO, AND I RUSHED THROUGH THE VOLLEY OF spells, Archivists, and illusions. Pum-eagles pounced. Spiders chittered. When Miry and I ran through, all of the creatures turned to us.

The Archivists got to them first.

Walls of ice crystalized themselves into shields, waves of flower petals sliced through the illusions, and rotten eggs exploded in miniature blasts of white, green, and yellow.

There were so many spells I stopped trying to keep track of them. My only goal was to get to the pyramid. Even as my legs started to burn and my lungs were crawling up my throat.

"Why are we going *through* the road of chaos!?" Miry shouted as we sidestepped a wall of blazing fire. "Can't we just go around?"

"Not when Chalchiuhtlicue's shield is up!" Lorenzo replied. "It surrounds the entire ruins, and the only way in or out is the entrance we came from!"

"Oh!" I panted. "Great! Definitely… not… inconvenient!"

We were maybe halfway down the road to the pyramid when we heard a very familiar voice.

"Lolo!" Daniel yelled. "*¿A dónde vas?*"

On our right, standing atop one of the dilapidated structures of what might've been a stone house, stood Daniel. He was in light blue jeans that were brand new, was holding a shining obsidian dagger in his right hand, and yet—I swear, I'm not making this up—he was still in that same AC/DC shirt.

Lorenzo snarled. "Daniel!"

"How the hell did *you* get here?" I cried.

I blinked, and where there was only one Daniel, there was now two.

I gasped as two clones of Daniel materialized ten feet in front of me. They were almost perfect copies of him, from the gelled hair to the faded t-shirt, and they both held shining obsidian daggers. They charged at us, their weapons poised to strike.

Lorenzo put himself between us and the clones. From a couple of small bottles hanging from his belt, he launched out two streams of water that hit the pseudo-Daniels. The copies vanished into a plume of mist, but they were immediately replaced by two more of them.

Lorenzo grunted as he launched his water streams again. The clones vanished, but just as he tried to guide us forward again, more pseudo-Daniels appeared to block our path. First it was just two, but then it was four. Then six. Then eight. All of them boxed us in and kept us from moving forward.

The clones rushed at us with their daggers. Some of them managed to dodge Lorenzo's water attacks. But when they did, Miry sent out her projectiles that made the skin on her forearm that still had arm hair turn red.

It wasn't enough. Every time a clone disappeared, a new one took its place a few feet away from us. It was an endless wave of Daniels. Lorenzo and Miry's magic kept them away from us, but it wasn't enough to give us an opening.

I raised my hands. But before I could attack with my barrage of needles, a green blur made the clones poof into mist.

Our rescuer was a woman. She had morphed both of her arms into giant cacti. More specifically, she had morphed her arms into spiky cacti hammers that were almost as long as her. The enormous mallets took out enough clones to make an opening in the horde of Daniels, and she turned to Miry and me.

I got a better look at her. She was around Lorenzo's age, with brown skin, a harsh scowl on her face, and her dark hair tied up in a high bun.

"Teresa?" I said.

"*¡Yo me encargo de ellas!*" Teresa waved Lorenzo away and pointed at Daniel. "*¡Distráelo!*"

"*¡Va!*" Lorenzo replied. "*¡Parece que vamos a tener otra revancha, Daniel!*"

"What is happening!?" I yelled as Lorenzo charged toward the remaining clones, streams of water flowing around his arms. "And where are *you* going!?"

Teresa said something in rapid-fire Spanish before Miry grabbed my arm and hauled me through the gap in Daniel's illusions.

"She says just shut up and run!" Miry translated.

"I can do that!"

We rushed through the rest of the crowd. Magic boomed and crashed all around me as the Archivists shielded my cousin and I from the illusions that jumped at us.

Well, the Archivists and Quetz.

The deity of light flew above us, his enormous eagle wings spread wide as he glided above the crowd in his disastrous battle outfits.

"Stand down!" Quetz bellowed at the creatures.

Twin beams of pure light flew from his fingertips. They extended across the waves of illusions, slicing through all of them like brilliant, deathly lasers.

"Haha!" Quetz laughed, sounding surprised at the force of his own attack. "I did it! Chalchiuhtlicue! Did you see that?"

The water dome above us glowed light blue for a moment, and I assumed that it was Chalchi's way of saying "yes".

I was almost at the big courtyard that led to the pyramid of the sun and the moon when the illusions cut us off.

A wave of ten pum-eagles stood in our way. Teresa screamed and rushed to the frontline. She swung her cacti-mallets in large, swooping attacks, crying out in victory each time her spiky hammers made a creature vanish.

But it wasn't enough. Each time a pum-eagle vanished, another one took its place. It was like Daniel and his clones but faster. Five of the creatures took to the skies to avoid Teresa's mallets, so I pointed my finger at them and shot my needles.

Next to me, Miry sent out her hair projectiles from her left arm. Our attacks hit the pum-eagles and made them disappear. With the immense speed of our attacks, we slowly slashed our way through the horde.

I glanced at my cousin. Every bit of her, from her toes to the tips of her hair, was encased in a blue aura.

I sent out another barrage of needles at a trio of pum-eagles who were coming in from our left side.

"You see that, right?" I asked Teresa. "That Miry's literally glowing!"

Teresa shouted something as she pulled her right cactus-mallet toward the sky. She brought it down onto a pum-eagle's skull, instantly making it vanish into mist.

"She doesn't," Miry translated. More of the skin on her left forearm turned red as she launched her hair projectiles at the illusions. "But *you're* glowing!"

"You are, too!" I said. "Blue!"

"You're orange!"

Teresa yelled something and swung her massive cactus-mallet into a set of five pum-eagles. She crashed into them with such force that all of them went flying to the side.

"She says focus on the pumas!" Miry translated.

I nodded and readjusted my aim. "Mystery for another time, then."

I sent out another set of needles that went flying, crashing into the pum-eagles' wings, paws, and legs. At the rate we were going, I was the one sending out the attacks that counted as the first one or two hits. Teresa was the one who stepped in and crushed them with her massive cactus-mallets. Miry was on clean-up duty, picking off whoever survived with a precise hair strike.

We slowly cut a path toward the pyramid, but the pum-eagles came from all directions. We didn't need to get rid of them—we just needed to get to the pyramid. But judging by the sensation of the magic depleting itself in my chest, I had a feeling that I wouldn't be able to keep up.

"I'm running out!" I cried.

Teresa said something as she brought both of her cactus-mallets down onto the floor, causing a miniature shockwave that had both the pum-eagles and me fumbling to regain balance. She swung her right cactus-mallet through a new horde of creatures. Almost all of them burst into mist.

"Miry, what's she saying?" I asked as I summoned more energy to my fingernails.

"She says feel the sun and—*Agh*!" Miry cried out and stamped her foot on the floor.

Some of the spiders had made their way through the Archivists' wall of ice. They targeted Miry, and she suddenly had to attack the floor with her stupidly long braids.

"Guadalupe!" Teresa yelled. "Hada!"

I turned. Though Teresa was still swinging her right hand through the pum-eagles, without Miry's support, the creatures she didn't manage to pick off kept coming.

I sent out another needle barrage. A wave of sudden exhaustion made my knees buckle, but my attack wasn't enough to keep all of the pum-eagles off Teresa.

One of them was regaining its balance. It aimed its massive claws at her head.

I raised my pointer finger. "Watch it!"

I didn't get a chance to use my needle. Why? Because Teresa sent a needle of her own.

In a split second, Teresa shot out one of the many needles

that made up her cactus-mallet straight toward the pum-eagle. It hit it in the face, and the creature disappeared.

I gaped at Teresa. This whole time, we were fighting wave after wave of pum-eagles, and I was getting more and more exhausted. But she was doing just fine. She was cutting through this hoard of pum-eagles like it was nothing. She wasn't even breaking a *sweat*.

"How aren't you tired?" I blurted.

Teresa glanced over her shoulder. She pummeled the pum-eagles with her right cactus-mallet, and she pointed at the rising sun with her left. She then awkwardly pointed to herself, the sun, and back to herself. Teresa took in a final deep breath before spinning around and smashing the skulls of three different pum-eagles.

I peered up at the sun. I knew it was the source of my powers, but it wasn't charging my energy fast enough. It just wasn't—

Wait, I thought, *maybe it is.*

Teresa was taking in long, purposeful deep breaths. Even as she was batting away the creatures, she kept up a steady rhythm. She focused on pulling air into her lungs.

No, I realized. *She isn't focused on taking in air. She's focused on taking in the sun.*

I followed her lead.

As I followed Teresa's steady breathing, I felt it. A sense of energy coming from the side where the sun was creeping its way up to the sky. It's like when someone tells you to focus on breathing and suddenly you notice what the air feels like. If it's dry or humid. Polluted or clear.

And now that I was actively sensing the energy of the sun, I was able to pull it directly into me.

I channeled the magic through my chest and to my hands. Needle-nails grew from both of my pointer fingers, and I pointed them at the pum-eagles. My projectiles flew and struck true. Pum-eagle after pum-eagle vanished into mist, and I didn't feel tired.

With every projectile I launched, the sun replaced the magic I used up. Well, not all the magic I used up, but most of it. It was enough for me to send out a barrage of a dozen needles that slashed through a new group of pum-eagles trying to flank Teresa from the left.

Now that some of the illusions had been taken care of, Teresa could focus on the creatures in front of her. She swung and slammed her mallets into the pum-eagles. When some of the remaining creatures took to the sky, Teresa lifted her cactus-hand and sent a wave of needles that made the illusions vanish.

Teresa glanced at me. But for once, she wasn't giving me a death glare. If anything, she looked like she was almost *smiling*.

"It's a flow!" I cheered. "A self-sustaining flow! That's why we waited until sunrise! That's brilliant! Miry, tell her that!"

Miry groaned and viciously slammed her braids against the ground. "Help me squash these spiders, and sure!"

I stamped on the spiders with my sneakers as I launched my needle-nails at the pum-eagles. Now that I could feel the sun's energy, I felt confident enough in my magic levels to send waves of projectiles at the illusions in the sky. That let Teresa focus on slamming the pum-eagles that were attacking us from the ground.

In less than two minutes, we'd finally cleared a way to the pyramids.

"*¡Muévanse!*" Teresa screamed as she motioned for us to run.

We sprinted across the courtyard. I glanced over my shoulder to see a new wave of pum-eagles run at us from behind, but we had just enough distance between us to get to the base of the pyramid of Chalchiuhtlicue. Also known as the pyramid of the moon.

Teresa put herself between us and the oncoming hoard of illusions.

"*¡Arriba! ¡Ahora!*" she ordered, pointing toward the staircase before turning to the creatures.

"*¡Okei!*" Miry replied. "She says—"

"I know!" I said. "Up! Now!"

MIRY AND I RACED UP THE GIANT PYRAMID, GOING UP THE many, many, *many* stone steps to the top.

Here's the thing. This pyramid, the pyramid of the moon, the pyramid of Chalchiuhtlicue or whatever. It is big. And it is *tall*. Which means that running up this thing is a workout. After literally fighting my way to get here, my lungs and legs were actively starting to hate me.

"I can't believe we're climbing this!" I shouted when we reached the who-knows-what goddamn stair. "I thought it wasn't allowed!"

Miry laughed over her shoulder. She sounded a bit tired, but she was way less winded than I was. "If these were normal circumstances, yeah, we'd be assholes! But this isn't normal!"

I sprinted up the next few steps to catch up to Miry. But when I reached her, I was offended to see her grinning at me.

"Why are you *smiling*?" I asked.

"Because you're actually wearing decent shoes for running!" She glanced down at my hot pink sneakers that were probably—no, *definitely*—a size too small.

"No mocking my fashion choices!" I yelled.

"I'm not mocking! For once, I'm complimenting!"

I rolled my eyes and trudged up at the last twenty or so steps.

We were almost there.

"Isn't this guy in the Spiritual World?" I asked. "We're gonna need another portal for that."

"I am not ready for that," Miry said. "It's a miracle I made the first one…"

Miry trailed off the moment we reached the very top of the pyramid.

Turns out, we didn't need a portal.

Because when we reached the top of the pyramid, an image appeared before us. An image of a man, in black and white, slowly appraising us.

I didn't need to extend my magic to feel how powerful he was. To know *who* he was.

It was him. *El Señor de la Tierra.*

The Lord of the Earth.

36

COLORS UNDER THE SUN

ADA

"Hello, Guadalupe. Hello, Miranda," the Lord of the Earth said in a deep voice. A voice I recognized. "I had hoped I wouldn't have to see you here."

The Lord of the Earth stood before us at the very top of the pyramid. He was in the center of a glowing circle that wove around him in waves of gray light. The circle was maybe ten or so feet in diameter—enough to walk in, but not enough to feel spacious. He had a long cloth that wrapped around his hips and was tied at the front, though it was barely visible beneath a long cape that covered his shoulders and ended at his feet.

But the standout piece of his outfit was the crown of eagle feathers that adorned his head. The feathers were immaculate, long and straight, and they encircled his entire forehead.

His face was long and weathered, but his posture was straight. He carried himself like a soldier who had seen his fair share of fights. There were also deep wrinkles around his eyes and mouth, like his face was used to frowning.

But he wasn't super old. If I had to guess his age from face alone, I would've said he was 40, 50 years max. He even had eye bags big enough to match Nando's when he was stressing over finals.

And for a guy calling himself the Lord of the Earth, he was pretty short.

He was about my height, and I'm 5'4. That should've made me feel less scared, right?

Wrong.

Because even though he was as tall as me, I could still feel the waves of power pulsing outward. Pushing, pushing, and pushing. It was dampened, but I could still feel it. Like the pressure of a water balloon that's one drop away from exploding.

"Um," I said dumbly, "I don't suppose there's a chance we can convince you to just let this whole 'I'm-gonna-destroy-the-city' thing go, right?"

Hey, I'd just run up like a million stairs and was physically exhausted. Give me a break.

Beside me, Miry growled. "*¡Pendejo!*"

Her long braids shot upward. She stalked toward the man until she reached the edge of the glowing circle, raised her braids to strike at him —

"You don't want to do that," he said in a very low, very assured tone.

Miry froze. It wasn't much of a threat, but the man said those words with such confidence and surety that it was enough to get both of us to stand still.

"If you make one move to fix the seal, I will bring forth a hundred creatures. Right here, right now. You know I have the power to do it."

"Oh, really?" Miry said.

"It is the power that lets me speak to you from my prison," the man said. "It is my power that created the illusions of daggers when you realized you were being followed. *I* tricked the Archivists into thinking your car was Daniel's. *I* created the spiders in the park, chasing you away from the ill woman who pretends to be an Archivist. *I* gave Daniel his powers, and

I was the one who sent you to your doom in a crumbling tunnel."

My hands shook. "So… you done giving us your resumé?"

"Seriously?" Miry hissed. "*That's* your response to all that?"

"Hey, I ramble when I'm nervous," I said. "Why's he even telling us all this?"

"I'm being courteous," the Lord of the Earth said slowly. "I'm giving you a chance to stand on the right side of history."

"What side?" I walked forward until I was standing next to Miry. "The side that lets you start a massive earthquake that could kill tens of thousands of people?"

"Hundreds of thousands." Miry kept her braids in the air, but made no move to attack. "At least. Probably more."

"Your city will fall one day," the Lord of the Earth said. "Be it today, tomorrow, or a thousand years from now. Cities fall. Just like mine did."

The pieces clicked in my head. "You were here," I said. "When Teotihuacán fell."

The Lord of the Earth opened his arms and gestured to the ruins behind us. "I cared for this city. I cared for its people. I grew to govern all of it. But when it started to collapse, I knew I needed help. I begged our so-called 'deities'. Our false gods. I begged them for help, but they just sat by and let my home *die*."

A hint of anger seeped into his voice. It was small, but with how measured and calm the rest of his words had been, it was enough to stand out.

The circle surrounding him flickered. That was the seal. It had to be. I wanted to go down and touch, see if I could figure out *how* to fix it, but the man's threat remained. If we tried anything, he'd launch a hoard of pum-eagles at us, no question.

So I bided my time and started talking. "I don't think the deities are the villains you're making them out to be." I pointed at the sky above us. "Chalchi's here!" I pointed another finger at the Avenue of the Dead, where, even from this height, I could make out Quetz's giant eagle wings and beams of light. "Even Quetz is here!"

"They are," the Lord of the Earth said. "And they are as hypocritical as they are useless. When I asked them for help, they denied me. They said that they could only help if it was magic destroying my city. But because magic was not the cause, they allowed us to fall into *ruin*." The man sneered. "Is that why they are here for *you*? Is that all it takes for the supposedly mighty 'gods' to grace us with a *fraction* of their powers?"

"Jeez, they're not gods!" I said. "Miry and I have been Archivists for less than a day and *we* get it. Quetz isn't the god of light—he's freaking *light itself*! It's not like he's omnipotent or anything, and I doubt he could've single handedly saved a whole city. I mean, what was he supposed to do? Help you pick out outfits?"

"He could have done *something*," the Lord of the Earth sneered. "But you are right. They are not strong. Can't you see? I am moments from breaking free of this seal and destroying your city, and they can't do anything themselves. No. They need to gamble on the prowess of two mortal children. They lack the power and will to do anything, so I stepped forward and claimed power for myself."

"And you got so power-hungry someone sealed you away." Miry chuckled, and the tips of her braids flicked outward. "That's what I'm getting from this."

"I can agree with that," I added. "Dude, you're just giving us better excuses to lock you away again."

The Lord of the Earth slowly, *very* slowly, shook his head. "You don't want to do that."

"Why not?" Miry growled.

The Lord of the Earth smirked. "Look down."

We did. And that's when we looked. *Really* looked.

Beneath the man's feet were the images of two people: A man and a woman curled on the floor and facing one another.

The woman was in her late 60s or early 70s, with gray hair tied into a short braid, a round face, and several moles on her neck and jawline. The man was around the same age. He had white hair and a clean-shaven face, and though he was lying down, I could tell he was short.

Their eyes were closed. Their faces were relaxed. Like they were sleeping.

And I knew exactly who they were.

"Abuelo and Abuela?" I asked, my voice cracking a little at the end.

Miry let out a choked sound.

"It is." The Lord of the Earth glared down at them. "When they were alive, their energy fed the seal. But now that they're gone—"

"They *are* the seal," Miry said, her eyes flicking back and forth between the images of our grandparents. "I-I can feel them. This energy—it's *them*."

The Lord of the Earth nodded. "That's right. Your grandparents… *Archivists*, reforged my seal 15 years ago. And now they pay the price. Instead of leaving for the underworld, their spirits are here. Dormant.

"If you repair the seal, they will stay here. But once I am free, so too shall they be."

My breathing hitched.

Vague memories came to me. I didn't know my grandparents very well, but I did have some memories of them. Memories of Christmas parties at their house, homemade *chilaquiles*, and old bedtime stories that I'd ask to get repeated over and over again. Those were the memories I cherished of my grandparents.

And now this guy was talking about them like they weren't even human. Like they were just an obstacle for him to get past.

I let all ten of my nail beds extend themselves into razor-sharp needles. "You—"

"Do you think reforging the seal is simple?" the man said, only taking a moment to glance down at my needle-nails. "Do you think you will come out unscathed?"

"I'm kind of hoping for that," I said, my fingers twitching with the urge to launch all my projectiles at his smug face!

"Think of your grandparents, Guadalupe. Think about what happened to them." The man's smirk grew. "If you and your twin try to reforge the seal, you will not simply fix it. You will also become part of it."

I blinked. "W-What?"

"What the hell do you mean 'become part of it'?" Miry demanded.

"It means," the man said, "that while I'm imprisoned, I will drain your life away from you. Piece by piece."

My body went numb.

"For you, Guadalupe, I will drain your mind. And for you, Miranda, I will drain your body. The magic required to keep me trapped will sap the life force away from you, breaking your bodies down until there is nothing they can do to fight it. You will live, but you will suffer. I will degrade Guadalupe's mind until illness makes her unable to remember, unable to think. I will degrade Miranda's body until sickness takes over, and her body is unable to fight back."

Miry shook beside me. Her braids twitched from side to side, and I knew that she was thinking about Abuela. About the sight of her going bald from the chemo and being so sick she was bedridden—sights I only occasionally saw when I visited during the holidays.

And me? Well, I was thinking about Abuelo. About the times when his mind was so far gone, he mistook me for my mom. About the first moment I realized he was so gone he couldn't even talk to me.

"And if you do take this burden, the curse on your family will remain," he continued. "If anyone in your family learns that you are tied to this seal, the magic will accelerate. You will die even faster.

"And your grandparents will remain here, trapped with me. They will remain barred from entering the abrasive underworld, frozen, unable to even know that the love of their life is right next to them."

The man kicked at Abuelo's face. His bare feet skimmed the surface of the seal, but did nothing to damage the visage of my grandfather.

Wait, I thought. *That did* nothing.

My brain finally started working again.

Here's my thought process. So, if I'm this guy from over a thousand years ago and I'm stuck in an eternal prison, and these two people come and reforge the seal holding me captive, I'm gonna hate their guts. And if I have to look at their faces while I'm still in prison? I'm *really* gonna hate their guts.

So, then I gather enough power to bust out of here. Call me petty, but if I started gathering power like that, I'd use some of it to smash the images of the people who kept me trapped. Or at least use some magic to cover them up. But this guy didn't do that.

More than that, this guy was staring at *us*. The only two people who could reforge this seal, and he hadn't gone through with his threat of sicking his illusions on us.

Which meant one thing.

"You're stalling."

The man's face twitched. Just a little bit. "What?"

"What?" Miry echoed.

"He's stalling," I said. "He's using all his magic to break the seal, and he used a bunch of his magic to cause that earthquake in the tunnel!" I pointed my finger at him and almost dug one of my needle-nails into my palm. "He used up all his extra magic to do that! Because if he did have the magic to bring out more illusions, he wouldn't be *threatening* to bring out more pum-eagles. He would've brought them out already!"

Miry gasped. "That… makes sense. That actually makes sense."

"It doesn't mean that I'm lying," the Lord of the Earth said quickly. "If you reforge the seal, your lives are forfeit. They will belong to the seal until it is destroyed, and I am freed. Do you want that? Do you want to give up your *lives* for this?"

Did I want to? No. Of course not! Why the hell would I want to practically sign away my life? No sane person would agree to that!

But then again, I was at the top of a pyramid talking to a man with the power to cause a massive earthquake. At that point in time, I was pretty sure all sanity had left me.

Which made this an easy choice.

I turned to Miry. "I can take it," I said. "That mental drain thing, it's nothing. And if it is, either way, we'll get it sorted out. One way or another."

Miry bit her bottom lip until it cracked open. A light trail of blood was seeping down her chin, and her eyes turned glassy.

But she wasn't beaten down. Not yet.

"What about you?" I asked. "Would you be okay, knowing your body's getting drained?"

The Lord of the Earth clicked his tongue. "Miran—"

"No," Miry said honestly. "But I could take it. It's just…"

"I'm okay with going through with this," I said. "But this isn't just about me. It's also about Abuelo and Abuela."

Miry looked down at the face of our grandparents. Her eyes stayed on Abuela, who looked like she did in the pictures from before the cancer.

"You and Nando were closer to them," I said, "but since Nando isn't here… you get to make the call. If you need some help thinking about it, what would Abuela do?"

The Lord of the Earth raised his voice. "Guadalu—"

"She's already done it," Miry said. She reached up and wiped the blood from her lip, and when her head rose to meet mine, I saw fire in her eyes. "She made her choice to stay and put this guy away."

"Listen to me —" the Lord of the Earth said, his voice louder than it had ever been before.

"You ready for this?" I asked.

"No." Miry chuckled. "But let's do it, anyway."

The Lord of the Earth stuttered as he searched for words.

Miry and I didn't stop to hear them.

The two of us stretched out our hands until our fingertips hovered over the edge of the seal's perimeter. Immediately, I felt how the electrifying energy of the seal coursed through my fingers, through my arms, and straight into my chest. It was like touching a live wire, but I wasn't getting electrocuted. The magic was accepting me, letting me in, but also telling me that if anyone else tried to touch this, they would get shocked with the force of a lightning bolt.

Well, everyone else except Miry.

To my left, Miry was glowing with waves of blue light that danced around her. She was able to hold her hands over the perimeter like it was nothing. More than that, through the seal, I could feel her magic. I could feel how it synergized with the seal's current, pulling her closer. Telling her to extend her magic until it could cover the entire area, creating a surface of magic that could coat the entire circle.

And the seal was guiding me, too. The magical current pulled me closer, guiding my power along the lines of the perimeter. Now that I was in contact with the magic, I could feel how the outer lines were cracking. How they were coming closer to breaking. The seal's magic guided me forward, telling me to harden it.

I suddenly realized why the seal needed both of us to fix it. One of us needed to create the magical base of the seal, and the other one needed to crystalize it.

If the prison were an envelope, then Miry's magic was the

wax that would close it. My magic was the flame that would shape it, turning that wax into a seal.

"Miranda!" the Lord of the Earth yelled, his voice louder than ever. "Do you understand what you're doing? You are trapping your grandmother in this seal!"

"Miry," I said, sounding amazed and terrified all at once. "Do you feel the current?"

"Yeah!" she replied, also sounding amazed and terrified. "It feels like the magic's pulling me in!"

"Don't let it! Just keep hold of it until I can harden the seal!"

"Don't tell me what to do!" Miry shouted back with a laugh.

Miry's magic grew until it was flowing across the entire seal, covering the area in an array of blue light that only I could see. I wasn't sure how or why I was seeing her power this way, but it let me know that she'd done her part.

Now it was time to do mine.

"Guadalupe!" the Lord of the Earth yelled. "Why are you following this? Why follow the false gods of a world you barely know?"

"Hey, Ada! Hurry it up!" Miry panted. "I know we're trying to stop a life-threatening catastrophe, but I'm running out of juice here!"

I laughed. "Can't tough it out?"

"I opened a portal! Give me a break!"

I extended my magic over Miry's, just enough to cover it all. While she held the fraying seal together, I focused on hardening my magic. Strengthening it to the point where it could no longer break unless I wanted it to.

The seal's power responded to us immediately. It guided us deeper, amplifying our magic so that it could weave with the energy of the earth. So it could tie *us* to the earth. To this seal. To this prison.

"Guadalupe! Miranda!" our prisoner cried. "I command you to —"

"Shut up!" we yelled back.

I focused on the seal. On the push and pull of the tethers that held it together. And then I saw it. I *saw* it.

My magic.

Waves of orange light, pulsing with a gentle heat, glided out of my arms and chest. It moved outward, mixing in with the blue waves of magic that had come from Miry. They swarmed together, spinning around in a kaleidoscope of colors that engulfed the Lord of the Earth.

Those two colors, blue and orange, spun together. Our magic mixed in with each other, creating something larger and stronger than either of us could have done on our own. I could feel it spread out across the entire pyramid. Across the courtyard at the bottom, beyond the Avenue of the Dead, and covering the entirety of the sunlit ruins.

The Lord of the Earth stopped screaming.

The glimmering gray seal that sat atop the pyramid faded. I could feel it travel back into the Spiritual World, where it would stay atop the pyramid of the moon. Invisible, but no longer breaking.

We lowered our arms. Our spell faded when the seal went back into the Spiritual World, but little wisps of orange and blue light remained. They glided around us, just for a moment, before disappearing into the wind.

"I... I think we did it," I said.

"Yeah," Miry said. "I think we did."

And with that, the two of us collapsed to the floor.

EPILOGUE
SOMETHING FORGED, SOMETHING MENDED

ADA

I DON'T KNOW IF IT WAS THE DELAYED SHOCK OF RECEIVING magical powers, the beginning of the seal's life drain, or the fact that we'd gotten completely soaked by heavy rainfall.

Whatever it was, after we sealed away the Lord of the Earth, Miry and I got sick.

It started out as a slight cough that turned into a cold that left us feeling exhausted and stuffed up for over a week. After we told the Archivists what had happened at the top of the pyramid of the moon, Nando booked us back home. We must've looked really sick, because my parents immediately went to buy an inflatable mattress for Miry's room so that neither of us had to stay in the sleeping bag.

After we sealed the Lord of the Earth, Daniel disappeared. He was fighting with Lorenzo when suddenly he poofed out of existence. The Archivists don't know how he escaped so quickly, but then again, there's a lot of things we're still trying to understand about him.

We told Nando what happened. All of it. We almost didn't, but then I remembered the letter our grandparents had left behind. Nando's smart. He'd piece things together sooner or later, and the curse that would accelerate the life drain would activate either way. At least this way we could be the ones to tell him.

When we did tell him, he hugged us and said that he'd figure something out.

I wanted to believe him; I *want* to believe him.

But when I was on that inflatable mattress in Miry's room, blowing green snot into yet another tissue, all I could think about was how much I absolutely hated being sick.

"Ugh," I groaned. "We seal away an evil spirit, and *this* is our reward?" I tossed the paper into the trash can. Well, I tried to throw it into the trash can. The paper bounced on the rim and fell to the floor.

"Being the hero sucks," Miry agreed.

Between the two of us, the cold was hitting Miry the hardest. By the fourth or fifth day, I had found enough energy to actually sit up in bed and talk to my parents, and I hadn't had a fever since day three. But it had been a week since we'd gotten sick, and Miry could barely make it to the bathroom before feeling like she was about to puke. So even though I won the *Smash* tournament, I'd moved over to the inflatable mattress so she could feel terrible in her own bed.

Miry also had a fever that morning. My mom, AKA Doctor Mira Rivera and our default family doctor, managed to get the fever down, but Miry still wasn't in the clear.

The Lord of the Earth said that the seal would drain Miry's body. Call me naïve, but I didn't expect it to start that soon.

"Jefe says we need to file a report about all this," Miry said weakly. "We save the city and we have to do goddamn paperwork."

I huffed. "Maybe we can convince Nando to write it."

"How?"

"I'll come up with something."

Miry chuckled and pulled out the remote from under her blanket. She aimed it at the CD player that hung from the wall, and after a couple of presses, the first song from *Map of the Soul: Persona* started playing.

"Why did I only learn you're ARMY *after* BTS went on hiatus?" I asked despondently.

"Because the universe is cruel and mandatory military service is crueler," Miry sighed. "We're gonna have to wait ages before they come back. Even longer before they can start touring again."

"I'd give anything to see them live. I'd fly halfway around the world if I had to."

"Where you gonna get the money for that?"

"I babysit kids! And I'm a pretty damn good math tutor. I've got some money rolling around."

"Enough for a transpacific flight?"

"Shut up." I vaguely kicked in her direction, only having the energy to somewhat move the blanket on top of me. "Bet I can score tickets faster than you could even dream."

"Any BTS tickets are a while off, Fresa."

"As if you could buy them on your own."

"I do commissions."

I huffed in surprise. "Wait, like art commissions?"

"Yep. You think that drawing tablet's just for show?"

"Please tell me you draw Jimin."

"He's my muse. Of course I draw him."

I grinned as I mouthed the lyrics to the next song. I was too sick to properly rap it, so I let my eyes wander around the room.

Since Miry had the "I'm sick" thing going on, when she asked Aunt Lupe if she could unpack the mystery suitcase from her closet, my aunt immediately said yes. Now, BTS merch—a lot of them being posters of Jimin—filled up the previously empty spaces. A collection of CDs sat on the desk next to the spot where the CD player hung from the wall, lanyards hung from a hook on the closet, and small figurines of each member were spread across the room.

I turned to the figurine of Suga that sat on the bedside table. "So this is what you were hiding in your suitcase?"

"Yep," Miry said, glancing at the Jimin figurine that sat by her drawing tablet. "Didn't know how you'd react to me being a K-pop stan. I should've been more worried that you're a Suga stan."

"You insulting my bias, Donaldson?"

"I'd never insult any member of BTS. I've just gotta accept that you're gonna be one of those people who actually knows every rap."

I opened my mouth to rap the next lyrics of the song that was playing, but my mind suddenly went blank.

Miry turned to me. "Ada?"

"I forgot what lyrics come next." I shook my head. "It's just because of this cold, right?"

Miry bit her lip. "Ada… You know what's happening. And me lying to you isn't gonna make either of us feel better."

Right. Because now the seal is draining my mind.

The two of us went quiet, the music the only sound in the room.

"I haven't been this scared since I was 12," Miry said softly.

I blinked as I realized exactly what my cousin was about to say. "You don't have to talk about it now, Miry."

"I want to." Miry swallowed the bile in her throat and stared up at the ceiling. "This guy saw me one day on my bus route. Started following me home. Everyday… for two months."

I winced. "You're serious?"

Miry huffed. "Yeah."

"What did Aunt Lupe and Uncle Luis do about it?"

"Nothing, at first."

"Why not?"

"Because I didn't tell them. Thought I could tough it out. Not be a wuss who was too scared to get on a bus. But then the guy… followed me until he learned where I live. Showed up on the corner one day."

A shiver crawled up my back. "Did he…"

"He groped me," Miry said in a tight voice. "I screamed loud enough for the neighbors to come running out of the house. That stopped him from—" Miry shuddered. "From doing anything else. Haven't been on public transit since."

"Until last week," I said.

"Yeah." Miry chuckled and bit her bottom lip. "I'm lucky."

"*How?*" I asked. "How would you *ever* count that as 'lucky'?"

"Because I've been able to *not* take the bus. Mamá works from home now, so she usually gets to drop me off places. And Dad earns enough that I can take Ubers or taxis when I need to." Miry chuckled darkly. "Perks of being an only child from a well-off family. I'm lucky."

"I don't think that having to avoid public transportation because you got groped is 'lucky'."

"I'm lucky that I don't have to risk it again. That's a privilege most women in this country don't get. And… I do."

I sighed. "I'm sorry. I didn't know."

"How were you supposed to?" Miry finally turned away from the ceiling to face me. Her eyes were dry, but there was a crack in her bottom lip. It bled, and Miry pulled her lips in before the blood could spill down her chin. "You didn't ask, so I didn't tell you."

And there it was. A summary of most of our lives. Ever since we were ten years old.

"And the groper?" I asked.

Miry shook her head. "They didn't catch him."

And there was only one thing I could say to that. "*Shit.*"

Miry laughed. "Yeah. Shit."

How in the world did we let it get to this? To the point where my own cousin got groped, and I had no idea.

Our whole adventure was starting to sink in. Our powers, this spirit, the seal that would slowly drain away our lives. When we were going through it, we kept going through a sea of adrenaline. But now the urgency was gone, leaving us with the cold, hard truth.

We were stuck in a mess. A magical, crazy, potentially deadly mess.

But…

"We'll figure it out," I said. "This spirit, this curse, seal, power, whatever. We'll figure it out."

Miry tugged at her messy braid. "You think?"

"We better," I said. "Preferably before you get cancer. I mean, no offense, but I don't know if you can pull off the bald look."

Miry stuttered for a second before letting out a loud laugh. "Yeah. And preferably before *you* get dementia. It'd be a shame if you forget Korean before you even give Spanish a shot."

"True," I said. An idea came to mind, and I grinned. "Besides, I can't get sick. I have a bet to win."

"Bet?"

"I bet that I can get BTS tickets before you. I'm gonna prove I'm right."

It took Miry a moment to process the words, but when she did, she laughed. "You can try. But what's a bet without any stakes?"

"What do you suggest?"

"If I get the tickets, you wear a Jimin shirt to the concert."

I snorted. "Sure. But if I score the tickets, you go to the concert in a Suga shirt."

Miry laughed, but her laughs quickly turned into a set of heavy coughs. "So… I guess this means that we're going to the concert together."

"Yeah. So that means we'll *both* get through this." I stretched out my arm and held out my hand. "Deal?"

Miry's breathing was ragged as her coughs died down. But when they did, she raised her hand and smirked. "Deal."

We shook hands, sealing the pact.

"I'm getting this in writing," Miry said, fishing around for her phone. "You're not getting out of this bet when I win."

I rolled my eyes. "*If* you win."

"*When* I win."

If someone had told me at the beginning of this trip that Miry and I would end up getting along, I would've thought they were straight up lying to me. If someone had told me we'd be planning to go to a BTS concert together, I would've thought they were getting paid by Nando in an attempt to have us get along.

But here we were. Actually talking to each other. It still wasn't like when we were really little, when we could spend the whole night talking under the covers, but it was something. And… I wanted it to get better.

There are still a lot of things I don't know about my cousin, and a lot of things she doesn't know about me. But if we can actually get through this mess, then maybe we can get back to being friends.

And as I delve into this world of magic and deities and spirits and ruins, I think it'd be nice to have a friend by my side.

Miry opened up a new document on her phone and typed in: *Ada and Miry's BTS Bet*.

I laughed in surprise.

"What?" Miry asked.

"You spell my name A-D-A. You don't add an 'H' to it."

"Yeah." Miry's fingers hovered over the delete button. "Want me to change it?"

I shook my head. "Nah. It's good just like that."

AFTERWORD
THE BET

FERNANDO

Thank you for reading our report. My cousins have told everything that happened last summer, but there are a few details I want to add.

After Hada and Miry recovered from their cold, they challenged me to a *Smash Brothers* tournament. Two versus one. If they won, I would help them write the report.

I agreed. They beat me in the final set.

I can't tell you how much of this I had to write, but I want whoever reads this to know that I had to write a *lot*.

And I also want to tell you who won the bet.

When BTS went back on tour, Hada got tickets the day they went on sale. But when Hada was about to call our cousin to say she won, Miry sent her a picture.

It turns out that Miry got tickets for the same concert.

In a way, they both won the bet. They asked

me if I wanted to go. I said no, of course, but they sent me a picture.

In it, Hada was wearing a Jimin shirt, Miry was wearing a Suga shirt, and both of them are grinning.

THE STORY CONTINUES

Ada and Miry didn't want to lie to their parents.

But when the lie literally kept them alive, they didn't have much choice.

After sealing away an evil spirit at the ruins of Teotihuacán, the two Mexican-American cousins became the magical wardens keeping him captive. But the seal drains the girls' life force, and if their family learns of this curse, their lives will get drained even faster. The only family member who does know is their cousin Fernando, and he grapples with the guilt of inadvertently advancing his cousins' decline.
As the girls from opposite sides of the border test the bonds of their new and fragile friendship, they race against the clock to find a way to destroy the spirit before he can cause a massive earthquake.

And if there's one thing the girls know for sure, it's that family is complicated. But mixing magic and family? Well… "complicated" is an understatement.

Follow Ada and Miry in their quest through Mexico, delving deeper into the fantastical world of magic based on the philosophy of the city of Teotihuacán.

ALSO BY ANDREA SEPTIÉN

THE ARCHIVES OF THE FORGOTTEN

Masks on the Water

The Sunlit Ruins

ABOUT THE AUTHOR

Andrea Septién is a writer, editor, and certified cat lady. Born and raised in Mexico City, she is a Mexican-American author who lives in Melbourne, Australia with her husband. She receives weekly pictures of her cats back in Mexico.

You can follow her on most social media here @septandrealis

GLOSSARY

- **Abuelo/a:** a Spanish word that translates to "grandfather/grandmother" in English.
- **ARMY:** the name given to the fanbase of the BTS, a popular South Korean boy band.
- **Aztec Civilization:** a Mesoamerican civilization developed in central and southern Mexico.
- **Bosque de Chapultepec:** a large urban park located in Mexico City, renowned for its historical significance, green spaces, cultural institutions, and recreational opportunities, making it a vital and iconic part of the city.
- **Carajo:** a versatile Spanish term that can be an exclamation of emotion or frustration, refer to the crow's nest on a ship, or, in certain contexts, be a vulgar expression similar to "damn" or "the devil."
- **Chalchiuhtlicue:** a deity in Aztec philosophy, often represented as a water spirit associated with rivers, lakes, and other bodies of water, and is considered a central figure in the Mesoamerican pantheon, symbolizing fertility and the life-giving properties of water.

- **Chapulines:** a type of edible grasshopper commonly consumed in some Mexican and Central American cuisines, known for their crunchy texture and often seasoned with spices, lime, and salt to create a popular snack or ingredient in traditional dishes.
- **Ciudadela:** a Spanish term that typically refers to a fortified or walled city or a housing complex, often used in the context of historical urban structures or modern residential developments.
- **Conquista:** the period of Spanish and Portuguese colonization and conquest in the Americas during the 15th to 17th centuries, which resulted in the subjugation and transformation of indigenous civilizations and the establishment of European colonial empires in the New World.
- **Gringo/a:** a colloquial term in Spanish, often used in Latin America, to refer to a female foreigner (often White/Caucasian), especially from the United States or an English-speaking country, and can sometimes carry cultural or social connotations.
- **Hada:** a Spanish term that means "fairy" in English.
- **Jefe/a:** a Spanish term that means "boss" in English.
- **Jimin:** a vocalist and dancer for the South Korean boy band BTS.
- **LLAMA:** short for "The League for the Latin American Magical Authority", a magical government overmatching the magic users of Latin America.
- **Mayan Civilization:** a Mesoamerican civilization developed in southeastern Mexico and Central America, also known as the Maya Region.
- **National Museum of Anthropology:** a Mexican museum that is the largest and most visited museum in the country.

- **Nieve:** a Spanish word that translates to "snow" in English, referring to frozen water vapor that falls from the sky in the form of ice crystals, typically associated with winter and cold weather. It can also refer to a type of frozen dessert similar to ice cream.
- **Niñas:** a Spanish term that means "young girls" in English.
- **Norteño:** a Spanish word referring to Mexican citizens that live in the North, and just south of United States border, who have a distinct accents from Mexico City (formerly known as the Federal District) and other regions of the country.
- **Parque de Chapultepec:** a renowned urban park located in Mexico City, celebrated for its historical, cultural, and recreational significance, making it one of the largest and most important city parks in the Americas.
- **Pendejo:** a slang term in Spanish, primarily used in Mexico and some other Spanish-speaking countries, and it is considered offensive and vulgar, roughly translating to "fool," "idiot," or a stronger derogatory term depending on the context, and it is not appropriate for polite or formal communication.
- **Periférico:** a Spanish term that typically refers to a peripheral road or highway encircling a city, often designed to facilitate traffic flow around urban areas and connecting different parts of the city.
- **Pirámide:** the word for "pyramid" in Spanish.
- **Prepa:** a colloquial term used in some Spanish-speaking regions, particularly in Mexico, to refer to "preparatoria," which is a type of secondary education institution that serves as a preparatory or high school level, typically attended by students before entering college or university.

- **Profesor/a:** a Spanish term that translates to "teacher" in English.
- **Pum-eagle:** a hybrid creature with the body of a puma and the wings of an eagle, sometimes known as a winged puma.
- **Quetzalcóatl:** a prominent deity in Mesoamerican philosophy, often depicted as a feathered serpent and considered one of the most important figures in Aztec and other ancient Mesoamerican cultures, associated with creation, knowledge, and various other aspects of life and nature.
- **Rancheras:** a genre of traditional Mexican music characterized by its lively and often sentimental songs, typically featuring themes related to rural life, love, and national pride, and are often accompanied by the use of instruments like guitars and trumpets.
- **Suga:** the lead rapper for the South Korean boy band BTS.
- **Teotihuacán:** an ancient Mesoamerican archaeological site located in Mexico, famous for its well-preserved pyramids, temples, and urban layout, and is considered one of the most significant pre-Columbian civilizations in the Americas.
- **Tío/a:** a Spanish word that translates to "uncle/aunt" in English.
- **Tláloc:** the ancient Aztec deity of rain and water, an important deity in Mesoamerican mythology associated with agriculture and fertility.
- **UCMP:** short for "The United Council of Magical Peoples", a magical government overmatching the magic users of the entire globe, similar to its mundane counter part: The United Nations.
- **UNAM:** short for "Universidad Nacional Autónoma

de México", a public research university with a
large campus in Mexico City.

www.ingramcontent.com/pod-product-compliance
Lightning Source LLC
Chambersburg PA
CBHW021243190726
48289CB00005B/1458